'The plot of this novel is intricate and beautifully turned, and echoes of Frances Hodgson Burnett and George MacDonald Fraser are entirely intentional – Fox's raids on the story-box cleverly enhance the sense of mystery'   *The Times*

'Dark secrets, hidden pasts and childhood mysteries are the focus in this sensual melodrama . . . an entertaining slice of Victoriana, rich in historical detail'   *Marie Claire*

'With just as many twists and turns as Wilkie Collins at his unpredictable best, Fox's take on the Victorian mystery novel will transport you to a world of intrigue and superstition . . . A gem of a read'   *The Lady*

'Delights in the underworld and exotica of Victorian Britain . . . Memorable and unusual'   *Sunday Times*

'A richly textured, highly coloured and entirely pleasurable read'   *Metro*

'The author captures the essence of Victorian life in this richly textured novel . . . hugely enjoyable. If you love all things Victorian, you will love this'   *Historical Novel Society*

'Beautifully turned and very beguiling . . . Fox cleverly weaves in real characters such as the widowed Queen Victoria and the Maharajah Duleep Singh, with Indian myths and legends, to produce a terrifically engrossing read'   *Saga Magazine*

'A dark enthralling story . . . I was totally engrossed!' *Essentials*

'A shadowy sensual world . . . [a] beguiling, imaginative and original tale'   *HELLO! Magazine*

Essie Fox divides her time between Windsor and Bow in the East End of London. Her debut novel, *The Somnambulist*, was selected for the Channel 4 TV Book Club and was shortlisted in the New Writer of the Year category of the 2012 National Book Awards. She is the author of The Virtual Victorian: www.virtualvictorian.blogspot.com

By Essie Fox

The Somnambulist
Elijah's Mermaid
The Goddess and the Thief

The Goddess *and the* Thief

ESSIE FOX

An Orion paperback

First published in Great Britain in 2013
by Orion Books
This paperback edition published in 2014
by Orion Books,
an imprint of The Orion Publishing Group Ltd,
Orion House, 5 Upper St Martin's Lane,
London WC2H 9EA

An Hachette UK company

1 3 5 7 9 10 8 6 4 2

A CIP catalogue record for this book is
available from the British Library.

ISBN 978-1-4091-4620-9

Typeset at The Spartan Press Ltd,
Lymington, Hants

Printed in Great Britain by Clays Ltd, St Ives plc

The Orion Publishing Group's policy is to use papers that are
natural, renewable and recyclable products and made from wood
grown in sustainable forests. The logging and manufacturing
processes are expected to conform to the environmental
regulations of the country of origin.

www.orionbooks.co.uk

A portrait of Maharajah Duleep Singh by Winterhalter
Commissioned by Queen Victoria

In memory of Isobel Thomson, née Duggan.

When we were at seven years old you told me stories about ghosts.

May those ghosts never exist.

May you rest in peace, dear friend.

His death in Benares
Won't save the assassin
From certain hell,

Any more than a dip
In the Ganges will send
Frogs – or you – to paradise.

My home, says Kabir
Is where there's no day, no night,
And no holy book in sight.

To squat on our lives.

'His Death in Benares' by Kabir

PART ONE

THE THEFT

THE LETTER – NEVER SENT

Benares

Tuesday, July 22nd, 1843

My Dearest Sister, Mercy,

How pleased I was to receive your letter, and to know that you and Mama have settled into the Windsor house, although Charles (and please, you must call him Charles – Doctor Willoughby is too formal by far!) says he will not countenance one more word of you being the 'poor relations'. He insists that Claremont Road is yours to do with exactly as you choose, and that when the time comes for us to return the house is perfectly adequate to accommodate the four of us – and any children too.

I only wish I were with you now, to select the new hangings and furniture – all those pleasures that I dreamed about before Charles was so prematurely called to return to his duties in India. Oh, Mercy, how I miss you! England is too far away, both in distance and in memory. I beg you not to tell Mama, but your letter has found me ailing and really at the lowest ebb. This homesickness consumes me. I am quite the abandoned wife, with my husband often travelling to the outlying districts on Company business. Almost a month he was in the Punjab, and now he has returned to Benares and says it is inevitable that a war with the Sikhs will come to pass. He says it is only a matter of time.

I can hardly bear to think of this. What on earth will I do if widowed here – if left with the care of an infant child? To have fallen in this pregnancy whilst we were still upon the boat, it seems to me the cruellest thing, and the symptoms worse with every day, which surely should not be the case. Perhaps I

3

harbour some hidden malaise. I no longer dare to look in a mirror to see a face so sallow and drawn, as pallid as the milky sweets and plain boiled chicken that I eat. (I cannot abide the spicy food – neither the taste nor the smell of it!) The flesh has fallen from my bones except for my belly which grows so fat. A wonder that I do not faint when having to lace my stays so tight to even begin to fit my gowns. If only I had more skill with a needle! There is a local tailor who can be hired for the smallest fee, but the native's interpretation of what we would consider a fashionable cut has led to the sorriest results. I think I would rather resort to the kurta, the loose tunic that some of the servants wear, though when I mentioned this to Charles he suggested I might turn Hindoo next.

Of course he was only teasing, but I sensed something serious beneath. I fear I am not the type of wife that my husband expected me to be. More than once he has expressed the hope that when this child of ours is born I will regain my joie de vivre and engage with the regiment's social life. I dearly hope that is the case. I dare not admit as much to him as I will now confess to you, but I find myself filled with a raging resentment to be always listless, always bored. I feel as if coming to India has placed me in some bondage. I cannot begin to grasp this place. It is never still, always spinning around. It is something like a kaleidoscope. It drains me. It overwhelms me. And the climate – that has me prisoner too, being nothing but detrimental to health. You hear about such terrible things. Why I had not known of this before, but Charles's own parents and sister died when taken with the dysentery; all gone in the space of just two days while he was at school at England. We went to lay flowers on their graves when we first arrived in Calcutta. Really, it almost broke my heart to walk past the stones in that cemetery and to see all the marble angels that marked the death of an English child.

Perhaps my child will also die. No life is safe in India! They say that a perfectly healthy man may wake with a headache at breakfast and be dead by three in the afternoon. I often wake with headaches! It is this wretched heat. Of late, there have been many days when I barely have the strength to dress and swelter here upon my bed. My flesh is sore and rough from sweat, but bathing is a thing to dread. There is no running water, and we may never use a sponge for fear of any scorpions that may be lurking underneath.

The vermin in this house! The white ants all but ate the piano, and its music my only pleasure here. I live in terror of the snakes (I often hear them slithering about in the thatching of the roof. And one morning, when Charles was dressing, one of them dropped onto his head – one of the small but deadly ones, and only by luck did he shake it off and trap it in the water jug.) I am plagued to distraction by the flies. Their buzzing wears my nerves to shreds, not to mention the creaking of the rope as the coolie tugs the punkah fan. That is, when he remains awake, not sleeping on the verandah.

The servants, you would not believe. To think Mama manages at home with no more than a cook and a housemaid! So many there are, for every need. A bearer – he is Charles's valet. A khansamah, or butler. A khitmutgar who serves at the table, and a musolchi to work in the scullery. There is the dhobi who washes the clothes, and – really, I could go on and on. Simply to remember their names is exhausting, and every one a heathen wretch with no desire to be trained, and no concern for privacy. I have told them not to do it, but these people will walk into a room, at any time, both day and night, no matter what state you might be in, and never a knock upon the door to offer any warning. And then there is their jabbering. If only I could understand. Charles tries to teach me. I have some words. I suppose I will learn as time goes by. But, Mercy, this is the truth of it. Deep down, I do not want to.

I want to come back to England. But I wonder if Charles would then resort to the keeping of a mistress? They say every man in The Company has one. One English wife, one Indian – and more often than not the Indian is the one that runs his household best, providing for his every need.

Another of the regiment's wives conveyed as much when she called on me. She spoke of the plight of one poor soul who travelled here from England (who endured all manner of scrapes on the way, including the wrecking of her ship) only to find that her husband already had a 'bibi, wife' and had fathered six little half-caste boys. She hung herself. How terrible!

When my visitor then heard of Charles's trip to Lahore, she could not wait to fill my ears with every scandal of that place. How licentious the Maharani is. How rumours claim that she was once a temple devadasis – one of the dancing prostitutes. How her morals are no better now, for she takes many lovers into her bed, both Indian and English men.

I asked that visitor to leave. I said I felt ill and indeed I did. But too late to resist the wicked seed already planted in my mind. I fear that her words had been specially chosen to imply that Charles might also be one of those immoral men. That night, I could not restrain myself from asking him about such things – to which he answered with contempt that: 'The devil makes work for idle minds, and idle minds have empty hearts, with nothing to do but cultivate their resentment for the natives.'

That is how he accused me! *As if I were idle here by choice! A terrible argument followed. I told him that I was not a child to be protected from the truth, that soon I would be a mother who needed to know the ways of the world and to understand her husband's heart – and if that heart was fickle then I should rather be aware than suffer the torments of ignorance.*

I went to bed and wept for hours and longed to be back in Windsor – with our lives going on just as before. But, eventually, Charles did join me and very sweetly wiped my tears and swore to his fidelity. And I do believe him, Mercy. And, in some ways, I do believe the two of us were closer then than we have been in many months.

He told me about his time in Lahore – all about the boy, but four years old, who is now the Maharajah. Charles says he is

*an innocent within a nest of vipers, where men have no
compunction in the murdering of rivals. Even their own
family members. And that is why these rumours abound
concerning the Maharani – who is forced to be so wily because
she must do whatever she can to ensure the protection of her
son, just as she once protected herself at the time when the
child's father died. For, even though it is frowned upon, quite
outlawed by The Company, when the Maharajah Ranjit
Singh finally breathed his last, four of his other living wives
and seven of his slave girls were taken along to the funeral and
immolated with the corpse. The Indians call it sati. The word
means Perfect Wife. To think of such a sacrifice! Charles says
that those women were carried along as part of the procession,
each seated on a gilded chair, each with a mirror set before and
a golden parasol above. They were then led to the sandalwood
pyre and concealed within a tent of shawls while everything
around them was drenched in a mixture of sulphur and ghee.
When lit, that became a fireball from which there could be no
escape – though Charles did assure me they felt no pain, being
stupefied with opiates. But even if that was the case, who
would willingly wish for such a fate?*

*Who could love a man to that extent? I know I would not
do it. This country is too brutal. Its women are but chattels.
However much I care for Charles, however true his heart to
mine, how can I think to settle here?*

*I know I must wait until after the birth. It would surely be
insanity to try and travel sooner, but I do not think it can be
long.*

Wednesday, July 25th

*I write by the light of a new day's dawn. I can hear Charles's
snores from the room next door, though I wonder he can sleep at
all after what happened to me last night. The shock of it
brought my labour on. All night I tossed and turned with
cramps, thoughts slipping in and out of dreams, and seeing the*

7

faces of the dead rising around me in the gloom. I am sure I saw our father. I could swear he was standing beside my bed, though perhaps that was the laudanum. But now the pains have abated and my mind is perfectly clear again, and I do so want to set things down, to complete this letter and have it sent, in case the birth comes suddenly. In case it is my fate to die. I wish that it were otherwise, but I have such presentiments of doom. I fear we shall never meet again. I fear that even if we do, the thing that happened yesterday will haunt me till my dying day.

The evening started off so well. I think with my decision made to come back home to England a weight was lifted from my mind. In the afternoon I slept for hours. I woke unusually refreshed. I even had some appetite when Charles and I sat down to dine, and more than happy to comply when, afterwards, he made the suggestion that we take a night drive into Benares.

Our progress was dreadfully slow. Such a seething mass of humanity. Such a din I am sure was never heard in the busiest parts of London. People shouting everywhere, not to mention the bleats of sheep and goats, and then there are the sacred bulls that wander anywhere at will. One blocked our path entirely. No amount of shouting or pushing could prevail upon that stubborn beast to move from the centre of the road. In the end, we left the carriage and walked about the place instead, heading into the tents of a bazaar where there must have been a hundred stalls, and every one of them piled high with steaming mounds of rice and dhal, with spices, fruits and vegetables, with jewellery and leather goods, and bales of such exquisite silks. There was one green, with threads of gold – the colour would have suited you, matching your eyes to perfection. We should have stopped to buy some, and then we should have gone back home. Really, I blame only myself. But I felt such a sudden sense of excitement to be part of that swarming chaos, to be following a surging crowd through the squalor of narrow *winding streets, to emerge and suddenly to see a scene from an Arabian fairy tale.*

There was a temple that looked like a palace right next to the banks of the Ganges. It gleamed like silver against black skies where a bright full moon was shining down upon the domes and balconies, and the ornate marble arches, and in every arch a deity, and every deity shimmering in the flare of torches set below. A pair of golden fretwork doors, each one as tall as an elephant, was at that moment drawing back to reveal within a golden god. The idol was sitting cross-legged upon a wheeled dais. It was hailed by a thousand beating drums, the crashing of cymbals, the blaring of conches, the ringing of so many bells. I smelled the perfume of jasmine and rose. I saw priests with shaved heads and yellow robes, all garlanded in marigolds, all chanting 'Om Shiva Mahesvara Mahadev', over and over and over again, until my head was swimming. But then a gust of air rose up and quite the strangest thing occurred. I thought, 'A gift. A blessing. A kiss from the lips of Shiva.'

Mercy, you may think me mad, but I felt as if I knew him. I could not drag my eyes away, even though the golden god's were closed. I kept thinking, 'He cannot see me.' And yet, I knew he could, as if he could look into my soul through the gleaming ruby in his brow, or the ruby eyes of the cobra that coiled around his throat. That put me in mind of the devil in Hell, as did the trident in one of his hands. But then, the way he raised one palm – that seemed a benediction. I felt such a swelling of joy in my breast. I thought of the love of Jesus.

What can such contradictions mean? If you were here you might explain my shameful, sacrilegious thoughts. I confess, at that one moment I could not have felt any further away from any sense of our Christian God. And perhaps my soul had been possessed, for I wanted to dance with the temple girls who began to shriek and whirl around, who scattered a carpet of rose petals on the ground before the idol. Their flesh gleamed like mahogany. Their eyes were ringed and black with kohl.

9

The bells around their ankles rang with every step those women took. I thought of that old nursery rhyme – the one we always loved to sing: 'With rings on her fingers and bells on her toes, she shall have music wherever she goes.'

That memory was swiftly lost when someone (I did not see them) hissed 'Feringhee' in my ear. It is their word for foreigner, intended as an insult, and horribly unnerving. But when I looked to Charles for help my husband did not notice me. His attention was fixed on the dancer who seemed to cast him in a spell, as she raised her arms above her head where oiled black hair hung down like silk.

I do not believe my husband has ever looked at me like that. But now I see through clearer eyes. All beauty here is treacherous; a thin veneer for the lust and sin that seethes beneath the surface. I could smell it on the dancers' flesh, the reek of musk and hot ripe sweat, and the only thing I could think about was the need to find some cleaner air, some air not yet corrupted.

I know that it was reckless, to leave my husband's side, when I pushed my way through all the crowds and then on down the steep stone steps that led me to the river's shore. How wide is it, that river? I could barely see to the other side where the flames of fires were burning high, and such strange shadows dancing. It must be one of the funeral ghats, where the Hindoos go to cremate their dead, before scattering their ashes in the waters of the Ganges. If only I'd not noticed the sudden stench of burning flesh. I felt sick. I felt frightened. I called for help. But how could Charles hear my voice when drowned in that cacophony?

Someone did, though. Someone heard me. I felt a hand upon my wrist, and that hand had fingers more like claws, its nails filthy, cracked and long. I saw them all too vividly in a moment of stillness that lasted an age. And there the horror did not end. In the other hand he held a staff, with a drum and what looked like a human skull tied upon the end of it. He wore nothing more than a loincloth. His flesh was black and wrinkled, stinking of blood and excrement. And the toothless face that leered above! Through long grey ropes of matted hair I could see that his eyes were yellowed, staring and wild with some intoxication. The noxious fumes upon his breath! A hundred fates ran through my mind. I fully expected that devil to strike – to rob, to beat me, or even worse. I could only watch when he dropped my wrist; unable to speak when his fingers spread and lowered to my belly. Just at that moment the baby kicked, and that motion so sudden and violent that I gasped at the very shock of it. But it did bring me back to my senses. I screamed and pushed that wretch away. He made no attempt to prevent me, only smiled as his hand was lifted, the palm extended forward, just like the golden god's before. And that was when he spoke to me, and it was the queerest thing, because, even though I would now swear that he did not speak in English, I understood him perfectly. Those words I never shall forget!

'I have a revelation. Do not fear thine death. Death is thine liberation. Death is the blessed sacrifice with which to glorify The Lord. The Lord will claim thy womb's new fruit, the goddess thus to be reborn.'

I am not sure what happened next. I watched him turn his back on me and melt away beneath some trees. It was then I began to tremble. My legs gave way and I fell to my knees, kneeling in the mud at the river's edge and wrapping my arms across my breast. I was rocking there like a creature possessed when I heard my name, a sudden shout – and the next thing I knew, Charles was there, at my side, lifting me into his arms, and carrying me up the river steps as he fought his way through the worshippers. And when he hailed a bullock cart, I cared not one jot at that ignominy, but was simply relieved to be on our way, to see the cantonment's whitewashed walls and to enter the doors of our bungalow.

There, Charles laid me on the bed and insisted I swallow some brandy to which he added laudanum, to help me regain a sense of calm. But what hope did I have of peace when he would persist in telling me that the demon who caused me such distress was one of the Aghori. One of Shiva's acolytes who inhabit the Hindoo burial grounds, who take strong drink to open their minds to messages from the spirit world, who believe they have the powers to exorcise demons and – oh, this is too vile a thing! – that to enhance such magic gifts they eat the flesh of the newly dead. They drink their blood from human skulls.

What hell I have found here in India, with its burning brides, its cannibals. To think such a creature touched my flesh! I feel as I have been cursed.

Will you pray for me, dear Mercy? Will you pray for your sister's soul? Will you pray that when you read these words her child will have been safely born and returning to England in her arms? And should God have some other plan, if we should never meet again, whatever wrongs I may have done, I beg for your forgiveness now.

I am and always shall remain, your loving sister,
Alice.

A NAME IN EXCHANGE
FOR A LIFE

Do you believe in other worlds, of lives ever after, of heavens on earth? My ayah did, and from her lips there dripped such honeyed promises. There was one tale she used to tell, and I heard it so often that, even now, I recall her every word by heart . . .

Far, far away, my heart's dearest, is a palace atop of Mount Kailash where Shiva lives in wedded bliss with his goddess bride, Parvati. But there was a time, long years before, when Shiva loved another: a woman made of mortal flesh whose name was Sati. Perfect wife.

Sati adored Lord Shiva. She worshipped the ground on which he walked. But her happiness was blighted when her father refused to accept the fact that his daughter, a lady of radiant beauty, had wed the god who was uncouth, with long, braided hair which was never combed, and his dirty flesh so often clothed in nothing but stinking animal skins. When Shiva was not invited to a festival her father held at which a sacred fire would burn and sacrifices would be made, Sati was filled with such grief and shame that she walked alone to her father's home and there, before his very eyes, she flung herself into the flames.

The devastation Shiva felt when he heard of this was terrible. He came to the place of his loved one's death and prayed for her soul to live again. He danced with her blackened, charred remains and washed her body in his tears. He smeared his flesh with her ashes, and then returned to his mountain home where he sat cross-legged in the snow and closed his eyes against the world and every pleasure it contained. There he mourned for a thousand years while the Pole Star glistened high above, around which the heavens all revolved, the hub of time, not life or death in which each soul shall be reborn. And so it was with Sati, when her spirit waxed like a springtime moon and entered the newborn, living flesh of a princess of the mountains.

That child was called Parvati – which means she who is of the hills – and from the moment of her birth, Parvati longed for nothing more than to leave her father's home and go in search of Shiva, to love him as Sati had before.

When at last she found the god she offered him gifts of flowers and food. She knelt in the snow to wash his feet, and prayed in freezing mountain streams. She was to suffer many trials before Shiva accepted her love for him, when at last he opened his eyes, and said, 'Oh thou bowed beauty. I have caused thee much misery and pain. Take my hand, and live with me in my palace, high up on the slopes of Kailasa. There thou shalt become Mahadevi. There thou shalt be divine.'

And there she lives to this very day, proving by her constancy that death is but a little dream. Death has no beginning. It has no end. It is only the mortal body that dies, our souls forever to be reborn, until every wrong has been righted, and every debt has been repaid, and then there will be the nothingness, which is Nirvana. Perfect bliss.

Those years I lived in India, I think they were my paradise. And Bhamini – that was my ayah's name – she was my guardian angel. I used to call her Mini. She called me Priyam – Beloved.

I will never forget that last summer when my father sent Mini and me to the hills to escape the city's heat and disease – and also the threat of another war, although I knew little of war back then, only that the first, against the Sikhs, had begun when I was still a babe. And when that was done, when the British prevailed, my father brought Mini and me from Benares to live in the city of Lahore.

My father began his army career when enlisting as a surgeon with the British East India Company. But, later, his role was 'political', aiding the work of the Resident who spoke for The Company's interests on the Punjabi Durbar, the council made up of Sikh generals and the aristocracy of Lahore, who ruled in the place of the boy Maharajah – the boy who was five years older than me, who was still too young to be aware of the simmering tensions and deceits that had led to the loss of his Golden Throne.

In the hills we were very far away from those dangerous games of politics. In the hills, we heard no bugle calls, no fifes or drums or marching feet to wake us in the mornings. In the hills we rose to the squawking of parrots, or the coos of doves on the windowsills and, sometimes, if my father was absent, then Mini would dress me as she did, in the *salwar kameez* – a loose tunic, with trousers secured by a string at the waist – with a gauzy *dupatta* to cover my head should we walk into the villages.

On those walks I liked to see the big houses with English names on the gates; names like Moss Grange or Sunny Bank, with gardens full of hollyhocks and roses trained around the doors. Our garden was full of roses too, but less constrained, more rampant growths that twined through trailing jasmine stems. Their perfume was dense and intoxicating when blowing through the window screens where, every morning, I liked to stand and look out at the saffron yellow skies, below which I always hoped to see the tiger that sometimes walked the lane – that sometimes stopped at the end of our driveway to scratch its great paws on the gateposts.

In the villages they often told of children snatched by tigers, and those children never seen again. And such a fate I might have shared, for there was one morning when Mini was sleeping, when none of the other female servants had by then emerged from their mud hut which was set at one side of the mango tope – and the gardeners who slept upon the verandah (charged by Papa with guarding me) were lying as silent as the dead. It was almost as if each one of them had been cast beneath an enchantment. Not a breath, not a snuffle or snore was heard, and had I wished, had I been so inclined, had I been some demon murderer, I could have crept along the rush matting and lifted the rifles stored under their charpoys and blown out the brains of every man – or else used the rifles' bayonets to slash any one of their sleeping throats. That's what the worst of the dacoits did. That's what Balkar, the coolie, always said.

Instead, I crept right past them, on down the wooden verandah steps, to wander across the dew-wet grass and then beneath the banyan tree where, within the basket weave of growth that was knitted together to form its trunk, there was a shrine to Shiva. It was the lingam, the stone phallus, of which Mini said I must not breathe a single word to Papa, although what that stone might signify was something then unknown to me. But I knew that it was sacred. It was where Mini went to pray each day, to pour water, or incense, or milk, or ghee upon the shaft's thick, rounded tip.

That dawn, when I'd looked from my window, it was very near to the banyan tree that I happened to spy a little deer. A hog deer, a doe I thought it must be. It had no horns as the males did, or else it might be very young, not yet having learned to be frightened of men because, as I drew closer, when it scented my presence on the air, it did not try to run away, only raised its head and stood quite still to gaze through baleful, moist brown eyes.

'Shush . . . I won't hurt you,' I hoped to assure it, reaching out with one of my hands, and just about to stroke its neck when it suddenly startled. And so did I, hearing the scream of alarm it gave, almost like a peeping whistle – after which the deer bolted away, the white flashing flag of its tail held high as it crashed through the shrubs at the garden's end. I watched until it disappeared, lost in the shadows of black and green and then, somewhat dejected at not having made myself a friend, I turned to go back to the house again – only to find myself face to face with the predator that had caused its flight.

Above my head the dawn sun throbbed. Its light glinted down through the banyan leaves. But my flesh was cold and prickling, frozen in that one moment of terror, with the tiger no more than three feet away, and so tall that its piercing yellow eyes were on a level with my own. There was nothing, nothing else in the world but the gleam of those mesmerising orbs, and the swirling stripes of gold and black each side of its enormous jaws – the jaws with white, barbed whiskers which were then stained and wet with blood, through which I heard a low, deep growl, a vibration of sound that filled my ears and continued when the creature moved. But, not to attack me as I feared, only to stretch and extend its legs, and to flex its paws, like dinner plates, through the stems of the grass on which I stood. I felt its claws, like razors as they grazed against the tips of my toes, as it lowered its head in a sort of salaam, after which, when the creature rose again it proceeded to circle around me. Its move-ments were slow and languid, but so close that I felt the ripple of muscle, and the fur, so much softer than I had expected when it brushed against those parts of me where the skin was not covered by my shift. I could feel its breath on the back of my neck, on the curve of my cheek, on my parted lips, and that breath smelled noxious, of fetid meat. I felt sure the beast would be eating me. But instead it did something very strange – something which, when I thought of it afterwards, created a mixture of dread and excitement, filling my veins with a rushing thrill whenever I recalled the way the tiger's muzzle rubbed my cheek, and then on down, along my arm, all the way to the wrist and back again. Another sound, deep in its throat, something between a groan and a purr, and then the tiger's rasping tongue began to lick my face, my neck – licking at all the trails of red that it had smeared onto my flesh, until, as if quite satisfied, it left me trembling, near to a faint, as it stalked away through the thicket of trees and followed the path of the deer before.

I ran back to the house and crept into my bed. I lay there, breaths shaking, pretending to sleep while I waited for Mini to wake me. When she came, when she dressed me and saw the wounds, she gasped and took me by the hands. Saying, '*Arrê!* My thumbling, what have you been doing? Have the rats been nibbling your toes?'

'Oh . . .' I looked down to see them, the lines of finely

crusted scabs. 'It might have happened yesterday, when I wasn't wearing any shoes.'

Well, it might! I had been barefoot, when Balkar chased me along the drive, and some stones in that gravel were very sharp.

'And you didn't even cry. Such a brave little *butcha*, my Priyam!' Mini smiled her relief and kissed my cheek, and the state of my toes was forgotten then, and very soon they had quite healed. But not so easily lost for me was the thought of the creature who'd caused those cuts – of which I dared not breathe a word. Not to Mini, not Balkar, or anyone else. If Papa learned that I'd gone out and roamed through the gardens alone at dawn, well, I couldn't imagine what he'd say. But, more than that: if it was known that the tiger had dared to scale our walls, then I feared that he would have it shot.

I did not want to see it die, even though I knew, deep in my heart, that the tiger could never be my friend. The tiger was wild and dangerous, a creature of instinct and appetite, a force of nature all its own.

I knew if the tiger had wanted to feed, my flesh would have tasted just as sweet as that of any mountain deer.

It was the third day of *Shuckla Paksha*. The Bright Moon Fortnight in Shravan. The time of the festival of Teej. The festival of Married Bliss. Balkar was driving the bullock cart, taking Mini and me to a mountain shrine where women from the villages were gathering to feast and dance – to celebrate Parvati and her perfect love for Shiva.

I was snuggling up to Mini's side, both of us batting away the flies that buzzed about around our heads. In a way, I was glad of those insects. They stopped me from dropping off to sleep, for it was very late at night and I was lulled by the rock of the cart, by the rise and fall of Mini's breaths as I rested my cheek upon her breast.

Through a yawn, I forced myself to sit, and asked, 'Mini, why do they call it Teej?'

'It is named for the little red beetles who know when the

monsoon rains will come . . . who burrow their way up through the soil and crawl across the ground above, to signify new life, new love.'

I thought I could hear those beetles then, rustling through the groves of pine where rising mists were swirling. I peered very hard through the veils of grey and whispered, 'Could there be tigers . . . crawling towards us through the trees?'

Balkar glanced back with teasing eyes. 'Not only tigers, little one! There have been ghosts seen in these woods, Rakshashas too – the demons who roam about in cemeteries!'

'Rakshashas?' Very slowly, I echoed this gleeful announcement, already fearing Balkar's words when his dreadful news was carried on.

'The demons who suck on children's blood, who can only walk at night, because the sunlight burns their flesh, but—'

'No more of this nonsense!' Mini snapped. And then, to lure my mind away, she suggested that we sing some songs – some Christian hymns that I had learned in the Sunday school, back in Lahore.

We sang 'All Things Bright and Beautiful'. We sang 'For the Beauty of the Earth'. And the earth was truly beautiful when we first caught sight of the mountain shrine, where the growth of the trees was sparser and the track began its steep descent. And there, in the bowl of a valley, was the gleam of clustered temple domes, all the pillars and arching terraces with statues of monkeys and holy bulls, with crumbling roofs and balconies where ancient trees had taken root. Glittering in the very midst there was the most enormous pool, and Mini told us those waters were sacred, having been formed from Shiva's tears when the god had been inconsolable at the loss of his first beloved wife.

Mini said, 'No one knows how deep it is. By day it is an emerald green. By night it forms a mirror, reflecting the stars and the moon above. And anyone who enters then may bathe in the waters of heaven, enfolded in Lord Shiva's arms . . . as if another goddess wife.'

'I want to bathe in Heaven!' Impatient and excited now, I could hear the sounds of laughter, of chattering and singing from those already in the shrine. I was tugging hard on Mini's hand. My hand. Her hand. Fingers entwined – along with the patterns of flowers and leaves that formed brown stains upon our skin – what Mini had painted the day before with the crushed leaves of henna, and oil and water; all coming together like mirrors then, until she lifted high my arms and shaped my fingers like a prayer. But a prayer with a space left in between, and in that space I held the moon, and the moon was as bright as a diamond – a vision that held me quite entranced as Mini leaned closer and murmured, 'A full moon, my dearest . . . that is an omen for thee to heed. But come, see its light in Shiva's pool.'

A thousand souls it seemed to me were gathered there around the pool, and every single one of them – every mother, sister, daughter, aunt – was dressed like me and Mini; each one as if she was a bride, in reds and pinks and greens and golds. They were singing, '*Om Namah Shivaya. Hara Hara Mahadeva*'. They were chanting the name of Parvati. Some of them were holding lamps. Some of them were holding bowls. Brass bowls full of honey, or sandalwood paste, or oil of rose, or sticky ghee. Some bowls they filled with Shiva's tears. They poured them on a lingam stone. I watched the water trickle down, to flow amongst the marigolds that formed a carpet on the ground. But where one woman's veil came loose and fell across those yellow blooms, that trailing silk, it looked like blood.

Dawn was already gilding the skies by the time we arrived back at the house. And how surprised we were to find my father waiting at the gates – he and several other men armed with guns and rifles, and every single one of them about to come in search of us.

We had not expected his visit. He had not expected to find us away. And, seeing us back his anxiety was replaced by a seething anger, when Balkar (poor Balkar, so afraid) explained exactly where we'd been – and then ran off while Mini wept, while my father refused to look her way when making the announcement that he could not trust her with my care – that he had decided to take me home.

I thought he was talking about Lahore, but very soon I was to learn that 'home' for my father was England – even though he'd not been there in years – even though his own mother and father had also lived in India.

The following day, when we made to depart, when Mini came to help me dress, and not in the coolness of flowing silks but in starched skirts and petticoats, I felt her fingers trembling, and I saw that her eyes were rimmed with red, and I heard the sorrow in her voice when she said, 'Go with the gods, my dearest one. I pray that Lord Shiva will care for thee and carry thee gently in his arms.'

'But Shiva will carry thee as well . . . for surely thou wilt come with us?' (Whenever my father was not around I often mimicked Mini's voice, what the memsahibs in the regiment church might scorn and call my 'chi-chi' ways – even though they spoke that way themselves when reciting their Bible verses, or during the singing of the hymns.)

'No,' Mini sighed as she lifted my wrist, around which she wound some coloured threads, and into those threads were knotted beads – little glass bubbles of red and green, and some seeds of the rudraksha tree: the rough, bobbled nuts which are sacred to Shiva, which I'd seen in a painting in Mini's room as being threaded at his throat, and through the plaits of his matted locks, along with snakes and flowers, along with the stars and the crescent moon.

'Always wear this, my dearest,' Mini said while she tied the bangle's threads. 'It shall be a token of our love. And every time you touch a bead you shall know that Mini thinks of thee, and that Mini shall be praying still for her beloved's safe return.'

I never imagined not coming back, never seeing my ayah's face again. But, I do sometimes wonder now if Mini knew exactly what my father planned to do with me. I think of her that morning, and how shocked and bewildered her lovely face when she stood by the tiger-clawed gateposts to watch our carriage drive between, when my father called out for the vehicle to stop, then left me alone while he went to her side. He placed a hand upon her arm and whispered something in her ear – something that I could not hear. But, I could see quite well enough how he reached a hand into his pocket and drew out a large brown envelope and pressed that into Mini's hands. And whatever it was – well, I think I know now, and Mini must have done as well because, when my father returned to me, when the carriage was setting off again and I strained to look back and wave goodbye, I saw Mini standing there, perfectly still. Mini just stared but she did not move, until she screamed my father's name – a sound that was shrill and alarming, a sound like the warning cry of the deer in the moments before the tiger appeared, during which she lifted up her arms, and holding high that envelope she tore it in two, then two again. Little scraps fluttered down about her feet.

My father said it was summertime when we first arrived at Southampton docks. But, so often I found myself shivering and oppressed by the dreariness of days when it seemed all the colours in the world had been bleached away to a dirty grey. My father left me yearning for the only home I'd ever known to live in a house like a darkened maze where, at first, I was very often lost in the claustrophobia of walls too close, of ceilings too low, of narrow stairs that led up and up to a bedroom where the walls had been papered with rosebuds. But those flowers were pale imitations, too regimented and prim by far when compared with the fragrant, blowsy blooms we'd left behind in India. I would lie in that bedroom and think of home, feeling hungry but never wanting to eat, with the food so bland and lacking taste. And the only thing to comfort me was to stare through the gloom to a gap in the shutters, where I sometimes saw the starlit skies and wondered if those self-same stars were shining over India. To sparkle in my ayah's eyes.

None of those stars could offer warmth when my first English winter came around, when, even with a fire to burn in the grate in the little bedroom hearth, the air was always much too cold – so cold that some mornings a layer of ice would form a skin in the water bowl. And then I would crawl back into the bed and bury myself in the blankets, and draw up my knees and bind my toes in the pocket made from my nightgown's hems. I would blow hot air onto my hands and when my fingers grew less numb, twist at the glass and rudraksha beads that Mini had wound about my wrist – just as I'd done when on board the ship, when I had been tortured by seasickness, where once I had been delirious when taken with a fever.

Hearing the constant creak of the paddles, I imagined that rhythm to be the sound of Shiva beating on his drum; the thrumming of eternity as he guided me through Limbo Land, that misery – not life, not death – in which I longed for Mini, to be lying again at my ayah's side and not in a cramped ship's cabin, but in an airy mountain house, where her fingers would softly stroke my cheek, the glass of her bangles tinkling, her hair like black silk as it wove through mine and spread across the pillow.

How I pined for what I'd left behind, for Mini's scent of musk and patchouli, instead of the ocean's salty tang. How I yearned for the music of Mini's voice as she told her tales of Hindoo gods – as I heard her whisper in my ear,

'*Far, far away, my heart's dearest, is a palace atop of Mount Kailash where Shiva lives in wedded bliss with his goddess bride, Parvati . . .*'

Once, those words were all it took for my heart to start thudding in anticipation, thinking of love and fire and death as I stared through my bedroom window to see amongst the banyan trees the roosting bats that looked like fruits as they clustered in the branches. And, if the skies were clear of cloud, then above those branches the stars would shine and the Pole Star would hang like a lantern, and the moon, round and ripe as

23

a mango, would gleam upon the snowy tips of mountains in the distant range.

My mother died when I was born. I suppose that is why I liked that tale, to think her soul might still live on, perhaps upon a mountain top, where the Pole Star glittered high above and crowned her head in silver light.

We followed the Pole Star to England. It looked like a beacon – a diamond. I saw it one night when my father insisted I leave the nest of my cabin bed and take some fresh air on the deck of the ship. He said we might see some flying fish. But while my hands clutched the wooden rail, all slippy from waves then spraying up, when I stared down at the sea below all I could see was a cauldron of demons who were splashing and raging, who roared in my ears. And over that noise I had to shout while staring up at the skies instead, telling my papa about the star, and the god on whom it always shone, and how I hoped my mother's soul might feel its light and be reborn.

Papa frowned to hear me then. He said that I was much too old to believe in the stories my ayah told, that they were no more than fairy tales. He had no faith in reincarnation. He refused to be drawn on my mother's soul or where it might be living then – in Heaven, Nirvana, or anywhere else.

Instead, he told me what was true, which was that my mother had died in Benares and that my father blamed himself for ever having married her, for luring her from England to live in a climate too arduous for one whose health was delicate, for whom there came the tragic toll when a childbirth fever claimed her life.

I always feel a pang of guilt to think that I lived when my mother did not – yet more because I bear her name. My name is Alice Willoughby. A name in exchange for a life.

24

THE BIRD WITH A STONE
FOR A HEART

It was early September, a Sunday. By then I was twelve years of
age and four of those years had already passed with me living
in the Windsor house; the house that, so I had presumed,
belonged to my Aunt Mercy; Mercy Matthews, my mother's
sister.

Sundays were sacrosanct, a day reserved for going to church,
with no visitors welcomed through the door of the tall, stuccoed
house in Claremont Road – though my aunt was not at all
averse to callers on other afternoons, to share tea and cakes and
'kindnesses' in the intimacy of her parlour. Those visits were
rarely surprise events, with flurries of letters received and sent,
with times and dates then written down in the book of ap-
pointments in the hall, in the pages of which I often looked to
discover if my aunt might chance to be occupied for an hour or
two. If she was, then I might creep upstairs and go on a visit all
my own, when I would enter the secret room that Mercy did
not know I'd found – or the friends that I had made there.

Since those very first days in Mercy's house I had found
myself being strangely drawn to the closet, the room my aunt
used as a wardrobe, which was set at the back of the first floor
hall. Really it was very small, being barely more than eight feet
in length, but large enough for a long bevelled mirror which
stood to one side of the window, and across one wall an
Indian chest, the drawers of which all overflowed with the
powders and paints that Mercy used whenever entertaining
'friends'. In one of the drawers she kept her jewels. The silver
and gold. The mourning jet. The precious stones she said were
paste. But no one would ever think to guess, for they glittered

so very prettily, the brooches and chokers and necklaces with which my aunt adorned herself.

I liked to try them on as well, whenever Mercy was not there, to see the transformation occur when I had completed the artifice by rouging my lips or piling my hair into tumbling curls above my head. *Is this what my mother looked like?* I would lose myself in a reverie, cocooned in that closet as if in a womb, in the hanging crush of Mercy's silks, all the velvets and muslins and gauzy lace that draped from hooks on the walls around. And perhaps some of those garments which appeared to be somewhat old-fashioned, my mother might have owned before – though when I asked Mercy about such a thing her lips only twitched in a frown of dismissal. 'There is nothing of my sister's here. Whatever she might have left behind was disposed of many years ago.'

A strange thing, to have so little care about the fact of my mother's death. I soon learned not to ask such things, not with Mercy's features so hard and closed, with her lips determined to stay clamped shut, as if the one sister hoped to erase everything of the other's memory.

If only the odour of Mercy's sweat could have been erased as easily, for even when doused in her perfumes, the violet being her favourite – that sickly sweetness much beloved of English ladies I had met – a sourer odour lurked beneath, exuding its way through the weave of her gowns, the sombre mourning blacks and greys that hung within the closet walls – through which, one day, I pressed my hands and discovered the door to another world: the world I came to call the Shrine.

In truth, it was only a bedroom, but Mercy always kept it locked, and the key that connected that room with the closet – the door that led from there to the Shrine – I'd found that one day when I'd dropped some pearls that I had been holding against my throat, when I'd had to crouch on hands and knees while scrabbling about to find that string, for fear of incurring Mercy's wrath should she happen to look and find it lost. As my palms were swept across the boards, wincing at the prick of a splinter or two, I lowered my face to squint under the dresser, where my eyes caught the glint of something else. Something metallic and iron black. Something that had lodged in a narrow gap between the floor and the skirting board. And that was the key to the hidden door.

Curiosity was my curse. I never could restrain myself. Very soon I'd entered the gloom where, despite the shutters being closed, sufficient light still dribbled in through the window of the closet behind to reveal the spinning specks of dust thrown up by the sudden disturbance of air when, with every cautious step I took on into that stagnant atmosphere, an inner conviction grew more intense that this was the room where grandmother died – the grandmother who'd shared this house while I still lived in India. I saw a big half tester bed. I saw a withered floral wreath that lay upon one pillow. On the other, the pale sheen of a nightgown, as if only recently laid out for the owner to pull on that night. On a marble stand set close to the bed there was an empty water glass, and a mixture of bottles, of potions and pills, just within reach of the fumbling hand that might extend to grab at them; the trembling hand with snaky skin and dark brown spots against the white.

Oh yes! I clearly saw that hand. I felt it brush against my cheek. But I wasn't the least bit frightened. I knew that my grandmother was kind. I could see the smile on her face when I plumped up the pillows on which she lay, or smoothed the creases from her sheets, or sat myself down on the end of the bed to listen to her whisperings. Through the muted creak of the mattress hair my grandmother would say to me – *Alice, my dearest, I knew you would come! I knew I had only to wait and you would find me in the end. Sit a little closer, child. Or perhaps you'd like to read a book? There are plenty of them on the shelves by the window. You may take whichever ones you want. You might like to look inside those drawers, or here, down underneath the bed. Who knows what secrets you might find.*

Later, on other visits, I explored that room for hours on end. I took a candle to aid my search while peering into the depths of the wardrobe, or rummaging through those dresser drawers to find any clues to my grandmother's life – and some that might have come from mine. Like the elephants carved from ivory, or the hair combs made of tortoiseshell, or the embroidered Kashmir shawls, the sort that Mini often wore. Such vibrant colours. Reds and greens. The same as those around my wrist.

Beneath the bed I found a box and in that, in a crumpled wrapping of tissue, there was a tiny baby's gown – *That was the Christening robe worn by your mother and her sister Mercy before her*, my grandmother sighed from the bed above. *I'd hoped to see you wear it too.*

Had I been christened in India? The truth was that I did not know, and while wondering about such things I lifted the gown and shook it out, holding it closer to my eyes, to see more clearly how the lace had yellowed in the darkness. I pressed the cloth against my nose. It was a little fusty, but perhaps the smell of that garment might draw my mother's spirit close. It did not. But still, I found some trace inside those books upon the shelves, the ones that bore the childish scrawl, the name of *Alice Matthews*. I stole her books up to my room. I liked to stroke the pages, to touch what my mother's hands once touched. I even placed them under my pillow to try and dream my mother's dreams, to see the things that she had seen. But any books with Mercy's name, I left those pages well alone. I knew enough of Mercy's thoughts. They could be dark and frightening.

The Shrine contained something frightening too. What a terrible shock it gave me, that very first day I saw it, when I knew my aunt to be downstairs, but then heard the front door's solid slam as, whoever had been visiting, departed much sooner than I had expected.

I dropped the ornament in my hands, about to rush out through the closet door, only to come to a gasping halt when I fell against a fretwork screen and spied what, till that moment, had been concealed behind it. The goddess – the idol of the Shrine – the idol draped in greying silk, her features hidden by the veils of lace that fell from head to waist.

Of course, when my mind had stilled from its reeling I knew that idol for what she was. An old bridal gown on a dress-maker's dummy. But the colour of those vestments. White! In India, in the Hindoo faith, white signified widows, or mourning. White was the colour of the dead. And only the dead had worn *that* dress, though my grandmother's ghost did not say as much. That was something I deduced alone – that the gown had been worn by my mother, and perhaps by my grandmother before. But never by Aunt Mercy, because Mercy was a spinster.

I knew those facts to be the truth, just as I knew that my grandmother's ghost only really existed in imagination. For all that I'd learned of my mother's life I'd heard from my father's lips before, or from whatever snippets that my aunt accidentally revealed – or else through the objects in the Shrine, the darkness to which I longed to return. Because, whenever I was there, unlike those hours that I spent in my Aunt Mercy's company, in the Shrine I never felt alone. In the Shrine I was not resented. In the Shrine I could think myself beloved.

My grandmother, the goddess bride, and me, we were a little trinity. Like Brahma and Vishnu and Shiva. Like God and The Son and The Holy Ghost. Like Alice, and Papa, and Mini. While my aunt and the rest of the world spun round, we three found a stillness in that core. We three were friends, were confidantes.

As to the other confidantes, those visitors who often came to share Aunt Mercy's kindnesses, well, as I mentioned earlier, no caller had been expected on that particular afternoon – that Sunday when I'd left my aunt sitting in her parlour, where the drapes had been drawn at the window and the air was thick with shadowed murk, whereas, in my room on the second floor, I lay on my bed with the shutters wide open, the sashes raised high to let in the sun, to feel its heat upon my face.

All through the preceding summer months the weather was nothing but grey and wet. But then, come September, it suddenly changed, and when we emerged from church that day to stand beneath a cloudless sky, my aunt's normally glacial demeanour had turned to something more like puce, to match the silk of the flowers and ribbons adorning her velvet bonnet's rim. Beneath that she squinted her eyes and frowned, 'I suppose this must be an Indian Summer.'

'Isn't it lovely?' I answered, very almost dancing for joy, wanting to spread my arms out wide when gazing up at the singing blue – as blue as the skies in the Punjab. 'Shall we go for a picnic?' I turned to my aunt, remembering those days gone by when Mini and I would spend whole afternoons in the Shali-mar Gardens in Lahore, when we'd spread our blanket on the lawns and sit in the shade of the palm trees, 'We could go to the park, or the river bank.'

'How vulgar!' My aunt's look was withering. 'Eating in public! Think of the wasps. They're everywhere! And in this heat! It really is too exhausting. I can't think it is good for anyone's health. Why, look at my hands . . . how they have swelled!'

She held one hand before my face and I saw how puffy and bloated the flesh, the veins a dark purple, distended like slugs – the slugs that left their mucous trails in the garden of Aunt Mercy's house, where the sun so rarely ever shone, and the slabs were always cold and dank, stained green and slippery with moss.

But I, I could never be warm enough, which was why I did not want to eat in Mercy's dreary sitting room where, for want of an actual dining room, a table was crammed against one wall, and upon its cloth there had been laid the plates of limp salads, and curled, dry meats. Most of that meal was left un-touched when my aunt went to sit in her parlour, to read her latest magazines, when I retreated to my room to doze in the lovely golden haze that flowed through the open window – though every quarter hour I woke, when disturbed by the ringing of the bells: that mellow punctuation that chimed from the church tower opposite.

That's how I knew it was four o'clock – and four o'clock

precisely – with the very last of the hour's tolls fading away to a thrum on the air, through which I heard the front door bell and then the front door's heavy thud, the vibrations of which travelled up through the walls, rattling the window in its frame.

At that moment I quite forgot myself. When I heard the deep tones of a masculine voice, I leapt from the bed and ran to the door, filled with a sudden rush of hope that: *this time – now – it might be him. My father, here, in Mercy's house, come to find me again, to take me home.* And then came the lurch of reality, when I remembered he was dead – that he had died two years before, soon after returning to India, when taken with the cholera.

To think of the day when the letter arrived to tell about that dreadful news was still too painful to endure. When she'd shown me the notification from The Company's office in Leadenhall Street, Aunt Mercy had said how lucky I was to be living in England with her by then, not left alone in a foreign land, surrounded by heathen reprobates. But it seemed to me her main concern was the value of my father's will, and her smiles – yes, smiles – when more letters came to bring news of the trust fund in my name and those monies, which, as my guardian, Aunt Mercy was able to access.

Not that I cared what my aunt might spend, if only my father could be brought back, and how I'd wished that it was him arriving on that afternoon. But, oh, that was a different voice. The same timbre, the same refined English tones. But you do not forget a father's voice, no matter how many years pass by.

Still, with my curiosity piqued, I made my way down the narrow stairs that led to the first-floor landing, and even though I could not see what might go on in the hall below, because of the turn of the little half landing, and the size of the fern in the Chinese pot which created a natural barrier, I could hear my aunt quite clearly, and the way she spoke: those softer notes reserved for the greeting of 'special friends'.

Was it my disappointment, or was it because I had risen too quickly from lying prone upon the bed, the reason for my dizziness and such a buzzing in my ears? And there was something else as well. It made me queerly nervous. That sound, that mechanical whirring, much like the winding of a clock. Wondering what the source could be, I continued to make my slow descent, on down the stairs to the front hall where, when I came to the very last step, I stood with my hands clutching onto the newel post, staring ahead to the console shelf where someone had left a tall silk hat. And there, in my aunt's appointment book, a brand new name had been inscribed, the ink still glossy on the page. But, if Mercy had a caller then why was the parlour door not closed? And where was the sign she always left, the red ribbon she tied around the knob when she was entertaining – the warning that no one left outside should knock or cause disturbance?

I never dared disturb her there unless I was invited. I knew my aunt was not as kind as 'intimates' might think she was. There had been maids who, by mistake, had opened up the ribboned door and later suffered reprimands that led to tear-stained notices. And one – her name was Sally, and I had liked her very much – one night, when I was fast asleep, Sally had come into my room to shake me awake and mutter on about her fears for my mortal soul 'in this house of unchristian blasphemy'.

Sally had packed her bags, was gone, before the morning light had come. But I remained in Claremont Road. I had no other place to go. And, I was already more than aware of what went on 'behind the door', and well before the moment came when my aunt thought to draw me into that profession.

You see, there had been occasions when I had disobeyed her rule and crept from my room and down the stairs, and then across the tiled floor, hardly daring to take a single breath as I pressed my ear against the door and heard those whispers, sighs, and groans.

But, on that day, that Sunday, the sounds were entirely different. First came the hypnotic ratcheting hum, and then the jerky, tinkling notes as the nets of a melody curled through the air, winding around me, luring me on, to walk across squares of black and white, to stand in full view at the parlour door – and there, the first thing to catch my eye was what I now think of as 'the bait' – the pretty little golden cage set down upon the mantelpiece, right next to the big black onyx clock.

It was gloriously oriental. It looked like a miniature temple or the church where my father used to pray in the Residency gardens; what had once been a Mughal tomb. The cage had a fretwork dome on top, and pillars spaced around outside. And inside, within the golden bars there perched a little silver bird, its surface engraved with feathers and flowers, very detailed, very intricate. Its eyes were two pieces of gleaming jet. A beak had somehow been engineered to open and close in time with the notes – until the music stuttered and died, which was when the bird's breast split in two and opened to reveal its heart. A green jewel in a nest of black velvet.

Our souls are like birds within a cage, they long for the liberty of the air.

Those words rang clear inside my head – and the voice, it was Mini's, my ayah's. I think I may have gasped in shock and Aunt Mercy, then sitting in a chair that was drawn very close to the marble hearth, she looked somewhat irked to see me there, staring in as I was through the parlour door. Her eyes which had been sparkling, as green as the emerald in its nest, were suddenly dulled and menacing. The smile on her lips became a frown, though she quickly regained her composure and cooed, 'Oh Alice, there you are. We have a guest . . . from India. And look!' Her hand was lifted to indicate the golden cage. 'He has been so kind as to bring a gift!'

India? It *was* someone from India! Might Mini have come along as well? I cannot begin to describe my excitement when, trembling with anticipation, I made to walk in through the parlour door, though my steps were deliberate, cautious, slow, for since I'd been wearing a crinoline beneath my skirts and petticoats, I was much prone to clumsiness, often bumping into the furniture. Aunt Mercy was always sighing at that, just one

33

more irritation that would lead to her sharp exhalations, to add to the myriad other things that held such importance in her mind: such as folding my clothes upon the chair when they were taken off at night, or kneeling to say my bedtime prayers, or wearing my gloves when walking out, or sitting with my knees tight closed, my hands tight folded in my lap.

My hands were clasped together then, so tightly that the knuckles ached, when, just like a shadow, the man slipped between us to appear from behind the screen of the door.

That first impression, so rapidly made, was of someone tall and spare of flesh with movements poised and graceful. The hair on his head was short and black. There were no whiskers on his face, which only emphasised the scar – so very prominent it was – the jagged diagonal line that ran from the lobe of his left ear to end halfway along his cheek. It did not reach to touch his mouth and the shape of his lips, they were not marred, but were full and firm and sensual. The eye above the scar drew down, if only very slightly, to where the skin was puckered red. Both eyes were framed by fanning lines, and yet I did not think him old – not as old as Papa, who had been in his forties. But he had that weathered countenance that men took on in India, and that deep colour of his skin was much the same as mine had been, before I came to England. Since then my face had turned quite wan, its hue a reflection of my aunt's – hers now having calmed from that morning's pink, though there still remained a waxy sheen.

I remember that sheen upon her face. I remember the way the stranger's hand extended then to reach for mine, the fingers long and elegant, the nails short and very clean. I remember how small my hand appeared, as if a doll's when held in his, and so white it might be ivory. I remember how I had been surprised at the coolness of the stranger's touch, and how my head began to swim when I smelled the odour on him, like sandalwood and something else. Something musky and thick and intoxicating.

His presence was very affecting. I found myself trapped in

34

his questioning gaze, daunted by eyes as black as the bird's – dark eyes within which the pupils dilated, within which there shimmered small pinpoints of light that sparkled like silver, like tiny stars. And, I know this may sound very melodramatic, but I must describe things as they were, and how, all at once I was overcome by such a sudden sense of dread, of some imminent danger to myself, something animal, elemental, cruel. It caused my heart to thump, thump, thump, its steady racing beat a drum. And that beat, it grew yet stronger as the stranger traced one finger across the beads tied at my wrist, where he lingered upon a rudraksha nut, until he spoke and broke the spell.

His voice was strangely soothing, my name wrapped in sleek and sonorous tones, when he said, 'You are Alice Willoughby, the daughter of Dr Charles Willoughby?'

My assent was silently nodded back, but otherwise I was motionless, listening when he carried on, 'My name is Lucian Tilsbury. Until recently I lived in Lahore, in the service of the East India Company. It was there that I once had the privilege of meeting with your father.'

He paused and looked down for a moment or two, but his eyes as soon lifted and fused with mine. 'He spoke very fondly about you. Which is why, now that I am in England again, I have taken this opportunity to call on you, and,' he glanced briefly back to where Mercy was sitting, 'your guardian – to offer my condolences.'

A shock to hear my father's name. I felt such a longing in my heart. My tongue was as dry as sand in my mouth, unable to utter a single word. Instead I glanced Aunt Mercy's way and saw that her cheeks were marbling, as red as the flock on the papered walls. Trickles of sweat ran down her brow, over her cheeks, her chin, her neck, to pool in the little hollow that was formed between her collar bones. I could see that her lips were moving, opening, closing, opening, though what she was saying I could not tell, not with that thudding in my head – and the clock's tock tocking in my ears, and the dazzle of the silver bird, and the gold of the bars around it, fracturing and blurring. All

35

sense of time and place was gone, for I was recalling another cage, one that I'd seen some years before, when my father first brought me to England . . .

I'm wearing my new red velvet dress. For the first time since leaving India I feel myself too sticky and hot – no longer shivering with cold, not coughing on the thick black fog that covers this city like a veil, that clings to the glass and the window frames, that tastes like metal on my tongue.

Today I feel that I can breathe. Today the air is fresh and clear. I am gazing up at the crystal dome that is towering above my head. I am dazzled by the midday light, all gold and glittering it shines through the gaps in the leafy branches of trees where little brown birds are flitting. I am turning around in circles. I am fizzing with excitement, just like the big fountain at my side as it sprays its coolness on my face. I close my eyes and lick my lips. I hear my papa laughing when he says I am covered in diamonds, and his fingers are brushing the wet from my cheek – and then there is only the banging of cannon, the blaring of trumpets, choirs singing, crowds cheering, and – whoosh! – Papa lifts me in his arms, so high that I can clearly see what now appears in the aisle below. A Chinaman with long black plaits, and a golden fan held in his hand. But Papa points beyond him, and says, 'Look, Alice, there is the Queen!' and I notice the tiny lady whose dress is a shimmer of silver and pink, with a garland of rosebuds upon her head instead of any golden crown. I see her and I whisper low, so low that no one but Papa can hear me: 'She looks like the Queen of Fairyland.'

After that we walk the aisles ourselves, for hours and hours or so it seems, underneath all the hanging red banners and flags, seeing wonderful things from all over the world. We stop and pose for a photograph, which is taken by a Frenchman. I like that man. He smiles and winks. He makes me laugh, and Papa too. But there are things I do not like. Things like the surgical instruments. I think it must be the way they gleam, the scalpels, the knives, the scissors – especially the scissors. But then, my Papa is a medical man, so I know he must have an interest, and I know I must be patient, because, if I am, Papa has said that I shall see the elephant.

The elephant is enormous, but not moving, not alive at all. Papa says it has come from an English museum, that is has been stuffed, and shabbily too. But still, I think it fine enough, and I desperately want to climb on up, up onto its back, to sit in the howdah, the canopied seat, more like a throne. A present from a rajah!

The howdah is carved from ivory. Beneath is a throw with threads of gold, with pearls and rubies and emeralds, all edged with tassels and little bells. I lift my hand to shake them. They tinkle, like Mini's bangles. I think if the elephant could walk, then whoever was riding on its back would hear that lovely sound all day.

But with so many others now gathering about us, Papa says we should move on, and he leads me to a small dark tent, in the centre of which is a table, and on that table is a cage. The cage is held in a big glass dome, around which are several jets of gas, and the sputtering hiss of those burners is almost as loud as the gasp I make when I begin to feel quite sure that this cage must hold some living thing. Perhaps a parrot that can talk!

But no brightly plumed creature is perching here. In the cage there is a diamond – and the diamond is enormous! Papa explains that the dark and the flames are to draw out the jewel's sparkle, that without them it would seem very dull indeed, no more than a bauble made of glass.

I don't think the stone is dull at all. I step just as close as I possibly can, and my fingers curl through the bars of the cage as I look at that diamond a long, long time. And there, in the middle of the jewel, is something that strikes me as very strange. I cannot drag my eyes away. I blink, and I think they will disappear. But no! When I look at the diamond again, those two black eyes, they are still there. Those two black eyes are fixed with mine. They know I am Alice Willoughby. They know I have come from India. And they know that I am frightened now – that I'm lifting my fingers away from the bars and reaching out for Papa's hand, that I'm winding my fingers tight through his and—

The press of more bodies, the clinking of dress swords, and when I look up I see a man who is dressed in a glory of scarlet and gold, with *a bright blue sash around his waist. His face is like my father's. He has the same big brown moustache. And looking at those whiskers, I start to giggle, then laugh out loud. I think my Papa has a twin!*

Papa's mirror is smiling down at me. When he speaks his words are stiff and gruff, as if he is not English. 'Good afternoon, young lady. As we are already holding hands, perhaps you should do me the honour of letting me know your name?'

I pull my hand away from his and turn to face the real Papa, and the real Papa gives a nod, and so I know I am allowed to answer the other one, to say, 'I am Alice Willoughby. I am very nearly eight years old.'

'Well, Miss Alice Willoughby who is very nearly eight years old, what do you think of this diamond?'

'I think it is very big and bright. But why have they put it inside a cage? It isn't alive. It can't fly away.'

'Ah, but this is one of the world's greatest treasures and this cage will protect it from damage – or thieves.' His head is tilting to one side, 'Do you happen to know what it is called?'

I am shaking my head, and my mouth is wide open, no words for once when the man goes on, 'This is the Koh-i-Noor diamond, also known as the sacred Mountain of Light. They say it was once a star in the heavens—'

'You mean this diamond dropped out of the sky?' I cannot help but interrupt. I am thinking of Mini's tales, and of Shiva high up on his mountain, and the star that shines above his head.

'Well, probably nothing quite like that. But it comes all the way from India, from Lahore to Bombay and the Cape of Good Hope, and then from the Portsmouth docks to here.'

'Oh!' I exclaim with excitement, 'I know Lahore! I live there, with Papa and Mini, my ayah.'

And that is when Papa says to me, 'Alice. I think we should go now and allow His Highness to continue with his tour of the exhibits, don't you?'

'His Highness, Papa?'

'Prince Albert.'

'Oh!'

This is a very important man. This man is married to the Queen. And thinking of what is best to do, I make a little curtsey, and when I dare look up again, I say, 'Goodbye, Prince Albert. When I go back to India I shall tell my ayah all about having met you today at the Great Exhibition, and how I saw the Mountain of Light. I know she'll like to hear of that.'

'Well, I have something else for your ayah's ears, though you must not tell another soul. Can you keep a secret, Miss Willoughby?'

I try not to laugh when Prince Albert bends down, to feel his moustache tickling rough on my cheek, and to see how his finger is tapping his nose, which means: Hush, hush, say nothing – these words are only yours to hear. 'There is another legend told, that only a queen may own this jewel . . . that any man who possesses it will be doomed to a dark and terrible fate . . . which is why it belongs to my wife, not me.'

My reply is as solemn as it can be. 'I promise. Only my ayah shall know.'

'Splendid!' The prince gives another smile and then he is standing tall again. He is walking away through the flap in the tent, and from there he looks back at me to say, 'Make sure you remember our secret. Make sure that you guard it well.'

I keep my promise to the Prince. I do not repeat one single word – not even to my Papa when, later that day, we are heading for Windsor, travelling there by railway car – a thing that still excites me, for we have no trains in India (though Papa says there will be soon). But here, there are so many, and the stations are great temples, and the engines are dragons, puffing smoke.

The dragon that pulls our carriage tonight will take us to Aunt Mercy's house. She is my mother's sister, but we have never met. So, I sit very quiet at Papa's side and wonder what she will be like. I lay my head on Papa's arm, and the rock of the carriage is soothing, and in no time at all I fall asleep – until I hear the whistle's screech, and wake from my dreams with a sudden cry, and try to look out through the window. But all I can see is Papa and me, our two reflections like silver ghosts, and behind them the clouds of hissing steam, and then all of the whiteness dissolving to blackness, and—

39

And there, in the Windsor parlour, my senses returned again as a bright shaft of sunlight came slanting in through a narrow gap in the window drapes. But no more whistles to screech in my ears, only those tinkling random notes that stuttered from the silver bird, over which Aunt Mercy spoke again. 'Alice, child, have you lost your tongue? Where are the manners I've taught you? Have you nothing to say to this gentleman when he's made such an effort to find you here?'

Looking down to avoid the sun's harsh glare, as well as the visitor's dark eyes – eyes which seemed much too intense while they were staring back at mine, eyes which reminded me too much of those I'd once seen in the core of a diamond – I pulled my hand away from his. And when looking up at his face again, how I wished it was Papa standing there – my Papa then crouching at my side, just as he'd done on that last night, when he had taken my hands in his and told me to be brave, not cry.

But it was not me, it was Papa whose eyes had been brimming up with tears. And his was the mouth that had crumpled when he'd struggled against the emotion he felt, when, in a voice unlike his own, a voice too cracked, too hoarse, too low, he'd said, 'Alice, I know this is hard. But, both of us, we must be strong.'

'Papa . . .' I *was* trying. I really was trying very hard to be strong enough to change his mind, and not to let him leave me there with the woman called Aunt Mercy; the stranger who looked sternly down at me from her place beside the open door, through which I could see an enormous church, very tall and very grey it was, and the blackness of the cab below that was waiting to take my papa home.

'Papa, what about Mini?' That was my final, desperate plea. 'I know she is waiting for me to return. She is praying to Shiva every day.'

My father sighed and dropped my hands. 'Alice – Shiva does not answer prayers. And Mini has always been aware that I would bring you here one day. It was selfish of us – of me, I suppose – to keep you so long in India. It is healthier. It is safer here. And you need to learn your heritage. What it is to be an English child. What it is to be a Christian. The years will pass before you know. And then, if you want to, then you might—'

'Come home again?'

'Come home again.'

Would I ever go back to India, now that my papa was dead? Would I ever see Mini's face again, or hear her stories of the gods? No mention had been made of her, not in the letters Papa sent, not in that dreadful formal one which had informed us of his death. But perhaps this stranger might have news, and with a burst of hope I asked, 'Do you – do you know my ayah? Her name is Mini – Bahmini. Did you meet her in Lahore? Did my father ever speak of her?'

'I'm sorry, I don't believe he did.'

Those few words, and my every hope was crushed. Still, I'd had to ask, to take that chance – after which it was all that I could do to say, as politely as I could through the knot of grief then in my throat, 'Thank you for coming to visit today. But I wonder if you will excuse me now? I should like to go back to my room.'

The stranger's eyes were mournful. Once again he extended his hand, but this time to touch a twist of hair that was hanging, unbound at my shoulder. I hardly knew what to do or say. That action was so intimate. I felt such a sweetness, a sliding sensation, deep within my belly. For a moment the world spun around me and I dared not glance Aunt Mercy's way. But then, perhaps she had not seen, for my aunt only smiled, made no comment at all, and in less than a moment the hand was gone and the fingers were reaching into his jacket as the man looked down at me and said, 'Before you go away again, may I offer you another gift?'

From his pocket he pulled a handkerchief. I thought he might mean to give me that, to dab the blurring in my eyes. But through my tears I clearly saw his fingers peeling back white folds to expose yet another bauble of glass, a twin to that

41

in the silver bird. Or could it be the very same? Could this man be some kind of magician? And the way he'd touched my hair just then, was that a trick to divert my thoughts, to ensure my attention was elsewhere?

I knew about such things, you see. They often went on in that parlour, all those times when Aunt Mercy performed her tricks, shuffling her tarots, conjuring ghosts, directing her theatres of the dead. And hers were the fingers that snatched the gift, her lips pursed in a thin grimace through which her voice was simpered, 'Ah, Mr Tilsbury, how clever you are, to have managed to steal this little heart . . . and from beneath my very nose!'

THE DIARY – NEVER READ

Final entry in the diary of Doctor Charles Willoughby

Lahore

The twentieth day of September, in the year of our Lord, 1851

The Governor's dinner was held tonight. It lacked the congeniality of previous affairs at the Residency, before Henry Lawrence left Lahore, before the Annexation.

The talk was all of Jindan Kaur, and her recent escape from Chunar to Nepal. Yet still, from such a distance, the Maharani continues to meddle, attempting to stir disaffection regarding The Company's dealings. She refuses to accept the fact that her son, Maharajah Duleep Singh, has been deposed from his Golden Throne. And then there is the Koh-i-Noor, the diamond that she will insist the Governor took illegally.

Governor Dalhousie is of the opinion that I should arrange to speak with her, to persuade her these matters will not change, and that all will go better for her son if she simply accepts his circumstance and the fact of their separation. I must assure her that the boy is perfectly well and thriving while confined in the hill fort at Futteghar. There, beneath the guardianship of The Company's Dr Login, he is kept far away from those in Lahore who might otherwise seek to use the boy as a pawn for political unrest.

I know it is a dreadful thing, to keep a mother from her son. But has she not brought this on herself? Even so, she must be shown respect. Her own circumstance may be sadly reduced, but if slighted, then I do not doubt that she will try to take revenge, whether through charm or ingratiation, or those swifter methods of fatal destruction. In the past she has proved adept at both.

To this end, Dalhousie has made the suggestion that Lucian Tilsbury accompany me. In the absence of dear Henry, this Captain is one of few Company men that Jindan has ever deigned to trust. And now, in preparation, I have been reading The Company records regarding this officer's past career. It has been somewhat unusual.

Tilsbury was born here, in India, the son of an English missionary and a native woman of Bombay. He was sent to England at six years old to board at a Richmond preparatory school. From there he went to Eton before gaining a place at Oxford, although a degree was never obtained – not for a lack of ability, but because of some misdemeanour, some event un-named but serious enough to merit his expulsion. However, he must have had friends in high places for despite not having attended either the East India College or Addiscombe, he was immediately sworn in when applying for a cadetship with the Bengal Native Infantry. Once enrolled his swarthy appearance and fluency in Hindustani, as well as other languages, rendered him eminently suitable for those roles where he might 'go native' and infiltrate enemy lines. (He is, by every account, an exceptional master of disguise.)

However, his career in surveillance almost came to an end in Afghanistan where, in 1841, he was captured while attempting to gain access to Amir Dost Mohammed Khan. Somehow he had the wit to survive, even being praised by his captors for his dignity and honour while others were murdered or horribly maimed. (This was the time when Dick Taylor had the ghastly misfortune to come across his brother's corpse strung from a tree, his genitals stuffed into his mouth.)

Tilsbury returned to Lahore unscathed when liberated by Pollock and his 'Army of Retribution'. However, the records do imply some mental affect from the hardships endured, which may be why he was then used in quieter diplomatic roles, specifically as an advisor to the Maharani, Jindan Kaur.

At that time she was strongly suspected of fomenting a war – plotting to set The Company against her own Sikh generals, those who had recently slaughtered her brother, and might very well betray her too — thus taking full advantage of her only son's minority. A coup would indeed have been her end, whereas, when that first Punjab war was done, we British proved to be her friends. Had she but respected that privilege, her position might be different now!

But, I digress from the subject in hand. These matters regarding Jindan Kaur are mentioned in previous diary entries and bear no repetition here. The subject here is Tilsbury, and at this point I must confess that he and I have met before, although he claims no memory.

The occasion was 1846, in General Gough's tent, on the field of Sobraon. I was there in the role of regiment surgeon. Tilsbury was reporting back on intelligence gained from the enemy's camp. The news he bore did not bode well. The ranks of the Khalsa outnumbered our own. Many were already crossing the Sutlej when, by the Grace of God, the river waters flooded up. The bridge collapsed and thousands of Sikhs were fated to drown upon that day, or be slaughtered in the aftermath.

Having last been seen caught up in that mêlée, Tilsbury was presumed as dead, his remains having been washed away. But now he has returned to us and again he appears to be unscathed, except for an injury to his head; a trauma he claims was inflicted on that day of battle at Sobraon, which has led to a state of amnesia enduring for these past five years.

I find that to be a questionable claim, more so the story spread about that his life was saved by disciples of Shiva; some vagrants with whom he since travelled about, surviving on alms and charity.

It is true, he bears a dreadful scar inflicted down across one cheek, and only partially concealed by the full black beard that he has grown. He has lost a great deal of flesh from his person, though I would say there is no loss to any mental faculties. He still exhibits those reserves of self-reliance and confidence that produced such a vivid impression before, being insufferably arrogant and yet also possessing a great appeal. On the surface, at least, he remains the type who Lawrence would claim as a natural hero, born for strong times and stirring events.

And yet, for me, there is something changed — something that nags, that is not right. I have seen this in battle survivors before. An inflation of the ego which over excites the animal parts, rather than the rational. Such men cannot be trusted. They are a menace to themselves, and any in the regiment. More than this, there are rumours that he has adopted the tenets of the Hindoo faith. He does have Indian blood in his veins, and these heathen proclivities will rise. He may no longer run quite 'straight'. I must therefore be vigilant when we two go to meet with Jindan Kaur. If Tilsbury is not our ally, he is the Maharani's friend. If so, he is our enemy.

It is my utmost hope that these suspicions prove unmet. After all, who am I to condemn? None of us can really know what torments this man may have endured. He has shown only bravery in the past, and every task he undertook was performed above and well beyond the call of any duty. I shall reserve all judgment until tomorrow night is done, and then compile an official report to present to the Governor General.

Let him decide the final fates of Jindan Kaur and Tilsbury. I no longer have an appetite for this world of political intrigue. I dare say my opinion is not helped by the whisky in my glass, but of late I would very happily say 'farewell, the plumed troop, and the big wars that make ambition virtue.' My ambition now would be no more than to take some Company clerical role in the offices at Leadenhall Street. Or else, to return to my doctoring, growing old in some pretty English town, somewhere with no risk of commotion, with nothing more to think about than who might be the local mayor or what jam to spread upon my bread.

If I did so, my daughter might join me. I miss Alice more than I can say. I look at her photograph on my desk, and as every day passes I grow more convinced that I should not have left her in the care of Mercy Matthews.

Such doubts, such maudlin thoughts I have. My conscience should be heeded. These wrongs, they should be righted, before those dearest to my heart become no more than memories. The whispering of faceless ghosts who haunt my drunken reveries.

IN WINDSOR,
I BECAME A GHOST

The only memento I possessed to remind me of my father was a photograph in a small brass frame. He left it with Aunt Mercy – the present he wished for me to have on my very first birthday in her house.

He was dead by then, or would be soon, which made that gift more precious still. It was a moment caught in time from our day at the Great Exhibition. It showed a suited gentleman who was sitting on an upright chair, and at his side a little girl, whose dress was swagged with lace and bows, a dress that looked grey but was actually red. And although her features were perfectly clear as she solemnly stared from the picture's frame, her father's face, that was a blur, as if someone had tried to smudge it out.

I feared that was an omen. I couldn't get it of my mind when I went to the kitchen later on, even though Mrs Morrison, the cook, had made a cake with candles, and strawberries and yellow cream. But I had so little appetite, no desire to blow those candles out, because Mini had always told me that every flame was sacred and to douse one only brought bad luck – like stealing the light out of the world. And, whatever Mrs Morrison said about being able to make a wish, I knew my wish would not come true, not with Mini and Papa in India. Not with them like the ghosts at the kitchen feast.

It was but a few months later that Aunt Mercy made a ghost of me. It was early one evening that she appeared, to stand in my bedroom door and say, 'Alice, I want you to come with me . . . come downstairs to the closet.'

I was almost quaking in my boots, quite certain that she had somehow discovered my secret intrusion of the Shrine. I fully expected a reprimand. But my aunt did not seem to be angry. Her voice was unusually light, really almost teasing when instructing me to close my eyes, and then to hold out both my hands.

And so it was the world turned black, and my mind become nothing but a blank when I heard the creak of the closet door, after which Mercy took my hands in hers and guided them until quite high, until my fingertips had touched something as smooth as water – which was when she said, triumphantly, 'You can look now. You can open your eyes!'

'What is it?' I asked, leaning forward, seeing that my hands had stroked what looked like yards of fine black silk, the fabric not made up at all, but hanging in drapes from a hook on the wall. Beside that was a length of muslin, very sheer and also black.

'It is for a costume . . . for you to wear. For you to join me in my work.'

'But . . . Aunt Mercy,' I stammered, as my hands dropped down, as I thought of all those sighs and moans that I'd heard coming through the parlour door. Retreating along the landing, my voice grew louder, more assured. 'I don't want to do it. The vicar was saying, just last week, when he spoke of such things in his sermon, that calling the spirits of the dead is nothing but the Devil's work.'

'Judge not that ye be not judged!' my aunt accused and then lashed out, the flat of her hand sharp on my cheek – an assault that shocked me deeply for, before that day, in all of my life, no one had ever so much as raised a finger to my person.

Stunned into silence, all I could see was the glassy agate of Mercy's eyes as her furious face went swimming through the tears then welling in my own. I feared that she would strike again, but she only sighed and shook her head before going on in a breathless voice, 'You have no option. I have heard from The Company again. Another letter from Leadenhall Street regarding your father's pension . . . and I am very sorry to say the news is not what I had hoped.'

'I thought—' What did I think? What did I know of pensions?

'We still have the trust fund,' my aunt carried on, 'but those monies are very almost gone. And those plans he had for your schooling, for the hiring of a governess? Well, I'm sure I can continue to teach you just as well myself. Haven't we made a good enough start? The piano, our weekly trips to church, all of those social niceties in which he considered you lacking before? And now, I can teach you something more – to aid my own endeavours – by which means you may contribute to the running of this house. I simply had not known before . . . the expenses incurred when raising a child. Why, your food and clothing, they alone—'

'But, I don't want to do it!' Again, I objected, then wished that I had held my tongue. Aunt Mercy was severely vexed. The way her hands were shaking, and then, the way she screeched at me, 'Who on earth do you think you are! To tell *me* what you will not do! You might have been the Miss Sahib, the spoiled princess in India. But now you are in England, and here in England you must stay – no clinging onto India's breasts! That venom has claimed your father. It took your mother's life before . . . though God knows I did the best I could to prevent her ever going there.'

She took a step forwards, to where I then cowered, and lowered her face very close to mine, so close that I saw the bluish tinge that spread around Aunt Mercy's lips. The colour of the Elixir, the sweetness of which was on her breath, the tonic she so often took to aid the fact that she'd been born '*with a double set of nerves. I am the most sensitive of souls, sensitive to the point of agony. Only the Elixir calms me.*'

I wished that it would calm her then. But my aunt's agitation, it only grew. She was panting, perspiring heavily. Sweat was staining the arms of her gown, two dark spreading circles that had me transfixed, unable to lift my eyes to hers. When I did, it made me shudder, to see how they glittered with her zeal – and how disconcerting it was for me to see her scowl become a smile, through which the words she uttered next put me in mind of missionaries, those English men I'd sometimes seen in the bazaar, back in Lahore, who'd preached about their One True God.

That righteousness in Mercy then – that passion was more frightening than any degree of wrath before, when she said, 'Alice, you must hear my dream, the one I had some months ago when we first heard the news of your father's death. It has consumed me ever since. It was my Revelation. You and I were in a room. We saw a cloud of pure white light, in the midst of which was a beautiful figure. The human form of Jesus Christ. The Divinity, He was dazzling! In His hair there were stars that looked like gems. He was bathed in the radiance of the moon. He was parted from us only by the filmiest screen, through which He reached out to embrace us . . . to fold us both within his arms. I believe that I was blessed that night. I believe that He has blessed you, too. You are, after all, my sister's child. You and I are bound by blood. And this is the purpose in His Will – not that I should cast you out, but that we should work together now . . . to work as one, to offer hope to those who grieve in misery. To tell them of the Mysteries, to show that Death is not the end, that every soul shall be reborn, to live in Bliss with those they love.'

I thought about my father, of his ruined face in my photograph. I said, 'But if Death is not the end, then where are my mother and father now? Why don't *they* come and visit us?'

She took my hands in both of hers. Her voice grew soft and very low, though I sensed that was simply a part of her act, that my aunt was only consoling me as she would any one of her clients. 'I cannot draw those spirits back who do not wish to cross the veil.' The faintest smile. A wistful sigh. 'I may only show the path by which their souls can choose to walk. But then, if you are with me . . . to see *your* own light shining . . . that beacon, it might guide them. We may yet see their faces here.'

And that is how I was reborn: to walk the path of Mercy's ghost, to act in Mercy's Mysteries, to hope to see my father's face. But even when that hope was dashed, when I knew that Mercy lied to me, that she lacked those gifts that she professed, for some years I colluded in her games – for fear of raising up her wrath, not knowing what my fate might be if my aunt should fail to find the funds to feed me, to clothe me, to keep me safe.

I became an apprentice in the trade for which she placed advertisements: discreet invitations in magazines for 'Tea and Table Moving' – though my aunt did not spread any local lures, not wishing to cause more offence to the vicar, not wanting to encourage those who might recognise her spirit guide as being so like the orphaned niece who had recently come to Claremont Road, to live there with her spinster aunt.

However, for the first few months there was no risk of being known. For then, she kept me well concealed, to spy from behind the sitting room door where I could eavesdrop on those 'guests' who sat in the hall and waited, until my aunt appeared on the stairs, as resplendent in her finery as any actress on a stage. I would listen to those visitors (nearly always women, nearly always old) exchanging confidential woes, and thus revealing vital clues. And later, when they had been called to sit beside the parlour fire, when the front door bell would chance to ring, requiring that Mercy be called out on a matter of some urgency – that subterfuge was all it took for me to show my aunt the page on which I'd scribbled down the facts that I had learned while hiding: those names and sorrowful events that might then drip from Mercy's lips.

When guests returned as 'regulars', when no more secrets need be learned, I wore the garments of the ghost; the hushing silks, the sheer black veils, the darkness of which obscured the face on which my aunt brushed silver paste, with ashes smudged around my eyes, to make me look half skull, half corpse. At other times a real mask transformed me to an infant child

51

whose tiny rosebud mouth would cry, 'Mama! Dear Mama – I am here!'

In daylight, it was pitiful to see such crude deceptions. I felt ashamed to play a part, to cause yet more unhappiness. But in the parlour's darkness, the power of those wicked acts! Truly, it was astonishing, and my aunt's every expectation exceeded by her guests' response when, at her given signal – a pre-arranged word, a certain look – her spirit guide materialised from behind 'The Filmy Veil of Death', which was generally the Chinese screen, or the drapes in the room's dimmest corner. From there, I would float across the room, leaving a trail of apports behind – the rosebuds, or other such fragrant blooms that might be construed as Spirit-sent: as were the kisses that I gave, the touch of veiled lips on tear-damp cheeks – the diversion of which then permitted my aunt the chance to fling some dust from her pocket, down onto the fire in the hearth. Those chemicals would cause the flames to crackle purple, orange, red, to then exude a dense grey pall through which I exited the door – through which my aunt would stand and chant:

Through the mists that hide the Light of God,
I see a shapeless form of Death.
Death comes and beckons me today to let me glimpse the Summerland.
And with commingled joy and dread, I hear the far-off whispers . . .

I hear the far-off whispers . . . I found myself repeating those words when I left my aunt in the parlour with the visitor from India. Something was wrong with me. But what? My eyes were stinging, hot with tears. And that slipping sensation I'd felt in my belly when the stranger placed his hand on mine, that was replaced by a dullish cramp, which, by the time I'd reached my room, had intensified to such an extent that I was almost doubled up; my breaths coming ragged and heaving so hard that I might have aged one hundred years. I might have climbed to a mountaintop.

I did not want to call my aunt, not with that man still in the

52

house – though much like the musical notes before from the silver bird in the golden cage, his voice had seemed to follow, a reverberation carried low through my rustling skirts upon the stairs, until I passed my bedroom door, and pushed it closed, and shut him out.

I went to stand before the hearth and looked at the photograph above, at the shapeless form of my father's face: the face where the features of the dead were hidden from the living still. It was the same with Mini: for deep within my memory her features faded more each year. My father and my ayah were nothing more than shadows then, but glimpses of the Summerland, that place too far beyond my reach.

Almost overcome by grief, I turned away and found myself staring down into my washing bowl. It was half-filled with water, the surface scummed and grey with soap, not being changed since yesterday, for we were then without a maid.

I don't know how long I lingered there, hearing sounds from the empty attic above – the shuffling scratch of what? *A bird? It could not be a snake.* But that was the last coherent thought that I remember having then, the rest a blank and for some hours, because, when I came to my senses again the day had darkened into night, and in the purple skies outside a bright full moon was shining. It crowned the spire of the Trinity Church as it loomed on the opposite side of the road. Its gleam pierced through my windowpanes to glimmer in the water bowl, in which my features wavered, a rippling that was transformed into the face of someone else – someone whose eyes were rimmed with kohl, whose blue black hair hung down like silk, whose lips were opening to say: *A full moon, my dearest. That is an omen for thee to heed!*

For a moment I had to steady myself. That echo again! My ayah's voice, as clear and sweet as it had been upon another moonlit night, when we visited a mountain shrine. And there, in the water's reflection, I saw some floating marigolds, and a veil grown dark with Shiva's tears. A trailing veil that looked like blood.

The next morning I woke in a panic. I felt such an ache in my belly again. There were bloodstains on my nightgown, yet more of them on the mattress sheet. I cried and called for Mercy. But my aunt showed little sympathy, only slapped my face to calm me, only scowled when she looked at the mess on the bed, after which she took a firm grip on my arm and dragged me downstairs to the basement floor.

Cook had not arrived by then. If she had, she surely would have tried to prevent the things that Mercy did – which began with the muttering of oaths, and then the remonstrations that, 'This foulness, this loss of blood is the blight of every woman, and all because of the sins of Eve.'

Releasing her grip upon my arm, she opened up a dresser drawer, and I wondered what she was about, rummaging through the knives like that. I started to shiver. I couldn't stop. The flags were like ice beneath my feet, and I should have thought to move those feet, to run back out the kitchen door before my aunt returned again, to hold me in a vice-like grip while, with the scissors in one hand – those gleaming, snapping, spiteful blades – she cut through the weave of coloured threads that formed a twist around my wrist; the twist which, only yesterday, the man called Tilsbury had caressed.

I pleaded for my aunt to stop, to give my bracelet back to me. But she made her way towards the range where some embers from the day before were still a glowing ruby red – the furnace into which she threw the treasure she had stolen.

I was shocked. All I could do was stare. I had not the wit to prevent her. I knew not what was the worse just then – the blood and the aching in my bowels, or the slashing of the steels, the hissing song that was resumed when she returned to grab my hair – the hair that Lucian Tilsbury had also touched the day before – great hanks of which she cut away to fall and curl about my feet.

When she was done, when the scissors were dropped with a clanging thud upon the slabs, she crouched down to gather the brown in her hands, the brown that looked like coiling snakes. And when she flung those into the flames, how they flared, and oh, the stench they made! A horrible odour, like rotten eggs, as good as any smelling salts to bring me to my senses.

A fury was rising inside me, through which I screamed such wicked things, 'I wish you were dead . . . like my mother before. I wish you were dead and burning now.'

Looking down through the open door of the range beside which my aunt was standing, I rushed towards her. I pushed her away. And while she stumbled backwards, I thrust my hands into the fire and snatched at all that I could find remaining of my ayah's gift.

The threads, they were entirely gone. The beads were ruined, black and charred. But, quite the strangest thing it was that, like the flesh upon my hands, when I drew the rudrakshas from those flames, it seemed they were not burned at all. I stared at those sacred, bobbled nuts and the fire of my fury dissolved into water – into the tears then in my eyes.

I was barely aware of Mercy, when she knelt on the slabs with a whining groan, when she wrapped her arms around my waist, and pressed her cheek against my ribs and begged for my forgiveness.

The words she spoke, though ominous, they came so sweet they soothed like balm, 'Forgive me, Alice. Forgive me. I only do what's best for you. It is well known that too much hair can drain a child's vitality. You are too young, too small, too pale. I fear you lack the inner strength to withstand the curse of the serpent. I do what I do to protect you. To keep you safe from sin.'

THE GIFT THAT NEED
ONLY BE NURTURED

Aunt Mercy was true to her word in this: in the coming years she kept me safe. And perhaps the cutting of my hair released some inner strength in me because, from that day onwards, I staunchly refused to play her ghost. I said, if she tried to make me, then I would expose her for what she was – a liar and a charlatan. I took the same shears that my aunt had used when raping my beads and the hair from my head, and used them to hack at my spirit veils. And then, those black and ruined shreds, I dumped them at her parlour door.

Even so, it often seemed to me that the veils in which she'd draped my face had never been removed at all, for I felt myself so distant, so alone and apart from the outside world. And perhaps I was only deceiving myself to imagine I had autonomy. In truth, since that fateful afternoon when Lucian Tilsbury first called – since when he often came again to share in Mercy's Circles – on each of those occasions my aunt insisted I stay away and remain in my room at the top of the house. And I was happy to comply, at first out of embarrassment, to hide my head of spiked short hair. But as the months and years drew on, I often sat up there to brood on what the attraction could possibly be for a man like Lucian Tilsbury to spend his time in our parlour, surrounded by grieving old women. I also had my suspicions where most of those women were concerned, that whenever Aunty Mercy fell into her trances, reaching out to touch 'The Dead', what she and her clients desired the most, the real allure of those events, was the chance for some close proximity with 'the handsome Mr Tilsbury'.

That was how so many referred to my aunt's enigmatic

friend, whenever they waited in the hall. And Mercy was no better. Whenever he was expected, she would take the whole day in selecting her costume, in arranging her hair, in pinking her cheeks, in deciding which jewels might suit her best. She said he was her mentor, that her spiritual powers were more intense whenever he was present, and that when his eyes were fixed on hers she felt as if she were possessed by the wisdom and strength of a goddess. She said he once told her an Indian priest had predicted that he would travel to England and meet with a powerful woman seer who would lead him to his destiny: to find some ancient mystery.

She should never have listened to what he said! Not that he specifically lied. I came to see that later on. He simply deceived her by saying as much as he needed to say, and nothing more. And all the while he exuded his glamour, that charisma, which, I must confess, had also bound me in its spell, and had done so since that afternoon when he first came to Claremont Road.

There were some nights I dreamed of him, of that moment when he touched my hand. And even during waking hours, though I took great pains to keep away, if I knew him to be calling, if we should accidentally meet, in the hallway, or on the house front steps – if he should come anywhere too near – I could not say quite how I felt, except that the air became too thick, as if whatever god looked down was holding its breath and waiting; waiting for something to begin.

It began, all that Tilsbury had planned, on one October evening when I was nineteen years of age.

I'd been a listless mood all day, and that mood only intensified when I chanced to look at the remains of what once wound around my wrist – the rough brown nuts, and the orbs of glass that were now as black as mourning jet. I was turning them over in my hands, counting those beads like a rosary, counting down the hours, the months, the years until I would be twenty-one, when I might attain my majority and inherit whatever then remained of my dead father's legacy – though what path I might follow then, who knew?

Just as I had done so often before, I went to gaze out of my window, to where, on the other side of the road, the Trinity Church blocked out the sky; oppressive, dark and ominous. In India the temples' domes had made them seem like palaces; marble visions conjured up from the pages of Arabian tales. But this church with its boundary of black iron railings, it looked more like a prison. Its tower resembled a fortress, its steeple an enormous spear that seemed to be threatening Heaven itself. Dull yellow bricks were fading to grey and a mist rose up from the bushes around, already obscuring the hands of the clock – though I knew the time when its chimes tolled out. Seven bells that came muffled and dull that night.

I thought my life rang just as dull. Most every day it was the same, beginning with bells, ending with bells, and with nothing of interest between – though there had been something different, something that occurred that afternoon, something so small that at the time it seemed of no significance.

I had been heading down the stairs, the fresh scent of beeswax filling my nose, and fully expecting to find the maid (another one, but newly hired), when I saw my aunt with a duster in hand, wiping at the dado rail, and with such a whirling urgency that when she glanced back to see me there I saw how her cheeks were flushed with exertion and how her hair had come undone, the long dark strands then falling free. One or two of them glinted silver. I had not seen that grey before. But there was something stranger, for where her sleeves had been rolled back I saw the bruised and reddened scabs that were scarring the inner flesh of her arm.

The sight of them caused me to cry in alarm, 'Aunt Mercy, you're hurt! What have you done?'

Glancing at what had caught my eye, she let her cloth drop to the floor and hurriedly dragged the sleeve back down, snapping, 'It's nothing! I had an accident. I fell. That new maid, that Nancy . . . she has no idea! She left a bucket on the stairs. How many times must I tell her? And I have such a valuable client tonight. Perhaps, just this once, you might think to help . . .'

She turned and reached over the console, across her big appointment book to where a crystal vase then stood, and I caught the sourest odour when she pressed that vase into my arms, saying, 'Will you take this on down to the kitchen. There are some lilies to be arranged. They were delivered hours ago, and I did ask Nancy to deal with them . . . but who knows where she has got to.'

Nancy had got to the basement, where she seemed to have not a care in the world, slouched over the kitchen table, drinking tea, blowing steam from her cup. Mrs Morrison was there as well, despite the fact that, normally, she would have been heading home by then. She was pouring herself a cup of tea. She was asking if I would like one too, while I stood at the sink to turn the tap and fill the vase with water, before carrying that to the table where, at the far end, the lilies lay, still in their paper wrappings.

Cook sighed and gave a little tut, 'Take care with that pollen, dearie. You don't want to go and stain your gown. Look at my apron – ruined, it is, with the horrible red of those blessed things.'

She lifted her hands to point at marks that streaked across her ample breast. At the same time little puffs of flour were scattered across three trays of tarts, some blowing up to ice the frizz of grey that curled below her cap.

One of those pastries I placed in my mouth, all melting butter, oyster and beef, so delicious I could have eaten ten – if only Cook had not stood up and reached across the table top to tap my hand and harshly chide, 'Alice, leave those tarts alone!'

She shook her head and grumbled, 'What on earth is your aunt about today? Not that I mind, it's my job after all, but I do like some notice now and then. And why is she going to such expense, ordering all this fancy stuff, when a pot of tea and slice of cake have always sufficed her guests before? Poor Nancy, here . . .' She paused for breath while pointing then towards

59

the maid, 'I insisted she sit and rest a while. Her fingers are nearly worn through to the bone. Show Miss Alice your hands – go on, girl!'

The maid duly proffered her fingers and I must admit I almost winced to see them as blistered and raw as that. Most maids had rough and calloused hands. But Nancy, she was different. Her shape was slight and delicate. Her features, apart from a small rash of freckles around her nose and on her brow, were pale and very finely made, in a sharpish, bird-like sort of way. Brown eyes were almost too alert, darting, quick and nervous – though that day I noticed how tired she looked, with shadowed circles round those eyes, as if she was an invalid, or someone much older than Nancy was. Because Nancy was more or less my age. Eighteen, I think Aunt Mercy said.

My aunt did expect a great deal of her maids and often worked them much too hard. Another reason why they left. But in Nancy, she might have met her match. For despite that look of fragility, Nancy could be brazen and was not averse to arguing, as shown when she lifted up a hand to push some dark red wisps of hair from where they fell across her brow – that brow then furrowed into lines when she glanced up at Cook and said, 'I can't be expected to work like this. I was hired in as a lady's maid, not some cheap skivvy or scullery girl.'

She dragged a sleeve across her nose, leaving a trail of snot on the cloth, which wasn't exactly ladylike! But I thought it best not to mention that, because Nancy did seem to be upset. And when one of the bells high on the wall gave out its tinkling alarm, its wires set off by the unseen hand of whoever was then at our front door, the maid let out a weary groan, during which the bell jangled all over again and Cook snapped, 'Nancy! Are you deaf? Go upstairs and answer that blessed door – though I dare say it's only our own Prince of Darkness arriving to spread The Word again. Not that it's any business of mine, but to hear the gossip going round! And your aunt . . .' She looked at me again. 'Charging the most outrageous fees for meddling in things that she should not. If not for you and the fondness I had for your dear grandmother before . . . well, if she's not spinning in her grave, my name's not Hannah Morrison!'

I'd heard Cook's complaints so often before – but whatever she thought of Aunt Mercy's profession she had only ever shown kindness to me – especially since that awful day when my aunt had chopped off all my hair. After that, Mrs Morrison often stayed and worked well into the afternoons: those hours for which she was not paid while my aunt met with her friends upstairs, when Cook and I would sit in the kitchen, talking of nothing, drinking hot chocolate, or nibbling on slices of cheese on toast: mine topped with the Lea & Perrins sauce that reminded me of India, which Cook had found in the grocer's shop and ordered in for me ever since.

But there was no idling that day as Cook went on with her complaints. 'And speaking of spinning round in graves, I hope you don't mind me saying, but would you take those lilies up. I cannot abide the smell of them! They stink of death and misery!'

I wondered if Nancy had also been upset by the fragrance of those blooms, if they had infused *her* with misery. But the maid's grudging mood had been thrown off the moment Cook alluded to whoever might happen to be at the door; when Nancy's face was one big smile, and she left the table in such haste that her cup was tipped and the tea was spilled.

'Well, I never! She is a flighty one!' Cook looked over her shoulder and motioned to the empty space where the maid had been. 'I imagine, the very first chance she gets, that one will be spreading her wings to fly. She'll disappear like all the rest, you mark my words, Miss Alice.'

I thought Mrs Morrison probably right. I no longer tried to make a friend of any of Aunt Mercy's maids. No sooner were they here than gone. And, musing on such matters, I left Cook mopping Nancy's spill and started up the service stairs, though nowhere as eager as the maid. I paused and clasped the vase to my breast when I heard the front door rattle shut, and then the deep tenor of Tilsbury's voice, though what he was saying I could not tell. But it must have been amusing. It certainly gave Nancy cause to laugh, a light, flirtatious musical sound, after which there came some murmurings that sounded far more serious – and every word too hushed and low to hear above the clatter of pans, and the oaths being uttered then by Cook, the racket of which was soon replaced by the swishing of silk and, when I turned, I saw my aunt on the stairs.

Haloed in a golden light that was shining through the open baize, she was quite transformed from her earlier self, her green eyes bright and glittering below the darkness of her hair, now tightly wound upon her head. She wore a gown of darkest blue, shimmering black where shadows fell. She looked elegant. She smelled fresh and clean, though her fragrance of violets was overwhelmed by that of the lilies in my arms. And yes, Cook was right, they were horribly pungent. Such a cloying, drenching sweetness. Their pollen caused my nose to itch. I had to sniff and tilt my head in the hope of staving off a sneeze.

Still, they suited the mood of my aunt's entertainments, my aunt whose palms were now pressed down upon the slope of the banister rail, over which she was leaning, calling out, 'Mrs Morrison, are you still there? Is the food prepared for bringing up?'

I knew all too well that brittle voice: Aunt Mercy's temper was simmering. At any moment she might explode.

In response, Cook's fleshy face appeared, poking around the kitchen door to offer her placid, slow reply, 'Old your 'orses, Miss Mercy, they will be soon enough. Send Nancy back down to plate them up. They're only cooling on the racks.'

My aunt tut-tutted her exasperation. 'Is that girl missing again? You and I will have to deal with it. And Alice . . .' Green eyes were cast my way, 'what are you doing standing there? Are you also deliberately riling me? Take those flowers on up to the parlour. Please!'

I held the lilies to one side while my aunt squeezed past to go on down. I made my way on through the baize and then across the hall's tiled floor. But, at the door to the parlour, I stopped and hesitated, because Lucian Tilsbury was there, standing at the window bay, one hand holding back a panel of lace while observing something in the street.

His concentration left me free to observe the man quite undisturbed, to see the aspect of the face that was not blemished by the scar – nothing to mar the profile so perfectly proportioned. A large but straightly chiselled nose, a smooth and cleanly shaven cheek. His hair, he wore that longer now, swept back from his brow and hanging loose to brush against his collar and—

And, whatever it was that had held his attention, he must have sensed my presence near, or perhaps it was when I sniffed again – when he turned his head, when his eyes met mine. Without a word, without a threat, I felt his gaze enslave me, as dark and intense as ever it was, as if he could see into my soul, as if we shared some secret; though the nature of what that secret was – what could it be but India? And yet, apart from the niceties – the hellos, or goodbyes, or how are you todays? – he had not mentioned the place of my birth, or anything of my father, not since the Sunday afternoon when I'd stood upon that very spot, where I dithered with the lilies then.

Five years ago I'd stood there, and Lucian Tilsbury touched my hand, and Lucian Tilsbury touched my hair. But ever since the cutting, since it had grown sufficiently, I'd never left my room again without ensuring that my hair was tied and well secured with combs, a style Aunt Mercy called demure – which was what I attempted to be just then, lowering my eyes when I turned away to set the vase of lilies down. And not on the parlour mantel as Mercy had instructed, but back in the hall, on the console shelf.

There, in the mirror hung above, I saw myself reflected back and recalled what Mini used to say: *Just as the fragrance is in the flower, so the reflection is in the mirror, reflecting who we really are, our pasts, our presents, our future fates.*

Behind my own reflection there were the eyes of Tilsbury, still staring at me through the parlour door.

An hour or so later, when back in my room, from below came the slam of the house front door, and then the whine of the garden gate. Going to stand at my window, I saw Tilsbury, out on the pavement. He was looking down the length of the road as it sloped its way on past the church. From there he peered up at the church's clock where the first of the hour's bells chimed out, and only when the seventh rang, and through its trembling resonance there came the clatter of iron hooves as a carriage drew up in the street outside.

Despite the failing evening light, my sight soon adjusted sufficiently to see the first passenger to descend. A gentleman in a tall top hat, and a black frock coat of a generous cut, very formal and rather old-fashioned, which made me think him elderly – as did his movements, so rigid and slow, when he stooped to lower some carriage steps and assist two ladies (also in black, their faces concealed by veiled hats) down to the pavement at his side. It was during this performance that Tilsbury bowed his welcomes. He motioned then towards the porch, to which the guests proceeded. But as he followed them through the gate – that was when he raised his eyes, to look straight up, at my window.

I couldn't be sure he saw me there, so quickly did I shuffle back. But I feared that he had, and if not me, then surely the marks where my fingers had been, where the tips had rested on the glass and smeared through dusty films of soot. And, when I crept near to the glass again, I saw him still there, on the path below – and the way his eyes were gleaming when caught in the glow of the street lamp. How oddly flustered that made me feel, yet more so when the faintest smile was playing then upon his lips – when that smile seemed to speak directly to me, to say in no uncertain terms: *I see you, Alice Willoughby*.

It was some moments after he'd gone before I felt myself free to breathe again, before my heart slowed in its racing beat. Now, only the carriage driver remained. I watched him reach into his overcoat pocket to extract what looked to be a pipe, and then to strike a lucifer. A tiny bright flame flared up in the gloom. I stared at that light a long, long time, almost as if I were hypnotised, seeing the tip glow crimson, then dulling back to black again when he tossed it to the gutter. He proceeded to puff upon the clay from which a plume of smoke rose up. It drifted as high as my window glass where it curled and seemed to hover – as if some spirit spied on me, as if the eyes of Tilsbury.

I was still staring at that smoke when, perhaps five minutes later, I heard a squeaking of the boards from just outside my bedroom door, that sound then followed by the traipse of weary feet on the stairs. Nancy was going to her room – to go to her rest and leave my aunt and Tilsbury with their guests alone.

I thought to go to bed myself. A stabbing pain was in my head. A gritty soreness in my throat. Could there be a tonic in one of the bottles – those potions cluttered on the stand beside the bed in my grandmother's room? Mrs Winslow's Soothing Syrup. I'm sure I'd seen such a medicine. A tincture used for children. What harm could it do to sip at that? But I should have thought to measure the dose, rather than simply unstopping the bottle and tipping it back to swallow down such gulps of sticky viscous brown.

Even so, in very little time I was feeling a great deal better, such a tingling warmth in my throat and breast, and – well – how soothed I seemed to be when I lay on my grandmother's quilt a while, having rummaged through her shelves to find a tale that I'd not read before. Soon I was entirely lost in some Penny Dreadful magazines – some musty yellowed papers that told stories of *Varney the Vampire*. Had my grandmother read those 'Feasts of Blood', or had they belonged to her daughters? Such salacious dark romances! And Varney's fate – how terrible – when, in the final instalment, when consumed by guilt and dark despair, the vampire ended his own life in the flames of a volcano, there to burn for the whole of eternity.

For all that excitement I fell asleep, but the vampire tale caused me to dream, and in that dream I saw a skull; a skull all burned and charred and black which then began to speak to me.

And its voice – it seemed familiar – when it asked, '*Why dost thou shrink from death?*'

That horrible vision, that talking skull: I cannot begin to convey to you how disturbed I was by such a dream. And then, to come to my senses again and find myself at the closet door, with both my hands upon the knob, as if about to turn it.

How long had I been standing there? I was much relieved when glancing back to see that the candle I'd set on the mantel had hardly melted down at all. Yet I did feel terribly muddled, as if I'd been asleep for hours, as if my head was filled with wool. My vision was affected too, become so dim and cloudy, as if wherever I might look was veiled in a dense white fog.

Shaking my head to clear my thoughts, I took the candle up again, retracing my steps through the closet door when I heard the faint rhythm of voices then rising through the stairwell, and that of my aunt so very clear, when she called, 'Why dost thou shrink from Death? Come what may, this night will bring the risen day.'

I took a deep breath, recalling my dream, and however unnerved I may have felt, I could not resist the compulsion to listen to a little more. With the candle set down on the Indian chest, I placed one hand on the banister rail, the fingers of the other scrunching and balling the cloth of my nightgown as my feet began to tread the stairs.

My progress was very slow. I flinched at every new descent, every hiss of the oil lamps, gleaming low, which cast my wavering shadow on – until I arrived at the final half landing, from which vantage point I could then see that the parlour door was open, the room within reflected back in the console mirror in the hall.

Though my sight was somewhat hazy I saw the parlour's brocade drapes which, as usual, were drawn across to conceal any guests from the street's prying eyes. No lamps had been lit within that room, only flames from white candles to glimmer and flash on my aunt's Egyptian crystal ball and the gilt decoration of the plates upon which many fancy tarts still lay entirely undisturbed. Inky shadows were flitting across the walls where the red and gold arabesque design created a dramatic backdrop for the lady whose hair appeared to be fair – or could it be a shade of grey? – who perched on the edge of the settle, very upright and stiff, clearly not at ease. And standing nearby, before the hearth, feigning an air of indifference, was the same mature gentleman seen before, who was dressed once again in a black frock coat, a high starched collar, a white cravat. His mouth was set in a fixed grimace which could not be concealed by the drooping tusks of a substantial white moustache. Perhaps he had been a military man. He had that stance, erect and proud. His eyes, despite being heavily bagged, I thought them watchful and astute when he surveyed those sitting at the table central in the room.

My aunt was dressed in black satin, and not one jewel as ornament. Her hair was equally severe, drawn back from her temples and bound in a chignon. At her side was Lucian Tilsbury, and as always he was immaculate, his suit dark grey, and his hair so oiled that it shone as black as a raven's wing. But the side of the face I witnessed then, that was the side that bore the scar; the flesh purple, and puckered, and ugly.

Of the woman then seated between him and my aunt, I saw but two hands on the table top, each one of them black-cuffed with lace. She wore a mourning shawl of crêpe, beneath which narrow shoulders hunched. But little else was visible: just the tip of her nose and a jowly cheek which quivered with emotion while my aunt began chanting some new incantation, its rhythmic message ringing out –

'Remember, death is but a charade, a thinly veiled door to enlightened lives where we are reborn and joined in bliss with those who have passed to The Other Side. The material and immaterial are never truly parted but bound by an invisible cord, delicate but immutable, linking the realms of the living and dead . . . those souls who exist in both Heaven and Earth.'

When this speech was done Aunt Mercy leaned forward, extending her hands with both palms facing upwards. Tilsbury took hold of the client's, placing them gently on top, at which point my aunt then closed her eyes, slumping backwards in her chair, her breaths coming deep and her head lolling forward until it was resting on her breast.

I had seen her do this many times before. But still, it never failed to alarm; to hear all that sighing, the grunting and moaning, and how, when she started to speak again, her voice was much deeper and stronger, as if it belonged to someone else, almost as if it was a man's. 'There is no pain, but grief lives on. He yearns to reach through the mists of time, to tell you he only sleeps and waits . . .'

A sob broke from the client's mouth, the depth of her anguish clear to hear. 'Is it him? Oh, I cannot bear it!'

Before she had even completed those words, the fair-haired woman made to stand, as if to go and aid her friend. But, with a dismissive shake of his head, the merest lifting of one hand, Tilsbury motioned that she sit, whispering firmly, 'Please. Be still.'

During that small disruption, my aunt's breathing grew more laboured, and how peculiar it was when my own lungs became constricted, when the drifting scent of the lilies caused me to feel nauseous, and the temperature seemed to drop so low that my flesh was prickling with cold. The scene in the mirror was motionless – before flaring, unnaturally bright, as if I was gazing into a flame – and that flame like a magnifying glass through which I saw, quite vividly, the lining of Tilsbury's jacket, as his fingers delved into claret silk in a motion that seemed relaxed and slow. However, in reality, I think it must have happened fast, with every visitor then fooled into thinking that all the man had done was to open his hand, to show what he held – what he seemed to have clutched out of thin air.

A golden ring it looked to be. It might well be the one of brass, the symbol of matrimonial love that Mercy sometimes conjured up when she spoke with grieving widows. That apport was then dropped to the table top where it twirled on the cushioning velvet, until gradually slowing to a stop. And there it glittered prettily while Aunt Mercy awoke from her psychic trance, to cry with wild abandon, 'The bridegroom is here! He has come for the bride. He has sent this token as his proof. But wait! I hear him . . . very near. He is speaking about a precious stone. Not some symbolic trinket . . . but the precious white jewel from India, and through its sacred energy his soul may yet materialise.'

The client's hands were then drawn back, one clasped to her breast, one to her mouth, through which she finally replied, 'I know what it is . . . what he speaks of! It is the proof. He is still here. My husband has not gone from me!'

There followed some soft exclamations, the hurried rush of comforting words, during which the gentleman by the hearth gave a small cough to clear his throat, and Tilsbury rose from the table, calmly informing the visitors of how draining the calling of spirits could be, and how Miss Matthews must now rest, to regain her vital energies – before any further communication could be resumed at a future date.

While he spoke, in such languid, polished tones, I distinctly heard another sound – the squeaking of something on the tiles, something that might be dragging feet. A clawed hand of dread gripped the base of my neck and, holding my breath, too frightened to move, when I finally dared to raise my eyes, I saw it, just under the arch by the door – something that gave me such a fright that I quite forgot any subterfuge and let out a long and piercing scream.

When that cry had faded, except for the ticking of the clock, there was nothing but silence in the house. It seemed to go on for ever. And my eyes, which were again a blur, now gazed through a narrow tunnel of light where I found myself looking at the eyes of the man then staring up at mine.

His face was pallid and dripping with sweat. His brown waving hair, parted low on one side, was plastered wet against his brow. The lids of his eyes were swollen. The flesh of his cheeks was oddly grey. Above his lips – quite blue and cracked – a dark moustache extended to whiskers that grew very low on the chin. And those whiskers were flecked with drools of white spittle when he opened his mouth to speak to me – just as he'd done all those years before, when I had been a little girl, when he had been full of vigour and charm, though his voice was now a dreadful drawl, as if time itself was decelerating, when he said, *'You must be wary. These things, they should be left alone.'*

With that warning he vanished away. Where he had been standing no more remained but a rippling of the air, like a haze on an Indian summer's day. Through that I recall seeing my aunt, standing in the parlour door, her mouth gaping and wide in shock, but otherwise quite recovered from what had been her exhausting 'ordeal'. Now, she was only mortified at what she'd heard and seen of me, clutching two hands against her breast and offering the plaintive gasp, 'Alice . . . it cannot be!'

I don't think she even noticed when Tilsbury swept past her to kneel beside me on the stairs, when speaking in barely a whisper, he said, 'You heard. You woke. I knew you would!'

I could barely concentrate at all on what was being said or done. I could only stare at Victoria. The Queen, in Mercy's parlour! How time and grief had altered her since that day in the Crystal Palace. Now, rather than wearing a garland of rosebuds her head was crowned with a mourning cap, and her hands appeared to be trembling while clutching at the wedding ring – the offering that should have provided the evening's dramatic finale, before my own contribution was made.

Through a fug of embarrassment and shame, I stammered, 'It . . . it was Prince Albert. He was saying that you must beware . . . that you must—'

'Go on!' The Queen rose from her chair, also pushing past my aunt to stand in the hallway from where she addressed me directly, 'Won't you get up . . . come nearer? Won't you tell me who you are?'

'Alice. I am Alice Willoughby.' Standing now upon the stairs, I looked down upon the Queen below, who was saying, 'Well, Miss Willoughby, perhaps you would like to explain –

and to lift that ridiculous veil away so that we may actually see your face!'

A veil? Was I wearing a veil? Was that why my sight had been so dimmed, because of what draped across my face?

In horror I snatched at the fraying hems and threw them back across my head – the greying lace that had adorned the head of the goddess in the Shrine.

My voice was trembling when I said, 'I'm sorry. I cannot think what I . . . I have never before done such a thing. I . . .'

'What nonsense is this! How could you be so wicked!' Aunt Mercy, still pressing a hand to her breast, was wincing now, as if in pain, and clearly furious with me. But her tone was far meeker when turning back to gasp, 'Your Majesty, I can only apologise for such an interruption. For my niece's audacious behaviour.'

'Calm yourself! What need is there for apologies? Not if your niece here speaks the truth. Though why must she dress herself like that? I had not thought for such cheap tricks. Or am I attending a pantomime!' The Queen gave Aunt Mercy a glaring look to denote her irritation before then turning back to me. 'Please,' she urged, more softly, 'you must not be afraid. I have a daughter, also called Alice. I am a mother as well as a queen . . . not quite the ogre you might think!'

A little assured, I told her all, only wishing that there could have been more, for so eagerly did she wait upon my every stumbling word, answering when they ended with, 'I believe you, Alice Willoughby. My husband deplored this communing with spirits. Why, even the more elaborate of our church's religious trappings he viewed as superstition and myth. His interests were in the here and now, in politics, social justice and science. All the great innovations of our age – not this meddling with the spirit world. Although,' she was then pensive, 'he did one time indulge me. At Osborne, it was . . . a Ouija board.' She paused, 'It was not a success – or rather, it was too much of one. The table began to levitate and was rocking so alarmingly that Albert insisted it be destroyed. And that . . .' she gave a

71

rueful smile, 'is why my husband would never approve of what has gone on this evening. Yet who could begrudge a heart-broken widow some word from her loved one, so sorely missed, so prematurely taken?'

The Queen began to weep again. Her lady stepped forward and took her arm, 'Come now, Ma'am. It is growing late, and this evening has been unsettling. You must consider your own health.'

'Yes! Yes, you are right!' Victoria sighed, shaking off the other's grasp, then turning to the gentleman who lingered still beside the hearth. He bowed his head to convey understanding before leading the ladies towards the front door, though, just as she was about to depart, while drawing down a net of lace with which to conceal her face again, Victoria looked back at the three of us remaining in that hallway – to Mercy, to Tilsbury, to me – and said, 'It has been a disquieting evening. It has given us much to ponder.'

Long after the carriage pulled away a surreal decorum reigned in our hallway. But my aunt's emotions could not be contained. Soon, she was pacing back and forth, her arms flung wide when she shrieked at me, 'How dare you appear like that tonight! Is it your wish to ruin us?'

She stopped, to turn on Tilsbury, 'Why did you say nothing to put matters right? This is surely the end of all we planned. You said that I'd win her patronage . . . the wealth and respect that would follow on. But now, everything is finished, before it has even had chance to begin. My reputation is bound to be—'

'Be quiet, will you!' He was abrupt; not calm and insouciant as usual. He pushed my aunt towards a chair and then, when she was sitting, placed both of his hands on her shoulders, and said, 'Stop for a moment and listen! Whatever the outcome of this night, our visitors will not divulge a thing. To do so would only invite the very gossip she must avoid.'

As Mercy relaxed, he loosened his hold, then took a step backwards, beginning to laugh. 'This evening has not been a failure. It has been the greatest success! I could not have designed it better myself. Can't you see? This is fate! For Albert to die . . . to direct the Queen into our hands! No events could have been so fortuitous, unless they were meant to be ordained by some higher power. Trust me. Trust in that power now, and in the end to which it leads.'

'Do you really think so?' Aunt Mercy asked, her voice subdued.

'I do not think – I know so. But,' he glanced towards where I still stood. He took a shawl from a console peg and draped it round my shoulders, 'we should consider Alice. She is cold. She is clearly in distress. Do you have anything to calm her nerves?'

Still much too dazed to offer objection I mutely complied when he took my hand, when he led me on down the remaining stairs, across the hall and through the door that opened to the sitting room. There, in the darkness, I sat on the sofa while Tilsbury set about making a fire. Hearing the thud of feet on the stairs, I feared Mercy was heading to the Shrine, to see how I'd managed to get inside and veil myself in the wedding lace. But, just as soon she came back down, emerging through the sitting room door and holding the candle that I had abandoned upon the top of the closet chest. She set that down on the cabinet from where she lifted a crystal decanter, pouring out three measures of port into three matching glasses – after which she reached into her pocket and drew out a bottle of medicine.

It was something from her own supply. Her bottle of Elixir – those drops I had tasted once before when my monthly curses first began. But I'd never asked for any since, disliking the way they made me dream, all those whirling visions, too vivid, too real, though they paled into insignificance compared to what I'd seen that night – after what I'd consumed in my grandmother's room.

Adding some tincture to one of the glasses, Aunt Mercy held the mixture high, circling the port around so that all the strands of syrup then melted from brown and into red. And that was the glass she offered me, even though she must have sensed my

73

reluctance, muttering, as if to herself, 'I wonder if this is right? Perhaps we should call for a doctor? Alice has never behaved like this. What if she had some sort of fit . . . some aberration of the mind?'

My aunt, the fake spiritualist medium, could not begin to comprehend that her niece may have seen an actual ghost. As far as Mercy was concerned, well, either my deeds were malicious, or else I really was unwell.

'What do you propose to tell the quack?' Tilsbury was standing up again, the fire in the hearth surging behind. 'That Alice has seen Prince Albert's ghost? Whatever she saw out there in the hall, whether real or imaginary, any physician you think to call would suggest making observations regarding your niece's sanity. And how would that influence the Queen? Would she wish to meet with *you* again? A medium whose family is touched by the taint of madness?'

Aunt Mercy acquiesced with a sigh. 'You're right. I know. You are always right.'

She came to sit beside me and offered that glass of port again, saying, in her sweetest tones, 'This will console you and help you to sleep . . . to rest . . . to forget all that happened tonight.'

As the rim was nudged against my lips I noticed the shaking of her hand, how some of that port was then spilled out to bleed through the lace of the wedding veil – how my nose then filled with its berry scent, and my ears with my aunt's urgent whispering, 'Hush, now. Do drink this down for me. Why, you are as pale as the dead yourself.'

I swallowed the wine as she bade me, still confused and disturbed by what I'd seen, hoping its contents might draw new heat to the blood that had frozen in my veins. And indeed, I soon felt its tingling burn when the liquid trickled through my throat, and I made no effort to resist when my aunt pushed my head back to lie on a pillow while the molten drug crept through my limbs, weighing them down in its velvety bonds. I felt safe and cocooned in the fire's glow. I found myself lulled by Tilsbury's voice: vowels linked and repeated like music, their

74

pattern a regular running beat attuned to that of my own heart as he stared at Mercy, then at me, when he said – to which one I did not know – 'You cannot deny the blessing, the gift that must be nurtured. It was only ever a matter of time.'

I struggled to keep my eyes open, to resist the engulfing darkness. I tried to object, but could not speak, though my aunt did protest on my behalf, 'But Alice has no interest in the workings of the spirit world. On the contrary, she has—'

'Whether she is *interested* or not, this night her destiny begins.'

A perplexed expression on her face, my aunt returned to the cabinet to lift, then offer him a glass, before adding more drops of Elixir to the one she had taken as her own. Her tongue was licked across her lips, moistened and slick with her anticipation. And then, when Tilsbury questioned the dose, her answer was almost childlike, meek and imploring when she said, 'But this evening has exhausted me. You know I must rest and calm my mind from the babbling torments of the dead . . .' She closed her eyes as if just then trying to shut some image out, 'Of seeing my niece upon the stairs and thinking my sister had returned.'

While she spoke, his own glass, with its purer contents, he placed that on the mantel shelf. And there it remained, not even sipped, while he stared down into the hearth below, his dark eyes narrowed into slits against the orange glare of flames that roared in the basket of the grate.

I also stared into that fire, too befuddled for any sense of guilt regarding what my aunt had said, about thinking her sister had returned. But before my senses had been drowned in the sticky grasp of the laudanum, I saw the strangest shifting shapes within those hissing, darting flames, those flames then glistening like gold. Gold, like the bars of a gilded cage.

And the coils of black smoke and the glow of red embers – were those the ruby eyes of a serpent rising up within its core? A core dense and white as a diamond.

THE MAN WHO WAS NOT THERE

A cold December morning. The world all decked in a sparkling white when I stood outside the draper's porch, resting my forehead against cool glass, seeing lace, shawls and ribbons, buttons and feathers – a whirling wheel of textures and colours. I closed my eyes against them, but no sooner was my dizziness quelled than I jumped at the sudden touch on my arm and heard my aunt's impatient voice. 'Are you coming back inside, or not? And where on earth is Nancy? I have more errands for her to run. How can she think to take so long, just to go and fetch a few ounces of tea?'

I took a deep breath and swallowed hard before giving my aunt an answer. 'I'll go and find her. She can't be far.'

In truth, I would have done anything to avoid going back inside that shop, with its darkly oppressive panelled walls, and the countless bolts of fabrics; like corpses laid out on mahogany shelves. Such sombre dreary hues they were, the blacks and greys, the purples and mauves: all the colours of mourning made fashionable by our very own 'Widow of Windsor', the Queen. *The Queen, who had come to Claremont Road.*

We might have been royalty ourselves, so fawning the shop proprietor, the diminutive man who had pranced all around us, flinging his arms this way and that while extending the lengths of material he considered the most appealing. In a high and lilting voice, he had drawn my aunt's attention to the shimmer of this cloth, the plushness of that, though I'm sure my own lack of enthusiasm was a great disappointment to them both. But the salesman was not to be daunted, setting down a roll of lace and appraising my person from head to toe. 'If I might be so bold,' he'd said, his smile so obsequious I'd squirmed, 'how handsome Miss Alice has grown of late – quite the elegant young lady.'

I did not think myself elegant. In the mirror that covered the shop's back wall, the reflection I'd seen might be a wraith. Clothes hanging too loose, grey eyes too bright in a face that was gaunt and very pale. More like some consumptive heroine brought to life from a tragic novella.

My aunt had answered for me, as if I was as deaf and dumb as the mannequins standing in the shop, each one of which put me in mind of the goddess in the Shrine. 'Well, her health has not been the best of late. But it's true, she has grown taller. I think we shall need an entirely new wardrobe if she is to be fit for public view. I trust your seamstress can comply.'

I had not been 'fit for public view' for more weeks than I could remember, my health not being good at all since that night when I had seen the ghost. And what Aunt Mercy said was true. I had grown prone to nervousness, often trembling and sweating beneath the bed covers while hours and days merged into misty confusions. More than once, I honestly thought that I might be losing my sanity – for what else could explain the sights and sounds to haunt my imagination?

That first morning, after the séance, I woke to a bleary confusion, my sleep only broken by Mercy's voice, 'Alice . . . Alice, can you hear me?' My aunt was standing beside the bed. 'You've been sleeping for almost three days.'

'Three days?' My voice was slow and gruff. 'I've had the strangest dreams. The Queen and—'

'Shush! Don't speak of that.' Aunt Mercy's eyes were dark and cold, her brow drawn down in pleats of doubt when she said, 'You weren't dreaming. Don't you remember? You came downstairs and . . .' She stopped for a moment before going on, 'Why did you do such a heartless thing? To have broken into my mother's room, to have worn my sister's wedding veil!' She stiffened and took a step backwards. Her next words sounded hollow and lacking conviction, 'You cannot know how cruel that was. Oh well . . .' she gave a heavy sigh, 'it is over now. What's done is done.'

What's done is done. I heard those words. I closed my eyes and fell asleep, only waking to see Nancy closing the shutters, to hear the rain thrashing on the panes, and the wind a howling beneath the eaves, wuthering like some anguished soul. Come morning, and Nancy was back in the room, a cold morning light dribbling around while she cleared the ashes from the grate, or set a tray on the stand by the bed, from which she offered me milk-softened bread or sips of a thin and tasteless broth. Now and then, I would sit in the fireside chair while she combed the knots from my tangled hair. And sometimes, when she'd gone away, then Cook might come up from the kitchens instead, humming a pretty lullaby, making me feel safe again – as if I was a little child.

I felt far from safe when, every night, Mercy brought more medicine – clear water laced brown with opiates which my aunt insisted would improve my strength and constitution. One time, I managed to prove her right, having the strength to lash out with my hand, knocking the glass to the floor below where its contents spilled across the boards. But to see her expression, so furious, I did not argue when she brought more, only swallowed that Elixir down, then watched through damp and stinging eyes when she left and slammed the door behind.

Lost in the sound of her feet on the stairs, I gasped at some movement beside the bed – but how foolish I felt to realise that it was only Nancy. She must have been there, in the room all along. She came nearer and touched a hand to mine – a gesture of friendship that caused me surprise, and which I was much too swift to refuse, snatching my fingers away from hers and ignoring the subsequent hurt in her eyes when I turned my face to the pillow and said, 'Go away, Nancy. Leave me alone!'

I had not meant to offend her. I felt so wretched, tired and ill. But, I have come to wonder since if my action caused Nancy to do what she did? Or had her demonstration of kindness only been based on the guilt she felt for the wickedness already planned?

Much later, when the house was still, when the greyness of night crept through the room, I heard the ring of the front door bell, then outside my door some shuffling steps, and some creaks from the attic boards above. But nothing more disturbed my sleep, which for once was empty of any dreams – until I was jolted to consciousness, when my eyes snapped open to stare through the darkness, and my mind was a flurrying panic of: *What was that sound? What woke me?*

Sitting up to peer through the soupy gloom, from nowhere that other hand appeared. Not the hand of Nancy. Not the hand of any phantom, but one of living, pliant warmth that was pressing then against my face, blocking the air to my mouth and nose. During that act its owner was speaking, his voice barely more than a murmured growl, 'Don't be frightened . . . don't try to make a sound. Your aunt is sleeping down below. I assure you there's *nothing* will wake her tonight. And, as for Nancy . . . she knows her place.'

Such a relief when those fingers were lifted. I honestly thought I might suffocate, falling back on the pillow and gulping for air when I really should have tried to shout. I should at least have tried to make some convincing show of objection. But I simply lay there in silence, as if I was trapped in a waking dream. And I did believe it was a dream, for I'd often had such fantasies, those decadent, lucid visions when my mind had embellished greatly upon the plights of romantic heroines in sensational novels I had read. Why, so shameful were my thoughts that at times I even imagined myself to be a victim of Varney the Vampire – when I would be lying on a bed with covers all in disarray, my lips moaning slightly, then gasping with fear when a figure appeared inside the room. I would try to scream but no sound would emerge. My bosom would heave in mortal dread, in the moment's exquisite anticipation of what profanity must come. I had not the strength, or the will in my heart, to resist when I thought of the vampire's mouth, and its press on my lips, and then my neck, and the gush of blood, and the hideous sound of sucking . . .

In truth, the only sound I could hear was the faintest scrubbing of a match, then the stench of the sulphur thick in my nose. I saw my candle flicker to life, its flame casting shadows all around. The vertical bars of my bed's brass ends were stretching long across the walls, the wavering cage through which I saw a face coarse with stubble of new-grown beard, as if that day he had not shaved. I saw his black pupils dilating, splintered with glistening flecks of gold. I thought, not of any vampire, but of the serpent, the Devil himself, risen up from the very fires of hell. And surely the guile of Satan was hidden in that melodious voice, when he said, 'Look, Alice . . . look into my eyes. Let your mind open and see your potential, the gift of the sight which is only beginning . . . for which I have been waiting.'

I was filled with a growing sense of alarm, protesting in a cracked, hoarse voice, 'No! You and my aunt . . . the things you do . . . I know that you are charlatans. I saw through your trick with that wedding ring. Hidden in your pocket all along.'

'You see many things you should not.' After stroking a finger across my cheek, he traced its tip around my lips. I felt his breath, warm and moist on my skin when his mouth drew closer, whispering, 'When you looked down from your window that night, when I looked up and saw you there, I knew that something would occur . . . though I never imagined quite how dramatic my ingénue's entrance would be. And yes, I do confess, I might practise some deceptions as a means of enforcing deeper truths, something to convince our clientele . . . but what is the harm if we bribe them with sparkles and pretty illusions?'

Struggling to free my eyes from his, I said, 'I don't want any part in this . . . in your world of illusions and . . .'

And I thought once again of a bird in a cage, and the bauble with which he first thought to bribe me, before Mercy's fingers snatched it away. And what she had done with it since, who knew?

'But you already are. You always were – and in time we'll possess the key to it all. No more pretending to commune with what *might* exist in the realms of death. You and I will be able to enter those worlds, to knock on those doors, for the gods to hear . . . just as I knock on this wall right now.'

His knuckle tapped lightly on the sprigs adorning the wall above my head – paper roses that juddered in candlelight, that might be swaying in a breeze. And, how strange it was, what happened next, when I heard a faint thrumming in the air, and one of those rosebuds started to swell, tight petals unfurling into bloom. I could not drag my eyes away but stared in sheer amazement when a worm (or could it have been a snake?) was born through the tips of the petals' folds, spiralling around the stem before slithering into the shadows below.

And that was the moment of his transformation, when Tilsbury changed before my eyes, when his hair appeared much longer, matted and threaded with flowers and beads, and his clothes were gone, and nothing remained to cover the shame of his nakedness but the tiger skin around his waist. In the glow of the candle his skin gleamed white, with a bluish tinge around his throat, as blue as the throat of Shiva in one of the stories Mini told – from the time when he fought the demons and drank all the poison in the world, and surely would have died of it, had not Parvati grasped his throat to stop that venom spreading more.

Something more astonishing was what I saw upon one arm, which was inked with patterns of flowers and leaves, around which a tattooed cobra coiled, up onto his shoulder, from there to his breast where, when the muscles flexed beneath, the snake seemed to quiver and come alive. Its eyes were two gleaming rubies. A forked black tongue tasted the air. I felt quite sure I heard it hiss, and through that hissing sound a name, a name that was mine, and yet was not . . .

And then the real Tilsbury was standing in the vision's place, words low, and hushed, and intimate, when he said, 'This is but a little thing . . . only the start of what will come. For now you must look into my eyes. Tell me what you see there.'

I swear, where the candle's dipping light was reflected in his pupils, it seemed to magnify and grow. Golden sparks were darting out, growing into tongues of fire that licked their way across his cheeks and caused his scar to glisten red, as if it was a flame itself.

'Do you see it?' His voice was tense now. 'Let the light pour from me and into you. Through this your own gift is ignited. For now, it will smoulder in your soul, but one day it will catch and begin to burn, and when that time comes only you will know. Wherever I am, you will find me.'

'I see it.' My answer was breathless, feeling the weight of his hands on the sheets, and how those sheets were then pushed back, and how cool his touch when caressing the cotton that sheathed my naked flesh beneath, until, at the hem, at my ankles, I sensed him pause and waver. But the fire I'd seen within his eyes, that fire was burning in my veins, and that fire, it possessed me. I heard myself moaning while raising my hips and pressing my belly against his arm. And, held in that moment of wanting, I watched as his hand lifted once more, as his finger and thumb pinched the wick of the candle, and the flame was doused. The darkness fell.

Sharp splinters of dawn were piercing through some gaps in the bedroom shutters. I pressed my head back on the pillow and stared at the papered walls above, where every rose was still in bud. The medicine Mercy brought last night, it must have been stronger than before. The dreams that had followed filled me with shame.

Dazed and thickheaded, I suddenly felt an overwhelming need to be safe. Without any other conscious thought I found myself climbing out of the bed where, groaning and giddy, I staggered and fell, crawling then on hands and knees until I reached the bedroom door. Mustering every ounce of strength, I stretched up an arm to turn the key, to hear the dull *click* as the lock was fixed. And there, overcome with lethargy, I laid my head upon the boards, not waking again for many hours, until the knob was rattling, over which came the sound of Mercy's voice, shouting at me from the other side, 'Alice, are you in there? Can you hear me? Open this door . . . at once!'

It took a few moments to understand and remember that the door was locked. It took even longer to turn the key, with my fingers shaking, fumbling, with me slumping back to the floor again when my aunt bustled in, dragging hard on my arm, crying out, 'What on earth are you doing? Get up! Look at the state of you!' She sighed in frustration, then screeched downstairs, 'Nancy! Come here – I need your help.'

It was then that I saw 'the state of myself' and all the rusted streaks of blood that stained the muslin of my shift. I thought of the pollen of lilies. I thought that my curse had come early that month, for my belly ached. I felt sticky and sore, and there was a fleeting moment when I wondered if Mercy would punish me by cutting off my hair again.

But no, how foolish was that thought. I would never let her do such a thing, no matter how doped with opiates – which caused my voice to be too slow, quite belying the rush of fear I felt, when I asked, 'Was Lucian Tilsbury here? Did that man come to my room last night?'

'What nonsense is this?' She was peevish, eyes glancing nervously around, as if thinking to find him standing there. 'Nancy . . .' She turned to look at the maid who had finally heeled to my aunt's command, though still panting and flushed from her rush up the stairs while Mercy went on abruptly, 'Nancy, did you hear what Alice said? Mr Tilsbury here, in this room last night?'

Nancy's brown eyes were cast downwards, at last rising to flit between me and her mistress, 'Well . . . he *did* visit the house, as you know. But I don't think he could have come in here. I saw him out of the door before you went to bed. Surely, you must remember? Although, I do admit . . .' Nancy took a pause for breath, 'it was around the midnight bells when I heard Miss Alice crying out. I thought she was having a nightmare. I did get up to take a look, but couldn't see her in her room. I found her in the bottom hall, with the front door wide open to the street, as if she was thinking of going out. Then again, she might have been coming in. I managed to get her back up here, but,' she gave my aunt a haughty glance, 'I am surprised *you* didn't hear, with such a racket going on.'

Aunt Mercy was clearly bewildered, but then announced more certainly, 'I always sleep so deeply. Nothing wakes me from my dreams. But, of course, I recall Mr Tilsbury coming to visit and say goodbye. He was catching the late train for London. He has business there, then Amsterdam. He may be away for quite some time.'

Could it be true, what was being said? Did I exist in some fraudulent world, with my dreams more lucid than reality? I looked at Nancy's face again, where her bottom lip was trembling as if she might begin to cry.

It was only when she'd gone away – sent off by Mercy to draw me a bath – that my aunt gave me a scornful glance, and said, 'There will be no more Elixir. You are too prone to delusions. I fear for your mind's fragility. Whatever occurred in the hall that night, when you interrupted the séance . . . it's high time you came to your senses again. Our lives must resume some normality!'

I felt very far from normal when I stood looking into the draper's glass and saw what I had then become – and hardly recognised myself. At least my mind was clearer, not addled by the grip of Elixir and the decadent thoughts that potion wove. And with Lucian Tilsbury gone away, it seemed I was granted some reprieve from the suggestion he had made that I was now ready to play a part within my aunt's professional life: a profession that, in his absence, she practised far less frequently. And, with our lives so quiet then, it was somewhat surprising that Mercy should become concerned with ordering new gowns to wear; with that visit to the draper's shop which seemed to last for hours and hours, during which I'd felt horribly giddy and sick and had to go and stand outside, to revive myself with fresher air – before heading off in pursuit of the maid.

So many people in town that day. Such a cacophony of noise! Since my illness I'd barely left the house and perhaps my mind was fragile, for it seemed that the slightest commotion could affect my equilibrium. I was distracted by any sounds that came too sudden, too loud or discordant. The shouting of costers, the clatter of hooves as horses pulled carts along Peascod Street – that rising clutter of shop fronts and the awnings beneath which the townspeople bustled, or else stood idly chatting, hugging their purchases to their chests.

I clapped my hands together for warmth. My breath left a trail of white on the air, little clouds dripping moisture that looked like pearls, and me only thinking how lovely that was when I noticed my cape being splattered by water thrown out by the butcher then sluicing his frontage. My stomach heaved when looking back at the carcasses hanging from his hooks. The red of the flesh marbled white with fat, the butcher's blue apron stained with blood. It was all I could do to avert my eyes, to try and suppress the nausea, when my eye caught another glimpse of red – this time the hue of Nancy's hair.

She was standing quite a way ahead, at the door of The Bull, the coaching inn. She was conversing with a man. I called out her name and the maid looked round, but her gaze was as frosty and sharp as the air, and I wished I'd said nothing, I wished I had waited, I wished that the pavement would swallow me up. But, before such a fate could be granted, her friend also chanced to glance my way and I stood there like a tongue-tied fool, my feet quite frozen to the spot as I watched a thin flurry of snowflakes dust over the brim of his tall silk hat, beneath which dark eyes were widened the moment they met with mine – as if my presence caused that man as much surprise as his did me. But then a conveyance went rattling past, and when that cab had disappeared, so had Lucian Tilsbury. Nancy was standing quite alone. Nancy was striding across the street. Nancy was standing at my side, and when I mentioned Tilsbury's name, she laughed. She asked, 'Are you going mad, to be seeing a man who is not there? He's off on his travels, Miss Alice. But then, you know that already!' The maid became more serious, 'Are you sure you're feeling well? Well enough to be out of the house again?'

I had no idea what to answer. I felt quite sure of what I'd seen. And, while walking back to the draper's shop I couldn't help but notice how Nancy kept glancing back over her shoulder, as if she was searching through the crowds, looking for someone who was not there. Someone with a distinctive scar upon the flesh of his left cheek.

THE ARRIVAL OF THE GODDESS

Time passed. My health was much improved, no longer plagued by vivid dreams, or the horrible morning nausea that had blighted my waking hours for weeks. But, that sense of well-being was only the lull, before other things began to occur, beginning with the wet afternoon when a letter arrived in Claremont Road.

At the time, I was in the sitting room where a pot of tea kept warm in the hearth, alongside a slice of half-eaten cake, though, much to Cook's consternation, I had lost my taste for sugary food. I had also lost my ability to concentrate on anything for longer than an hour or two. The page of the book I was reading had been resumed at least three times. In the end, I gave in to my indolence, set the book down, kicked off my shoes and tucked my feet beneath my skirts, lying back on the sofa's cushions while staring down at the fire's flames.

I thought once again of the night of the séance, and the snakes I had seen within those flames – of the snake on the arm of a man in a dream – only startled from that reverie when the wind got up and gave a howl. That made me feel nervous, though I cannot say *what* daunted me. It was not the thought of Albert's ghost, for common sense had then prevailed, and I had quite convinced myself that the Prince's apparition – that any dreams that followed – had almost certainly been caused by phantoms of the laudanum.

The wind died down and for some time there was only the crackle and spit of the fire – through which came the clang of the porch's bell, then the rattling creak of an opened door. Some brief exchange of voices before it thudded shut again, when I made my way out to the hallway and found Nancy standing in front of the console, the maid hardly taking any heed when I asked, 'Who was that . . . at the door just then?'

She walked towards the basement stairs, already at the green baize door when glancing back at me to say, 'Just someone bringing a letter. A letter for Miss Matthews.'

When sure that I was quite alone, I lifted the envelope from the rack in which the maid had placed it. I saw no stamp or postmark to hint as to its origin, but the writing was familiar, and when turning it over in my hands I saw on the back a black wax seal, in its centre a curling letter *T*.

Should I dare to open that envelope? What if Nancy came upstairs again? What if Mercy should come back through the door and catch me red-handed in such a deceit? Only a moment I dithered. Very soon I returned to the sitting room hearth where, next to the partially eaten cake, a pearl-handled knife lay on the plate. All that it took was some small concentration, a delicate lift of the tip of the blade, and there – I exhaled a long, slow breath – the envelope opened in my hands, and not even the tiniest tear on the paper from which I then began to read.

November 20th 1862

DEAR MERCY,

I trust this letter reaches you safely and that you, and Alice, are both in good health.

I lowered the page for a moment. I could almost think he addressed me directly, that he knew that I had been unwell – or was that my shame conscience for prying so illicitly? Still, stronger by far than the guilt I felt was the lure of curiosity, and so I continued to scan the lines.

For myself, I am able to confirm that I shall be returning soon. The object is perfect and in my possession. I only implore that you hold firm and have faith in all that has been planned.

> *As a token of my confidence and also a symbol of my intent I have arranged to send a gift. It will arrive in Claremont Road on the very same day as this letter.*
>
> *Believe me, I do remain,*
>   *As Ever,*
>   *Lucian Tilsbury*

No address was written on the page. Who knew the truth of his whereabouts. But the gift, the 'symbol of his intent', that was delivered to the house just as he had promised – though before its arrival my aunt returned, by which time I had heated the blade of the knife in the flames still burning in the grate, melting again the disc of wax by applying the metal to its back, thus successfully sealing the letter once more before setting it back in the console rack.

Even so, when Mercy came into the room with Tilsbury's letter in her hand, I feared she might only glance my way to know exactly what I'd done. How I cringed at the rustle of paper unfolding, at the great blast of heat then rising up when I prodded the coals with a poker, pretending to be engrossed in that task while, all along, I was anxiously praying that my aunt might find nothing amiss with her letter. Meanwhile, when a fountain of sparks flew out, very almost setting my skirts alight, I swiftly stood and brushed them off, hoping to sound all innocence when I asked, 'Have you any interesting news?'

At first she did not answer. She remained very still, staring out through the window, at the gardens there, so bleak and bare. She took a deep breath before turning around, her voice artificially bright when she said, 'It is Mr Tilsbury. He mentions a present being sent. Something to arrive this very day!'

No mention then of other 'plans' and unless I exposed my duplicity, my only option was silence as I watched her open a bureau drawer, and place the letter within it – just as a hammering came at the door to announce the delivery of a crate.

It was brought up the path, and with no little struggle, by

two burly men who cursed and swore at the weight of whatever might be inside – though Mercy ignored their rudeness while issuing instructions for the box to be placed on the table that she used for parlour séances.

The moment those men had gone away Aunt Mercy sent Nancy downstairs to the kitchen, telling the maid to fetch a knife with which to hack at the ropes and slats, after which a great deal of straw packing was scattered all over the rug below – causing the maid to go off again, this time to look for a dustpan and brush while Mercy stepped back to more clearly observe what her endeavours had revealed.

Through the room's encroaching gloom we saw a shroud of dark red silk secured at the top with a corded knot, though my aunt soon had that tie released and swiftly drew the fabric down to reveal a silver figurine.

Lit by the sputtering glow of the street lamp, its gleam shining in through the window glass, was the form of a Hindoo goddess. She was all of eighteen inches tall. Her head was domed in an ornate crown and in the centre, just over her forehead, a single red ruby glistened. Snakes coiled like bracelets around her limbs, yet more of them writhing at her breasts where the metal glinted white and gold as if some fire burned within. She exuded such a sensual air. I wanted to reach out and touch those breasts, to stroke the raised and bending leg where one foot came to rest on the opposite knee, as if she was about to dance. One of her hands pointed down to the ground where the base was engraved with flowers and leaves. The other supported a tilting chin, below which a red satin ribbon was wound. And to that was attached the small white card which, when my aunt had worked it free, she carried to the window bay, to read by the glow of the street lamp:

'*This is my gift to you. Parvati, Hindoo goddess, Mother of all the World, holding mystery, riches and promise for the future, the secrets of deliverance and marital harmony.*'

Mercy was breathless, her excitement contagious, and I

noticed the tremor in her voice when she said, 'Is she not beautiful! Such a very unusual gift.'

It felt as if an iron band was wrapping then around my heart, and I found myself thinking about a dream in which I'd been given a different name, a name I had not remembered, even though the not knowing had gnawed at me. But at that moment, I suddenly knew –

'Parvati,' I whispered, as if to myself, circling the table and viewing the goddess from every possible angle, until I arrived at Mercy's side, when I looked at my aunt and cautiously said, 'She is very lovely. But, it seems an odd sort of gift to me . . . a goddess of marital harmony.'

In truth, the significance of those words had been lost on neither one of us, and I think that was just as the donor intended. I would have to face the fact that, sooner or later, wherever he was, Lucian Tilsbury would return – and then he would make my aunt his wife.

I looked at her with different eyes. She could no longer be classed as young, but I saw how handsome Mercy was, how oblivious she was of me when placing a hand on the window-pane and staring at the church beyond. In that glass her reflection wavered, as if it was in water, and the starry black heavens that glittered above reminded me of those once seen being mirrored in a pool of tears, in a mountain shrine, in the hills that rose above the city of Lahore.

I looked at the silver goddess, and I thought of my ayah and ached with loss.

Where are you, Mini? Do you still live? Do you still remember me?

On December 12th, a Friday, a second letter arrived at the house, and that one delivered while Mercy and I were in the sitting room again. We were eating our lunch at the table where a silver candelabrum divided the space between us. There was only the clinking of spoons in our bowls, or the hissing crack of the wood in the hearth to disturb our mutual silence – through which we heard the doorbell ring.

I held my breath and waited, fearful of what that jangling hailed when Nancy came bursting into the room, saying, 'There's a messenger come from the castle, ma'am! I'm instructed to return with an answer at once. He will not leave without it.'

My aunt gave the maid a dour look, but it was with quite indecent haste that she snatched the white envelope from her hand, and then withdrew a black-edged card. She said, while rising in her chair, 'A request for us to visit the Queen . . . to visit Windsor castle, on the anniversary of Prince Albert's death.'

I knew not what to say, but soon enough protested, 'Aunt, must you reply at once? Perhaps you should consider more . . .' I paused and looked at Nancy, only wishing the maid might leave us alone, so that we could talk more openly, 'all of the implications of such an invitation.'

But Mercy ignored my reluctance, speaking with quiet authority, 'Of course, we must answer – and accept. It is the greatest honour!'

Acutely aware of Nancy's stare, angry that Mercy should be indiscreet, I answered back immediately, 'But why must *I* go? I cannot think that I can contribute to—'

'Nonsense!' was my aunt's reply as she swept from my view to the hallway, where she offered our acceptance to whoever had been waiting there. And then she returned to the sitting room, a smile of triumph on her face when she looked at me, and then the maid, saying, 'Nancy, go down to the kitchen, and button your lip if you know what is good for yourself – and any wages due. You may clear the lunch things later on. For now, I must not be disturbed. I need to write some letters.'

Nancy did as instructed, and I followed her out to the hallway, from where I then wandered on into the parlour. Walking past the table where the goddess gleamed in pride of place, her silver polished every day, I went to stand in the window bay where I drew back the lace and found myself entranced at the sight of a little brown bird then perching on the outside ledge. Seeing its eye of glittering jet, for a moment my mind swam in circles, thinking back to that first day when Tilsbury came to visit us in Claremont Road, and the silver bird in its golden cage. I'm sure I heard music in my ears – just a few mechanical, stuttering notes – but then, shaking my head to try and dispel what was surely no more than a memory, I looked past the bird on the window ledge, past the lawn and the laurel hedging, to where the railings and garden wall divided the house from the street beyond.

Out there, all life's dramas went on as before, but whatever scene I chanced to view, it might as well not exist for me. It might as well be nothing more than the light from a magic lantern show. The real world, that was a stage upon which I could play no part – because I lived on the other side, behind the folds of the red damask. I was the puppet whose strings were pulled by the whims and desires of her aunt. And such a foreboding hung over me at the thought of the Queen's invitation, a premonition in no way eased when I made to leave the room again, when I glanced at the goddess Parvati and could swear that her metal lips had moved, and what's more her smile did not look kind, more like a cunning, contemptuous sneer. As if she knew something that I did not.

A HORNED AND
HOWLING CREATURE

Outside carriage windows soft snowflakes were swirling. They laced the bare branches of skeletal elms that formed a straight guard either side of the Long Walk, that narrow driveway dissecting broad lawns that led to the Queen's private entrance gates, and from there to the grounds of the castle.

Just as the invitation advised, at six o'clock, on December 14th, a carriage arrived at Claremont Road. But then, rather than driving us through the town, it took a much longer, circuitous route, even venturing through some forest lanes until emerging onto the Walk. While waiting for the castle gates to be opened, while the driver conversed with a guard, I looked at my aunt who sat at my side, who stared straight ahead into the gloom. No lights had been lit on that carriage, no doubt to conceal us from prying eyes – of any who might chance to see my aunt, and the tapestry bag in her arms – what was bulging with the tricks of her trade: a crystal ball and tarot cards, and who knew what else she had brought along.

I wondered at Mercy's serenity. I was beside myself with nerves and had been the entire afternoon, my fingers trembling so much that I'd had to ask for Nancy's help when fixing the clasps of my new black gown. The maid had sighed at the shimmering velvet when she'd stood at my side and gazed into the mirror – where all at once my aunt appeared, as if to form a trinity. And there she announced with a gracious smile, 'Yes, I think you'll do very well . . . very well indeed!'

But I felt like a lamb to the slaughter, and would never have gone along at all, had it not been for Mercy's pleading on the evening that followed our summoning, when, with many tears spilled from her eyes, she swore upon my mother's soul that if I did this thing for her then she would never ask again for me to aid her in her work.

I had never seen her so distraught, so desperate and so anxious. Still, I wished we were visiting anywhere else when, at last, we rumbled through the gates to approach an arch with a tower each side, both capped with several chimneys from which grey smoke was pluming. Windows below them twinkled with light, like the glinting eyes of some watchful beast which observed as we entered a quadrangle surrounded by yet more turrets and towers. A sprawling, storybook vista it was, reeking of history and myth, and all defended by battlement walls over which the snow continued to fall: a smothering white oblivion.

The elderly mustachioed man, he of the military air who had come to our house with the Queen before, was waiting at some open doors. There he assisted us out of the carriage though, how very strange it was, the way my aunt paid him so little attention; not a glimmer of recognition when he offered to carry her bag, then led us through long corridors where shadows pressed in from panelled walls and the damp struck up through cold slab floors. At last we ascended some carpeted stairs and came to a gas-lit passageway, but still no others to view our procession except for the glassy eyes of stags whose heads were mounted high on walls, their antlers thrusting wide and proud.

Those beasts made me yet warier. I started when the royal aide suddenly came to a halt, when he reached to take our cloaks and hats and arranged them on a stand nearby. Having by then returned the bag into Mercy's waiting hands, he knocked upon some double doors. Without even waiting for any reply he turned the handles and walked inside, only then to be met by the yelping bark of a little brown dog that ran out to greet us, its mistress's voice ringing brittle behind when she called, 'Dacko! Come back . . . at once!'

Despite her imperious command, how frail and small the Queen then looked within the opulence of that room. Above her blazed a chandelier, its crystals dripping, a thousand stars, all prismatic feathers, spangles and spires. Silk curtains were puddled like water on carpets. Every wall was a mass of portraits and mirrors, and some of those glasses as tall as the ceiling beneath which embroidered settles and chairs were placed by occasional tables, and every one of those table tops was cluttered with random yet prosaic items such as newspapers, playing cards or books – as if any normal drawing room. But a larger table was left quite bare, the only adornment a cloth of black, much like the one in our parlour at home. I guessed that must be for the evening's use – if there was to be any circle held, for the Queen had barely glanced our way, being more concerned with her dog just then, after which her attention turned to the child who was kneeling at her feet.

Aged six or seven years at most, her tartalan skirts spread over the floor, her head of brown ringlets resting limp on the black crêpe folds of her mother's lap. I was moved to see that little child and remember myself around the time when I knew of my own father's death, when I had been left in Mercy's house – though I'd never sat with my aunt like that, and the only times she'd held me or shown any signs of affection at all were during the aftermaths of rage, as expressions of guilt rather than love. But such musings were interrupted when the gentleman, still at our side, made the formal announcement, 'Your Majesty – Miss Matthews, and Miss Willoughby.'

As if irked by his interruption the Queen looked up with a tight grimace, at the same time pulling the child to her feet and chiding softly in her ear, 'Come, Beatrice . . . it is well past your bath time. I have other matters to attend.'

A woman, perhaps a governess, who was sitting in a chair nearby, set down the sewing in her hands and stood up to take the child's hand, though the princess looked grudging when she whined, 'But Mama, you will come and say goodnight?'

Victoria inclined her head in response, her cap's black ribbons dangling across one plump and sagging cheek, those silks pushed aside when she answered sharp, 'Off with you now. Go on. Chop chop! We all have an early start in the morning.'

With the child and governess gone from the room the Queen at last turned to greet us, still sounding somewhat irritable when she said, 'I understand that Mr Tilsbury will not be joining us tonight.'

My aunt answered without a moment's pause, 'Ma'am, that is correct. He is travelling on business concerns and will be overseas for some months to come. I know he regrets not being here, being fully aware of the significance of this, the first anniversary of your dear husband's passing. But, if I am able to offer some comfort, then that would be the greatest of honours – though I make you no false promises. It is not always possible to see into the Darkness of Beyond. And without Mr Tilsbury's guidance, I confess I am somewhat limited.'

While this little dance of manners went on I found myself distracted by one of the paintings on the walls. It was very large, as if life-sized. It depicted an Indian prince. A youth on the cusp of becoming a man. His hair, that was not visible because of the folds of a turban secured at the front by a jewelled aigrette, beneath which a vivid flash of red could just be glimpsed below the white. Two thick black brows framed large brown eyes. An aquiline nose above full lips. A moustache, and the fine, precise line of that then echoed by whiskers clipped close at his jaw. His native ceremonial clothes were gorgeously draping coloured silks. In one hand he held a sabre – golden handled, golden tipped, its long black sheath of ebony. Behind him, misty and pale in the distance, there were temple minarets, and the towers and domes of a palace fort – and that was a building I recognised, having seen its grandeur many times from the roads which ran around Lahore. *My home! My home and Mini's. The place where my father returned to die.*

How poignant was that scene for me. What a stab of longing in my heart. I was only brought back to the present again when suddenly nudged by Mercy's arm, and turning then to realise that the Queen had been addressing me –

'Why, Miss Willoughby,' she smiled, 'you are in quite the

reverie. He is very beautiful, do you not think, my Maharajah, Prince Duleep?'

'Duleep . . . who once sat upon the Golden Throne?' The words came rushing from my mouth with no thought for any tact or decorum. 'I saw him once, when I lived in Lahore, at a party at the Residency. I was really very young at the time, and I didn't speak with him as such, but I saw him ride in on an elephant. He was wearing robes of yellow silk, and a rope of pearls around his throat, and my father was . . .'

. . . and my father was with the Resident's wife and she wore a straw hat over rose petal cheeks, and children were running around on the lawns, laughing and shouting, throwing balls. But I – I stood apart from them, nibbling down through the fingertips of the new lace gloves that I had worn, yearning for Mini to be at my side, or to join the white-turbaned waiters, one of whom looked like Balkar, who held silver trays with glasses of lassi – the drinks of which Papa was so fond – the sweetened sherbets with spices and nuts that Mini always used to say were 'the very ambrosia that gushes from Shiva's topknot'.

Aunt Mercy's gaze was fearsome to see when my eyes were raised to hers again, which led to my muttered apology. 'I am sorry. That was too forward. I did not think to . . . I . . .'

'Not at all!' said the Queen. 'How interesting it is, to know that you come from India too. But then, when I look more closely . . . yes, it is something about the eyes.' She smiled and raised one brow, before going on confidentially, 'Do you know that the Maharajah now also resides here in England, and has done so for many years? Before that he was in Futteghar. Did you ever know that place? It was there, in the care of our dear Dr Login that Duleep became a Christian, just like the Princess Gowramma before. I had such hopes to see them wed. But Gowramma's morals are *not* what we hoped. Why,' the Queen's blue eyes grew wide, 'she dared to flirt with the Prince of Wales! They warn me that the Eastern mind can be unnaturally disposed to . . . to these hedonistic tendencies. We must rise in

God's grace, or we will fall. Do heed those words, Miss Willoughby.'

I was feeling somewhat flustered to suspect that Queen Victoria imagined me an Indian – to have such 'hedonistic' ways. But then, I was also thinking that whoever the Princess Gowramma was, if I was ever in her place then I would all too willingly fall into the arms of Prince Duleep. But the Queen was then far more concerned with thoughts of the loved one she had lost, shaking her head and muttering, 'Enough of such idle gossiping. The memorial service has left me drained. Oh, such a dreadful, dreadful day. May we hope for some consolation now?'

'If I might be so bold, Ma'am,' I hoped to make my position clear, before my aunt sought to involve me more, 'I do not possess any special gifts as far as the spirits are concerned. It was only that once. It has not happened since.'

'Young lady, you look quite petrified. You make me feel cold with your shivering. Go and sit by the fire and warm yourself. But, should anything occur to you . . . well, I hope you will think to share it. If my husband's spirit appeared to you once then there is a chance he may do so again, here in his own home, and on such a night. The date must surely augur well.'

She rose from her seat and walked towards the table draped in the velvet cloth, looking just as hunched and drawn as she had done in Claremont Road, and sighing while she carried on, 'You may not think it to see us now but Christmas was always the happiest time for my family here in Windsor. This year I cannot bear to stay . . . Which is why, at first light in the morning, we shall make our way to Osborne House.'

All the while, as the Queen was speaking, the aide who'd led us to that room was drawing two upright chairs from the table. The Queen and my aunt then sat – after which he returned to the double doors, from where I felt his eyes on me, though rather than looking back at him I was engrossed with watching Aunt Mercy unpacking the contents of her bag.

She drew out two black pouches. From the first – which was

99

the largest – she extracted her crystal ball, its surface polished to a shine, though always with a residue of bubbled greyness in its midst. From the second she took her tarot cards, a very gaudily painted deck. But the varnish captured the gleam of the lights in a way that made you want to look, to try and decipher the meanings, those secrets that the pictures held, though – in truth – Mercy rarely used them, except to create a sense of allure.

She then extracted a small white bowl with a thick tallow candle set inside, and while placing that at the table's edge my aunt looked back at the gentleman and asked in supercilious tones, 'I wonder . . . would you light this, and then dim the rest of the lamps?'

'Of course, madam,' he answered, no expression discernible in his voice as he walked to the hearth and drew a spill from a jar upon the mantel's shelf. He held its tip against the flames and when it caught he moved away, first lighting Mercy's candle, then dousing the lights as requested. During this my aunt was preoccupied with placing her palms on each side of the ball and, as the room darkened all around, the jets no more than purple wisps, the shuddering of her candle's flame distorted her features dramatically. The hollows and mounds of bones that lay beneath Aunt Mercy's flesh were all at once much too pronounced. Her face became a living skull and, in that mask, she closed her eyes while still caressing the glassy orb, letting out a low and tremulous breath and then exclaiming with surprise, 'Ah . . . I see you and Albert . . . both very young, walking hand in hand through the gardens here in Windsor. You smile at his love for the beauty of nature, for the peace and the calm of the castle grounds which always fills him with delight.'

'It is true!' the Queen interrupted. 'He far preferred to be here than in London.'

My aunt continued as if unaware that the Queen had commented at all, 'He asks if you remember how he taught you the names of the flowers and trees . . . how you sketched them in your journals?'

Victoria expressed astonishment. 'How can you possibly know such a thing?'

Again, my aunt ignored her words, continuing in greater haste, 'He is glad you saw the ring, the token that he sent before. But he speaks, so very urgently, of the stone, the Koh-i-Noor – the ancient and sacred vibrations of which may lead his spirit to align upon this earthly sphere.'

'I have it! I heeded his message.' The Queen spoke in barely a whisper – during which I saw how nervously she twisted at the wedding band that was worn on a chain around her neck. Was that the ring from the séance before?

She went on, 'My advisors, they all disapprove. They would have me keep it locked away. But the jewel was so dear to my husband's heart . . . and now I wear it next to mine.' A sad smile as she lifted a hand to her breast where pale fingers fluttered across the black mantlet. 'And yet, it is but an ephemeral thing. Without Albert, my life is worth nothing at all. I think on this matter again and again. If only we'd known he was so ill. If only he had not left his bed. How often since have I also wished to die and follow in his path.'

My aunt was speaking boldly, 'You cannot blame yourself. It was his time to be taken. But as to yourself, I do believe it is *your* royal destiny to live for many years to come.'

The Queen's answer was heavy with dismay. 'You will have me grow old on this lonely throne, having lost the only man I love?'

'Your husband may yet return again . . .' My aunt appeared to be deep in thought. 'But my crystal is too cloudy. Would you care to draw the Tarots next? Perhaps you would like to shuffle them.'

Victoria did as Mercy asked, and rather expertly I thought, before setting the deck on the table again where my aunt took up the first four cards and arranged them face down on the velvet cloth.

'Ah, yes . . .' she sighed, when she turned the first. 'Here we have the Empress. The symbol of fertility. A kind mother. Clearly Your Majesty.'

The Magician was the next to be drawn. 'A man of skill and action.' Mercy was smiling defiantly. 'Someone now destined to enter your life, to have the greatest influence and—'

The Queen broke in abruptly, 'That is preposterous! I can assure you of—'

'Please,' Mercy urged, 'allow me to finish.' She flipped up the third card. It showed The Sun. She smiled serenely before going on, 'This card predicts a marriage.'

The Queen bristled, but Mercy seemed unaware, raising the final image while pronouncing, 'The Last Judgement. The end of all loneliness. A joyous union. A sense of rebirth . . . of the mortal body as well as the soul.'

At that point the Queen lost all patience. Her anger was more than apparent when she snapped, 'What you are implying is scandalous! After my husband, no other man shall have any influence on my life! Can you have any concept of my grief? How *dare* you imply such things? We will hear no more of such nonsense tonight. Albert was right all along. This dabbling is ridiculous! This audience is at an end!'

Mercy responded calmly, 'It is not my way to lie, or to offer unwarranted flattery. I only tell of what is to come. But should you prefer to ignore the cards, then we could refer to the stone . . . the sacred jewel from India.'

'You wish to see it, to hold it?' The Queen lifted her hand again, this time reaching beneath her shawl and drawing out a diamond brooch.

Could *that* be the Koh-i-Noor, the diamond once owned by Duleep Singh, his kingdom's sovereign symbol – and here so lightly handled? I was too far away from the table to see with any clarity, but the stone I had viewed in a gilded cage with Prince Albert standing at my side now appeared to be set in claws of gold. Its shape was much diminished, and almost like a pear, with a uniform pattern of little cuts criss-crossed upon its surface. The design was fashionable, formal, and neutered, whereas the original Mughal stone had been something magnificent and raw – its shape then mostly flat on top, with an intricate border of facets around. Like a crystal mountain rising up above the sloping hills below.

The Queen placed her jewel in Mercy's hand. My aunt stroked a finger across the gem's surface as if it was a living thing, and then, with her head inclined forward, she peered into the diamond's depths, and said, 'The energies are vital! Look, and you shall see him! I sense the husband's presence near.'

'What is there to see?' the Queen broke in suspiciously. Her eyes were darting around the room, searching through every corner: the corners where nothing but shadows moved. And that was the greatest relief for me. Not to feel any change in the atmosphere. Nothing like the night in Claremont Road.

'Please,' my aunt urged, 'be patient.' She laid the brooch on the table where its whiteness contrasted vividly with the hues of the ebony velvet. Mercy then began to chant, 'The jewel's light waxes and wanes with the moon. Every new moon is a time of rebirth, of the mortal body as well as the soul. Every full moon will lead our souls to the fulfilment of their dreams, when . . .'

She paused and smiled serenely, and perhaps she was thinking of herself and her dreams of wedding Tilsbury, but the Queen interjected sourly, 'What is this silly talk, of waning moons and waxing moons? Do you take me for some naïve girl?'

My aunt responded calmly, 'The spirits speak in riddles, through symbols and natural phenomenon.'

The Queen ignored her protest, looking back to find her gentleman, demanding, 'Take this candle away from the table. I find its perfume sickening!'

The servant came forward to lift the bowl which he then took to one of the windows, placing it down upon the sill where the flame drew long, was wavering, while he held a length of curtain back and stared out into the quiet night, before pinching the wick between finger and thumb. I had seen another man do that, when he doused a candle beside my bed. Had that act been real, or was it a dream, when that thin plume of smoke passed over his lips, when it looked like a kiss, as it entered his mouth?

My aunt let out a long, low groan, her fingers pressed hard to her temples, and it seemed that she was listening – though in truth there was nothing at all to hear, only some coals shifting in the fire beside which I was standing then, from where I was quite mortified to see Mercy's body, as still as a statue's, and her eyes become so tightly closed that I feared her lost in a psychic trance, or was it the pretence of one? I thought to try and rouse her, but then came the awful commotion outside, all those echoing shouts in the courtyard, and what might have been a wailing wind – or was it the call of some creature?

The little dog began to yap, and Aunt Mercy, she came to her senses at last, looking up when a knocking came at the doors, where one of the guards then burst inside, crying out, 'Your Majesty. Take care! An intruder, on the castle walls!'

Soon, he was dragging back more drapes, stabbing a finger towards the point where a silhouette could clearly be seen, theatrically lit by the low full moon then shining down through a gap in the clouds. The dog's barks turned to whimpering yelps as it cringed beneath the Queen's black skirts. And it wasn't just the freezing air that came rushing in through the open doors that chilled me to the very bone. Below that luminous disc of moon, the creature's naked arms were raised, and I could see more clearly then that, although his body was that of a man, from the straggling hair at his forehead there extended a pair of antlers, like those that branched from the stuffed stags' heads seen mounted in the corridor. One of his hands was holding a chain. Such a clanking and rattling it made. The other grasped a hunting bow, and when he opened up his mouth, the terrible screech that issued forth might well be the song of a banshee.

When it finally stopped, through the silence, Victoria was heard to moan, 'Oh dear God! It cannot . . . it cannot be him!'

'No, you must not say it, Ma'am,' her gentleman swiftly responded. 'Such tales . . . they are but legend.'

'Well then, you shall explain to me how it is that we all see him there! What else could it be but the spirit of Herne? And does Herne not come when the sovereign is threatened . . . to warn of some great peril?'

Mistress and servant stared at each other, locked in what seemed a moment of dread. And, meanwhile, more voices were ringing out as guardsmen emerged, holding fiery torches, running this way and that along battlement walls while attempting to capture the ghoulish intruder. Gunshots were fired as he fled away, though none with hope of finding aim, not with the lash of a rising wind, and the veils of sleet then spiralling, through which the creature vanished, as if wrapped in invisible magic.

A terrible stillness fell in that room, through which I could not prevent myself from suddenly asking, 'Who is Herne?'

Still staring out through the window, the Queen spoke with little emotion: 'He is a spirit . . . half man, half stag. The story says that, centuries past, he was the chief huntsman at the court. One day, while out hunting, he saved the king from being attacked by a stag at bay. But, in doing so, Herne was fatally wounded, and then his own life was saved in turn when a mysterious man appeared. A magician, he was said to be. He stepped from the bole of a blasted oak and proceeded to cut off the dead stag's head. That head he then placed on the hunter's . . . after which he disappeared, leaving Herne miraculously cured . . . not so much as a scratch upon his flesh.

'But that gift of new life proved to be a curse, for Herne was never trusted again, reviled as being touched by black magic. In the end, they say the man went mad. He died after hanging himself from a branch of the very tree where his saviour appeared. They say that ever since that day his spirit has haunted the castle grounds. Always in the guise of a hunter. Always with the horns of a stag on his head. And, when he comes it is to warn of treason . . . or else the monarch's death.'

I was entirely at a loss as to what to offer in answer. And there was no aid from Mercy, who by then was only intent on the packing of her bag, placing the pouches back inside, and afterwards crouching down on the carpet, collecting any tarot cards that might have fallen thereabouts. But I do not think she had been unaffected by that vision on the castle walls. I noticed how her fingers were shaking, and really so very violently that it was all my aunt could do to grasp the edges of those cards. I think, like me, she desired no more than to leave that room and go back home – though, how haughty and rude she sounded when she rose to her full height again and announced, 'Would your gentleman kindly arrange for us to be shown the best way out? And we shall not require a carriage. We would prefer to walk.'

Victoria's response was cold. 'Naturally, you do understand, that we shall expect your utmost discretion regarding *whatever* occurred tonight.'

'You may count on that,' Mercy assured. And then, her bag clutched to her breast once more, she headed towards the double doors through which we had entered an hour before. I followed meekly after, only wishing I knew what formalities might happen to be expected when taking one's leaving of a queen.

But it seemed that the evening's unnerving events had dispensed with all previous decorum, for the elderly courtier was sitting down in what had been Victoria's chair, his face drained of colour, glistening grey, with the little dog quivering in his lap.

Not that the Queen seemed the least aware, either of him, or of us, when she also returned to the table's side, where she stood and stared down at what remained – at the diamond brooch still lying there. An age, it seemed, till she lifted her eyes, during which my own were lured again to the Maharajah on her wall – the prince who had once owned that stone. Could those painted brown eyes see what I saw? Could they see the precious Koh-i-Noor now reduced to nothing more than a glittering prop in a spiritualist show?

Did the Queen really believe that gem might lure her husband's spirit back? She had certainly hoped for that miracle, and how anxious her voice had been when she raised her eyes and addressed my aunt, 'Well, Miss Matthews, you have conjured up one ghost tonight, if not the one we were hoping for. I wonder, do you still insist that I shall live for many years?'

'Yes, Ma'am.' My aunt's tone was confident, though I noticed her hands, still trembling, 'There is not one moment of doubt in my mind.'

'Then I am cursed,' was the Queen's reply.

A CHRISTMAS BELL. A GHOST.
A SKULL.

A low mood fell over the house following that visit of ours to the castle. My aunt swore me to secrecy and then did not speak of the evening at all, turning in on herself, often rising late, refusing to see any callers.

My nights were filled with vivid dreams in which I was always being chased by a horned and howling creature. And that ghoul had the face of the vagrant, the old man who accosted my aunt and I when, after taking our leave of the Queen – when we had been made to wait an hour in a cold and dreary anti-room until the castle was deemed secure – we were finally shown to the main front gates from where we trudged our way back home; a journey for which no one seemed to care if we should be observed or not.

I had been glad of the cold sharp air to draw me back to reality. But the town was unnaturally quiet, as if it slept beneath the snow, or also mourned for Albert's death. While anxiously listening for more of those cries that had echoed out from the castle walls, it seemed to me that my aunt and I were the only living souls on earth. Every shop front we passed on Peascod Street had long been closed and shuttered up, their porches drenched in blackness. Even the public houses were oddly devoid of revellers. It was only on reaching Claremont Road that the vagrant suddenly appeared, to stand directly in our path.

It was too dark to see him well, too far from any street-lamp's glow, though clear enough to notice when a hand snatched out for Mercy's arm. Shocked, she almost dropped her bag, protesting with a stifled cry, 'Get off! Get off, you filthy brute!'

The assailant turned his face to mine, though the eyes

through which he must have looked were cast in shadow from his hat. His words were oddly accented, groaned through a thick white hedge of beard: 'May the gods look down and bless you – all that you are, all you possess.'

What a peculiar thing! To ask for nothing from us, to offer only blessings. I could not help but think about something that Mini used to say, which was that when we lived in Benares, before Papa took us to Lahore, there used to be an Aghori – I think that's what she called him – one of the religious zealots whose hair and beards were never cut, who chanted Shiva's blessings while robed in rotting funeral shrouds that they stole from the corpses at burning ghats. For whatever reason, such a man was obsessed with Mini and me, following as if a guard whenever we happened to leave the house, even loitering at the gates on those nights when my father was away. And there he was found one morning, having died while sitting cross-legged on the ground, as if in something of a trance, with his eyes still open, staring up – up at my bedroom's window frame.

I'm sure I never saw him. If so, I had forgotten, having been so very young back then. But still, Mini's story filled my mind when I saw that man in Claremont Road. I was overcome with a haunting dread – though of course my nerves were already frayed from that evening's earlier events.

And yet, Mercy's initial fright seemed to quite dissolve away the moment the stranger spoke those words. She gasped a sudden, 'Thank you!' at which he nodded, then turned away, shuffling across the road, limping back the way we'd come, leaving us free to walk on home with nothing to disturb us but the sounds of our boots as they crunched through snow.

Christmas morning came around, and with Nancy taking her holiday – and who knew where she might have gone – there was no maid to wake us. More falls of snow during the night had muffled any outside noise and only the pealing of the bells alerted us in time for church. We dressed in haste, and not even the time to make ourselves a cup of tea before scurrying across the road, to where the bells were tolling still, the church doors standing open wide.

It seemed the whole neighbourhood gathered that day, and such a great swelling of song there was, with carols soaring high above and rising through the battle flags. For, as well as serving parishioners, the Trinity was a garrison church, with many a military parade – and so often I thought about India when I heard the soldiers marching past, their stamps, and shouts, and bugle calls. But then, to sit inside that church and to see those emblems of war and destruction displayed side by side with that of the cross, the sign of a peace-loving Christian God – I found that a discomfiting compromise.

Of late, there was something else in church that caused me more uneasiness, and that was the fact that my aunt's profession had somehow become more widely known and whenever we went to worship (and nowhere as regularly as before) the vicar would stand in his pulpit, delivering his sermons, staring down at Mercy's face while condemning the wicked practices of those who were 'mystical mediums', who trod the path of evil and disavowed the word of God by conjuring demons up from Hell.

All around us were disapproving looks. Whispers were hissed from behind kid gloves. My aunt and I were ignored or spurned, even by those who used to smile, who had shown only kindness when Papa died – who might well have been in that very church when he and my mother once stood at the altar and made their vows before their god; where they might have walked out one sunlit day to a shower of falling rose petals.

That Christmas morn sharp flakes of ice fell on my head and stung my cheeks when Mercy and I emerged from the church (where the vicar had refrained that day from any condemnation), and completed our circle of prints in the snow, to walk back up the house's path and shelter a while beneath the porch. There, while my aunt pulled her key from her pocket, I looked up at the mistletoe hung from the lantern and wondered why Mercy had put that there: just who she expected to visit with kisses?

But then, I thought there might be one. I thought of Lucian Tilsbury.

While we'd been sitting in the church, Mrs Morrison had laid up the table. She always joined us at Christmas, with her husband being dead for years and having no family nearby. She would conjure up a splendid meal, then come upstairs to share it – and that afternoon she proudly served a small turkey, a pheasant, and even quails, with vegetables of just about every description, not to mention the cheeses, fruits and nuts, the champagne jellies and mince pies. More than enough for twenty souls! She had even arranged an ivy wreath around the candelabra's base, and everything very festive indeed when my aunt lit the new red candles, when pretty shadows danced around as we sipped at Cook's brandy and lemon punch. My aunt drank several glasses in rather quick succession. A very rare event it was when she became so merry, though she did look sour when Cook announced, 'There's been some gossip going round, about recent events at the castle.'

'What's gossip is that?' Aunt Mercy was brusque – a warning glance then cast my way to ensure that my tongue remained quite still.

'Well,' Cook gave a slow, sage nod, 'its something just up your street I'd say . . . though you know I don't generally believe. But there's been another haunting . . . that ghost of Herne seen out again. That's what's sent the Queen away, rushing off to the Isle of Wight.'

'Has anyone seen him since . . . this Herne?' I asked in no more than a whisper.

'Word is that he vanished into thin air after running over the battlement walls, howling and screaming to wake the dead. And every shot the guardsmen fired appeared to pass right through him. But, I ask you,' Cook raised a knowing brow, 'even *if* Herne did exist, what use could any bullets be against a phantom, dead for years?'

'Enough of such gloomy nonsense! We should go on through

to the parlour.' My aunt stood up, quite determined it seemed to put an end to such a tale. 'We should think of more pleasant matters today . . . such as distributing my gifts.'

Gifts? In all my years in Claremont Road, I had never received a Christmas gift. But that year Cook was the recipient of a dainty lace-edged handkerchief – with which she did seem very pleased. For me there was a reticule, worked with tiny beads of jet, with threads of gold embroidery.

'Oh, Aunt Mercy . . . it is lovely!'

'Your mother made it. She gave it to me, when she left us to go to India. The work is very clumsy. She really had no needle skills. But still, you might like to have it.'

I was moved to receive such a precious gift, whatever Mercy thought of it. I wished I had something to offer back, though my aunt did not seem to expect it, only suggesting that we sit before the parlour fire – that cast a glow on every cheek and added a glisten to every eye, and not the gleam of misery so often found within that room whenever a séance was performed. Even so, Mercy fidgeted in her chair and then got up to pace about, eventually coming to a halt beside the silver goddess, at which point Cook wryly exclaimed, 'Well, I hope you don't mind me saying, but in the absence of a tree perhaps we should set *her* up in the window, deck your goddess in fancy ribbons and candles. That should get the vicar up in arms . . . though I dare say it might catch the eyes of thieves. It must be worth a penny or two.'

She chuckled and reached out a plump pink hand to lift another glass of punch, having brought the jug along with her when we left the dining table. Meanwhile, my aunt's fingers brushed against one of the silver idol's limbs and over the snakes that coiled there, as she said, 'I dare say its financial value would be a matter of some dispute. But she has a certain worth to *me*. And as to those in the Trinity Church, the vicar, and the rest of them . . . I do not need my crystal ball to see that by this time next year I shall have left those wagging tongues and gossip well behind me. I shall have made a life elsewhere, where minds are not so closed and small.'

'Oh!' Cook exclaimed with indignant surprise, the wind quite taken out of her sails. 'Well, I'll thank you for letting me know, when I've worked for this family all these years. I trust that you'll give me fair notice – enough time to find a post elsewhere.'

My own surprise was locked inside. I wondered if that decision was the cause of my aunt's generosity. Were our presents to be her parting gifts, when she left to marry Tilsbury? What other reason could there be for such a strange announcement? And what would become of Claremont Road, of Cook's position, of Nancy's too? And what about me? Where would I go? All that I could think about was the cryptic message once attached to a ribbon at Parvati's neck, the neck that Mercy now caressed before heading towards the piano, where she then sat down and proceeded to play the notes of a popular melody.

In the past, Cook might have sung along, warbling the words in her fruity contralto. But that day her lips remained tight closed, not even her usual reference as to how well my mother once used to play the instrument. And my aunt, her mind was clearly elsewhere, for before she had even finished the piece she sighed and left the piano stool.

I don't know why I took her place. I had never been blessed with a musical gift and at first my fingers were clumsy. And yet, how odd it was to find the piano come to vibrant life when I played the carol, 'Brightest and Best'. It was one we'd sung in church that day, and, though I'd never learned it, my fingers seemed to know the notes, moving mechanically over the board as if they had a will of their own. And when I began to sing the words, it was as though I heard my voice but quite another took control, another soul was singing . . .

Brightest and best of the sons of the morning,
Dawn on our darkness and lend us Thine aid;
Star of the East, the horizon adorning,
Guide where our infant Redeemer is laid.

Cold on His cradle the dewdrops are shining
Low lies His head with the beasts of the stall;
Angels adore Him in slumber reclining,
Maker and Monarch and Saviour of all.

Say shall we yield Him, in costly devotion,
Odours of Edom and offerings divine?
Gems of the mountain and pearls of the ocean,
Myrrh from the forest, or gold from the mine?

Vainly we offer each ample oblation,
Vainly with gifts would His favour secure;
Richer by far is the heart's adoration,
Dearer to God are the prayers of the poor.

The performance was over, but there I remained, motionless upon the stool, my hands still hovering over the keys, the notes' vibrations thrumming on – until Aunt Mercy broke the spell, her fingers pointed beneath her chin as if to mirror Parvati's pose, when suddenly calling out to me, 'Brava, Alice! Brava! Though I find myself inclined to ask what made you choose that *particular* carol? Such a favourite it was with your mother too.'

'I don't know .. . .' And I didn't. What could I say?

It was Cook who came to the rescue, easing her substantial flesh up from the sofa's cushions, wheezing a little when she asked, 'Well, what about some plum pudding? Come on, Alice, you can give me a hand and carry it up from the kitchen.' And then, looking back, towards my aunt, she said in rather pointed tones, 'No peace for the wicked in this house!'

No peace, no heat and no goodwill when we left the fuggy parlour's warmth to find the sitting room fire burned out. I could not help but shiver when I watched the blue of the brandy flame as it licked around the pudding plate. And no more than ten minutes later, when my aunt and I had eaten but the tiniest portions possible, when Cook had consumed an enormous slice and then pronounced herself to be 'as stuffed as any Christmas bird' – she started to gather the dishes up, then stopped to ask in an anxious voice, 'Did no one find the sixpence, then? A sixpence lost in the pudding means a year of bad luck for all of us. There'll be no more health or happiness. We might as well turn up our toes – if they haven't dropped off from the cold in here! Then again,' she shot a sly look at Aunt Mercy, 'for those heading down that way, the fires of Hell might bring some warmth.'

Very soon after that my aunt retired, wishing Cook and me goodnight, even though it was very early, not even the hour of seven o'clock. I was not in the least bit tired, but feeling very full inside and much in need of exercise, I decided to walk along with Cook when she set off to go back home. At first, she seemed glad enough of that as we ambled down the garden path, one of her arms entwined through mine, really most companionable. But we'd barely reached the end of the road when she insisted I go back, for the night was bitter, dark and cold, the snow grown icy underfoot, and though her boots held firm enough, mine were much too slippery.

Back in the hallway, my fingers numb, I struggled to remove those boots, the laces unyielding when grown so damp. But at last I had them kicked aside, my stockinged toes upon the tiles when I looked at myself in the console glass. Strands of dark hair had come loose from their pins and were sticking damp against my cheeks. My lips were stung red from the freezing air. I looked wild and dishevelled, not myself at all. I looked a little anxious too. And, in truth, I was, for although I had not thought of him when setting down the road with Cook, on my return, when on my own, I thought I saw that tramp again.

It was only some shadows across the street. I knew he wasn't really there. But what if he had been? What if I had been followed? What if that man was outside the house, watching and waiting – waiting now?

In an attempt to divert my thoughts I padded downstairs to the kitchen floor where great piles of china still stood on the drainer, with pots and pans in the sink to soak; many of them still caked in grease. Poor Nancy would have to face that chore when she returned next morning. For then, apart from the dripping tap and the comforting shushing of coals in the range, there was nothing and no one to give me distraction while I picked at cold pheasant and made some tea, and then went upstairs to the parlour – and wondered how my aunt could sleep with the hands of the clock at barely eight.

But then, if I'd known how that Christmas would end, with a skull, and a ghost, and a tolling bell, I would surely have followed Mercy's lead – no matter how cold my room might be, with no Nancy to light the upstairs fires.

The parlour, that was cosier, some coals still glowing in the grate, the occasional flame still flaring up so that flashes of light were flickering across Parvati's silver form. While gazing at her beauty I sipped the tea that I had topped with Mrs Morrison's special punch – what drops remained there in the jug. But I think I took too much of it, becoming drowsy, nodding off – only waking hours later.

My head felt thick and groggy. I felt the need of cooling air. I got up and walked to the window bay where I heard the street-lamp's shushing hiss and, through its hazy radiance, I saw, with the greatest sense of relief, no stranger lurking by the gate. But I did hear a distant shout, and started at some howling sound, through which the Trinity Church bell then struck the morning hour of one.

So many times I'd heard the chime, but *that* bell, it was different. There was a pricking in my hands but not from any sense of cold. This sensation was something alien. Some tremor that tickled through my palms, then up my arms to my shoulders, crawling around the base of my skull, like something living, like insects, like beetles burrowing through my scalp – like minute buzzing impulses then stealing into my every thought, until replaced by the sudden awareness that:

This single note has not ended. The bell is continuing to toll, an echoing low vibration of sound that has me frozen in its spell as I

look into the mirror and see myself, and the room behind a swim-
ming mass of shadows that are swelling and bending all around.

*The bell tolls on. I notice the table upon which the goddess
Parvati is standing, and how the ruby in her brow is suddenly
pierced by a moonbeam, a spear of light which seems to shift, and
when my eyes follow its path they rest upon the bony thing that
someone has placed on the mantelpiece — where once there stood a
golden cage.*

*The skull, for that is what I see, has been turned up, upon its
end, to form a sort of bowl, and in that bowl appears to be some dark
and viscous fluid. While I stare at that, quite horrified, the strangest
compulsion comes over me and, as if they belong to another, my
hands reach forward to grasp the cup. Feeling the warmth of the
liquid within it, I lift the vessel to my lips and even though my
stomach convulses, gagging on the taste of bile that is then rising in
my throat, it is only when I drop the skull that I find myself come to
my senses again. I stare at the wetness on my gown, the crimson
spreading to the hem. And from there I look up at the mirror where
my eyes are wide and round with shock, not only because of the sight
of that blood, but because of what stands behind me now.*

*He looks exactly as he did when I saw him that night in the
hallway. Very slowly he raises an arm, though the effort to do so is
clearly enormous, as if the atmosphere in that room is too heavy and
dense for the ghost to bear. But, at last, he succeeds, and while his
eyes are still intently fixed on mine, his finger points at the ruby
embedded in Parvati's crown. He opens his mouth as if to speak, but
I can't hear his words, I can't hear anything but the constant tolling
of the bell, that note surging in and out of my mind, ebbing and
flowing, ebbing and flowing, until, when I think it will drive me
mad, the world becomes silent and still again. There is only a
lingering resonance; an echo chiming on the air. The room within
the mirror's frame is empty of any soul but mine. And how strange
it is that I moan with regret when I see the skull of blood is gone,
that the silk of my dress is as dry as bone, no crimson staining any
more . . .*

It took a few moments before I was able to rush from the

parlour and out to the hall, and then up the stairs to Mercy's door – thinking to tell her about the bell, and Albert's ghost, and the skull of blood. But, despite being frightened, half out of my wits, my hand was drawn back before it knocked. Because there was something I feared yet more – and that was my aunt being convinced that I possessed the 'abilities' that might lead me to join her profession.

So, I mentioned nothing of what had occurred. I went on upstairs to my room instead. In darkness I fumbled my way to the stand, where I found and lit the candle stub. And by that flame I then undressed, gasping and quaking with the cold as I dragged the nightshift down over my head and plunged beneath the covers. There I sat with my back to the bed's brass bars, my knees drawn up, my arms wrapped round, until my eye fell on the beaded bag that my aunt had given earlier, which she must have placed on the end of my bed, although I had not seen it in her hands when she left me and Cook in the hall below.

I held it in my own a while and then got out of bed again and went to stand before the hearth where I lifted the frame of my photograph. I placed that in my mother's bag, and then the remains of Mini's braid. I set the bag down at the side of my pillow, as if it might somehow be a charm – after which I blew out the candle's flame and placed my head beside it. But despite the lateness of the hour I found it impossible to sleep, thinking on and on about the bell, and the skull, and the ghost that had returned: the ghost whose hand had pointed at the ruby in Parvati's crown.

Surely it had been dream. One of those lucid imaginings as clearly seen as when awake. But if not a dream, if it had been real, then what could such a vision mean?

AN UNEXPECTED DISCOVERY

That April had been wet and cold. A relief to wake one morning and look out to see some clear blue skies, though a gusting wind was fuelling still the tense and fractious mood in the house. Nancy was at the kitchen door, muttering curses under her breath, bent double when knocking clods of mud from a pair of battered leather boots. I was lost in the rhythm of those thuds and almost choked on a bite of toast when Mrs Morrison bellowed, 'Nancy! For goodness sake, girl, will you think to close that door!'

I was thinking the heat from Cook's bubbling pans might do very well to escape the room, with thick streams of condensation trickling over the windows and walls, over the dresser's piles of white china, the copper saucepans, the tea tins and jars. But, she seemed inured to the atmosphere, and when she had done with blaming the maid for all of the dirt and the cold in town she turned her grouchy attentions to me, her dripping spoon pointing accusingly. 'And a good thing *you've* got some appetite back. I won't say I wasn't worried towards the end of last year. But at least you've regained your bloom since then, so I dare say everything is well . . .'

She nodded in Nancy's direction, and her frizzled curls were quivering when she spoke with such emotion, 'Now *that* girl has become too thin by far, what with all of the housework and laundry she does. Your aunt should take care. It will end in tears. You mark my words. I'm never wrong!'

Nancy snapped back immediately, 'I have got a pair of ears, you know! At least *they* haven't wasted away!'

'Yet!' concluded Cook, determined as ever to have the last word.

I couldn't say Nancy looked different to me: a little surlier perhaps, if such a thing was possible. And while watching her clomp away at those boots, as more lumps of earth went flying free, I was suddenly moved to ask, 'Nancy, whose boots are those?'

'They're mine.'

'Well, they're a disgrace,' Cook said. 'You should get some new and throw them out. Anyone would imagine you worked on a farm. I can't think where you've been to, to get yourself in such a state.'

My aunt was working at her desk, going through her appointment book and responding to any letters sent enquiring of her services. When she'd done, she called for Nancy and asked her to run an errand. 'The same place as usual,' she said, and Nancy nodded in response while stuffing an envelope into her pocket and then disappearing back down to the kitchen.

Very suspicious I thought it was, the look that passed between them both. And when, very shortly afterwards my aunt retired to her room, to rest before she must go out to visit clients later on, I went to stand in the parlour bay from where I saw Nancy pass through the front gate, after which I hurried back out to the hall and grabbed my shawl and bonnet.

When sure that she'd gone far enough not to notice if any should follow on, I carefully opened the house front door and closed it quietly behind, setting off like a dog on the trail of a fox, determined to run the maid to ground. All the time I feared she might glance back, as she headed past the Trinity church, then scurried past shop fronts and houses until heading down the slope of a hill where the road was replaced by a scrubby path that led across stretches of pastureland. At one point, I lingered behind a cart, emerging to find my quarry gone – and, forced into making a rapid guess, I skirted round pig pens and huddles of geese, at last climbing over a stile, to find myself on another road. But there was no sign of Nancy and I was about to admit defeat when I caught a brief glance of her shawl again, halfway down a narrow lane that was signed with the name of Adelaide Square. It was but moments later that I came to an alley, very bleak, hedged by bushes and randomly paved – and at its end was Gloucester Place. There I saw more dwellings, five or six cottages, all set apart, and one of those was clearly the place of the maid's destination. For, although the day was milder, the dankness being blown away, where the ground was still boggy from recent rain I saw footprints and wheel furrows scarred through the mud – and the freshest of those leading to a gate. It was quite rotten and loose on its hinges, and through the swinging creak it made, I suddenly heard some voices, and then approaching footsteps.

Glancing about for somewhere to hide I saw a door in the alley wall and, thinking it led to one of the gardens and hoping it might have been left unlocked, I pushed against it, very hard, and all but fell through to the other side. Cringing at the scrape of wood on stones, I managed to drag it closed again, after which I spied over a creeper-clad wall and pinched my nose between finger and thumb, doing my best to stave off a sneeze brought on by the leaves' dank odours – not to mention the urge to cry out loud when I saw the very vagrant who had accosted Mercy on that night of the castle séance. The same tattered coat and unkempt beard, but in the brighter light of day how could I fail to recognise those two distinctive bold dark eyes beneath the brim of a wide felt hat?

The shock would have rendered me speechless – had I dared to try and speak! Such a sickening wrench in my gut there was, as I watched him, with Nancy at his side, the two of them walking down the lane, and he taking up the limping gait affected by the tramp before, as if to ensure the disguise complete.

They were deep in conversation and Nancy was earnestly asking, 'And Miss Matthews? Do you still say that I must continue to work for her?'

His voice held no artifice that day, nothing to disguise the elegant tones that could belong to no one else but Mr Lucian Tilsbury. 'Yes. She may be useful yet . . .'

Though I strained very hard, I could hear no more. The two of them disappeared from view, at which point I crept back out to the alley and stood for a while in a state of confusion. What was Nancy's connection with Tilsbury, for him to command where she should work? And why should my aunt be useful to them?

The questions galvanised my mind, and when sure of no others lurking nearby, no sounds but the birds in the branches above, I plucked up my courage, along with my skirts, and squelched through the puddles of sucking mud to enter the whining wooden gate through which that pair had just emerged. Inside, upon the garden path, the high hedge of yew that grew around permitted me the luxury of being able to stare a while at the straggling grass and mildewed weeds, at the tarnished bell hung in the porch, at several broken window-panes, where the frames were nailed or shuttered within, all of which suggested that the house had been abandoned. Creeping nearer to the door I held an ear to the peeling paint and rapped very lightly, then knocked again – and when sure that no one was inside, I walked to the back where the hedge was replaced by empty swathes of meadowland. Beyond was the green of the Queen's Long Walk which led to the castle's private gates, above which threatening dark clouds were scudding quickly through the skies, to warn of yet more rain to come.

I tried the back door but it was locked. I saw a large stone beside the step. Its weight was enough with which to smash some smeared and filthy panes of glass, through which I could then reach inside to turn a key and lift a latch.

A scullery kitchen was dimly lit. I shuddered to look at the ceiling where, among thick hanging cobwebs there was an enormous spider, its trap littered black with countless husks of what were surely long-dead flies. Quickly moving on to the hallway I saw two rooms either side of a staircase, but nowhere did there seem to be any signs of habitation. Perhaps a mouse scratched in the gloom, but the hearths were cold and appeared disused.

I winced at the complaining stairs as my feet began their slow ascent, arriving on the landing to see that there were two more rooms, each set above the lower ones. The first of them was just as bare. Peeling paint upon the walls. A broken window stuffed with rags. But, the second contained an iron bed, its legs elevated on blocks of wood. Some embers still glowed in the iron grate, and there on the narrow mantelpiece was a plate with some cheese, a loaf of bread, an apple, and a water jug.

I took a few steps into that room and paused at a table set under the window, upon which was a stack of books, a pen and some ink, and a bundle of papers, some of them scrawled with writing. Most of those books were plainly bound, but a few were gorgeously embossed, with golden letters on the spines. I could read very few of the titles which appeared to be in the Sanskrit text. I think that the handwritten papers beside them had perhaps been some form of translation work.

One page was still entirely blank but for a title at the top – *The Vedas: The Search for Divinity*. On another a poem had been inscribed, as if a dedication.

> *Who says the eternal being does not exist?*
> *Who says the sun has gone out?*
> *Someone who climbs up on the roof,*
> *And closes his eyes tight, and says,*
> *I don't see anything.*

I found that strangely moving. I paused a while then lifted up those books printed in English. *The Art of Mystical Spiritualism* was one that I had seen before, when being read by Mercy. The same with *The Occult And The Art of Clairvoyance*, and *The Inspiration of Mesmerism*. But the book that most intrigued me, I had certainly not seen that before. Its title was *The Hindoo Gods*.

The leather of its cover was worn and soft and velvety when

stroked beneath my fingertips. When I opened it up to look inside the papers gave off a strange odour – some notes of vanilla and almonds, but also something musky. It reminded me of Tilsbury and I found that disconcerting, imagining he might be there. I kept glancing back at the empty door, but the lure of the gods within that book were more compelling than my fear as I flicked through the pages to find the one that held such a fascination for me. And, thinking he'd never notice it gone and that, even if he did, he would never know the thief was me, I tore that page away from its binding and folded it neatly into a square, and pushed it into the pocket sewn into the gathers of my skirts.

At that moment, I heard some sound below. Was it a key being pressed in a lock? I stood very still, trying not to breathe, dreading the prospect of being discovered. Cold waves of sickness gripped at my belly. I sat on the bed with my head lolling forward, seeing nothing but dancing white flashes of light until, at last, the retching passed.

While one hand was wiping the sweat from my brow, the other brushed the floor's rough boards, and my sleeve was snagged on something sharp, something protruding from under the mattress. It looked like sticks of grainy wood. I lifted the edge of the blanket high and tried to wrench the object out, cursing when I realised that the mattress's underside had torn. But still, I had it free enough to stand and look more carefully at what by then had been revealed – at which point my mind's clanking calculations might very well have been audible.

What I saw was a pair of antlers, crudely fixed onto some kind of helmet, with leather ties and buckles hanging loose below it. I'd never seen anything like it before. But then, of course I knew I had, and not so very long ago – when visiting the castle, when such a contraption had crowned the head of the phantom that howled upon its walls.

Why had he done it? It made no sense. He could have been shot. He could have been killed. But, for then, the riddle would have to wait, for I suddenly heard more rustling sounds. It was probably only birds or rats who nested in the roof above, but knowing that time was moving on I forced those horns beneath the bed, then left without a backward glance, running down the narrow stairs and on into the scullery. There, in my haste, I quite forgot about the hanging spiders' webs, gasping with horror to think myself trapped when that gauze clung to my face like glue. But at last the panic subsided. I had the worst of it brushed away, spitting out any residue while my boots crunched over broken glass to emerge through the house back door again where, when sure of no voices or footfall approaching, I made my way to the battered gate, splashed across the muddy track, and then along the brambled path that would lead me back to Claremont Road.

Arriving there, I realised that I had forgotten to take a key. But I knew of a spare to the kitchen door that lay beneath a flowerpot, and with Cook long having gone back home, I used that to enter the house again.

Inside, I managed to find a rag with which to clean my muddy boots, and while immersed in such a task my head was filled with wondering if I should dare to tell my aunt of where I'd been, of what I'd seen. But then, what secrets did *she* keep – for surely she knew about Tilsbury's presence or why would she be sending him letters? And what about Nancy? What was her part? What conspiracy could involve her too?

Heading upstairs and into the hall, I called for my aunt, and Nancy too, but the house was still and silent, no other within those walls but me.

I walked on through to the parlour and stared very hard at the goddess Parvati, and thought of my Christmas vision again, when a sudden notion entered my mind, and I wondered why I had lacked the wit to think of such a thing before.

Approaching the table on which she was standing, recalling Albert's pointing hand, I leaned forward, inspecting more closely to see, where the crown was attached to the head, there was a flaw in the silverwork. Or, was it not a flaw at all, but something more deliberate? With one hand firmly gripping the base of the idol, the other began to twist the crown which slowly unscrewed, like a cumbersome lid, and once that was off and set aside I was looking down at a hollow bowl, its interior lined with a satin cloth – as red as blood that fabric was. As red as the ruby that then gleamed in Parvati's silver crown. But what a shock it was for me to see what that chamber had concealed, for even in the fading light the glamour of it stole my breath. And even though it was reduced, but half the size it used to be, and constrained within the clasping brooch, still the diamond glowed with light, a pulsing vibrant energy.

Was I mad to think such things? How could a diamond pulse with life, like the faintest drum, like a beating heart? But I could swear that this one did, and I pressed my hands against my ears so as to make myself quite deaf, so that I could try to gather my senses, to screw the crown back on the deity's head. And with that act accomplished, I left Parvati quite alone. I left her in her silent role as keeper of the Koh-i-Noor – what my aunt had surely stolen when Tilsbury caused his distraction, when disguised as Herne the Hunter, when howling on the castle walls.

I went to my room and remained there for hours, still hearing no sounds of life below, during which time my every thought kept coming back to the silver crown. I *knew* I had found the Koh-i-Noor. What I did not understand was how there could be more than one. For I had seen another, and Victoria staring down at that when my aunt and I had been dismissed on that night of the castle séance.

Had Mercy used a replica? Is that what Tilsbury's letter meant? *The object is perfect and in my possession.*

Considering that, I then recalled what *I* had stolen earlier. I drew the torn page from my pocket, unfolding and smoothing the creases until they were entirely flat – which was when I came to realise that I had removed not one, but two. I stared at what then lay on top. The faded illustration of a goddess who rode on the back of a tiger. A goddess with four pairs of arms, and there, grasped in her many hands, weapons of war were brandished. A trident. A bow and arrows. A thunderbolt. A gleaming sword.

At the base of the page I read the words that told me this was Durga – *she who protects all devotees from the evils of the world. Her left eye represents the moon. Her right eye represents the sun. Her central eye is knowledge, the knowledge that is known through fire. Surrender all actions and duties to her and she shall release thee from thy fears.*

How fearful Durga seemed to me! I knew from Mini's stories that Parvati sometimes took her form when she became a warrior. But I preferred to see her depicted on the page beneath, the only page I'd meant to steal – in which the goddess stood alone upon some snow-capped mountains, her flesh draped in lengths of pure white cloth, with strings of pearls around her breasts, yet more of them threaded through her hair which was long and loose and very dark. And how my hands then trembled, to see how much she looked like me, which made it hard to read the words.

The goddess Parvati, symbol of fertility and marital devotion, consort to the great god Shiva with whom she resides in Mount Kailash. Through her love Shiva gains immortality. Her yoni calms and nurtures his lingam, which once blighted the earth in passion and fire to burn every living thing in its wake. But, should Shiva dare incur her wrath, then Parvati will call on The Ten Mahavidyas. The furies will rise and wreak revenge.

I folded the papers once again and placed them in my mother's bag. In my wretched state of confusion it seemed to me appropriate that my father's image and Mini's beads, as well as the gods that Mini loved, should be buried in darkness, side by side. And later, when the darkness fell, when I was cold and shivering, I dragged a sheet from off the bed, and wound that white around me, sitting by the unlit hearth, where I lit a candle and listened hard, in case the others should return – when I must have drifted into sleep.

Such fitful, restless dreams I had, in which I saw Parvati, just as she was in that picture, her eyes staring very hard at mine as if she was trying to enter my mind, to *know* me, even to *be* me. Her arms were twisting as she danced to the tune of some shrill and reedy flute, a mournful but familiar sound that made me think of a musical box. A silver bird in a golden cage. And every word she sang I knew, and I woke to find myself whispering:

I am mother of the world, holding mystery and riches. I am the goddess of deliverance and marital harmony.

THE TERRIBLE REVELATION

'What's that? What on earth are you talking about? Are you reciting poetry . . . or have you gone demented?'

I came to my senses with a start, jumping at Nancy's questioning, hearing the clatter of the tray she set upon the table. I must have slept so deeply – not to have woken in the night, still to be sitting in the chair. There was such an aching in my neck. I was too hot and somewhat dazed, unsure of who or where I was – very glad of the breeze that blew into the room when she opened the shutters and lifted the sashes, when the sun filtered in through the lace like gold to cast a trellised cage around. Through that the maid then turned to me and laughed, 'Well, Miss Alice, I have to say, you certainly look a sight for sore eyes with your hair all stuck on end like that, and your face just as red as a beetroot.'

'What time is it?' My voice was hoarse.

'Gone eleven. Didn't you hear the bells? Miss Matthews has gone out . . . again.' An intake of breath, a slight sneer on her lips, and then, as if reciting by heart, 'She says that she'll see you at supper this evening. Well, I think that was more or less the gist. In the meantime, Cook's sent some eggs and toast, seeing as you've missed your breakfast.'

'Where has she gone, my aunt? Did she say?'

'She mentioned a visit to Park Street.'

'Park Street? Not somewhere I've heard of before.' Or had I? My head was too bleary and dull.

'No.' Nancy was smiling brightly, full of all the joys of spring she was. 'But I think she may be visiting there more often in the future.'

*

That day was filled with anxious hours, most of them spent in the kitchen with Cook, to whom I almost did confess – thinking to ask her for advice. But I feared she might not be discreet. And I might yet chance to learn some more if I remained in 'ignorance' – by playing the part of detective, by watching Nancy carefully for any signs she might reveal. Although later, when Mercy returned to the house, when we ate our meal in the sitting room, I was almost afraid to look in *her* eyes, in case she might see the suspicion mine held.

I went to my room very early again, but found it hard to rest – so many thoughts whirring around. And then, on the very cusp of sleep, it seemed that my spirit rose up from my body, escaped from the prison of mortal constraints to look down from the ceiling's shadowy corners, to spy on the Alice who sprawled on the bed, her eyes staring back and into mine – until that strange reverie ended, when I was jolted to consciousness by a twisting sensation in my gut.

I sat up and lit the candle stub, and by the glimmer of that flame experienced such a sense of dismay when I lifted my gown and saw the flesh. So bloated and fat it had become – and those small rounded shapes pushing under the skin, as if some creature lived within: as if it was trying to escape. My fear was spiralling by then, recalling Mrs Morrison's tales of tapeworms that grow as large as a horse and destroy a man from the inside out. I heard a horrible high-pitched whine, only stopped when I clamped a hand to my mouth to try and stifle what came out. But too late because, very soon after that, Aunt Mercy appeared at my bedroom door.

She was wearing her nightgown, all creased it was, and her words were slow and thick with sleep, when she asked, 'Alice, what is it? Have you been dreaming again?'

Raising the sheets, and then my shift, I exposed the horror underneath, at which Aunt Mercy looked appalled, mouth stretched to its limits in disbelief, through which she finally said the words, 'When is this child to be born?'

This child? She made no sense. 'Aunt Mercy, what are you talking about? There's something inside me – can't you see?'

'I can see very well.' She seemed to be entirely calm when coming nearer to the bed. And, I thought – with utter disbelief – that my aunt may be going to hug me, to comfort and hold me in her arms. But instead, she grabbed my shoulders and began to shake me very hard, so hard that my head hit against the wall and only the sudden bang of that caused my aunt alarm enough to cease that violent onslaught. She stared at me in silence – except for the gasping of her breaths – and the venting of her anger, when all at once she shouted, 'How could I be so blind, not to notice what's been going on, right under my nose, in my own house?'

Flinching back, fearing she would strike again, my spine was crushed against brass bars as I tried to protest. 'I don't understand.'

But I think I did. I started to. I thought of the dream that I'd once had, when Lucian Tilsbury came to my room, and the soreness I'd felt, and the stains of blood when I woke the following morning. The blood that had not been my curse. Not the curse that I presumed . . .

I think my aunt remembered too, when she leaned even closer and whispered with venom, 'Tell me the truth. How long has this been going on? This shameful, sordid secret of yours!'

The next thing, she was standing again, pacing the room in small, preying circles, her voice coming sharp and staccato. 'To think you both deceived me! And, this!' Her finger was jabbing, striking as sharp as any knife into the flesh of my belly, making me wince and cry in pain, over which she screamed, 'This is your ruin, your punishment, the end of your every hope for a future. And what about *me* and *my* reputation? What about—'.

She stopped short, and my own voice was pleading, 'What you say . . . it can't be true.' I was weeping and holding my arms out towards her, hoping for any sign of affection, receiving no more than a withering glance when she left me there, alone again, when the door to my room then slammed so hard the whole house seemed to shudder with her disgust. After that, all I heard was her stamping below, doors and walls banging, ornaments smashing – my aunt's rage then far more frightening than the terrible thing she had claimed as its cause.

First thing in the morning, Nancy was sent for the doctor. I stood at my window and watched her leave. Her feet splashed through puddles in the street, her head beetle-domed underneath an umbrella. I wondered that she could see or hear a thing that was going on around. I hoped she had been deaf last night when my aunt had been screaming her cruel accusations, and if she had heard, then I hoped and prayed that she would not mention a thing to Cook.

But, why should I panic? Why should I fret? Surely, when the doctor came, he would find some other cause of complaint; he would prove my aunt's suspicions wrong and then he might make me well again.

The doctor arrived at eleven o'clock. I was told to lie back on the bed, to expose my stomach and spread my legs. I cannot express my embarrassment or the anger I felt towards my aunt, to think she could so willingly permit those cruel indignities, while that doctor, no more than a stranger to me, invaded my most private parts. Not once did he look into my eyes while enquiring about my monthly shows, or whether I'd had any sickness – at which response he heaved a sigh when I said I had seen no fresh blood since last year, how since then I had often felt queasy and faint.

'Well, you're still very small, but I'd say you've advanced at least five or six months in this pregnancy. No option but to accept your fate.'

'My fate! No! It can't be true!' I looked up at my aunt, at the end of the bed, standing quite still, staring down at me.

The doctor replied with a snort of derision, followed by a

brief explanation of what he so curtly named my 'dilemma', all the while implying that I must be perfectly aware of how I had come to be placed there. But his words were so technical, rushed and vague – really, I was left none the wiser, only wishing to look at some medical books, to research all the symptoms and causes myself. But as there were none in Mercy's house, what choice did I have but to accept this doctor's diagnosis, when two serious and pale blue eyes stared over his wire spectacle rims, where I searched for a glimmer of sympathy but found only professional detachment.

'How could you bring such shame on this house?' My aunt's eyes were moist and reddening. 'What would your father think? I thank God your parents are both dead!'

'You don't believe they can see me then?'

She glared to hear my insolence. She lifted her chin, her jaw clenched hard, as she turned her face away from mine, to follow the doctor out again.

When they'd gone, I got up from the bed, quite dumbstruck, in a state of shock. I was tying my dressing gown tightly around, not wanting to do so much as glance at the body then concealed beneath for fear of what tricks it might play next.

I picked up my beaded reticule. I drew out a rudraksha seed, and while gripping that tightly in one hand I reached out with both my arms to embrace what was the empty air, wishing that Mini might appear, to stand at my side, to hold me, to tell me that I was a brave little *butcha*; to call me her Priyam. Beloved.

I was only despised by Mercy. It might be better if I was dead. Dead, just like my parents. How hard would it be to lift the sash and climb onto the window ledge? There would be less than a moment of falling and then it would all be over. For me, for the parasite within. The punishment for my night of sin – for my hedonistic tendencies.

As my shaking fingers drew back the catch, I looked down at some stems of white lilac, the blossom very early that year, and already turned brown on the rain-battered branches. While straining to push the window up I felt the wetness of that rain, soft splashes like tears falling over my face – the tears that mingled with my own when I knew myself a coward, when I turned and walked towards the bed, and covered myself with the blankets and tried to drown in darkness.

How many hours had passed by when I heard a voice calling my name. 'Alice. Alice . . . can you hear me?'

Pushing the blankets from my face, I saw Aunt Mercy peering down and, at first, with my mind so befuddled, I thought I must be dreaming, for Mercy was smiling, hands clasped to her breast as if to contain the excitement she felt, when she said, 'I have some news. I have met with Mr Tilsbury . . . who is recently back from Amsterdam, and he feels – we both feel – that this problem of yours might yet reach a happy conclusion.'

'A happy conclusion?'

'Yes! We mean to keep your condition concealed, for *no one* must know of this disgrace. And then, by the time the child is born I shall take it on as if my own.'

I lay very still, staring up from my pillow. I spoke with utter disbelief, 'You have forgiven him for this? For that night when he must have come to my room? For what that man has done to me? And how can you think to take on this child, to take any blame away from me, when you have no husband to act as the father? Or will you call it a spirit child – an immaculate conception?'

My aunt's green eyes fixed hard on me while my acid response was vented, but nothing and no one was going to spoil her glorious moment of triumph, when she took a deep breath to control herself and slowly began to explain to me, 'We've talked it all through, very carefully. I had suspected . . . I will confess, but Mr Tilsbury admits to no knowledge of this predicament. And Nancy has assured me that he never came to your room that night. It was wicked of you to seek to blame a man of such fine character. Who really knows where *you* have been, what sordid things you might have done! I've afforded you too much liberty when I should have been more vigilant. I certainly will be from now on! As yet you are a minor, still only nineteen years of age. I would be remiss, as your guardian, if I were to abandon you. We are where we are. The deed is done. And now, Mr Tilsbury and I shall endeavour to make things right again. We shall be married, as soon as we can, and when any others chance to ask, we shall simply say that the wedding took place some time in the previous year, that we did not announce it at the time because he was suddenly called away to attend to some business overseas. I doubt that any will be surprised. Lucian has wooed me long enough. But the main thing is, when this child is born, it will assume a legitimate name, and your own will remain unblemished. I think you must begin to see how admirable our compassion is. And when you are recovered enough, we shall find a place for you to go. You are well read and clever enough to take on the role of a governess – if not that, then perhaps a companion . . . though,' she lowered her eyes to my belly again, 'not quite clever enough, it seems.'

So, my destiny was decided. How convenient it was! My aunt would become Mrs Tilsbury, just as she'd always wished to be. She would also command my obedience. She would hold me in debt for her sacrifice. But then, what option did I have? How could I think to cope alone, if I should be homeless, without any income? How could I ever hope to survive? I was trapped. I must be grateful and strive to play the dutiful niece, the cousin to my bastard child – for ever more forced to live my life in abetting my aunt's deceptions.

THE TIGHTENING OF THE ROPE

Could it possibly be right, what Lucian Tilsbury told my aunt, that he'd had no involvement in my fate? Had I taken to walking out at night when I was asleep and dreaming – just as I had when I had worn the lace of my mother's wedding veil? Just as I must have done again when Nancy had claimed to have found me, downstairs in the hallway, the front door wide open. Where had I been? What *had* I done? Was I really so immersed in a sordid world of fantasies, dreaming of vampires and human skulls, of gods who dressed in tiger skins with tattooed snakes upon their arms? Had I been raped, or given myself to some filthy stranger on the street? The very thought of it made me retch.

I believed I should know when I saw him, when I next met with Lucian Tilsbury, when I looked for the guilt behind his eyes. So, when Aunt Mercy appeared one day and told me to wash and dress myself and prepare for a visit to his house, I went there all too willingly.

It was a pleasant warm spring day when we walked through the town, to the castle walls, and then along the High Street until it forked into three prongs – like the spikes on the end of a trident. The middle way was Park Street, the address that Nancy mentioned before, as being somewhere that my aunt would visit more often in future. There, on either side of the road, several tall brick houses stood, and at its end were stable yards, and a tavern, and then the iron gates by which to enter those public parts that led to the lawns of the Long Walk. All conveniently close to the castle, and not so very far away from the hovel with horns beneath the bed – where I had last seen Tilsbury.

Aunt Mercy ascended the steep stone steps of a house where

the lower windows were faced with painted iron bars. She waited beneath a pillared porch while a great deal of rattling came from within before the door was opened by a maid in a pale blue uniform; and that maid had barely opened her mouth to offer any greeting before my aunt swept on inside.

My entrance was more tentative as I followed up the front steps and waited for a moment there until my eyes acclimatised to the dimness of the hallway. And such a strange illusion there was, when a sudden ray of light shone in from the brighter street behind me. It flickered across the polished boards – slithering, golden, like a worm. It gleamed upon the rise of the stairs where a newel post was carved as a serpent's head, and the curving rail that rose behind was etched with the serpents' diamond scales.

A serpent once crawled from a rosebud upon my bedroom's papered walls. But, no time to think of such things just then, as a pair of inner doors swung wide – and my legs almost buckled beneath me to see the man between them.

No longer decked in his beggar's disguise, he could have been an angel there – a dark angel though, with that scar on his cheek – who welcomed us so courteously and asked if we would join him to take tea in the drawing room.

We entered a large rectangular space where daylight flowed in from the front to the back and shimmered like water on pale blue walls. Gilt mirrors were arched with flowers and birds. There were black japanned tables, and tall Chinese vases, and intricate carvings made from jade. A cabinet held butterflies, such delicate things, cruelly impaled; their wings iridescent in greens and blues, like glistening, oily, vibrant jewels. On the walls there were paintings suspended from chains. Some were portraits of many-limbed gods. Some of them were landscapes: barren worlds bleached white beneath glaring suns, where camels walked across the sands, past the ruins of long lost temples. Others showed gardens with palm trees and fountains, with the domes of great palaces far in the distance, where men in turbans lounged on thrones, carried on the backs of elephants. Such gorgeously tented howdahs they were, like the one that I'd seen at the Great Exhibition, that last day I'd spent with Papa – that day when Papa held my hand, just as I wished he could right then.

I closed my eyes. When they opened again I found myself dazzled by rays of light that shafted through the muslin drapes on either side of two glass doors that opened up to a balcony. From there steps led to broad green lawns, their boundaries surrounded by high brick walls, each wall then topped with metal spikes, I supposed for deterring intruders – or perhaps those inside who might wish to escape?

Tilsbury drew my attention back, inviting my aunt and me to sit. There followed solicitous idle talk, during which no mention was made at all of my new 'situation'. And despite all my earlier bravado, I found I could only avoid the eyes of the man who was planning to marry my aunt, to save my reputation.

I was glad when the maid appeared again to cause some small distraction. She was holding a silver tray in her hands, though my aunt, as if already mistress there, told the girl to go away and went on to pour the tea herself. She dropped several sugar cubes into the cups, and the thought of that sweetness – I felt quite sick. It was all I could do to sip from mine until, at around four o'clock, Aunt Mercy set her cup aside and said we should be leaving, to attend some spiritualist meeting.

'We?' My question was abrupt.

'The Dalrymples will be there . . . you know them, dear.' My aunt's face was bathed in her falsest smile. 'They used to visit regularly, coming down from London. They did so like my spirit guide, though, sadly, when she disappeared, their interest also seemed to wane. Still, they have now written to say that their friend, no less than Lady Garsington, is currently leasing a house here in Windsor and would very much like to meet with me . . . and also Mr Tilsbury. It seems she has heard some rumours regarding our royal connections. Such valuable introductions may lead us to those households where I feel our skills are suited best.'

Was this then to be the day of my public initiation, this role to be my chosen path, not a governess or companion? Was my entry into her psychic charades the price that I was now to pay: the fee for Mercy's kindnesses?

I looked at my aunt in some alarm. I stated that I felt too tired to join in any séance. Clearly irked to hear that claim, she firmly insisted I should go, until Tilsbury suggested she show some compassion, pointing out the paleness of my face, and how it might be just as well if I remained there, in his house, to rest until restored again.

He showed me the bell beside the hearth, in case I should wish to call for refreshment or happen to have any other need. And then, without much more ado, he and my aunt left the drawing room – and left me sitting there alone.

Some moments passed before I decided to make my way back to Claremont Road, before which I thought to look out through the window, to be sure that they were safely gone. But, it was not unpleasant to linger a while in that lovely room, to wander across the Turkey rugs and lay my hands upon the keys of a piano that stood against one wall. My fingers touched on random notes which hung upon the air like jewels as I made my way to a marble-topped table upon which was set a lingam, the shape of it sculpted from pale grey stone. Beside it were some figurines, their detailed and exotic forms all cast from silver, bronze or brass, though there was one, the largest by far, which appeared to be made of solid gold.

That idol was shown in the motion of dance. One of his feet was lifted high, the other planted on the ground to crush the little demon that lay at the statue's ornate base. That creature was very ugly, but his conqueror was beautiful. His waist was small, his breast as broad as that of any monkey god. But the face above was human, and the hair that coiled upon the head was towering as if a crown. He had two legs. His arms were four. The palm of one hand was extended, as if it was in blessing. A second wielded an axe. A third one held a little deer. A fourth a trident and a drum. A garland of skulls hung at his breast, and like a rope around his neck there was a coiling serpent. Surrounding all there was an arch. A ring of fire, or so it seemed, with tiny pointed tongues of flame that blazed about the golden god. The god that Mini always loved.

I had no doubt this was Shiva. Shiva The Destroyer. Shiva The Slayer of Demons. Shiva The Cosmic Dancer, whose wheel of fire constantly turned to bring balance and harmony to the world. The light and the darkness, the good and the bad, all were found in Shiva's mind.

My fingers touched the lingam stone, then circled the bowl in which it stood. I thought of the page I'd stolen from Tilsbury's book of Hindoo gods, how that told of the goddess Parvati, and how it is through her love for him that Lord Shiva gains immortality, how 'her yoni calms and nurtures his lingam . . .'

I felt dizzy. My head was aching. I went to sit upon a chaise where a breeze then stirred the window drapes. The softness of fabric caressed my face. I was lulled by the sweet throbbing song of some bird, the street sounds of horse hooves and footsteps on cobbles . . . and when I opened my eyes again the room was much darker than it had been. Lifting my head from a cushion, I yawned and stretched both arms up high, only noticing then that the front window's shutters had been unfolded and secured.

Who could have come in and done such a thing, without causing any disturbance? Whoever it was, I suddenly sensed that they were still there, in the room with me.

Looking about, I noticed the man who was sitting in a chair close by. His face was concealed by its high winged sides. One hand rested limp upon a knee, and the fingers of that hand quite still, though its owner was surely aware by then that I was awake, and aware of him.

All at once he made to stand, then walked towards where I was sitting, where he knelt on the carpet at my side and said, as if simply discussing the weather, 'I didn't mean to wake you. Your aunt was somewhat tired, too. The result of her psychic exertions. I persuaded her to go home and rest. She will join us for dinner . . . later on.'

My heart was hammering in my breast. I was shuffling backwards in the seat, away from the eyes that stared into mine – the eyes that were splintered with flecks of gold. And I knew then, without any question of doubt, that I *had* seen that light before, when he came to my bedroom in Claremont Road, when Nancy must have lied to me, for the sake of Lucian Tilsbury. And further distressed to face that truth at last I managed to accuse, 'It *was* you. That night was not a dream!'

His head was tilted to one side. His hair fell forward across his brow to cover the scar upon his cheek. He lifted a hand to push it back, at the same time beginning to speak again, and I heard the catch of nervousness when Tilsbury almost seemed to plead, 'Alice, believe me . . .' He glanced down at the dome of my belly, the swelling all too visible beneath my skirts and petticoats. 'I never intended this outcome.'

My ears filled with a rushing of blood, recalling that cold dawn morning when I woke with my nightgown streaked with blood. 'This "outcome"? You mean my ruin!' I tried to rise. I raged at him, demanding in a breathless voice, 'Does my aunt know what you have done? Or is she really such a dupe?'

An icy chill ran through my veins to hear the words he spoke just then, 'It matters not what Mercy thinks.'

I felt the heat of his breath on my lips as he placed his hands on both my arms, restraining me there while he leaned even closer. But, oh, the sadness in his smile. How could that not affect me? For all of my bravado, I was too easily seduced when he lifted his hands to cup my face, to draw my mouth to meet his own – when there was no decorum, no holding back, when the passion and sweetness in that kiss caused memories, sup-pressed till then, to stir such yearnings in my flesh. I did not need to cast my eyes upon the sacred lingam stone to know exactly what it was that object represented.

How could I act so sinfully, so willingly to give myself to this man who had surely doomed my life – this man who claimed himself to be a friend to my own father, this man who had con-vinced my aunt that he had never touched my flesh? And what lies did he tell to me? Did he mean to keep the both of us? Two wives for this one husband? Did Nancy make that number three?

'Stop! This is wrong!' I pushed him off.

'Alice?' He touched my cheek again, and such remorse within his eyes when he said, 'You have no cause for doubt. You must trust in my intentions.'

'What intentions?' I was standing then, turning to look back down on him, thrusting a hand to my belly and shouting, 'I am carrying your child, and yet you plan to wed my aunt.'

'I have no choice!' He also rose, reaching out to grip my arm, twisting me round to face him. 'She is your guardian and you are a minor. You may marry no one without her permission. Of course, I could take you away, I could leave your aunt here, elope with you, but then . . .' he gave a lengthy sigh '. . . I am not so sure that *you* can be trusted. By marrying Mercy I keep you close, ensuring the good repute of all.'

He lowered his arm and stepped away, heading then towards the door. 'Your aunt will soon be arriving for dinner. As you know, she is entirely convinced that some stranger has fathered this child of yours, and for now you must believe me when I say such a view is convenient. Should you speak out . . .' he paused again, 'then I fear the result of Mercy's wrath. I fear that we might both be lost.'

And then something steelier entered his voice. 'Before she arrives there is one more thing. I have something of yours that should be returned, for I never take that which I do not own, what is not freely given.'

From his waistcoat pocket he withdrew a small object, and at first I thought it was a coin, glistening there in the flat of his palm. But, no, it was a button, from the dress I had been wearing, on the day when I went to his other house – when I had found his Herne disguise.

'I think we both know where I found this. You may also wish to know that all evidence within that house has been entirely destroyed. But I suggest that you are more careful about leaving clues when you next play detective? You should keep your

142

counsel in *all* these things, not only for your safety, but for any that you care about. Those living now . . . and those to come.'

'I saw you that day. I saw you with Nancy. You were dressed in that beggar disguise. Why did you go about like that? Does Nancy know what's going on?'

'Nancy knows as much as she needs to know. That and nothing more. And as to my disguise . . . it was not convenient for me to be thought of as being in Windsor then. Always best to have an alibi, a means of making a swift escape should circumstances so require, if events do not go along as planned. However . . .' he continued, resting one hand upon the door, 'I believe enough time has now elapsed to be confident that all is well, the campaign about to meet success.'

The turn of a key gave a muffled *click*, and something clicked inside my mind as I watched the window's muslin drapes when they bloated into the room again. Like phantoms they struggled to enter, to bind me and blind me in the crimes of this man of whom I knew nothing at all, who seemed to know so much of me. This man who, had my aunt been caught while attempting to steal the Koh-i-Noor, would have abandoned her – and me – to leave us condemned for that crime alone.

Did he know I was aware of that? That I knew of what lay in Parvati's crown?

It was impossible to tell. For now I would speak not a word of it. I would keep my secret safe inside, and, perhaps, in time, that knowledge might yet lead me to my liberty.

When Aunt Mercy arrived we sat down to dine. It was all I could do not to run from the table, noticing the sphinx-like ease with which Lucian Tilsbury fell into the part that she expected him to play, and how, when the maid who had waited on us had finally gone away again, he enquired so solicitously, 'Did you rest well, Mercy? I think Alice did. She looks more refreshed now, don't you think?'

'Yes, she looks well enough, I suppose.'

'During your absence we discussed her reluctance to use her abilities, her awareness of what is The Truth.'

The knife in my hand – might I stab him with that? My hand shook and I had to take a deep breath to keep calm at the tone of his insinuation. I felt sick to the pit of my belly to imagine Mercy in his arms. I could not swallow one ounce of food, even though the aromas were fragrantly spiced. How I had once loved the Dal Makhani – the lentils with butter – when I was a child. But now the aroma distressed me. To my ears, every sound was amplified – the cutlery clanging, the scraping of china, the wine being poured into glasses. And, outside in the gardens, that shrill cry of alarm, the panicked warning of a bird as a cat climbed through branches to plunder its nestlings.

My plunderer smiled and lifted his glass. In return I gulped my wine to the dregs, as if it were welcome poison. Mercy watched. She sipped more demurely, then clinked her glass against his own, during which she made her toast, 'To our happiness . . . to our future lives!'

She could never have known what she wished for, how that sham of a happy family filled me with nothing but fuming resentment. And that's when I saw the new ring on her finger, a garland of emeralds and pearly white opals. And, presuming that was their sign of engagement, and although I would come to regret such thoughts, I wished that those opals would bring her bad luck, would lead to nothing but grief and tears, just as the old wives tales said.

Spiteful words welled in my mouth and I wanted to spit them in her face, to crush every lie, every smug expectation. But, recalling Tilsbury's earlier warnings, I somehow managed to hold my tongue – because I knew one thing for sure. Even if Mercy was aware of the guilt of Lucian Tilsbury, there could be no guarantee that she would choose to stand by me.

When that ghastly dinner was over and done our host suggested we retire, to sit once again in the drawing room. He led me to the very chaise upon which I had lain before, when he had found me sleeping. I felt myself blush. I was very hot. My hands were twisting in my lap. Couldn't Aunt Mercy see my distress? Couldn't she sense the shame I felt? All I could hear was her trivial chatter as if we were back where the day had begun. All I could think was, *Is Mercy blind?*

And then, something else diverted my thoughts, when I saw how, high above us, the chandelier's candles had all been lit to glow upon the room's blue walls, their light also glittering on the gods that stood on the marble table top. And there, beside the lingam and the golden idol of Shiva, there was another figurine that had definitely not been there before – Parvati, the silver goddess, who had graced the front parlour in Claremont Road. She was now here, in the Park Street house.

Who had brought her in, and when? Had Tilsbury done that while I slept? Did the diamond still lie in her silver crown?

On another table there was a tray, and on that a glass decanter from which Tilsbury was pouring measures of some dark amber liquid, passing a glass to both his guests before taking his own to the high-winged chair that, now, had been turned to face the room. More specifically, it was facing me.

I felt so very conspicuous. And the brandy, I swallowed it down in one, just as I had the wine before, as if it were but water – soon coming to regret that act when choking at the burn in my throat, coughing and pressing a hand to my breast and closing my eyes against the pain. A sudden draught rushed in from the garden and caused me to shiver violently, and when I opened my eyes again I saw how the candles' flames shuddered and dipped. My breathing grew shallow and laboured. The air smelled pungently of wax. My head felt so light I thought I should faint, and I sensed myself rising up from my seat where nothing was solid beneath my feet, where my body was floating, was weightless. At least, that's how it seemed to me, even though that was impossible. But then, I could see, quite clearly, the winding blue silk round the chandelier's chain, the fluffing grey dust that had settled there, and how that chain was creaking as, slowly, it began to sway, which in turn caused the candles to drip hot wax, great scalding gobbets of molten white that fell onto the rug below. I heard a humming, low in my ears, something that could almost be a song, and that accompanied by the sound of glasses and ornaments tinkling on tables, as if every atom of their creation had been disturbed by the subtle vibrations. And the source of that thrumming, that strange emanation, it was the marble table top, upon which the gods were trembling, as if they were about to dance – as if they had somehow come to life.

Aunt Mercy looked around the room, and then she glanced back up at me, her mouth gaping open to see me like that. But like what? Was I actually levitating, or was I simply standing? Whatever the reality, her shocked expression broke the spell. Every pulsation came to an end, but not before a Chinese vase toppled from its place on the mantel, crashing to the hearth below where a hundred shards of blue and white were shattered at Lucian Tilsbury's feet.

Whatever the strings that held me, that enchantment also broke. I fell back. I was sprawled upon the chaise.

Aunt Mercy's voice came high and tense when she asked, 'What was that? Alice? What happened just then?'

'I don't know, I . . .' I stopped, but not from fear. I was seething with anger all over again, suspecting that Lucian Tilsbury had engineered this happening; that somehow he'd managed to mesmerise me, or perhaps his maid was now upstairs to manipulate the chandelier. I wanted to scream. I opened my mouth, but my voice, that was not the thing I heard. I heard something that was mechanical. Something that was musical – and the three of us turned, as if we were one, and our six eyes fixed on the source of *that* sound: the piano that stood against the wall.

The stool set before it was empty, but the keys were rising and falling as if being played by invisible hands. At first those notes were light and slow but soon they became much faster, a random, discordant and chiming crescendo that was joined by my own hysterical laughter – and that only ending when

Mercy's hand was slapped so hard against my cheek, when, holding my own to the stinging flesh, I asked, 'Why did you do that, Aunt? Don't you like that particular song? Wasn't it "Brightest and Best" . . . the carol I played at Christmas? I begin to see its significance now. Those words, I begin to understand: *Gems of the mountain. Richer by—*'

'Stop this insolence!' Mercy glared at me. She may have looked and sounded fierce, but the flash of terror filled her eyes, whereas I – I felt a power, a thrilling rushing in my veins to know it was *my* fury that caused that music to occur. Some malice inside me now wanted more mischief, and so I got up from my seat again and walked across the length of the room to the table upon which Parvati was standing. I closed my eyes as if in a trance, and just as Albert's ghost had done, my arm slowly lifted to point at her crown, and all the while I was chanting, 'Parvati speaks of her burden. She tells of the mystical light within, that yearns to escape the darkness.'

The moment that cryptic allusion was made I felt strangely drained and exhausted. I thought that, much like the idol itself, I also carried a burden, a secret within the dark bowl of my body: the new life that was waiting to be born and, at that time, to steal my own.

I asked in a small and shaking voice, 'What's happening to me? I don't want this "seeing". I don't want this child.'

While my aunt remained silent, still staring at me, her knuckles clenching at her sides, it was Tilsbury who answered, and he spoke quite plainly for all to hear, 'I'm sorry, Alice. Forgive me.'

How could I ever forgive him? I was running towards him, arms flailing, fists striking hard against his chest. And yet he did nothing to stop me, calmly accepting every blow, waiting until my rage was spent – when I slumped to my knees with my face in my hands and saw all too clearly the error I'd made, and how, by alluding to Parvati's secret, the crime that neither he nor my aunt could ever afford to be exposed, I had only managed to tighten the rope already knotted at my throat.

THE MAHARAJAH'S PROPHECY

Over the course of the following weeks I took to staying in my room, sometimes not getting dressed at all. And my aunt, she did not breathe one word of what had occurred in the Park Street house. She even encouraged my idle behaviour, her anger expressed in other ways, by suggesting I stay well away from the kitchen, 'In case Mrs Morrison should see the shameful state of your vile degradation.'

At first I was defiant. I wore a corset laced so tight that Cook would never know what lay concealed beneath those whalebones. But when I took it off at night, my flesh would be scarred into angry red furrows that barely had the chance to fade before the next morning's torture began. At times, I could barely catch my breath when heading up and down the stairs. And so I gave in to my aunt's demands, and she brought me food and drink on trays. And when I asked where Nancy was, no longer seeing her in the house or hearing creaks from the attic room, my aunt told me the girl had been dismissed, for fear of seeing 'what she should not'; for fear of any gossip spread. She said there would be no other maid until we returned to normality – and that word, for some reason, it made me explode, crying out, 'Normality? Will you tell me what normality means? Will it be resumed when my child is born, or will it be on your wedding day . . . or when your next séance is arranged? And just what will you steal then?'

I expected her to deny the theft, but my aunt's response was brazen. 'Are you not impressed, that I held my nerve and accomplished the act, exchanging the brooch with a replica, and that *she*, not for one moment, had the notion to tell the difference?'

'So, there *were* two diamonds! But . . .' I could not quell my interest, 'how could two jewels be so alike?'

'The duplicate is made of paste, by a specialised method, and much refined from the usual fakery. Truly, only an expert would know. And as Victoria will insist on keeping the diamond as a brooch, it is not at all likely that anyone else should think to look as close as that – at what adorns the royal breast!

'Lucian knows about such things. He used to deal in precious gems – a part-time trade to enhance his pay when in the army, in India. Many soldiers do it. So many jewels to be found there . . . taken as booty in the wars, or used as bribery. I recall your father telling once of a ruby given as a gift which fetched a thousand guineas when auctioned here in London. The natives are too ignorant. No sense of the value of what they have. But then, I assumed you'd know all that, that Lucian would have told you. No?'

Her question was loaded with venom. I knew then that Mercy loathed me. There had always been resentment, but to see the hatred in her eyes – those green eyes, full of jealousy. She was not blind. She knew the truth, and that was why she relished this chance to see me wither beneath her gaze. She could not resist this moment of exhibiting her dominance. She could not help but carry on and tell me everything she knew . . .

'When Lucian travelled to Amsterdam, it was to visit a jeweller there . . . the very same craftsman commissioned before when Prince Albert had him remodel the stone, supposedly for any new facets cut to expose its inner brilliance . . . though Lucian says it only served to render the stone a duller thing, much easier to counterfeit than the original design.

'He offered that selfsame jeweller sufficient financial recompense to create an identical mould for him – working from those drawings kept that showed the new shape and measurements. From that, a glass imitation was formed, with certain chemicals applied to enhance the colours locked within. Quite faithful to the original – as was the golden clasp in which the replica has now been set.'

'And what do you and Tilsbury plan to do with the original? You cannot think to sell it? A diamond so notorious! You would most surely be found out.'

'He has no intention of selling it. He has other ambitions for the stone . . . one of which is to visit a shrine in the Himalayan mountains. He says that the summers are beautiful, not at all unpleasant or too hot. And there we shall go when we are wed. Do you not think that romantic . . . that my husband will take me to the place where the Koh-i-Noor diamond once graced the head of an ancient Hindoo god . . . where we shall then replace it?'

'Far, far away my heart's dearest, is a palace atop of Mount Kailash, where Shiva lives in wedded bliss with his goddess wife, Parvati.'

I had not meant to speak my thoughts, but clearly I had, for Aunt Mercy asked, 'What? What did you say?'

'It is nothing – just a story. A story my ayah used to tell. But . . .' I almost pleaded then, so desperate was I to hear the rest, those other facts she claimed to know, 'if that is one reason for stealing the diamond, then what can the other be?'

'He wishes to redress the wrongs that were done to the Maharajah, for whom the diamond signifies the power of his sovereignty.'

'The Maharajah Duleep Singh? But his throne was lost in the Punjab Wars. How can he think to regain it now without another conflict? And this theft, should it be discovered, then you would be charged with treason. And, if that is so, then . . .' I was suddenly struck by the awful thought, 'then I would be implicated too! I was there, at the castle séance. What if you had been discovered then at the time when you exchanged the stones?'

'No one was concerned with the diamond – or me! Not when Herne was there on the castle walls. It may have been an extravagant act, but it was one that was quite sure of achieving complete attention.'

'He must be mad to take such risks. No sane man would

behave that way. And you . . . are you deluded too, to join in such tricks, so willingly?'

'If I am deluded then so are you.' She was pointing at me accusingly. 'He is right when he says you have the gift. You have something that I would give anything for, and yet you choose to spurn it. You have been blessed in many ways, and yet you only seek to harm. That incident with the piano . . . your abhorrent behaviour afterwards! What if his offer is withdrawn? What if he abandons me . . . if I am left here, on my own . . . with you . . . with *your* delusions? Well, I warn you, Alice Willoughby, if that is to be the case then when the time comes for this child to be born, some other arrangements will be made. Your bastard will be given away and—'

'No! I countered boldly, and quite without any conscious thought I placed both my hands on my belly, the fingers spread wide to form a cage, as if to protect the child within. 'I would rather starve upon the streets.'

My aunt replied with smiling scorn, 'You know nothing of the real world!' And then, before she left the room, she said in calm but chilling tones, 'There is a local convent, run by the Sisters of the Raj. Is that not appropriate? They take in homeless waifs and strays, those bastards born to reprobates. I should have left *you* at their door, all those years ago when your father died. What gratitude have you ever shown for the sacrifices *I* have made? I think you should consider that . . . and any future you may have.'

With that she left me quite alone, 'considering my future', sitting in the hearthside chair and listlessly holding a cup of tea – when suddenly she reappeared to show me the letter in her hand, the contents of which had magically succeeded in brightening her mood.

No longer furious with me, Mercy was brimming over with smiles, her free hand clutched against her breast as she gasped from exertion, from all the stairs, 'He has not thrown me off! We have both been invited to Park Street, to attend a small gathering of friends. I believe this will be the occasion when he makes the formal announcement . . . to say that he and I are wed.'

'But you are not.'

'But we will be, and I think it must be very soon.'

The cup fell from my fingers. Tea spilled in my lap. But I hardly noticed the scalding burn, only said, 'I would rather not come with you. I would rather stay here in Claremont Road.'

My aunt was severe when she replied, 'He specifically asks for you to go . . . though goodness knows why that should be, after your last debacle there. Still, you must be prepared to show gratitude, not to spurn his generous nature, his willingness to forgive and forget. I cannot force you to comply. But, I do suggest you consider this. Lucian Tilsbury and I *will* be married and well before your child is born. Best you accept this and act with grace . . . that you play the part of the dutiful niece . . . that you affirm to any who ask the veracity of this marriage claim. You should also consider the consequence of denying this or speaking out – because once I *am* legally his wife, what is to prevent me from changing my mind, from withdrawing my protection from you?'

Mercy was standing at Tilsbury's side. She was dressed in a dark green satin, her lips and cheeks aglow with rouge. But I needed no powder to offer a blush and would gladly have fled back out to the street when so many eyes turned to look our way.

Nervously glancing towards the wall where a piano had once stood, I was enormously relieved to find the instrument removed. How mortified I would have been to create such a scene as that again, to draw such attention to myself.

I thought to hide in some dimly lit corner, but it seemed there were hundreds of candles lit, hundreds of spotlights all shining on me. When a maid approached with a tray of food, my vision became a swimming blur, seeing so many fingers of all shapes and sizes, some snatching at *palak*, or *gobi pakora*, or the little skewers of chicken breast – and then it was Lucian Tilsbury's hand, taking my arm to lead me away.

I did my best to shrug him off, but his grip was like steel as he steered me on, past huddles of chattering, staring guests, towards two ladies beside the hearth – and I already knew who they were, even if they did not recognise me. But then, when they'd seen me years before I had worn the black veils of the parlour ghost, which meant I could now feign ignorance when Tilsbury introduced me to the sisters, the Miss Dalrymples, the two women advanced in middle years who pouted and tittered and beamed with delight when he asked them to act as my chaperones.

They had always been eccentric. More peculiar still they looked that night. One wore a tiara stuck high on her head with a mass of white ringlets around her ears. Her sister's hair was more lustrous, though tinted a strangely bluish-black, that stain also smeared on her forehead and neck. It was she who took my hand, loudly admiring my grey silk gown and the pearls that glistened at my neck – the pearls from Mercy's closet, the pearls that my aunt had insisted I wear.

After paying me such compliments, the dark-haired sister began to pronounce on her own *marvellous* abilities – of how she and my aunt were long known to each other through their mutual study of 'other powers', all of those ghosts who surely knocked upon the Iron Doors of Death. She claimed to have no peace at all from the heavenly perfume that smoked from her candles, the signs of devotion from lost spirit lovers. Her sister then went on to refer to the odours that wafted from under their floorboards, indicating the movements of restless souls. I presumed they must have rats or mice and, silently, I imagined that if those aromas were nearly as strong as the perfume in which those two were doused then, truly, the strangest thing of all was that any ghosts un-exorcised were not gasping and choking while running back to find that Door of Death again.

When they asked if I shared my aunt's psychic skills, I shook my head and tried to smile, to practise sweet temper and patience. But the older refused to be put off, trilling, 'Oh, come now, my dear, you must tell the truth! I can practically smell the gift on you. You have quite an aura about you, you know. Much like our own dear Mr Tilsbury – and he such a force of nature, so very charismatic, so very . . .' She exhaled a sigh, seeming unable to carry on.

I was wondering how *he* could tolerate to listen to such silly talk – though my aunt, she seemed to thrive in the company of sycophantic admirers. That night she was her sparkling best, mingling with the other guests. And no doubt she was only awaiting more pleasure, when her mentor might take *her* by the arm and announce to all and sundry that Miss Matthews was now Mrs Tilsbury – the fact that I must then confirm, or else suffer the 'consequence'.

With every passing moment, I dreaded that announcement, but then there fell a sudden hush when someone else entered the drawing room, and I'm sure that I was not alone in that quickening thud within my breast. Why, I thought my spinster friends might faint to see such a strikingly handsome man – to see Victoria's 'beautiful boy' – the Maharajah of Lahore, whose portrait adorned the castle walls.

He was older now, become a man. But those were the very same brown eyes, the same full lips and black moustache – though the beard had now been shaved away to expose the firm line of the chin beneath. He was exotically attired. On his head was another elaborate turban with a ruby and feather fixed on front, with tassels of gold to frame his face. Around his neck was a string of pearls. The affect was nothing but masculine. His trousers were trimmed with gold at the sides, and a tunic embroidered with silver threads was worn loose and fell to brush his thighs. Over that was a black velvet jacket, with a glittering brooch in the shape of a star: a cluster of diamonds and pearls it was, attached to one of the lapels.

At the sight of this grand apparition, Tilsbury smiled and stepped forward, between two other Indian men who seemed to be there to guard the prince. But I noticed little about them then, except that they wore turbans too.

Tilsbury proceeded to make introductions to those around

who simply gawped, as if mesmerised when he announced, 'I hope you will join me in welcoming the Maharajah Duleep Singh . . . whose late arrival here is due to the fact that he has dined tonight with somewhat more illustrious friends. But, please, do raise your glasses now . . .' He lifted his own. He smiled at the prince. 'To long lives. To redemption. The now and hereafter.'

Many guests in that room appeared bemused. But they were all polite enough to echo the action of their host, raising their glasses, repeating his words as if to chant a mantra.

Meanwhile I watched as Duleep Singh began conversing with my aunt, and how, when he drew her hand to his lips, her new ring caught the candles' gleam. I thought of the Koh-i-Noor diamond again. Was it still concealed in Parvati's crown? Had Duleep Singh come to claim his prize? So openly. So brazenly!

While the chatter around me resumed and grew louder I went to sit by the garden doors, inwardly groaning when glancing back to see myself trailed by the Dalrymples, and the sisters fizzing over now with new sources of whispers and scandal. The one with white hair began to gush, 'Oh isn't he magnificent? Little wonder they say that the Queen is entranced, though I hear Duleep visits less frequently since bringing his mother to London.'

'Our good friend, Lady Garsington, she met with his mother recently,' the raven-haired sister was speaking now. 'It was one afternoon in Kensington. Lady Garsington couldn't believe her eyes. Such rumours there were of Jindan Kaur . . . of the Maharani's beauty. But hard to imagine such a thing . . . especially when Lady Garsington says that the rani can barely walk today. Such a tiny, wrinkled, pockmarked old woman who had to be carried into her house while sitting on a pallet. And, just wait until you hear this, my dear, for it is the most peculiar thing: on top of all her silks and veils, and all of the pearls and precious stones, she'd fixed herself up in a crinoline, a shawl and a bonnet flung on top. And that ensemble then festooned with a crown of feathers and flowers! Can you imagine the sight of it? The poor woman, so encumbered! I dare say she could hardly have moved if she'd tried. And, once taken up to the drawing room, she simply ignored all other guests, sitting cross-legged and mumbling like some lunatic bundle of rags. She even began to puff on a pipe, refusing to eat a thing that was offered, but bringing out her own little pouches and nibbling on what appeared to be birdseed! Lady Garsington said she was speechless. She has been trying to work it out, quite convinced that the Maharani can hardly be more than forty years – and yet she looks a hundred! Of course,' she covered her mouth with a hand, 'they do say she's riddled with syphilis! And how could she not be. The life she's led!'

'Well,' the white-haired sister chided, glancing nervously at me, 'I think we should be more discreet. We should not repeat such gossip here, not in the present company!'

But a great deal more gossip was to flow, during which I drank much more champagne and looked for Duleep Singh again but saw no further sign of him. The same with Tilsbury, his friend. With every successive chime of the clock I watched my aunt play the smiling hostess, though that smile was now frozen on her face and I sensed her disappointment when, for whatever reason, her bridal status remained unannounced. And then, it was surely much too late, for my aunt was receiving words of goodnight instead of congratulations. And the Dalrymple sisters, who were among the very last to leave the house – how I cringed when they approached my aunt to say how proud she must be of me, to have raised a niece so polite and demure, the very embodiment of grace. At that point it was more than clear to me that their gift of 'the seeing' did not extend to what was bulging at my waist, even if it was constrained by the lacing of my corset strings.

How relieved I was when those sisters left. How I longed to return to Claremont Road, to be free of that corset, to breathe again. The sense of discomfort I felt just then was not helped by the temperature in the room which, despite it only being May, had become oppressively heavy and warm, so much so that I walked to the garden doors which by then had both been opened up – from where I looked back to see Tilsbury re-emerging from those to the hallway. And there at his side was Duleep Singh.

The prince was speaking, caught in mid sentence, and his voice, which I had not heard till then, sounded very English and aristocratic, with the slightest trace of an Indian accent. He glanced about the room and said, 'Why . . . has everyone departed? I was hoping for more entertainment. I've heard so much this evening, about Miss Matthews's special skills. Do you think she might call down some spirits for me?'

'It is rather late,' my aunt quickly replied as she followed the gentlemen into the room. 'I had not expected this evening to be—'

'And, who is this?' Prince Duleep asked, ignoring my aunt's reluctance and turning his gaze to me instead. 'Perhaps *she* might be persuaded to amuse a Maharajah?'

'This is my niece, Alice Willoughby.' Aunt Mercy's introduction was brief, displeasure causing her lips to twitch as the prince then raised my hand to his, my palm caressed by his beautiful mouth. And how bold he was – and how shocked was I – when he touched a finger to my pearls, then stroked on down to the swell of my breast, and said it must be an omen that we both chose to wear identical strings, that those small beads of white must bind us both in some common union of fellowship.

'Perhaps,' his eyes glinted with mischief, 'we should be wed, Miss Willoughby. I have a wager with my guardian's wife, and Mrs Login does not believe that I shall find myself a wife before the rest of this year is out.'

Of course, he was only teasing, but I took a step back in some alarm, for what could I say in response to that? Was Queen Victoria right – about the oriental mind? Even so, if that were the case, and despite my lack of experience regarding the etiquette ruling romance, it seemed to me a thrilling thing, for a gentleman, so glamorous, to be looking at me so ardently – until I recalled my 'condition', and why I could never return his affections. Not his. Not those of any man. No man but Lucian Tilsbury . . .

And with that awful thought in mind, I said as lightly as I could, 'But I am not a princess, and a prince may not wed a commoner.'

'This prince will marry whoever he wants! My mother began her life as a pauper . . . born to the palace gardener. Jindan came from nothing and yet she rose to be a Maharani, to bewitch Ranjit Singh with her beauty and wit.'

She rose – and now she has fallen. And I had fallen too. I stared down in remorse at the waist of my gown, only glad that so many candles around had already died and flickered out. I hoped that darkness might hide my shame – of which I was only reminded when I looked back across the room and saw the ice of Mercy's gaze, through which she called to Prince Duleep, 'If you wish to commune with the spirits tonight then I shall need to prepare my thoughts. Perhaps you will spare me some moments alone?'

One more furious glance at me and Aunt Mercy turned upon her heel, sweeping back out to the hallway, with Tilsbury following in her wake. But even when she'd gone away I felt the shadow of her gaze, the weight of her disapproval.

And so, in an effort to draw the prince away from his flirtatious ways, I asked, 'How long have you lived here in England?'

'I was sixteen when they brought me here. Imported by the East India Company . . . brought straight from Calcutta to Claridges!'

'Claridges! I once stayed in that very hotel when I travelled here with my father. We also sailed from Calcutta, along with some other East India men.' *And then went to the Great Exhibition, and saw your diamond, the Koh-i-Noor.*

'Your father is an East India man?' The prince's expression grew serious.

'He was, but he did not fight as such.' I went on when I

158

should have held my tongue. 'He was an army surgeon. And then, he worked at the Residency. I believe I might have seen you there . . . when a garden party was once held.'

'Indeed! There were many parties before I was exiled to Futteghar. What was your father's role back then? Perhaps I may have met with him.'

'His name was Charles Willoughby.' I looked down for a moment and closed my eyes, struggling to control the well of emotion that was, even then, too quick to rise. But when I had it quite subdued I did succeed in going on, 'He died in Lahore . . . some years ago.'

'And you expect *me* to regret this loss? To mourn for those who took my throne?'

The time for pleasantries was gone. As far as Duleep Singh was concerned that talk of the British Residency – of my father – had been tactless.

'I'm sorry. It must be hard. Not to feel a great deal of resentment, not to—'

'You claim to understand?' I heard the incredulous tone in his voice. 'Then you form a more enlightened view than many of your countrymen. I wonder, are you a little too honest, or simply a fool to discuss such things?'

He paused to glance down at his jacket sleeve, to which he slowly raised a hand, to flick some invisible trace of lint from the lustre of its velvet nap. 'Personally, I feel a mixture of emotions. Your Queen has always shown kindness to me. The Prince of Wales is a loyal friend. I attended his wedding a few months ago.' He smiled. Another teasing look, and the volatile clouds that had darkened his brow were replaced by warmth and light again, when he continued to enquire, 'I wonder, does that surprise you?'

'I see that you are an enigma, sir.' I was wondering if the desire for a diamond affected the bond of his royal connections – with the Queen, or any others with whom he might recently have dined. 'Will you stay in Windsor . . . with the Queen?'

'No, I shall travel to Kensington, which is where my mother

now resides, and where she will be missing me. Before that, I was something more of a nomad. At one time they called me "the black prince of Perthshire" so often was I hidden there. But that's how The *Honourable* Company liked it, keeping their hostage well away from any seditious idealists who might subvert his loyalty. Why, I was even refused the chance to continue my studies at Cambridge. And yet I was forced to hear Bertie's accounts regarding *his* freedoms and pleasures there.'

'You are unhappy?' How audacious I was, to express my thoughts so openly.

Duleep Singh gave me a serious look and I felt quite sure of his honesty when he finally said, 'I am not free. I need to do more, to fulfil my life. A great deal has changed since my mother was found.'

'Found?'

'We were parted when I was a child. I watched as they dragged her away by her hair, screaming and holding her arms out towards me, the child she had nurtured in her womb removed from her so callously. I saw many terrible things in Lahore. My own uncle was murdered before my eyes – not by the British, that is true. *Their* aim was to keep me safe, to *anglicise* me . . . to bring me here.'

Before going on he looked over his shoulder, back at the mirror above the hearth. What did he see there that gave him pause? The man he was now, or the child in Lahore? His past, his present . . . or future life?

His face was turned again, to me, the young woman then standing at his side, who saw how the muscles in his face became somewhat tenser when he explained, 'My future was planned with military precision. They took a boy at a vulnerable age. They thought to subdue and mould me, though . . .' his expression softened, 'I will not deny being indulged. Your society brings its advantages.'

The air hung heavy with his suggestion. His fingers were circling my wrist – the wrist where some Indian beads once wound – then stroking on up to the elbow. This was a young man who had no inhibitions when dealing with the opposite sex. And yet, I must admit, his attentions were not unpleasant. I cannot deny the response I felt, even though I knew that it was wrong, though I feared Mercy's wrath, should my aunt return to find me not the least demure.

I pulled my arm away, seeing the slightest knit in his brow while I tried to find the courage to ask what was then the uppermost thing in my mind, which was to discover what part he played in the theft of the Koh-i-Noor diamond – the diamond that my aunt had said was stolen on Duleep's behalf.

But how to broach the subject, with this young man so sensitive? It was all I could do at that point to ask, 'And your mother . . . is she happy now, to be living here, in England?'

'She would prefer to be in Lahore. She would prefer to be a queen, to see her son upon his throne. But at least we have come to meet again – though that arranged but recently when I was permitted a trip to my homeland. For a tiger shooting party! Can you believe the irony?' He snorted with derision. 'But then, how the British love to hunt. If only I'd thought of it earlier! Such a ruse and I might have returned all the sooner, to hunt my very own mother down.'

He paused and looked pained for a moment or two. 'She has been much neglected. She has gone blind. She is aged beyond all recognition. And yet, it was only under duress that The Company let me bring her here. Then again, perhaps they were right to be cautious. Since then, she and I have spent many hours discussing the insults of our past. My mother has told me many tales, many truths as to *who* and *what* I am. I begin to see things differently. I see that England is not my home, and—'

He stopped short when Tilsbury reappeared. In the merest blinking of an eye, Duleep's expression changed again, smiling broadly when he called, 'My dear friend, where have you been? This young lady and I were discussing my mother . . . which reminds me, I had quite forgotten. Jindan wished me to express her remorse regarding the death of a colleague of yours. A mutual friend who she last met when you dined together in Chandigarh – when she made a visit from Nepal.'

Tilsbury looked a little alarmed. His voice was unusually slow when he answered, 'Perhaps you will thank your mother for reminding me of her concern. But I hope she will also understand how . . . in the current circumstances . . . how impossible it would be for us to ever meet again.'

'Come now, my dear fellow,' Duleep laughed, 'she understands that perfectly. But, no more of such dreary matters. Miss Matthews has promised to call up some ghosts. How long will she keep us in anticipation?' He turned back to me and earnestly asked, 'Are you also a part of the repertoire?'

'I am not, sir,' I quickly responded, thinking of the piano again. 'I am more dubious than my aunt of meddling with the unknown.'

'Oh, please do meddle a little tonight.' Duleep caressed my arm again. 'It would be too lonely without you. Such a jewel should not be hidden away. Promise me that you will stay?'

I did not look for Tilsbury's reaction, and just at that moment my aunt returned, seeming more confident than before, with that old relaxed languor about her that often followed a dose of Elixir. Her eyes were glassy and very dark as she drew nearer to my side, when her fingers squeezed upon my arm – what I took to be a warning, for there to be no re-enactment of our previous visit's dramatic events.

What Tilsbury might expect of me, I really had no idea at all, for he and one of the prince's men – an older man with pitted cheeks, a white beard like the sheerest gossamer – were occupied with collecting chairs, five of which were soon enough arranged beneath the chandelier. He then gave instructions regarding the seating. Tilsbury, the prince's two servants, myself, and, of course, my aunt, were to be placed in that circle of chairs. But Duleep Singh, he was to stand caged as it were within our midst. And that seemed unutterably poignant to me, as if it symbolised his fate, imprisoned between two peoples, in a place where he would never belong.

Such thoughts were interrupted when my aunt reached out to take my hand. Her palm was warm and moist on mine, whereas Tilsbury's flesh was dry and cool – and at his touch I felt a surge of tingling passion in my veins, so very much more powerful than any induced by Duleep before. While despising myself for that response I heard my aunt begin to say that the five who then surrounded the prince must all hold hands to form the chain, and that chain must not be broken, no matter what might next occur.

The others obeyed and completed the circle and for some time there was nothing to hear but the living breaths of those around; some fast, some slow, some wheezing – though their origins I could not tell. My eyes glanced sideways, towards my aunt who awaited her 'possession' then. For some time she said nothing at all, her breaths coming deeper and slower, her face become entirely blank, and her eyes rolling back in their sockets until only the whites were visible. As if that was not alarming enough, my own vision began to swim, as if seeing the world through water, and all the while, I was panicking. I was think-ing, *No! I do not want this. Not this feeling come upon me again.*

Dragging my eyes away from my aunt's, in the light of those candles remaining, I looked ahead to see Duleep and thought his flesh like burnished bronze, like one of those gods on the console top. It was then I strained to glance back at Parvati, and to see that the ruby in her crown no longer shone a gleaming red, but appeared to be as black as coal. It was the same with the precious stone then fixed above the prince's brow, which glittered in his turban's folds.

My nose filled with the odour of sandalwood, during which I could swear that other hands were stroking my hair, my cheeks, my arms. But when I looked around again I saw no more than empty air. My throat felt too dry and constricted. Moisture was trickling from my brow, to run into my eyes, stinging, sharp. But I had no free hand to wipe it away. It was all that I could do to blink, to look up, to see that the chandelier's crystals were absolutely motionless. But I heard a faint ringing in my ears, as if all of the empty wine glasses still scattered around the room had started to vibrate and hum. And above that tinkling melody Aunt Mercy started to proclaim, her voice deep and gravelly when she said, 'I am Ranjit Singh, the Lion of Punjab.'

Duleep sighed and folded his arms. 'Oh really! My father? How very predictable! I had hoped for some originality.'

Undeterred by his scorn my aunt went on, her words now become a confusing rant of which I could make no sense at all. It was not a tongue I'd ever heard, although now and then there were some words I might perhaps have recognised – a sudden inflection, a certain stress that could have come from Mini's mouth. Had Tilsbury primed my aunt for this? Is that why she needed to go and prepare? Is that why he followed her out of the room; to coach her in these new deceits – to be sure of convincing Duleep Singh?

When her speech had finally ended, the glasses continued to rattle on tables and the picture chains swayed upon the walls, the frames beneath them shuddering. And that was when Tilsbury spoke out, seeking to reassure us, though he did not sound assured himself when he said, 'Be still – everyone, stay calm. Do not break the circle's bond.'

My eyes were drawn back to the ruby that was set in the Prince's turban – the ruby that might be mourning jet. My mouth opened. My voice began to recite, but none of those words just then were mine.

'I stand in the White Room at Buckingham Palace and stare at the ceiling above me, the high curving sweep of the trellised dome. I look down at the sheets spread over the floor, a rippling canvas sea of white. How long must I pose for this portrait, wearing these ceremonial clothes? These golden slippers pinch my feet. The emeralds that hang at my ears are too heavy—

'Duleep . . .' She appears, she calls my name. I look up to see her enter the room and those round blue eyes are fused with mine, and Victoria smiles through her small, pursed mouth, 'Has my beautiful boy grown weary with all of these hours of posing?'

She talks to the artist and tells him to leave. Where afternoon sunshine shafts in through the windows it flashes over a glass on the wall. My reflection there is dazzling. The ruby I wear might be a wound, a vibrant red splashing of blood at my brow.

In that reflection I also see the white-coated man at Victoria's side. In his white-gloved hands is a small golden casket. She reaches out and opens the lid, and her words come low and formal, 'Maharajah, close your eyes. Hold out your hands. We have a gift for you today.'

I do as she asks. I feel something heavy and cold in my palms. When I open my eyes I cannot prevent the gasp that then escapes my mouth.

She asks if I remember. How could I ever forget? The symbol of all that I once owned, of everything I ever was. I had not thought to see again the glory of the Koh-i-Noor. I cannot drag my eyes away, gazing into the blue-white depths, at the fragmenting prism, a rainbow of lights, skittering, dancing around the room. Even the chandelier above, dripping with hundreds of crystals, it is but a bauble compared with this . . . with what this diamond represents. How can she know the ache in my soul? How can she know the insult – to see how it has been reduced, its facets remodelled, its size cut down, but a bauble in a trinket box!

As such, am I so different?

I have to try and understand what it is that Victoria might want. But then, what choice do I have? What is this but a trial of allegiance? In Lahore, the East India took it as ransom. In England, it must be tendered again, and this time directly, from me, to my Queen.

So, I bow, and I place it back in her palm, and she smiles with relief, and her guilt is assuaged, and the happiest outcome is achieved. She keeps me. She keeps the diamond – even though, when she placed it in my hand, she knew it was never mine to take, only my Queen's . . . not the English one, but the one left behind in India. Jindan Kaur, my Maharani . . .'

When I spoke that word, *Maharani*, a great surge of breath tore from my lungs. I felt a searing pain in my breast where my heart beat too fast and irregular. The clearest picture had formed in my mind. Not that caricature that the Dalrymples painted, but one of a woman in robes of silk, encrusted with rubies and emeralds, her oiled black hair loose at her back, and her eyes – deep brown and almond-shaped – so very much like Duleep Singh's. But filled with an evil cunning when, in my vision, she lifted her hands and began to unfurl a rolled piece of parchment.

The paper was faded, in places torn, as if of great antiquity. The text, I could not read at all. I thought she would recite the words, but no sound came out when she opened her mouth, her lips stretched back so very wide that I saw the red of a serpent's eyes glittering in the darkness, its forked tongue flicking through the air, preparing to strike and—

Prince Duleep broke the silence, his voice then but a whisper, imbued with incredulity. 'How do you come know these things . . . to speak as if from my very soul?'

I wrenched my hands free from the others. I said, 'I'm sorry. I . . .'

'I'm sure no offence was intended.' Tilsbury spoke on my behalf.

Meanwhile, my aunt looked to be upset, the medium rising from her chair and leaving the room without a word. Tilsbury watched her, then stood himself, muttering in the prince's ear before he followed after – though I wanted to scream for him to stay, and I almost did but was restrained by Duleep's hand upon my arm. Holding it firmly he turned to his friends. He bade them leave us and wait in his carriage, and when they had also departed the room, he sat in the chair next to my own and spoke with great sincerity. 'You saw the secrets of my heart . . . those things I have told to no one else. How did you do it? How did you know?'

Still thinking of his mother's eyes and the cruelty I had witnessed there, I said, 'I think you must take care. I suspect that you came for the diamond tonight. I know that your mother has dreams of past glories . . . of other glories yet to come. But her ambition may ruin you.'

At first, he made me no reply – and then it happened very fast, when I felt the sudden rush of air and expected the prince's hand to strike. I think he would have done so, but managed to restrain himself, when his face was brought up close to mine and his muttered response was full of threat. 'How dare you say such things? Have they told you to play some game with me? I know that The Company watches and waits, wherever I go, whatever I do. But, I am not the fool they suppose me to be. It was never my intention to take the diamond away tonight. The knowledge of its liberty is quite enough – for now. And so it will be for my mother, until we return to India, when Tilsbury will bring the stone, when the Maharajah of Lahore will be restored to the golden throne.'

My voice was barely audible. 'But they say that the diamond is cursed, that no man can own it . . . only a queen.'

He threw back his head and laughed out loud. But there was no humour in that sound. 'And that's why I am already doomed – since the moment your Queen, your own Mrs Fagin, placed her stolen goods into my hands. The stone should have been returned to my mother, for all those years of her humiliation, removed from a world you could never imagine. She was waited upon by hundreds of servants, desired by every man in court. We lived in marble palaces. We walked in gardens, like Paradise. What does England have to compare? When I think of my childhood I see a world bathed in a glowing golden light and, in its centre, my mother sits, the ruby in the harem's crown. Every morning, before she even dressed, great silver platters were brought to her bed. They overflowed with jewels and pearls and her greatest concern was which to wear. What must she have felt when her infant son, who was simply too young to understand, was instructed to give up the diamond . . . a performing monkey who smiled and bowed as he handed his throne to the Governor of the oh, *so* Honourable Company. And then, as if that was not enough, Dalhousie took everything we owned. He had it auctioned . . . every possession, even the bowls from the kitchens! "Lahore confiscated property". And then, he confiscated *me*!

'You must see what I have been reduced to. The pointless tedium of my life. I am nothing but the exotic prince who provides the glamour at society events, the bauble for drooling old women to pet. Well, my mother Jindan may now be blind, but since coming to England she's opened *my* eyes. Now, I know where the truth of my destiny lies.'

'But, how can a diamond reclaim a lost throne?'

'My mother was given an ancient scroll. That scroll foretold a prophecy, in which a child named Duleep would be dispossessed of all he owned and taken to live in a foreign land. But when a man, he would return, bringing with him two sacred things . . . the Koh-i-Noor diamond . . . the corpse of his mother. The stone would be returned again to the ancient temple from which it was stolen over a thousand years ago. And, as a reward, Duleep would be crowned, the Pure One. The Punjab's true Maharajah. The one to cast all invaders out.'

Is that what I had recently seen, seen but been unable to read? That prophecy written on the scroll held up in the Maharani's hands?

I made no mention of such a thing when I gave my reply to Prince Duleep. 'By invaders, you mean the British. But that's just a story. How can it be true? You would risk your life to attain such a thing – and those of everyone else involved?'

'Ah! Does she fear for the safety of her den of thieves? Well, don't worry, Miss Willoughby. For those who serve me loyally I promise a glorious future. If not – then I will see you damned. Make no mistake about it!'

At that, he stood up, and so very abruptly, his chair toppled over to its side. He did not attempt to pick it up but simply left me there alone. Alone, but with his final words still ringing loudly in my ears when I rose and walked towards the doors that led out to the balcony.

There, I tried to still my thoughts while I stared at the black silhouettes of trees. From their leaves came the rustling patter of rain that had just then begun to fall. I heard the hoot of a night bird. Was it an owl? Mini always used to say that was an inauspicious thing – to hear the hoot of an owl at night. The warning of evil things to come.

That hooting sound, it came again, during which I was startled to realise that Tilsbury was at my side, and he was reaching out, saying, 'Alice, you are crying. I'm sorry. Please, don't be frightened. I only thought to amuse Duleep . . . not to cause you any more distress. But the prince has seen what he needed to see. Now, it is only a matter of time.'

'A matter of time, until what? Until the prince's mother dies? Or is it until my child is born, when you and Mercy will take it – take it with you to India?'

'*You* are to come to India. Only then will you realise what it is that the diamond means to me, and what I have suffered to get this far. But, you will understand, Priyam, you will.'

Priyam. He called me Priyam. Priyam . . . it meant Beloved. Only my ayah called me that. How could he know? Could he see my soul as I had seen Duleep's before?

My fingers gripped onto the balcony rail, already slippery and wet as the rain became much heavier. I watched as it bounced off garden slabs, off the tall black spikes on the garden walls – the walls built like a fortress.

I turned to Tilsbury again and spoke with a calmness in my voice that entirely belied what I felt inside. 'I am not your beloved.'

His hands locked onto my elbows, drawing me closer to his breast, looking down through burning eyes. The scar on his cheek gleamed livid red in what light then shone out through the drawing room doors. A vein in his forehead distended and pulsed with whatever emotion he might have felt.

But I could offer nothing back, pushing against him, then stumbling to fall against the house's wall, where some jasmine flowers scattered down. They looked like stars about our feet. They might have been bridal confetti. And, thinking then of Mercy, I looked at Tilsbury to implore, 'You and my aunt may marry and follow whatever dreams you have. But I beg you . . . won't you let me go? I could say I was a widow. I could say that my child's father died. There would be no shame in that. But I fear that my aunt will not be a kind mother. And this work of hers . . . this seeing . . . can't *you* see I want nothing to do with it? And I do not want my child raised in the home of a woman so obsessed.'

'Alice, you must be patient. I swear that—' His voice broke off at some sounds that came from the room behind us, some sudden quick footsteps, then Mercy's voice, and Mercy's face on the balcony, and Mercy's eyes so wide and shocked to see me there with Tilsbury.

'Ah, here she is,' her insults began, 'the little whore of Babylon! Did you see her before, with Prince Duleep? Worse than any bitch on heat!'

At that moment, something inside me broke, like a wire that was strung too tight. In my mind, I'm sure I heard its *snap*. I felt such a need to get away, unable to stand one moment more of what fell from my aunt's malicious tongue.

I ran past her, I ran past him, on down the iron balcony steps and across the lawns towards the walls. But they were too high, too slimed and wet. My fingers found no purchase there, or else were stabbed by vicious thorns. And, in no time at all I was drenched to the skin, my clothes all sodden, clinging, cold – as ruined and filthy as I felt.

PART TWO

THE RANSOM

THE THOUGHTS – NEVER HEARD

I can hardly bear to look at her! Like some sleeping princess in a fairy tale. Like some innocent virgin bride. Who would dream of the reality? A tigress, a harridan she was, screaming out there in the rain tonight, threatening to tell of what we'd done – done to her – done with the diamond.

Thank goodness every guest had gone. We had to fight to restrain her. Lucian had to subdue her with drops. And the state of the girl when we dragged her in! Soaked to the skin and caked in mud, covered in scratches from thorns in the bushes, from trying to scale the garden walls.

Her hair is still wet now despite all the rubbing. She has my sister's fine dark hair. She has the hair Charles Willoughby chose to unpin on his wedding night. Through her heart there beats the blood of the sister for whom he cruelly threw me off.

How I despised my sister then, no less when hearing of her death. My mother had wished me to forgive, to show charity and kindness. But was she ever kind to me? She always preferred 'sweet Alice', even giving support for her marriage to Charles. If she'd known the pain that brought me! And to think that God should mock me more, to burden me with my sister's child, to have Charles die and leave me bound forever to this incubus.

And now, the betrayal, it starts again. This Alice is stealing Lucian. I see it – I see it in his eyes.

My eyes – I know he thinks them blind. But only a fool could fail to see the way he was with her tonight; how he had the gall to stand and look when I removed her filthy clothes, when I took the pearls from round her throat – when he dared to accuse me of being rough!

I would say he is too tender. That reflection in the armoire door.

The way he gazed upon her flesh. How did I not scream and smash the glass!

But I must not panic. I must stay calm and think how best to rid myself of this rival. She may well share my sister's name. She will not share her destiny. And Lucian has assured me that he and I shall still be wed, that he would have announced the thing tonight but for the moment being lost on Duleep Singh's arrival.

I told him we should do it soon. We should do it tomorrow if we can. We should not waste one moment more, but take the stone to India and wait for Prince Duleep to come. It is the one sure way to be safe, with Alice now knowing, now making her threats.

But he insists that we shall stay, living here in England until her bastard has been born. This bastard that belongs to him. Does he really think I could believe that Alice went wandering in her sleep, walking out through the night in a state of undress, and that no one ever saw her, or thought to bring her home again?

Let her do whatever she will when we've gone. The house in Claremont Road is hers. Her father's before, his daughter's now. But surely it is mine by rights, some recompense for what I lost, for the marriage my sister stole from me! For her sins, I shall reclaim my life and start anew with Lucian. I shall steal Charles Willoughby's grandchild and raise it as my own. I think that a pretty enough revenge! And perhaps other children may follow on. I am not yet too old for that – even if I must risk my sister's fate. I would rather die than be thwarted again. I would rather face trial and imprisonment. And I will, if Lucian spurns me. I will see him doomed, and Alice too.

No threat of this has passed my lips, but he knows my mind, I know he does. He knows he must be true to me. Only then, will his secrets remain untold.

GREEN ROOMS WITH BIRDS AND BUTTERFLIES

He forced me to take some drops. I tried my best to spit them out, but he covered my mouth and pinched my nose until I had to swallow them. He carried me up to a bedroom – a room that was painted to look like a forest, with parrots and purple butterflies, with peacocks with their tails spread wide amongst the trailing branches.

I lay on covers made of silk, their hues like the most vivid jewels. Amethyst. Ruby. Emerald. The ebony bedposts bore carvings of women, women who looked like Parvati to me, and every one of them dancing, shameless in her nakedness.

Averting my eyes, I found myself gazing up at my aunt again – the other aunt, the kinder one, the one who then perched on the mattress edge, hushing my sobs and stroking my brow while pushing wet tangles of hair from my face. She must have taken off my clothes. I was wearing a nightshirt, much too large. Surely something for a man. Something that Mercy said she'd found in the chest that lay at the end of the bed.

The lid of that chest was still open. My childhood wafted out. Perfumes of patchouli, jasmine, rose. But Paradise was far away, this fragrance but a memory. In the present, my hands and arms were sore from the stinging scratch of bramble thorns, and when I looked up and saw Tilsbury standing there at the open door, I struggled to rise from the pillow. I accused him of ruining my life.

My aunt gripped my hands and urged me to stop, saying, 'Alice, be quiet! You'll do yourself harm . . . not to mention the baby you're carrying.'

'I don't care! I wish the baby were dead. I wish that I was dead as well!'

'Oh come,' she coaxed, squeezing my fingers, and so very hard that I thought she would break them. 'You have everything to live for. I know how emotionally draining a spiritual possession can be. But . . .' she sighed, and smiled benevolently, 'we don't choose the gifts that God bestows, even though they often feel more like a curse than a blessing.'

She leaned forward and pressed her lips to my cheek, seeming content that such pearls of wisdom might contain the power to ease my distress. 'You must forgive me, my dear, for not being more watchful, for failing to protect you when—' Breaking off, she shook her head, 'Your future is what is important now.'

'My future! What future?'

'Alice!' Tilsbury's voice was low. His next words were cryptic and carefully chosen, a reminder and also a warning for me to be sure to hold my tongue. 'Remember those things we spoke of before, about caring for you *and* those you love . . . now, and in the days to come? You must understand the risks involved. Have I made myself perfectly clear?'

I gave the smallest, the faintest of nods. And seeming content with that outcome, he took a step back into the hall, where Lucian Tilsbury disappeared, melted into the shadows of his house.

The drug's effect seemed to come in waves. It was when the child twisted and kicked in my belly that I fully revived again, for a moment not knowing where I was. A candle still burned on the stand nearby and where its radiance happened to fall across the green of the painted walls, the birds appeared to hop on their branches, the butterflies' wings to be quivering. And what was that rustling, creeping sound? Could it be beetles burrowing? Little red Teej beetles coming to life and crawling through the undergrowth? And was that a sudden purring growl, and those golden orbs of burning light that flickered in the corner – could those be the eyes of a tiger?

It must have been the dying flame that caused the light to play such tricks. It was by such an eerie illumination I threw back the covers and crawled towards the chest that was placed at the end of the bed, where I lifted the lid and smelled again those gorgeous, drifting perfumes.

There was little of interest to see within, just some plain linen sheets and pillowslips – until I delved yet deeper, and found the treasures at the base: the gorgeous lengths of coloured silk, their edges embroidered with wires of gold. And then, the little wooden box where a border of rose and iris flowers created a frame for the miniature. A Mughal portrait, I think it was. The profile of a black-haired girl who wore a veil upon her head. A *matha patti* adorned her brow – the jewelled pendant with a chain that was worn through the parting of the hair. A *nath* – a ring pierced through her nose. Rubies were hanging from her ears.

Inside that box were earrings, exactly like those in the picture. And a necklace mirrored their design, the ornate patterns of the gold within which rubies had been set.

I wondered who had worn such things, and why they were hidden in that chest. But the candle flame guttered and threatened to die, so I set the jewels back in the box, replaced the box beneath the silks, and lay with my head on the pillow again – from where I imagined that all of those women who danced around the bedposts were moving in time to the beat of the rain as it pattered on the window panes. And, as I drifted into sleep, the musical hiss and splash of the gutters seemed to be burbling watery secrets. Secrets about trust and commitments, about destinies, about prophecies . . .

I opened my eyes to see my aunt, standing at a window, having unfolded the shutters there to let in a dull and dreary day.

Climbing down from the bed, I walked to her side, only then coming to realise how very high in the house we were – at the back, overlooking the gardens which were misted with an aqueous grey, still damp from all of last night's rain.

Wandering towards an internal door I twisted the knob but found it locked, during which effort Aunt Mercy called, 'Alice, you look very flushed, and that shift . . . it is soaked through with sweat! You must have caught a chill last night. Whatever were you thinking of, running out into the storm like that?'

Had she forgotten her ranting spite, from which I'd been trying to escape?

But looking down I saw she was right. The garment I wore was sticky and wet, clinging close against my flesh.

Aunt Mercy opened more cupboards and drawers, and then the tall door of a mirrored armoire where she found another nightgown. She told me to lift my arms while she dragged the damp one high above – which made me feel vulnerable, for all too clear for me to see when that shift lay crumpled on the floor was the look that formed on Mercy's face: her disgust at my swollen nakedness.

But there was another who held no such qualms, and I should have defended my modesty against the hunger in his gaze. I should have tried to hide my shame, or told my aunt that he was there. But my eyes locked with his in a long, silent stare until he was eclipsed from view, when I snatched the clean shift from Mercy's hands and yanked it down over my head.

During that action some buttons were snagged, tearing through knots that had formed in my hair, causing me to gasp in pain – that sound to be echoed by Mercy's lips when Tilsbury made his presence known, when he said, 'I hope you slept well, Alice. It is important for you to recover . . . for when the wedding is arranged.'

'Do you really think that necessary?' Such a tone of resentment in Mercy's voice, to which he made no comment, only turned his back to leave us. But my aunt remained and snapped at me, 'I suppose he is right. You must get well. Won't you try to eat something? At least drink a cup of this coffee I've brought?'

I looked at a table and saw a tray. A plate of toast. A silver jug. A porcelain saucer and a cup. The coffee she poured tasted horribly sweet, but Mercy insisted that sugar was good to strengthen and speed my recovery. And I was so thirsty, I drank it all, and too late did I come to realise that the coffee contained some sleeping draught.

Overcome with a yawning fatigue, I almost fell when trying to stand, which was when Mercy led me back to the bed where I lay and watched the forest walls swirling all around me, where I felt the softness of sheets at my neck, and then heard the solid clunk of the door as Mercy closed it up again. And then, nothing more for several hours, when – *what was that rattling?*

Holding my breath, glancing about, I saw that the knob of the internal door was moving; twisting back and forth. And then, a figure appeared in its frame, a jumble of clothes hanging over an arm.

'Nancy? Is that you?' My sight was slow to focus, squinting through streams of yellow light that now replaced the morning's gloom.

'Yes, it's me,' she replied, and with such a lightness in her voice that implied it was perfectly normal for me to be there, in that strange room, for her to suddenly appear when my aunt had most distinctly said that the maid's employment was at an end.

'Whatever was going on last night? I've just seen your dress, downstairs in the laundry. Ruined it is, the silk all torn. Covered in mud and grass stains! Miss Matthews has gone back to Claremont Road, but she's asked me to bring these things for you.'

'But why? I won't be staying here.'

'Everything has been arranged. Miss Matthews says that a move may be bad for . . .' Nancy's face turned very pink, 'for you, in your present condition.'

'My condition is not an illness! I want to get dressed and leave this house.'

Climbing down from the bed, walking slowly towards her,

I picked through the garments that Nancy was holding. But when I found only shifts and shawls the realisation truly dawned, saying as much to myself as her, 'They mean to keep me prisoner here. They mean to stop my tongue that way.'

'You're to rest and get well, that's all. I shall be sleeping along the hall, on hand for anything you need.'

She set the linen on a chair, retreating into the room behind which, now that I could see on through, had walls that were painted like those of the bedroom. In there, Nancy nodded towards a low table, her voice somewhat dourer when she said, 'He's sent up some flowers from the garden. I suppose he thought to cheer you.'

A vase contained white roses. Most of them were still in bud, their lustre like satin, still dewy and fresh, but their stems a mass of pointed thorns – and those thorns perhaps the very ones that had torn into my flesh last night, when I'd tried to climb the garden walls. I looked at the scratches on my hands and laughed out loud at the irony, that Tilsbury should send me such a gift! – at which Nancy gave me a worried look, though she quickly resumed her chattering. 'Are you hungry? I think you must be. After all, you've not eaten a thing all day. Tell me whatever you fancy now and I'll get it made up in the kitchens. There might be some chops left from earlier, or—'

'Eat, and find myself drugged again? I've no doubt you are in on their scheming. I saw you that day, with Tilsbury, when he was disguised as a beggar man. I know that you have lied for him. Do you know of their other deceits as well?'

'Other deceits? I don't know what you mean. I was a maid here in Park Street before. That's how I know Mr Tilsbury. And yes, I have met him from time to time, when taking letters for your aunt and—'

'And yet, how very strange it is that you, my aunt and Tilsbury never once mentioned your previous employment, not even when your previous employer so often called at Claremont Road!'

Her answer was made with a sullen defiance, 'There was no

reason to mention it. He sent me there when your aunt was in need, when she was without a housemaid. He thought the position would suit me.'

She was pressing her palms down over her apron as if to smooth the cotton's folds, during which she stepped forward and urged again, 'Come on through, Miss Alice. Come and sit down and wait in here while I get on and change your bed. Mr Tilsbury was most insistent. He wants you to be comfortable.'

Due more to my curiosity than any degree of obedience I walked past the maid and into that room, and there I saw another door, and thinking that must lead back out to a landing, and so prove a possible route of escape, I turned the knob which, once again, I found was locked against me. In an effort to keep myself grounded and calm I closed my eyes and curled my toes down into a rug where thick white wool was soft and warm and comforting. And while listening to the thumpings and swooshes of Nancy's bed-making efforts next door, I found myself suddenly moved to call, 'I suppose you know they are to wed.'

Nancy came to the doorway to hear me go on, and very matter-of-fact I was, 'And then, Aunt Mercy will take my child.'

She lowered her eyes and bit down on her lip. 'I'm sure they only mean the best.'

'The best for who?' I stared down at my belly, hardly noticing when the maid drew near, when she touched a hand to my shoulder and said, 'Please, Miss Alice, don't go getting yourself upset like this. Sometimes it's best to forget what's past . . . to try and start afresh again.'

Looking straight into her eyes, I said, 'I wish I could. I wish that Lucian Tilsbury had never come into my life.'

Fresh colour rose into her cheeks. She was plucking at her apron skirts. She was fiddling with something underneath. It looked like a pocket secured at her waist, and beside that the jut of a metal chain from which some keys were dangling.

Nancy has the keys to the door. Suddenly, lunging forward, my hands reached underneath the cloth, attempting to dislodge the keys. But, despite being slightly smaller than me, Nancy was wiry and very much stronger. And Nancy was not the one with child. And she was not slow with opiates.

All at once, overcome with a dizziness, I slumped to the sheepskin on the floor, and there at my side was some other item; something fallen from out of her pocket. It was a twisted curl of hair. The colour was red, very like her own, if perhaps a little lighter. In great haste, she ducked down to retrieve it, snatching it up, then standing again, her breaths coming laboured and very fast when she thrust that twist before my eyes and said, 'Shall I tell you what this is . . . the terrible thing *I* can't forget? This is a lock of my mother's hair, taken from her head when she'd bled to death, when she'd forced a hook inside herself trying to loosen the bastard child that had rooted itself inside *her* womb. She had no husband then, you see. He'd long gone off, and who knew where. He left my ma all on her own, with the care of me, and a brother too. She was what most of you fancy types might call "no more than she ought to be". But, for me and George, she was all we had, and we loved our ma, and she loved us too. We never minded what she did. If she had a gentleman come to call, it meant food in our bellies and coal for the hearth, and a bottle of gin to soothe her nerves.

'Two empty bottles there were that day, there on the floor at the side of the bed when we woke and went to find her. There was blood in the bed, and over the floor, and our ma lying there in the middle of that, and already as white as any ghost. I sometimes think she is a ghost, that she lurks in the shadows to haunt me. She never was laid to a decent rest, not even a stone to call her own. They buried her with the paupers and no prayer was said across that grave. They said our ma would burn in Hell . . . burn for all eternity for committing the sin of self murder. But she never would have sinned at all if her husband hadn't left her. And she never wanted to die like that. She was only trying to survive.'

'Oh, Nancy . . . I'm so sorry. Where is your brother now?'

'Dead and in the ground as well. George and me, they sent us away after that, to live in some country orphanage, a place not fit for animals. They put us girls to making lace, or plaiting straw for baskets. The boys were rented out to farms and worked like slaves from dawn till dusk. That life, it was too much for him. He'd always suffered with his lungs. If ever the air was cold or damp he used to find the breathing hard. He passed away one winter. They told me it was peaceful. But I never did believe them . . . not when I saw my brother's face.'

She brushed a hand across her eyes, the brown then wet and glistening, but something harder clouded them when Nancy looked at me again. 'So, *you*, Miss Alice, your whole life being waited on hand, foot and finger . . . you think how lucky you happen to be. Not having to rid yourself of this child and risking your life in the process. Not being thrown out to fend alone when you were less than fourteen years, being told to find yourself occupation or else make your way to the workhouse. But then, I was luckier than most. I was taken in at the convent here . . . me and some other orphan girls. And that's where Mr Tilsbury came, giving us a brand new start, when he hired us to work in Park Street.'

'Nancy, I never imagined . . .'

My voice was barely audible, not knowing what to do or say, only listening mute when the maid went on, 'I came here, and I thought it was Paradise compared to what I'd known before. Always food in my belly, always clothed and warm. And I'll tell you the truth, Miss Alice, I would do *anything* to repay him, for what Mr Tilsbury did for me.'

Had she already repaid him, by lying and saying he wasn't there when he'd come to my room in Claremont Road? By acting as my jailor now? I wondered, but I did not ask. I knew I had no need to. I only watched when she left again, going by way of the bedroom door. I heard its sudden banging slam: the rattle and turn of a key in a lock.

A CEREMONY IS PERFORMED

The hours and days rolled into weeks, during which Lucian Tilsbury did not deign to show his face again. My aunt said he was often out, out and about on his business concerns, whatever those concerns might be. During that time it was Nancy who became my constant companion, bringing in trays, taking out slops, or fetching hot water in which I could wash, her every arrival and every departure accompanied by the sound of keys.

At first, I spent my waking hours in trying to devise some means of escape. But the window in the sitting room overlooked a slimed brick wall: a covered passage as high as the house, and enclosed at each end by solid doors. The view from the bedroom was that of the gardens, and beyond them orchards full of trees. On either side were stable yards, but the only vehicle I ever saw was Tilsbury's black brougham, and the two grey mares that drew it, and the bowler-hatted driver who sometimes looked back up at me – a sneering leer upon his face. There was a maid who carried out washing to hang at the end of the garden. But, however much I shouted to try and gain attention, she never so much as looked my way, only scurried back inside the house, her face turned down, her cheeks flushed red. And then there was the turbaned man who occasionally followed her onto the lawns. I think he must have been the cook. Or could he have been a valet? Whatever he was, he did not respond, even when I flung down trays or plates, the china smashing at his feet – those objects not thrown at the armoire door where the glass was now cracked, its reflection distorted. The most he did was to pick up that debris and carry it away again. Whatever I called, however I screamed, I suppose they must have thought me mad. Who knew what tales my captors told? My every protest reached deaf ears.

In desperation, one night when it rained, when I heard the drainpipe's gurgling, I thought to use that pipe as a ladder by which to climb to the ground below, knotting sheets and lengths of silk to aid me in that enterprise. But no matter how far I stretched my arms while reaching through the window frame, the distance was too great for me. And I'm sure the things I ate and drank were constantly laced with sleeping draughts that altered my sense of awareness, of space and time, and common sense.

I almost came to welcome that state, the dreamy solace of senses dulled, the dark oblivion of sleep – though in rarer moments of clarity, I yearned for something – *anything* – to relieve the languor of those days I spent within green forest walls. Sometimes I even fantasised that Prince Duleep might rescue me. But I was no Rapunzel – and how could I forget the way of our parting, when the Maharajah left with threats, saying that he would see me damned rather than risk any danger posed to his future plans with Tilsbury.

The other accomplice in crime, my aunt, she claimed that her days were occupied with seeing her clients in Claremont Road. But most evenings she came to visit me, she and Nancy sitting side by side while exhibiting their needle skills, with the sewing of tiny baby gowns, with tiny lace collars to decorate – which only upset me all the more, hardly able to bear the knowledge that within the tightening drum of my belly something was biding its time to be born, to be dressed like a doll, to be washed and fed – for my aunt to steal away from me.

I did my best to try and forget, burying my head in the pages of books which my aunt brought from Tilsbury's shelves below. If she read, it was her Bible, to memorise those verses from which to weave more séance spells – those quotes which pledged of lives to come.

I had no wish to think about what life might lie ahead for me. I lost myself in poetry, in fantasy worlds of adventure and myth. And how affected I became when I chanced to come across a tale once heard from the lips of my father – on that day when we went to the party held on the lawns of the Residency, the day when the boy Maharajah had arrived on the back of an elephant.

Mini had not been there. Servants were not invited. That had caused me some distress, so much so that, when we first arrived, Papa took me to the rooms in which he had his offices. There, he dabbed at my tears with a handkerchief, then collected some seed kept in a drawer, after which he took my hand and we walked to the Residency church – to the gardens where Papa often went, to feed the birds, to sit alone.

It made me smile to see them, the parrots and the budgerigars, to hear the flutter of their wings, the whirling colours, blues and greens. Some of those birds, they were so tame they flew right down from the palm trees and ate the seed from Papa's hand. And one of the parrots, it perched on his arm. It squawked, 'Hello, dear Willoughby! And how are we today?'

That made me laugh, and Papa smiled. He said that he would teach that bird to say hello to me as well. I don't know if he ever did. For then, he squawked the words himself, 'Hello, Miss Alice! How are you?' And when the birdseed had all gone, when the parrot had flown from my father's arm, my fingers settled there instead and we went to look inside the church.

It was not very English, more like a miniature Indian temple, being rectangular in shape, with columns holding up a dome. Papa said that was because it had once been a Mughal tomb which marked the final resting place of a girl called Anarkali.

I hung upon his every word when he told me that Anarkali's name meant Pomegranate flower, to hear that Anarkali had been a favourite in the court of the Mughal Emperor, Akbar. But when his son, the Prince Saleem, declared how much he loved the girl, Akbar said his son must die. Anarkali was distressed, so much so that she offered her life instead, and all she asked in return was to spend one night in Saleem's arms. It was during that night she drugged his wine with seed of the pomegranate bloom, so that Saleem failed to wake in the morning and therefore prevent her sacrifice – when Akbar buried her alive – on the very spot where I then stood!

When Papa reached that part of the story I remember clapping a hand to my mouth, and gasping with the shock of it. But nevertheless, I wanted more, still gazing up through wide-stretched eyes when Papa told me Prince Saleem had never recovered from his loss. And later, when his father died, when Saleem became the emperor, he constructed a tomb on the very site of the ditch where Anarkali lay. And on that tomb had been inscribed:

> *Ah! Could I behold the face of my beloved once more,*
> *I would thank God until the day of resurrection.*

I almost cried to hear those words – the depth of yearning they contained. They made me think of Shiva, and how he felt when Sati died. But when I went back home again, Mini consoled me with other tales in which Anarkali had been saved, then taken to a secret place where she and Saleem often met, to join in bliss, as man and wife.

I'm not sure I believed her, even at that tender age, when 'happy ever after' seemed the surest end for everything, when every story Mini told would have some scene of married bliss. But, if Anarkali had lived on, then why would Saleem build that shrine? Why would he have inscribed those words – the words I'd seen with my own eyes?

How bittersweet it was for me to think of Anarkali's fate, to think of what I had become; buried alive in forest walls.

When I set the book down with a heavy sigh, Aunt Mercy looked up from her Bible and smiled at me indulgently and asked if there was anything that I might want from Claremont Road – the house where she returned each night, still sleeping there in her own bed. A fact that Nancy had divulged.

I answered with some passion, 'There's nothing I would

want from there, except to have my freedom back – and to see Mrs Morrison again. I miss her terribly.'

'Mrs Morrison has been dismissed, and on the very best of terms. I'm sure she will have left by now . . . gone to live in Margate where her sister has a lodging house.'

'Did she give no address, so that I could write?'

'I'm so sorry, my dear. If only she had.' My aunt twirled a hand dismissively. 'She sent you her love when she left, of course . . . but I had to explain how ill you've been, and how if we tried to move you now your health might well be compromised. I could not think to bring her here, when . . . well, have you looked in the mirror of late! Mrs Morrison would be appalled!'

She rose from her seat to leave the room, shaking her head as she passed the armoire, and the glass which, even with its cracks, could not conceal my pregnancy. And, stunned to hear that news of Cook, too late I thought about Papa; his photograph in Claremont Road, within my beaded reticule. I called from the other side of the door in the hope of making Mercy hear. But, if she did, she ignored my plea.

When she returned next morning, she brought something else entirely.

I was standing at the window, breathing the scent of wisteria, the summer sun warm on my face, when I heard the familiar rattling key, but Mercy's voice, not Nancy's, and Mercy calling out my name, 'Alice – look! What do you think?'

In her hands she was holding up a gown; the same grey silk that I had worn on the night of Tilsbury's party. And, seeing that, I felt some hope, asking, 'Am I to be free again, permitted to dress and leave this house?'

'You are . . .' My aunt was hesitant, then going on more surely, 'We have been making some repairs . . . letting out the bodice seams. I think it should fit you well enough, though,' she paused and set the garment down, 'it would not be appropriate for you to be seen about in town, but Lucian thought you might enjoy a drive into the countryside.'

The song of a blackbird piped in through the window and I thought it so clear, so vibrant, it could have come from those creatures painted on the bedroom walls. Over that oppressive green the golden rays of a July sun created the mirage of a trail. How I longed to follow, wherever that path might lead me. I would go anywhere, I would do anything to leave that room, to breathe fresh air.

So many stairs to the hall below, and every step along the way Nancy's arm supported mine. She led me through the house front door, under the porch and into a cab where she sat at my side, where I stared through the window and thought it strange to see the world: still turning without me.

As the vehicle skirted the castle walls, then over the river to Eton, we passed the school's great gothic mass to travel through secluded lanes that opened to stretches of common land where the sky expanded high above, a bowling dome of cloudless blue. We turned onto a narrow track – by which point I really was convinced that I had been deceived again and now about to be confined in yet more isolation. But, at the very farthest end, beyond some ramshackle cottages, a small grey church came into view – a very poor, dejected place with flinty walls and a low wooden tower, and a tiled roof where slates had cracked, most of them mossed and lichen green.

It was at that sight I realised the reason for our country jaunt, for we were not the only ones to make a visit to that church.

No sign of any driver, but there was Tilsbury's brougham, the horses grazing on some grass and, just a little way apart, a man and woman standing.

Mercy was wearing a purple brocade, her bonnet trimmed with violet blooms – a colour that signified mourning rather than celebration. Such a hue normally suited her, but on that day she looked too pale, dark shadows smudged beneath her eyes; those eyes too glassy, too intense.

Tilsbury wore a plain dark grey. One hand was reaching into his waistcoat to withdraw a golden watch and chain, observing the time before walking towards us, to help me and Nancy descend from the cab. He paid the driver and told him to leave – and barely a moment after that a clergyman emerged from the church to hasten down the weedy path. He was painfully thin and stooping, with greasy brown hair and hollow eyes. He was rubbing his hands together – whether eager or nervous, I could not say, though his greeting was cheerful enough when he called, 'Good morning, good morning, Miss Matthews . . . Mr Tilsbury. Shall we go on inside now? Shall we begin the ceremony?'

That was when Mercy took my arm, her fingers gripping there like iron, during which act she muttered, 'Lucian insisted you come along. I trust you will not let us down or try to cause another scene. This marriage means everything to me. I hope you will respect that.'

The vicar walked back towards the church, with Tilsbury and Nancy just behind. My aunt continued to hold my arm as we followed on that scrubby path, observed by no more than the gravestones, around which grass grew very long. Did no one ever tend them?

Inside was just as desultory. The air smelled mouldy, felt clammy and damp. The pews were set on either side of a tiled and dusty aisle. The altar was draped in a plain white sheet and adorned by a tarnished silver cross. A low ceiling was vaulted with crudely cut beams and rough wooden panelling lined each wall. It looked like a place of penance rather than one of worship.

At the altar, the vicar prepared himself to face his little audience, looking particularly anxious by then as if he had never performed such a task. Mercy and Tilsbury were standing before him. It was Nancy who then held onto my arm as she drew me into one of the pews. And when sitting there, gazing about, I suddenly saw two other souls: two men I had not noticed before who had seated themselves across the aisle, and before them a scrawny old woman who was wearing a shabby tartan shawl who began to thump an organ, its notes wheezing and very flat when she played Aunt Mercy's favourite psalm –

> *'The Lord is my shepherd I shall not want,*
> *He maketh me down to lie . . .'*

Nancy sang the first few lines, though she merely hummed along with the rest. The two gentlemen mumbled and grunted the words. But I – I refused to join them, lost in the thoughts of my own 'lying down', and how that one act with Tilsbury had resulted in my current woes. And when it came to the final lines –

> *'And in God's house forevermore,*
> *My dwelling place shall be'* . . .

I thought they were the perfect choice. I was forced to dwell in another man's house, and that man was my corrupter, and he held such a sway on my future life that he might as well be called a god – who reigned not in Heaven, but in some Hell, where chaos ruled in place of sense. Why did he wish me to witness this sham? Or was it a sham? I had no idea what was going on, only that this marriage was the very thing I'd come to dread since my aunt had announced her engagement.

At least the service was not long. That was something to be thankful for. During the vows my eyes looked down to see the bare flesh of my arms and wrists, where every scratch had long been healed. I counted frayed stitches on plain faded kneelers. I lifted a hymnal and turned the foxed pages, only glancing up when I heard the 'I do's', after which the vicar and the bride and groom headed towards the back of the church, and on through the door of a small dark room – I supposed to sign the register. Those two strange men, they also rose and made to follow after. But, no one gestured for me to go, and the moment that Nancy and I were alone I started to mutter under my breath, 'You must have known . . . you tricked me! I would

191

never have willingly come here. I feel ill in this church. I need some air.'

She sounded alarmed when I left the pew. 'You can't leave . . . not now! You'll have to wait.'

But I did not wait. My feet were echoing on the tiles as I made my way towards the porch – though only halfway when a beam of light streamed in through a window to fall on the font, a crudely hewn bowl that bore no decoration except for a few strands of fragile grey. The dusty lace of a spider's web. Where holy water would normally be the sunlit stone was shimmering, and just for that moment I was transfixed, imagining Aunt Mercy there, holding my child in her arms. My child in the christening gown from the Shrine, its brow gleaming wet with baptismal water. The promise of Christ's eternity.

Making my way on out of the doors, I was startled to see two crows fly up from the bushes that grew beside them.

A bad omen it is to see a crow, if it should fly from left to right. See the wicked glitter in its eyes. Black at birth and black when grown. What is bred in the bone will come out in the flesh.

That was what Mini would have said, and indeed, those birds did give me a turn. If one brought bad luck, what omen two? The sound of their raucous, cawing cries. The snapping threat of their flapping wings. Raising a hand to shield my eyes, I watched them alight upon a fence. Two heads then cocked to the one side, two glittering eyes fixed hard on mine, and I had the strangest fancy that those birds had been sent to watch me, their mission to guard me from running away. But, if that was the case, they failed. I headed straight past them and down the path, past the brougham and along the rough mud track. Half walking, half running I made for the common, though realising, all too late, that there was not a hedge or ditch in which I might conceal myself. There was nowhere to hide when they followed me, when I heard the thudding of the hooves and the rattle of the carriage wheels, when the carriage pulled up beside me, when Tilsbury lifted me in his arms.

I did not even struggle. So encumbered I was by my

pregnancy, as sure as any iron chain. But there were no chains upon my lips and I opened them and spat at him. My contempt gleamed wet on his scarred cheek. He did not even wipe it off. He gave no answer when I said through what were tearful, gasping breaths, 'There will come a time I'll make you pay for the shame that you have brought to me – for the cruel humiliation of being in that church today!'

The wedding luncheon, such as it was, took place in the Park Street garden. A perfect summer afternoon; the sort of heat for which I'd yearned when I'd first came to England. The air was scented green with grass. Bees hovered and buzzed through lavender mists. A dove obligingly cooed from the eaves and, below them, brick walls were rampant with wisteria, rose and jasmine. I suppose you might say that scene was idyllic, and the gardens as fragrantly scented as those I'd roamed when in the hills, the hills that rose above Lahore – if not for the sun-dazzled panes of my window, that window from which I so often stared down and which now, when I chanced to look back up, could only remind of my incarceration.

A table was already laid, with bread and salads, meats and fruits. A blanket was spread upon the grass, half in and half out of the canopy formed by the branches of a tree. A young maid, no more than fourteen years, brought jugs of minted lemonade, some *lassi*, a bottle of champagne, after which she left us quite alone – just as Nancy had done when we first returned. The same with the vicar, and those two men, all three abandoned at the church.

In the brougham few words were spoken. Tilsbury was driving, and so was set apart from where I perched on a folding seat, my skirts crushed into that confined space along with Nancy's and my aunt's. I refused to give an answer when Mercy scowled and demanded to know why I must always set my mind on spoiling her every happiness.

I remained just as mute in the garden when her petulant tones were resumed, addressing her new husband with, 'I

193

do think it is a shame. Not to have invited any friends . . . not even *your* acquaintances . . . those gentlemen who were in the church.'

'A marriage needs its witnesses,' Tilsbury scowled and looked away, no attempt to disguise ill temper when he threw off his jacket and rolled up his shirtsleeves, exposing dark hair on sinewy arms – upon which I could not fail to see the vibrant design of a coloured tattoo – the flowers and leaves and the cobra's scales that had been inked upon his flesh.

It was all I could do not to cry out, recalling a time when I'd seen that snake in a sensual and dangerous dream – except it had not been a dream. I lowered my head and closed my eyes, trying to forget that night while Tilsbury then carried on, 'Those men . . . those witnesses I trust, but they have no other significance. You seem to be forgetting, this occasion requires privacy so that, later on, no questions are asked regarding the *actual* wedding date.'

I could not hold my tongue at that, looking up again to ask, 'What questions would those happen to be? Are you thinking of my captivity, or is it the parentage of my child?'

My aunt, who by then had settled in a wicker garden chair, sighed, 'Oh, Alice . . . please! No more of this.'

She took up a glass of champagne to drink, and while she did that I looked at her face, so prettily dappled in green it was from the leaves of the shading tree above. And I decided she was right. I should do no more to spoil her day. Not because I was happy for her. Not because I felt any sense of forgiveness, but because I was relishing my liberation, being outside in the light of the gardens, well away from dark green forest walls.

But they were not the only walls. I looked at the gardens all around, and above them the guarding iron spikes. I knew I could never climb them. How foolish I had been to try. Instead, I sat on the blanket that had been spread at Mercy's feet; and there I watched her husband as he made to refill her empty glass.

He smiled when passing one to me. Mercy assumed that

smile was for her and extended her hand, which he then took, bringing it against his lips which brushed against the new gold band now set above her engagement ring. But, he did not return my aunt's fond gaze. All the while he stared into my eyes.

Did she notice that? I think she did. When she drew her hand away from his, she glanced at me suspiciously. I felt distinctly uncomfortable and shuffled my way across the rug to find a cooling spot of shade, where I pulled off my bonnet and threw it aside, and then turned away from both of them.

I don't remember dozing off. When I woke the world was blackness. But, the cause of that was the parasol that someone had placed above my head to protect me from the glaring sun that, by then, had moved in skies above. Beyond the fringe of that dark shade the afternoon air rippled and hissed, to leave me yet more languorous – to leave my aunt relaxed in ways that I had never seen before. Twisting my head to look back again, I saw, with some element of surprise, that she was no longer wearing shoes, that both of those items had been kicked off to lie in the grass beneath her chair. Higher still, her fingers were stroking the twisting stem of her wine glass, the glass which was quite empty now, and above which her eyes became intent on the husband who was some way off – sitting cross-legged upon the grass, his back against the trunk of a tree, reading a book, ignoring her.

When she attempted to rise from her seat she fell back rather clumsily. Her words were stumbled when she complained, 'This heat is exhausting. I think I'll go in and rest for a while . . . before we . . . before we leave.' And, looking then towards the house, she called out somewhat feebly, 'Nancy . . . where are you? I need you here.'

Pushing the parasol aside, while sitting up I stifled a yawn, and asked, 'Where are you going to?'

Tilsbury answered brusquely. 'A business meeting I must attend. It requires a visit to London. Your aunt insists on coming too.'

My aunt, who was then standing, holding her shoes in one of

her hands, swept the other through the air. I saw the tracings of swollen veins when she pointed towards her husband and said, 'I think I must – after all, this is our wedding night.' She turned to me and stated, 'We are to leave at six o'clock, taking the evening train from Slough, then staying the night in a hotel. But first, I need to have some rest.' She wavered a little then gathered her poise, walking away with her purple hems lifted, exposing her white-stockinged ankles.

'Do you mind?' He was addressing me. 'Would you prefer your aunt to stay?'

'Why should I mind what your wife does?'

'But in the circumstances. Considering your condition . . .'

My aunt called back from the balcony steps, determined her plans were not to be thwarted, 'I can't see any problem in leaving Alice alone for one night. She has Nancy . . . and the other staff. They are quite able to care for her. And where is Nancy, anyway? I need her to go to Claremont Road to collect my evening gown . . . my jewels.'

She made her way up the iron steps with a careful and slow precision that reflected the state of her inebriation. But even when she'd gone from view, her voice, that was still audible, hectoring and much too shrill when she called for Nancy yet again.

I closed my eyes a moment more before deciding, with some reluctance, that I should follow my aunt inside – or else be alone with Tilsbury. But even with my back to him, while I walked away across the lawn, I felt his eyes upon me still, burning, as hot as the sun itself.

When Shiva, the Mahesvara, opens his third and sacred eye, the flames that shoot out will consume the world. All will be destroyed in flames. Love and death and desire and hate will be reduced to ash and dust.

Another of Mini's stories; and those words still running through my mind when I finally climbed the last of the stairs and entered through the green room door – the door which was unlocked that day. Inside, I stood to catch my breath and thought that the painted flowers and leaves appeared to be wilting in the heat, the parrots and peacocks sleeping, the colours of feathers all bleached in that torpor. The bed was made and on the quilts there were fresh sprigs of lavender. The window had been opened wide to welcome in the garden air. A fly buzzed and stopped, buzzed and stopped – or was that some painted insect that sought to escape from the forest walls? Otherwise, all was peace and quiet, except for the groan of shifting boards, the wood expanding in the heat. Or, could those sounds have been my aunt, her movements in some room below? Strange to think that I'd spent all those weeks in the house and still had no idea at all as to where it was that Tilsbury slept. But now – now that he and my aunt were wed, wherever that room might happen to be, I presumed that she would share it.

Trying not to think of that, I stripped to no more than a thin lawn shift, my clothes a discarded heap on the floor when I lay upon the covers, and pressed silk fabric to my cheeks, and relished the slippery chill on my limbs – not noticing when the door opened, not hearing when he came inside, though I jumped in alarm to hear him ask, 'Do you like your bed, Alice? It comes from a palace in Jaipur. The prince it once belonged to had the faces of all of his favourite whores copied into the carvings. If you look closely enough,' one of his fingers ran over a post, 'you'll see that each one is unique.'

'It seems you collect *all* things Indian,' I answered, while trying to calm my breaths, and tugging down on the hem of my shift while he pushed some sweat-dampened hair from his forehead. Very briefly – I think unconsciously – he touched a finger to his cheek, to the scar where my spittle had long-since dried.

'This house once belonged to an uncle of mine. A nabob. A Company man. How convenient that has proved to be . . . with you now also residing in Windsor. One might almost say it was meant to be.' He smiled, and then went on again. 'He brought back many treasures from India, and they were added to my

197

own, when he died and named me as his heir. But then, one does acquire a taste. And, after all, much like yourself, I do have an affinity.'

A bitter tone entered his voice. 'I was born the half-caste bastard son of a Bible-thumping missionary whose only vocation in this world was to convert the heathens from their lives of sinful decadence, though,' he gave a small snort of derision, 'he was not so very fastidious that he didn't sire a son himself on one of the local women, then beat that woman to death one night when she would not kneel before his god.

'I saw him do that with my own eyes. I was a child of just five years when I witnessed my mother's murder – and very often after that my father's ire was spent on me, in the form of a buckle, a fist, or boot. Luckily, when I was old enough, he persuaded my childless uncle to sponsor my education here, where my interest in Oriental studies, particularly the languages, pleased my father inordinately. He believed that my abilities could only aid him in his work, that I might return to India and join him in his mission – to stand at his side and quote from the Bible at Hindoo fairs and festivals. What was it that he used to proclaim? Ah yes, I have it now . . . Providence has entrusted the Empire of Hindustan into the care of England, in order that the banner of Christ should wave from one end to the other.

'I had no intention of waving the flags of that sinful hypocrite. I last saw him when I was nine years old. I never intend to see him again. But that does not make me a faithless man. And I did go back to India . . . where something extraordinary happened to me, which deeply affected my beliefs. It changed me. It made me what I am. I saw things I could never have dreamed about, and those dreams were the reason I came back here, and—'

'Oh yes, your dream of a diamond!' While making that interruption I was sliding down from the mattress edge, feeling much less vulnerable once my feet were planted on the boards, from where I continued to rail at him. 'The diamond that led to the madness of screaming on the castle walls, and then to hiding a priceless gem in the crown of a silver goddess. But you could have been caught. You could have been killed. You could have lost *everything* you are. *Everything* that you believe!'

'Perhaps . . .' He paused a little while, and then: 'Do you know this poem, Alice? It is a very ancient one. I translated it from the Pakhtun. It has always struck a chord –

I despise a man who does not guide his life by honour
The very word drives me mad.
And when a man is mad, what does he care if he wins or loses a fortune.

His lips twitched in the faintest smile. 'I have so much to gain, and I mean for you to share my dreams. But all of that will come in time. For now, how apt it is that, just as Parvati once guarded the stone, now she may work her more natural magic . . . which is that of marital harmony.'

'Marital harmony! You should go and speak of such things with my aunt. Is it not time for you to leave . . . to take her on her honeymoon?'

My words were harsh. They quite belied the wretchedness I felt inside.

'Oh, we have another hour or so before Mercy needs to be disturbed. I dare say she will be sleeping now.'

I thought of my aunt glugging back her champagne, I thought of the tincture of black drop that she often took to aid her rest. And, feeling somewhat less assured, my voice dropped to barely a whisper, when I said, 'You should go. You should not be in here.'

But Tilsbury did not leave me, and I made no further protest when he moved towards the end of the bed and opened up the lid of the chest, then reaching in to extract the box which held the jewels that I had found on my first evening in his house. With the ruby necklace in his hands, he came to stand beside me, so close that I could feel his breaths, their soft caress upon my cheek. And then the sudden coolness when one of his hands gathered up my hair, twisting that into a coil. He lifted it above my head, baring the skin at the nape of my neck where I shivered to feel the brush of his lips, and then the chill weight of gold and stones as he secured them at my throat.

'A Mughal prince once had this made . . . a gift created for his bride.' He spoke while lowering an arm with which he then caressed my waist, the arm on which the snake was inked. His palm then stroked the swollen mound beneath the sheerness of my shift – during which there came the stealthy drip of his sweet poison in my ear . . . '*You* are my Parvati. *You* are my goddess, a ripening fruit about to split.'

What happened next, I cannot pretend that Lucian Tilsbury forced me. I cannot say I was not aware of what we were both doing then – when his other hand exposed a breast, so much heavier than it had been before. But I felt no shame at what he saw – only a latent, animal hunger – a desire which, now, I realise, had only been waiting to escape, had been biding its time to rise again since that very first moment when we met, when he reached out and took my hand, when I stood at Mercy's parlour door. I felt the same sliding want in my belly. I moaned when his fingertips circled my nipple. I felt my eyes grow wet with desire when he lowered his mouth to nuzzle there – though some of my tears were surely of shame, to know that my aunt was in that house, oblivious and ignorant. But, I closed my eyes against that thought, against any thought of anything – anything but him, anything but me. I wound my fingers through his hair and clamped him tighter to my breast – and when he pulled me to the floor, when he'd flung off his waistcoat, his shirt, his tie, when he had unbuttoned his trouser flies and gently pushed my thighs apart, I sat above to straddle him, to ride him like an animal. I no longer had a conscience. I was nothing but touch and sight and smell as we two groaned and gasped and sighed, and wrapped each other in our arms, and rocked, back and forth, like a lullaby – until it was done and our passions were sated, when we lay on the floor and our pulses slowed.

How the sun anointed our decadence, seeming to turn our

200

flesh to gold. But that moment of bliss, it did not last. It was broken by the two short words that brought such pleasure to an end, when Lucian Tilsbury said, 'My wife—'

'No!' I cried out, and then more hushed, 'I am *not* your wife. You made sure of that! Your wife lies elsewhere in this house, and you should go! Go back to her.'

Dragging myself from his embrace, I stood up and stared at the bedposts, at the whores who danced around them, and again I fought against the tears that threatened to escape my eyes, because I knew myself to be as decadent as all of them.

'You are mine . . .' He was also standing then, and I saw at the centre of his brow a tiny bead of sweat had formed, the crystalline gleam of a god's third eye – when he said, 'You are my goddess.'

Those words were imbued with such passion, but a passion that was swiftly crushed when we heard the sigh, then a rustling sound, then a creak on the stairs, in the hall, by the door. We became like statues, holding our breaths, holding our gaze until, somewhere lower down in the house, a faltering voice called out a name.

'Nancy . . .' Mercy cried again. 'Nancy, is that you? Have you come back from Claremont Road?'

I exhaled. I was able to breathe again. My aunt had woken from her sleep, but not to know what we had done.

As Tilsbury dressed, then left the room, I unclasped the rubies at my throat. I felt relieved to take them off, as if released from a spell. I flung them back into the chest, closed up the lid and returned to the bed where I drew up the covers to hide my face, to try and become invisible. I inhaled the scent of lavender, but however sweet that floral scent, it could not conceal the stench of corruption: the odour of Lucian Tilsbury that was clinging to my body still, as if I was yet embraced in his arms, long after the man had disappeared.

And he would be gone for three more days, during which my life would change again, and in ways I could never imagine.

THE BABY AND THE BIRTHMARK

I heard the steady *plip, plip, plip* that leaked from the spouts of big brass taps – like teardrops, those miniature echoes of sound. I lay in a deep copper bathtub where above me light was filtered dim through the patterns etched in the window glass. I stared through a misty fug of steam at the skin of the water then lapping at my torso, washing away the stickiness in which I had woken to find myself. I'd been frightened, my body curled into a ball when Nancy came in to find me, in sheets made wet with the fluid that, at some point, during the night, had broken and gushed between my legs.

Nancy was very gentle. She helped me out of the soiled bed and then led me down one flight of stairs and through the door of a bathroom. There, when she had turned the taps, while hot twists of silver went splashing down to fill the empty tub below, I dragged off my shift and stared into a mirror and felt such a loathing for what I saw: the bloated skin, the swollen eyes, the face all blotched and red from tears.

When the glass veiled with steam to set me free, I wandered back out to the landing and entered through another door to find myself in a lavish room where the walls were painted cobalt blue. The blue of the ceiling was adorned with hundreds of little golden stars – though to see them only made me sad, recalling a shrine and a pool of tears, and the stars and the moon reflected there. Below this sky was a large gilt bed with intricately fretworked ends. A tiger skin lay on the floor, the head of the creature still fixed to the pelt, its mouth yawning open as if it was roaring, and its eyes two blind and glassy orbs – which made me shudder to think that those marbles might replace the eyes of the wild beast that had once fixed its gaze on me, the beast in which the life force purred.

I forced myself to look away, lifting my eyes to an ebony press where the doors were carved with curling leaves, their patterns inlaid with ivory. A matching chest to one side of the window was littered with masculine effects: tiepins, a tortoiseshell comb, some bottles of hair oil and cologne, a jar of sandalwood pomade, its fragrance hanging on the air – all the clues that led me to believe that this was where Tilsbury must sleep.

From the bathroom next door I could hear Nancy singing, a pretty accompaniment it was for the sudden intake of my breath when I felt a thrumming beneath my feet and heard a percussion of tinkling as the window rattled in its frame.

'Nancy . . . what's that?' my voice called out, faltering a little when my eyes glanced at those of the tiger again. But they were no danger. Still glassed. Still cold.

The maid appeared in the bedroom door. 'What's what?'

'That buzzing. Do you hear it too?'

Nancy only looked confused, 'Could it be the water pipes? But really, you shouldn't be in . . .'

Her voice fell off when, as if in a dream, she walked towards the gilded bed where her hand brushed over the covers, trailing in the air behind when she went to look out of the window. And perhaps she *could* hear the same as me, for drawing one of the drapes aside she stared down at the street for a very long time, and something peculiar happened then. Nancy held out both her arms, grabbing each side of the window frame. And her face turned very pale as if all the blood had drained away. She took on a queerly bluish tinge, within which her mouth was gaping, and her eyes became entirely blank – until the strange vibrations stopped as if to release her from their thrall, when she turned away from that window again and wandered back, straight past me, as I wasn't even there, as if I was invisible.

I could not help but shudder, and yet I also felt compelled to go to the window and look outside, to see what had so intrigued the maid. But then something else distracted my eye, something that lay on top of the chest – something that I would have sworn had not been there a moment back.

Could it be the very skull that I'd seen in the parlour, in Claremont Road? This time the vessel was empty, and common sense told me it was no more than an *objet de curiosité*, if a rather gruesome one. But, how disconcerting it was for me to remember that horrible vision when I'd lifted such a thing in my hands and seen it full of curdled blood. And now, when recalling that event, rather than feeling self-disgust I found myself racked with a raging thirst.

What an unnatural desire that was, to have such monstrous cravings! My pulse thudded heavy and slow in my ears, like a ticking clock then counting down to some imminent, unknown event. Or perhaps it was not so unknown, because it was then I noticed the tickling between my thighs, and the splatter of wetness on my feet, and when I glanced down to see what it was I gasped at the running trails of red which dribbled on the tiger skin. Again, I thought of that day in the hills when such a beast had grazed my toes and drawn out ruby beads of blood. I heard a voice, inside my head, though it seemed to come from the tiger's jaws, and the voice of the tiger, it said to me,

Priyam, my dearest . . . dost thou remember the story of Durga? Durga the Mahadevi? Durga who is the warrior? The form of the goddess Parvati when she wishes to slay the demons, when she rides upon the tiger's back and emerges in a blaze of light? Surrender all actions and duties to her and she shall release thee from thy fears.

Those words – those words I remembered from the stolen pages of a book. Might they give me the courage to endure the trial from which I could not run?

In a daze, I returned to the bathroom. There Nancy helped me into the tub, after which she disappeared again, to find a clean nightgown for me to wear. Meanwhile, I lay back in the water and watched how its heat turned my flesh to pink, how the water turned pink where my blood flowed out, and such morbid thoughts were in my mind. *Water can kill you. In water you drown.*

Slowly sinking down under surface, my head filled with echoing, amplified sounds. Long strands of my hair floated round like weeds. My mouth opened wide and the water ran in. I'd heard tell that such deaths could be peaceful. Would it give Tilsbury peace of mind to know that I'd died, in his own bath, with his child still unborn in my belly?

Gazing up through the swirling lens of the water I saw Nancy's red curls hanging down like ropes. She might well have been a Medusa, her head a coiling mass of snakes. Her face was made ugly by gravity, the flesh weighed down in creasing folds, and the way her mouth opened and closed like that – it might be the maid who was drowning, not me. It might have been Nancy gasping for air while I was floating, quite serene – until a violent stabbing pain made me rise up like a creature possessed.

When Nancy helped me from the bath I slumped at her side upon the floor, waiting for the spasm to pass, groaning, 'No . . . no! I'm not ready for this.'

'Is it the baby coming, then?' She snatched up a towel and wrapped it around me before running out through the door again and I heard a clattering on the stairs, and then Nancy's shrieking cries for help.

She soon reappeared with the younger maid, both of them dragging me up to the green room, the other running off again to go and fetch the doctor while Nancy tore the wet sheets from the bed, remaking it while I crouched nearby.

I was still there when the doctor arrived, examining me for a second time, peering over the tops of his spectacle rims to assure that the birth was a long way off. Patting my arm in useless support, he instructed Nancy to stay at my side and promised to come back later on, when he might administer chloroform, but for then, 'You must let nature take its course, bearing the labour as best you can. You are young and healthy and strong enough, and sedation may be the fashionable thing but, in my long experience, these matters progress more reliably without using drugs to dull the brain.'

He glanced at the ebony bedposts, shaking his head, mumbling under his breath. But, whereas I might once have been mortified, right then I could not care one jot, panting and moaning as I was, swearing the vilest of curses.

In due course he left and, once again, Nancy and I were quite alone. During those hours she was my friend, doing her best to console me, wiping my face with cool, damp cloths, giving me water to sip upon. But nothing could ease my distress, and sometimes I felt myself slipping away, the room become almost as dark as night, during which I saw Mini beside the bed, though my ayah, she did not say one word. She only stared down, shaking her head. She placed a finger to my lips, and then she touched it to her own, as if to signify to me that we must keep some secret.

It was from very far away I seemed to hear the doctor's voice, 'Alice . . . can you hear me? You must endeavour to stay calm. All is going as it should . . . though how your aunt could think to go off and leave you with this inexperienced maid! Now, listen to me, and do your best. When I say, you must push, and as hard as you can. Soon everything will be over and done – this pain no more than a memory.'

I wondered that anyone ever forgot a torture as all-consuming as that, but I ground my teeth and gathered my strength, pushing and pushing until he cried, 'Stop!'

And I did. And I heard a screeching wail.

Much later, in the evening, a telegraph message arrived at the house. Nancy brought it upstairs for me, so that I could read the words set down: *REGRET TO INFORM STOP RETURN DELAYED STOP LT STOP.*

Nancy was fretting terribly. 'We should send a reply. They should be told . . . know that the baby has been born.'

'Where would we send an answer? I have no idea where they're staying. Do you?'

Nancy shrugged and shook her head, after which she set about busying herself with finding the baby clothes she'd made, and then with other practical things, such as pulling a drawer from a dresser and constructing a makeshift cot for the child, into which she laid some cut down sheets, with shawls to use as blankets.

All through the hours of that night it was Nancy who held the child in her arms, tenderly cradling his head as if it was something that might break. It was Nancy who sang to soothe his cries. It was Nancy who changed him and swaddled his limbs. And when I refused to offer my breast, it was Nancy who dipped a rolled up rag into some sugared water, coaxing his tiny mouth to suck, saying that's what they did in the orphanage – though for the most she urged me to try, begging, 'Please, Miss Alice. You are his mother. If you don't feed him this babe will die.'

'Do what you like. Get him a wet nurse. I don't want him anywhere near me.'

I thought of his father's mouth at my breast, and I had no desire to suckle the child of the man who had seduced me, the wicked consequence of which had caused such pain and misery. How could I bear to hold this child when my aunt would return to take him away, to claim she was his mother? First grief, then a numbness, spread though my veins until every emotion had turned to stone. When I looked at that tiny, defenceless thing, I felt nothing, nothing at all. All I wanted to do was to close my eyes, to pretend that my child did not exist, to sleep and never wake again.

Little hope of any rest! At dawn, I woke with such a start when the child was wailing to wake the dead, and with Nancy nowhere to be seen I propped myself up on an elbow, peering down to the end of the bed where the drawer had been set upon the chest. I shushed the red-faced tyrant and pressed my palms against my ears, trying to block the noise of him. But all too soon I was crying as well, and my breasts felt so hard and sore to touch. In the end I did the only thing that might hope to stop his screeching.

Groaning at the ache in my muscles, I reached into the makeshift crib and, in the dreary morning light, I lifted the baby in my arms – relieved when his crying became but a whimper, when he rooted his mouth at my nipple to suck. And while he did that, when I looked at his face, where the redness now paled on the downy cheek, I saw that the natural hue of his skin was more of a dusky olive brown. I traced the rosebud of his lips, then stroked my finger down his neck – and that's when I noticed the birthmark, the stain that looked like a narrow red ribbon that had been wound around his throat, like the ribbon that Mercy used to tie on the door of her parlour in Claremont Road. Could that be the sign of her ownership?

I drew the shawl up higher, just below his chin, and stared instead into his eyes – eyes so like Lucian Tilsbury's, unblinking, liquid, black as coal – except that these eyes were innocent, and these eyes had an open, mute appeal, and that look, it scratched into my soul, deeper than any rose's thorn. How could I not love this child, whatever the sin of his origin?

The next day passed peacefully enough, and when the doctor made his call I mentioned the mark at the baby's throat and how that was of concern to me. But he said it was nothing, that it would fade, that such things were often seen at birth. He then pronounced both patients well. He looked my way and smugly said, 'I can tell we'll have no worries here!'

But he really should have worried, as to why my aunt had not returned.

Nancy fretted all that day, though she was calmer later on when she held the baby in her arms and then looked straight into my eyes, and said, 'I know who the father is. And I know he was with you, the other day, after the wedding ceremony. When I came back from Claremont Road, I found your aunt in such a state. She said that she'd seen you . . . together, in here. She said she'd heard him call you "wife".'

There were some moments before I could give any coherent answer. 'I thought I heard something . . . someone at the door. Do you think that's why she's not come back?'

My voice was then much stronger, and filled with a bitter resentment. 'But *you've* known it all, right from the start, from that very first time in Claremont Road. You knew that he'd been in my room that night . . . when you claimed that I'd been sleepwalking!'

Her answer surprised me. No attempt at denial. 'At least he desires *you*.'

My laughter was contemptuous, 'Then why don't you go and leave me here . . . go and join his harem? He and my aunt have deserted me. Why shouldn't you make that one more?'

During the night, I woke with a start. The baby was whimpering in his sleep. I climbed out the bed, still a little sore, but nowhere as bad as I'd been before when I lifted him up from his drawer bed and then wandered out to the landing, passing through the bedroom door which had not been locked since the fateful day when my aunt wed Lucian Tilsbury – as if no one any longer cared if I should stay or leave the house.

I saw beams of moonlight shine faint through a window. It felt as if time itself stood still. I held my child much closer, cradling his tiny, fragile neck while pressing my lips to his silken hair. And while doing that, I heard them – the muted voices down below. I was sure that one was Nancy's. But who was she talking to?

Resting a hand on the banister rail, while peering down through the spiralling well I leaned too far and almost fell, almost losing my grip on the baby. And, shocked to think what might have been, had he slipped from my arms to the hall below, I managed to turn around again, my spine sliding down the length of the stair post until I was sitting on the floor, as limp and useless as a doll, my child clutched tight in trembling arms. I knew I could never bear his loss. And yet, if those voices hailed Mercy's return, then he would be taken, and all too soon.

Gripped by a sudden urgency I managed to struggle to my feet and walked on down the corridor, to where another open door revealed a narrow wooden bed. Draped over the end of that was the blue of Nancy's uniform. Could I quickly put that on? Could I dress and leave the house, get out before they found me, perhaps make my way to the refuge that Mercy had once mentioned, where nuns took in the homeless, the fallen and the destitute?

I placed the child up on the bed and, lifting the dress, stepped into its skirts and dragged the bodice to my breast. But Nancy was so very slight that the buttons refused to fasten, no matter how hard I tugged the cloth. And through my anger and distress I heard a rustling sound behind, and there was Nancy watching me, her fingers plucking at the fringe of the shawl drawn tight around her, that covered the nightgown worn beneath.

Behind her, there was Tilsbury. Insubstantial, he looked, in the hall's dreary light, his face wan and strained with exhaustion – and I knew then that something was terribly wrong, calling out, 'What has happened? Where is my aunt?'

He walked past the maid and into the room, attempting to take my hand in his when he said, 'Alice . . . your aunt is . . .'

'Don't!' Such fear was in my voice when I stepped back towards my child, as if to create a barrier between him and this shadowy stranger. As I did so the folds of blue cotton cloth fell from my hands and to my feet, to puddle there like water, to trap me when I shouted, 'Don't touch me! Don't *ever* touch me again. Don't touch me *or* my baby.'

Nancy walked past us and went to the bed, taking the baby in her arms, where he woke and made some mewling whines, at which Tilsbury gave a lengthy sigh and said, 'Take him away, Nancy. See to the child. Alice and I must talk privately.'

THE DECEPTION
AT THE FUNERAL

That July was my twentieth birthday: a date I have since preferred to forget, just as it was forgotten then. Except that is by Fate – and how generous was her bounty, to grant me three unwanted gifts: A birth. A death. A funeral.

I sat in a trance, not eating, not sleeping, because Tilsbury had told me that Mercy was dead, that the reason for his own delay in returning from London to Windsor had been due to the legal necessities: waiting for the autopsy to be performed, to confirm the attending doctor's presumption that Mercy had died from a heart seizure.

Two days later he took me to Claremont Road, to where her body had been returned in readiness for the funeral. The night before my milk had dried and the baby was hungry and fretful for hours, his cries almost driving me to distraction. I found myself wishing that he would die too, disappear just as my aunt had done, to leave me in peace to find some sleep – though very soon I was weeping again, for how could I think such dreadful things?

The day dawned and saw me calmer. I sat in a chair, staring mutely up at what was hung from the armoire door: a black bonnet, and a long black veil that Nancy had found in Mercy's room when she made a visit to Claremont Road – because veils were worn by mourners. They were not just for brides and spirit guides.

She had also brought a selection of gowns, but only the black was appropriate, even though it really was too warm for the velvet I had worn before when attending the castle séance. I was struggling to put it on when Nancy started to pester me, saying that I should feed the child who seemed to be too listless, his skin grown pale and clammy.

I did try, but my efforts failed again, and when she saw how hopeless it was, Nancy said, 'I must tell Mr Tilsbury. Something will have to be done.'

She went. I finished dressing. Within the hour, the maid returned. She carried a bottle containing white liquid, something the apothecary recommended. And, just as when he had first been born, it was Nancy who took my babe in her arms, coaxing the rubber teat to his mouth, laughing out loud when he started to suck, his little legs kicking in delight. She stroked her fingers through his hair, so dark and fine and downy. She mused, 'I am drawn to this little one. I could take to him as if my own.'

I was thinking of Aunt Mercy then, and her plans to steal my child from me. Even so, it was irrational, the terrible rage then rising up, when I dragged the child from Nancy's arms and knocked the bottle of milk to the floor. I was dizzy and breathless. I frightened myself. What on earth was I doing, behaving like that, almost in a state of hysteria while attempting to soothe his screaming cries, holding him tight against my breast while I heard Nancy's mumbled apology, 'I'm sorry, Miss Alice. I meant no harm.'

When Lucian Tilsbury appeared in the room, some sort of peace had been resumed. Nancy was holding the baby again. His father smiled down, saying nothing at all, though that was the first time he lingered, to really look at the face of his son, and whatever his guise of serenity I saw the twitching of the eye drawn down towards the puckered scar, as he touched a hand to the baby's neck and traced the line of the birthmark.

For some reason that made me feel alarmed, and my voice was beseeching when I said, 'Later . . . time enough for that later.'

Tilsbury looked back at me, his face etched deeply with remorse when he said, 'You're right. We should go, if you still wish to see the coffin, before . . .'

'Yes,' I answered curtly, 'I would like to see my aunt. I owe her that much, to say goodbye.'

He reached a hand into a pocket and looked at me through bloodshot eyes, saying, 'I almost forgot. I think she would wish you to have these rings.'

In his palm lay the emeralds and opals, the stones with which I'd cursed my aunt, and also the plainer golden band given on her wedding day.

'But why would I wear her rings?'

'As a token of remembrance.'

Did the grieving wear rings for remembrance? I had no idea of the customs of death. And in a state of confusion, I said, 'I will wear the opals, but only today. The other . . . I think she should have it back. She should take it with her to the grave.'

I made to put the opals on, but the only finger they would fit, and much too tightly for comfort, was the fourth finger of my left hand. That should have given me warning, but for then I forgot about it, clutching the golden ring in my hand while Tilsbury drew my veils down.

The funeral hearse was already waiting outside the house in Claremont Road. Its darkly caped driver was sitting erect, a black scarf draping down from his tall silk hat. Now and then that fluttered in a breeze but otherwise he was motionless, staring over the backs of the black, blinkered horses who wore black plumes upon their heads, standing as patient as death itself.

'How strange,' I spoke my thoughts out loud, 'to place my aunt inside this hearse . . . to make all of this fuss and bother when the church is only across the road.'

The church bell answered, tolling slow. It sounded like a dying heart. And there, below the tower, a small group of mourners were clustered like vultures. How did they know about today? Had a notice been placed in the newspaper?

I felt the weight of a hand on my sleeve, looking back to see Lucian Tilsbury, whose lips spoke softly in my ear. 'Alice. You should come inside.'

I don't know what I expected to see, and at first I couldn't see a thing, not with those veils across my face, not with the shutters all closed up, the house so prematurely dark.

'There's nothing to harm you,' Tilsbury said, when I wavered at the sitting room door.

He was right. No ghosts in the shadows that day, only the spectre of memory, of the things he had done, to her, to me.

As my eyes adjusted to the gloom, through the gauzy weave before my eyes I saw the white cloth on the dining room table, and on top the open coffin lay. The air was stagnant. It smelled of decay, that putrid aroma more cloying still when mingled with the scent of the lilies arranged around the corpse. Cook's words came back to haunt me then: *They stink of death and misery.* I had to grab at the table's edge, waiting a while to steady myself until I felt able to lift my veils and clearly see Aunt Mercy's face – although it wasn't really her. That corpse was devoid of any life. It was no more than a mannequin – like the dressmaker's dummy upstairs in the Shrine. The one who wore the wedding veil.

Should Mercy have worn that when she wed, just as her mother and sister had? Should I put that veil in her casket now, along with my aunt's wedding ring? In death she looked more like a bride than she had upon her wedding day. She wore a white nightgown, frothy with lace, over which her dark hair was brushed loose at her shoulders, the few strands of grey like silver. Framed within that, when I dared to look closer, her face in repose was smoothed of all lines. Like parchment, it stretched across her cheeks, against which her lips were too prominent, stained a vivid bluish-black – that sign of the Elixir. Her fingertips were blackened too where the blood had congealed and stilled beneath, but I held my breath and plucked up the courage to reach into the casket then; to lift the hand on which I placed what had been Mercy's wedding ring. I don't know what made me think about those scratches once seen upon her arm, but lifting her sleeve to the elbow I found, just as

I'd feared I would, that the flesh below was a lurid rash of crusted scabs and pinpricks.

'What killed you?' I whispered, knowing in my heart that those marks must surely hold the proof of what had enthralled my aunt for years, what I feared had led to her demise. I wondered if she had meant to die, this tragedy the fault of me, because of what Aunt Mercy heard. Because her husband called me 'wife'.

I jumped at the touch of a hand on my shoulder. I heard Tilsbury's voice when he softly said, 'The undertakers are waiting. They must close up the coffin lid. Won't you come and wait in the parlour?'

At that, I whirled around and cried, 'You should be an undertaker yourself. A rather related trade, don't you think, this little industry of death that you and my aunt always loved so well?'

He did not give an answer, only steered me back out and to the hall where I dragged my arm away from his, all but flying up the stairs to open the door that led to the Shrine, the door that had never been locked since the night when I had donned the bridal veil. But when I went to seek it now, the dummy remained but nothing else. The dress and the drapes of lace had gone. Something else that my aunt had disposed of? Had it also been burned in the kitchen range, as had my hair, as had my beads?

I ran down the passage to Mercy's room and stood in the doorway, panting, my eyes casting round through the drab half-light at what had already been closed up. Dust sheets were draped on the furniture, looking like so many ghosts. Had she never intended to return?

Another deep breath to contain my emotions, after which I ran up the narrow stairs that led to what had been my room. And there, still on the mantelpiece, there was my mother's beaded bag and everything that it contained, the ties of which I sealed once more, the ribbons wound around my wrist.

I made my way back down the stairs – where I was almost

overcome by a sudden spell of dizziness, having to clutch at the newel post until Tilsbury stepped forward and took my arm and led me through the parlour door.

There the shutters and curtains had been drawn back, just enough to let in a faint glimpse of day, to see that the mirror was draped in black velvet; to see that the hands of the clock had stopped. In the mirror set above, my eye caught a movement beside the piano where two gentlemen were standing. I knew them at once from the wedding day. I supposed they had come to support their friend in this, his widower hour of grief. But surely they should have been in the church? Neither were family members.

Behind came the thud of the closing door, after which I heard Lucian Tilsbury's voice, 'Alice, I don't believe you were introduced to my colleagues before. This is Dr Thomas . . .'

He nodded towards the shorter, who was wearing a monocle at one eye, who had a thick head of straw-like hair, and the brush of a dirty-yellow moustache. The other he named Mr Fletcher, his lawyer, and he was of a larger build, with a clean-shaven face and small blue eyes almost hidden beneath their drooping lids. He looked like some monstrous, milky-faced child, with his bald head and shiny pink features – and those features then looming above me when he took a step forward, extending his hand, expressing trite words of sympathy.

I did not offer an answer for I felt distinctly ill at ease, both in my body and my mind – gripped by a sense of urgency, that here some danger threatened me, and that foreboding only enhanced when the doctor softly said, 'My dear Mrs Tilsbury, may I take this opportunity to offer my condolences?'

His accomplice was as swift to add, 'Indeed, Mrs Tilsbury. How tragic, to lose a loved one, and so near to the joyous event of your wedding.'

I was shocked. I took some time to say, 'I'm sorry. I think you misunderstand . . . my aunt, who lies in her coffin next door, she is . . . she *was* . . . Mrs Tilsbury. I am her ward. I am her niece. My name is Alice Willoughby.'

Tilsbury circled an arm at my shoulders, a sudden gesture of ownership. 'Come, Alice, this is a difficult time.'

'Take your hands off me!' I stepped away. 'Can't you hear what they're saying?'

'Sshh,' he hushed, turning to speak with his cronies. 'It is very hard, coming so close on the birth of our child. And now, having to face—'

'You're lying!' I shouted. 'Why are you lying?'

The man called Fletcher then interjected, 'Dr Thomas and I were there at your marriage. We saw the ring placed on your finger – the opals and emeralds that stood for your troth, witnessed in the very presence of God.'

I lifted my hand to my face and stared at the ring I was wearing, placed there of my own free will, and barely more than an hour before. How could I deny its existence without appearing to be insane?

I tried to run towards the door, struggling from Tilsbury's embrace. But in no time at all the others were on me, a hot sticky hand covering my mouth, both of my arms held in firm restraint. Panting with terror and anger, the moment my lips were free again I screamed and tried to call for help. But no one came. No one answered. The undertakers, all inured to such harrowing cries from the newly bereaved, were well-practised at turning blind eyes, deaf ears. The only reply that came for me was the toll of the melancholy bell, reminding me of Christmas night, creating an eerie suspension in time, an unreal mood on that unreal day – through which the doctor spoke again. 'It is the trauma of childbirth, compounded with such sudden grief. I suggest she does not attend the church. I cannot say what profound effect that may have on a mind so jolted.'

Reaching down to a brown leather bag at his side, he raised a bushy yellow brow. 'It is always an unseemly thing, to have women attending funerals, and in circumstances as trying as this I find that sedation is a help.'

A knot was tightening in my breast, the dread of what might

next be done. 'No!' I appealed to Tilsbury, 'Not that. I'll be quiet. I swear it. But I *will* attend this funeral. Surely, you will not deny me that.'

'Well,' his quack of a friend went on, 'I can always sit nearby in church, be on hand should events prove too stressful to bear . . . should Mrs Tilsbury happen to need any medical intervention.'

'I'm sure that won't be necessary.' Tilsbury was severe in his answer. 'I'm sure that Alice understands.'

'Understand!' I stared into his eyes. 'How can you treat me with such disrespect?'

'I must know that you can be trusted. If any should ask, *you* are my wife. Mr Fletcher has the proof at hand.'

As if on cue, the tall bald man then drew something out from his pocket, unfolding a paper certificate which he then held before my eyes. Where his stubby pink finger was pointing, its thickly ridged nail bitten down to the quick, I saw the name of Tilsbury. The name of Alice Willoughby where Mercy Matthews should have been.

What was this cruel deception? Had Tilsbury disposed of my aunt? Was it the hand of a murderer that now tenderly pushed some hair from my face, straightened my hat, re-arranged my veils? Like some stiff-limbed mechanical doll I found myself walking out of the house, through the front door and down the steps, and then along the narrow path where Tilsbury's hand cupped my elbow, where he drew me back at the garden gate, and said, 'I won't keep you away from this funeral. I care nothing for propriety. But . . .' he glanced at his friends on the path behind, though the threat in his statement was all for me, 'if what I ask of you today proves to be too difficult, then I'm sure the good doctor can arrange for one of his colleagues to visit my house . . . to offer a second opinion.'

His meaning was perfectly clear. He would claim I was mad. He would put me away if I thought to expose his duplicity.

As we two walked behind the hearse, as my aunt's coffin was driven away – that shortest of distances, over the road, to the doors of the Trinity Garrison Church, even with Tilsbury at my side, I felt so alone, I felt chilled to the bone, stripped of every certainty that I had ever known. I heard the strike of our feet on the cobbles; a slow tapping in time with the funeral bell, and I did not think of Shiva's *damaru*, the drum with which the Hindoo god once beat the rhythm of life in the world. I thought of nothing more than death. I thought of the beat of Satan's drum. I thought that if I was not mad, then how much longer would it be before this man had pushed me to the very brink?

Standing in the cemetery, when my aunt had been laid to her final rest, my handful of soil scattered like rain upon the wood of the coffin lid. And how surprised I was to see that her grave was shared with other bones – with the grandparents I'd never met, whose names were inscribed on the headstone to which, as far as I was aware, my aunt never went to lay flowers, or any other offerings.

Apart from the pallbearers there was no one to witness that sorry scene. Only the vicar, Tilsbury and me. While some doleful prayers were said I shut my eyes and listened instead to the sounds of birds singing, the soughing of leaves which rustled in branches above our heads. If I pretended hard enough might those be the leaves of a banyan tree?

When I had stood in the Trinity Church, the flags of war had hung above, like giant bunting for the dead. Below them, great shafts of harlequin light had beamed through the tall, arched windows; a rainbow of colours that fell on the altar, adorning the cross and white petals of lilies. When I first walked in and saw those flowers through the filmy black mist of the veil I wore, as I walked down the aisle on Tilsbury's arm, I noticed that most of the pews were still empty. Those faces I did see were vaguely familiar. Some neighbours, and some of Mercy's past clients who had called at the house from time to time. And there were the Dalrymples, the sisters huddled in a pew, and next to them, Mrs Morrison. She turned her eyes to glance my way, the saddest of smiles upon her lips.

I was glad they cared not for propriety, those women at the funeral! I was looking forward to seeing Cook later, but even that hope was to be dashed when, at the start of the service, the vicar announced that the family – Mr and Mrs Tilsbury – regretted that there would be no wake, and asked for understanding regarding their wish that the burial should be conducted privately. After that, with my new name so publicly spoken, with Fletcher and Thomas so close behind, I kept my eyes fixed straight ahead. I said no prayers. I sang no hymns. I kept my lips clamped tightly shut.

When it was over we went outside and I watched as the coffin was placed in the hearse. Tilsbury waited, a small distance off, talking with the vicar. His two vile friends lingered nearby. I felt their eyes fixed hard on me and, hoping to evade them, retraced my steps back into the porch. There, I heard many consoling words, most of which I felt quite sure were simply said for manners' sake, not for any true expression of loss. My aunt had had many acquaintances, but she had known no real friends – except for Lucian Tilsbury. And he had proved no friend at all.

When the Dalrymple sisters approached me they twittered their duet of sympathy, though rather than simpering with admiration I noticed their sternly quizzical glances when they looked at Tilsbury that day. I feared the rancour of their thoughts – sensing they must be scandalised, to think that Mercy's demure young niece should have usurped her older aunt in the arms of her blessed mentor. Even so, the sister with stained black hair – somewhat more faded on this occasion, with more than an inch of grey now seen beneath the edge of her bonnet brim – suddenly took my hand in hers, into which she pressed a *carte de visite*, all the while muttering low in my ear, 'Do keep this, my dear. Should find yourself in need of friends, you are always most welcome to visit with us.'

'Indeed!' the other added. 'We have tried to speak with Mercy but we fear that her spirit has already passed. We have received one message, though, from where . . . from whom . . .

we do not know. It came to us both in a dream last night, and no confusing what it said. *"Take care of Alice Willoughby."'*

Such a sense of relief I felt when Mrs Morrison sought me out, pushing past the sisters and standing protectively at my side, saying, 'Alice! How I have missed you. How can I say how sorry I am? And what a terrible thing it is, for Mercy to be taken so . . . for Mercy to have such a weakness, just the same as her mother before her. I was saying to these two friends of hers, who would have guessed at such a thing, with your aunt so hale and vigorous!'

Mrs Morrison, she did not look hale. She appeared to have lost a great deal of weight; her teeth and her eyes somehow too large, nothing quite fitting any more.

I asked, 'Have you been unwell?' to which she heaved a sigh, as if it was just the two of us, still down in the kitchen in Claremont Road, chatting across the table top, 'That doctor . . . he has no idea as to what it could be that's ailing me. But more than once I've had the thought that someone found that sixpence, the one in the Christmas pudding mix – and that someone must have been me. Must have swallowed it down without even knowing and then had it lodge like a cork in my gut. That's my explanation anyway! But to see you here in church today, no matter how sorry the circumstance . . . it's as good as a tonic for me, it is.'

Suddenly, her expression changed, a great deal harsher when she said, 'And what about that Nancy? Did she not think to come today? I had heard that she was in Park Street now, employed as one of the maids up there.'

What to say without having to mention the baby? I hated to lie, but what could I do when thinking of Tilsbury's threats again? 'She is . . . she is in Park Street. But she is indisposed. She has been rather ill of late.'

'The Tilsbury effect!' Cook quipped. 'I was told the very same of you, when Mercy refused to let me near.' And then, just as soon, forgetting the maid, the old woman's tone was softened. I had to strain to hear her words: 'Certain matters have come to reach my attention. I should have liked to think them wrong, but . . .'

'What have you heard?' I felt alarmed.

'Well, back there, in the church, for one thing, to know that you've gone and got married! But hark at me! My rudeness! I should offer congratulations, though the good Lord knows it was a shock. It was always your aunt I thought would be the one to end up with Tilsbury . . . as did everyone else in the church today. I've always said he's a dark one, and in every sense of the word!'

At that she strained to peer outside, to where my 'husband' could now be seen, standing nearby the arched porch doors and a sour expression on his face when engaged by the Dalrymples. He spoke to them but briefly, before turning his back and beckoning to one of the undertakers, and after a word with that gentleman, he waved for his carriage driver.

Cook had noticed that – the fact that I would soon be called to join him at the cemetery. After sniffing and dabbing a cloth to her cheeks – the dainty, lace-edged handkerchief that Mercy had given on Christmas day – she managed to force a smile and say, 'Now, push back that veil and show me your face and give this silly old woman a kiss. And make sure to remember this. You have more friends than you realise, and a friend in need is a friend indeed. Do not be afraid to call on them, at any time, both day and night.'

We embraced and she pulled me close to her bosom, no longer as plump as in years before. But still I was glad of the warmth of that, during which I mumbled back, 'Oh Cook, whatever you may have heard, please don't think too badly of me. Things are not always what they seem.'

She lifted a hand to stroke my brow, the brow now free of the draping veils that fell behind my head instead. She wiped at my eyes with her handkerchief, then pressed that into my own hands, and said, 'Indeed they are not, my dear . . . which is why we must set them right again.'

SHIVA TURNS EVERY
THORN INTO BLOSSOM

We were driven away through the cemetery gates. I sat in the carriage's corner, as far away from Tilsbury as I could possibly manage to be, and glad of the veils drawn down again, to hide my face from his piercing gaze. He stared out through the window, motionless and severe in his silence, his unscarred profile then in view, until he glanced my way again, and asked through the devil's countenance, 'Does the child have a name?'

'No!' My reply was surly. 'Not unless Satan names his own!'

'I'm sorry that we were away for the birth. You should never have been left alone. But the child's name must be registered. The formalities must be settled.'

'Settled? How settled?' I asked, disbelieving. 'Settled that my aunt is dead? How did it happen? Tell me the truth. Tell me if your conscience is clear on that count.'

That nerve was twitching beneath his eye. The scar was flaring, an angry red – the signs of his discomposure through which he spoke but calmly, 'I told you before, what the coroner wrote. What it says on the death certificate. It was a weakness of the heart, and—'

'And is that death certificate as valid as what I saw today? That document with my own name!'

'The hotel management called in their own physician. Would you imply that he was bribed? Although, I confess, he did prove to be most understanding with regard to the social niceties . . . the need to uphold your aunt's reputation, regarding her liberal consumption of certain affecting substances, not to mention the wine consumed that day. How should we adorn her memorial stone?' His voice was raised, alarming me, 'Here lies Mercy Matthews, Windsor occultist and opium addict, who brought about her own demise, who shames her name for ever more?'

I was seething to hear such a blunt response. 'I wonder who brought her to such a state . . . how long she was controlled that way, through the habits *you* encouraged!'

His reply was more desperate than angry. 'Alice, you must believe me. You speak from a place of ignorance. But there is one thing that you should know. I will not allow the death of your aunt to affect any plans for *our* future lives. She never was a part of them.'

It was still early afternoon when I stood in the Park Street hallway, looking through the open drawing room doors to those that led out to the balcony. I heard Nancy's laughter come in from the garden, and then some squealing cries from the baby. I wondered if Nancy was aware that I had been passed off as Tilsbury's wife.

For then, I was too exhausted to care. Such a desperate need to be alone. And so, with one hand on the stair rail, the rail that was formed of serpent scales, I began my slow ascent while Tilsbury followed on behind, his voice rising up to reach my ears. 'I know you disliked the green room. I've had your things moved to the floor below. Would you like me to show you where?'

'Do I have any choice?' I turned back from the landing, but still followed when he walked ahead, too weary to offer objection when he opened a door into a room that did not have walls of green or blue, but was yellow and airy and filled with light, with bamboo-framed paintings of peonies, and delicate lacquered furniture. Even so, I held back from entering, looking over my shoulder to ask, 'Did Mercy ever sleep in here?'

'No.'

A simple answer. If he lied, how could I know? I went inside and slammed the door, then pressed my ear against the wood, listening for the turn of a key. But that clicking sound, it did not come, only the passage of his feet as he headed down the stairs again.

I dragged off my hat and the mourning veil. I would never wear that gauze again. I undid the ties of my mother's bag and lifted out my photograph, placing my father's likeness upon a mirrored table. I went to the window and closed up the shutters, trying to block out the natural light, along with all sounds from the garden below. And when that was done I lay down on the covers, consumed with a terrible sobbing fit as my fists beat against the pillows, calling for Mercy to appear; for my aunt to speak and so to prove that spirits really did live on, were something more than waking dreams, or phantoms of the laudanum.

How long I wept, I do not know. My aunt, she did not come to me. She did not come then. She has not come since. But that does not mean ghosts don't exist.

And as for those who see them – for whom it is more than mere pretence – I wonder to this very day, are we blessed, or are we cursed?

My head throbbed at the temples and jabbed at the back where I'd lain with my hairpins still in place. The first thing I saw was the staining of red where my hand lay against the lace edge of the pillow. The flesh of one finger was stinging and raw. In my sleep, I must have been trying to force Aunt Mercy's ring over the knuckle. But it was stuck fast. It would not budge, that little circle of green and white in which Lucian Tilsbury had me trapped.

I must think of a way to escape him. Could I go to Mrs Morrison? But where Mrs Morrison happened to live, I simply had no idea at all. All those years she had worked in our house and I had never been to hers! Perhaps I could go to Claremont Road where the spare set of keys might still be found under the pot by the kitchen door. But then, he would know where to find me. And he had his illicit proof of a marriage. What if I could not prove it false? As a wife, any husband would legally own me.

I was but a chattel in his house. He would own my body, own my mind, own anything that I possessed. And he would also own my child. If I tried to object, he could claim me mad. He had already threatened to do as much – to put me away if I disobeyed.

I felt ill at the thought of that. I needed to breathe some fresher air. I went to the window and drew back the shutters, seeing the deepest pink sunset above. A sky flecked with stretches of wisping gold. A wood pigeon burbled and, somewhere far off, a dog barked three times. From the room overhead I heard footsteps. Nancy must be there with the baby. *My baby!* I felt such a longing to hold him, overwhelmed by the culpability that I, his own mother was so self-absorbed, to think so little of his needs.

Leaving the yellow room, I was making my way up the next flight of stairs, when I paused at a rhythmic squeaking sound. Creeping on, when I came to the landing above, while standing outside the green room door, I saw not Nancy, but Tilsbury – and I stood and watched him for some time, hardly daring to move from my place of concealment, from where *he* had previously spied on me. And there, as the light grew dimmer, the room within was shadowed green – as green as Mercy's eyes had been – as green as the sting of jealousy that entered my heart when I saw that scene.

A mother should not feel resentment to see a father so at ease, so adoring of his offspring. But I did. I felt such anger to see him sitting beside that new cradle – the source of the whining, repetitive sound. But my baby had not been rocked to sleep. My baby's eyes were open still, locked with those that stared back down. And, did I imagine those specks of gold, the splinters of light that glittered like metal, that were shining so brightly in his own?

I dreaded to think that my baby might inherit his father's corruption. And yet, this father seemed nothing but kind, this father who whispered endearments, and who was then so rapt in his child that he failed to notice the mother there. And she –

she felt nothing but alone. She felt like an intruder, which was, after all, what she would have been, had Mercy still been living. But Mercy was dead. Mercy was gone. She no longer owned me, or my child. And neither would Lucian Tilsbury.

I crept back down the stairs and into the room with yellow walls, where I stood staring up at the ceiling for what then felt like hours on end, hearing more movements, muted conversations, which I guessed to be Tilsbury speaking with Nancy. And when heavy footsteps descended the stairs, I feared he would come into my room. But he didn't. He didn't disturb me that night. As the house became still and silent I listened for the church's bells, to hear them strike and know the hour. But, I had forgotten that I was in Park Street. The Trinity bell did not toll for me there.

I woke the next day, very early, still dressed in my black velvet gown. But no matter how crumpled and dirty it was I had no thought of changing. I did sit for a while on the dressing stool, looking into the mirror set above while I picked up a silver brush and worked it through my tangled hair. My face was swollen and waxy white, except for some angry spots of red that were then burning at my cheeks. If not for my situation and the shock of all the recent events, I might almost think myself feverish. My head felt too light, a strange shaking inside; that sensation only intensified when the brush suddenly dropped from my hand – when my eye chanced to fall on my photograph.

Lifting the frame, I rubbed the glass, just over the spot on the print below where, before, a blurred residue had formed – where, now, the face of the man was restored!

But if that was the face of my father, I had not seen Prince Albert's ghost. The warning I'd thought then for the Queen – *You must be wary. These things, they should be left alone* – had those words been intended instead for me, spoken through the lips of my father: the very same man I looked at now, when he had been handsome and healthy and strong, not the ravaged sick spirit I'd seen in that hall.

Being so engrossed in his face, I hardly noticed the knock on the door, not even having a chance to reply before Lucian Tilsbury entered the room, and drew so very close behind that he must have observed what it was I held.

I said, 'I want to be alone.'

'Of course, I won't detain you long. But, as any good husband, I wanted to ask if you were well and—'

'How can you hope to prolong this deception? Nancy saw you wed my aunt. She knows that I am not your wife. I will ask her to be my witness . . . I will go to the constabulary and accuse you of theft . . . of kidnap . . . of murder . . . of—'

'Do you really think that would be wise?' His eyes met with mine in the mirror. 'You would only implicate yourself in the fraud of that séance with the Queen . . . and the theft that visit led to. What would become of your child, if you and I were jailed now? Have your considered his future . . . or yours? I apologise for any hurt that my arrangements may have caused, for that cruel charade of a funeral. But I would do the same again. I have no intention of risking my freedom, of losing the diamond, or you . . . or my son. And never imagine that Nancy would deign to speak against me. She knows and accepts what I have done. She understands that Mercy was wed only to protect my child's name, and that, now, for the sake of him again, I have claimed you as my wife. That may not be the entire truth, but *that* is what Nancy understands. And that is enough for her to know . . . until we leave for India.'

'India? You still mean to take us there?' I swallowed. My throat felt hot and sore, my voice croaked with the emotion. 'You mean to take what is not yours.'

'I only take that which I own . . . that which is freely given. Surely you must remember? But, yes, you are right in that virtues are won. And for now,' his tone grew tenser, 'have you thought any more of a name for the child?'

'He is a bastard. What does it matter?'

'His *legitimate* name is Tilsbury, the very same as yours. But if you have no preference then you may leave the choice to me.

These matters must be reconciled. They are required for the paperwork, to make the arrangements for our trip.'

Once such a journey was all that I longed for, to find my way back home again. If only I knew where Mini was. If only my father was living still, living and waiting in Lahore.

I looked again at my photograph, then said, 'Let the child's name be Charles.'

For a fleeting moment Tilsbury baulked, before meeting my eye in the mirror once more. 'Very well. Let it be Charles.'

With those words, he placed one hand on my shoulder, then raised it to gently cup my chin. He tilted my face towards his own, then slowly stooped forward and kissed my lips. The briefest of pledges that token was, and something more chaste than passionate. But I understood him well enough. That was the sign of his intent.

Much of the morning I spent with Charles, sitting beside his cradle, disturbed by no sound but his snuffling breaths. Inhaling his milky fragrance, I stroked my fingers through his hair, so black against the white of the pillow. I remembered Mini's fingers, and how they once caressed my cheek when she was soothing me to sleep.

Towards noon, I think it must have been, Nancy broke my reverie, telling me that Tilsbury had gone out to meet his solicitor. How she came to know every detail about his daily arrangements I did not know and I did not care. But I did know that I mistrusted her, that this maid was still her master's spy, and that she would support him in any lie.

I asked if she would feed the child, saying I needed to go and rest. She took him gladly in her arms, though just as I passed through the bedroom door, she called out behind me, 'Oh, Alice . . . you should be made aware, in case you are thinking of trying to leave, the rest of the staff have all been told that you are ill . . . ill in your mind. Nothing but a risk to yourself, or the public. Miss Matthews often used to say that you should be cared for in an asylum . . . . that Mr Tilsbury keeps you here only out of the kindness of his heart.'

My heart sank to hear her threats. But they made me more determined still, to find a way to leave – and soon.

On my way down to the entrance hall, I heard some chattering laughter coming up from the basement floor below where 'the rest of the staff' must be at work. A brisk patter of feet from nearer still, and I ducked behind the rise of the stairs, from where I saw an unknown maid, in her arms a basket full to the brim with the brushes and pans for her cleaning tasks. She kicked her foot against the baize, and as that door swung open the sounds from the kitchen were amplified. But then she was gone and the voices dimmed and I quickly moved across the hall and placed a hand on the front door latch – only to find it was secured.

That did not surprise me. Neither did it unduly distress me. Even had it not been locked I would never have left without my son. But then, how could I leave at all unless I found a key to use? A key that was more accessible than any chained at Nancy's waist.

I looked under a newspaper left on a salver. I opened up the long-cased clock, and then stood high on tiptoes as my fingers searched along the top – finding no more than woolly dust. Casting around, I noticed then the room from which the maid had come – the one with the door standing ajar – the gap which exposed a large grey hearth, and on its mantel a globe of the world. *Where is India on that?* Lured yet nearer by such a sight, I took a step into that room, and then saw the rest of the mantelpiece and the large glass dome displayed there – in which there was a stuffed black crow. Incongruously mawkish and ugly it was, very much like those birds of ill omen that I had seen at the country church on the day of the fraudulent wedding. This bird's beak was open. It seemed to be jeering. Its eye was glinting down at the mouse that was lying prone at its blackscaled feet, eternally caught in that moment of peril before it was to be devoured.

Dragging my eyes from that cruel tableau, they fell on a rust-coloured velvet chaise, and beside that a stack of newspapers. Two walls were made entirely of shelves, and every one was full of books – and some, like those in the hovel before, appeared to be very old indeed. There were books on religion. Books on the occult, on medicine, history, and art. There were travelogues, maps and dictionaries, novels and volumes of poetry – some of which Mercy had brought for me, during my confinement.

I walked towards an enormous desk, almost as broad as the room itself and set beneath the window that faced onto the street outside. The window, I knew it to be barred, and more than that, its shutter, which was one that drew up from beneath the sill, had been lifted halfway and secured with nails. What light spilled in through the panes above was shining on a cabinet where, behind a door of glass there lay a collection of precious stones. How those treasures glittered! Such blues, and reds, and greens they were. I thought again of Mini's beads. I touched the wrist where once they'd gleamed, and wished and wished for what was gone, for what was buried in my past. Buried like Anarkali.

But what about the present? What secrets might be buried here? What might I find in those desk drawers?

A page of stamps. Some sealing wax. Bottles of ink. A silver pen, and – what was that? I froze to read Aunt Mercy's name upon a death certificate. I had to take several deep breaths and force myself to carry on – leafing through letters, bankbooks and statements, accounts in various company names. Did those papers also conceal the recompense for a diamond's theft? Surely, there must have been a fee? Surely the Maharajah paid. Such risks the thief had taken!

It was then, when I thought of the diamond again, I had the distinct impression that I was no longer alone in that room, when I saw a movement on the wall, a shadow that flitted past me, then faded away through the open door. I followed its trail with a thudding heart, suspecting that Nancy spied on me, or had the other maid returned? I walked across the empty hall and heard a sigh, like the wind in the trees. But when I looked in through the drawing room doors, those to the garden were firmly closed. And yet, the muslin fluttered, as did the shape upon the wall – the silhouette then hovering beside the table with the gods. It was the shadow of a man. A snake was extending from his neck. The snake's great jaws were gaping wide, and its forking tongue was quivering. I heard a hissing in my ears and closed my eyes and held my breath, and when they opened up again the vision was entirely gone. But the presence – there *was* a presence – remained in the form of a whirring hum that surely came from Parvati's crown, where the ruby was glowing, as red as blood. Another sigh. A breath on my face. A breath that smelled salty and ferrous. I heard distant music, like violins whining, their strings being tuned for . . . for what? For a dance? All around me vibrations were subtle, entering every pore in my body, playing my nerves like an instrument; so sensuous a stirring, and through them a whisper – a whisper that sounded like a spell . . .

Open your eyes and you will see. Shiva turns every thorn into blossom. You are the spring flower, the bright sparking of life, always dying and always returning to him. Everything turns and changes, and yet, nothing changes at all.

Something *had* to change. How could I remain in that Park Street house, being prone to such delusions, imagining messages from the gods? How glad I was when another voice brought its own message later on when, that very day, mid afternoon, there came a loud hammering at the door.

I was back in the green room by then. Nancy had left me alone with Charles, but at that sound I went out to the hallway and heard the front door opening, and then Nancy's voice, then a different one. But one just as familiar.

It belonged to Mrs Morrison! And Mrs Morrison was asking for me – and what if Nancy told her to go? I ran like a fury, down all of the stairs to find the front door open still, and my friend, she was standing beneath the porch, exclaiming at the sight of me, 'Alice, my dear . . . there you are! Forgive me for coming unannounced, but I thought I'd take the chance to call, to invite you round for a pot of tea – tomorrow, if convenient.'

Nancy's agitation was plain to see, yet more so when Lucian Tilsbury came walking through his study door, when the twist of his heel on the wooden floor sounded like the squealing of a rat – over which I very quickly said, 'Oh, Mrs Morrison, I would love to come and visit you, unless my . . . my husband may know about some prior engagement that we have.'

Tilsbury remained inscrutable, brooding in his silence when Mrs Morrison replied, as if she was oblivious to the presence of the other two, 'I quite understand, my dear. You are a married woman now, and with all of the obligations that such a role entails. But I do hope you'll try to come along . . . just to make an old woman happy. We had so little chance to chat at your poor Aunt Mercy's funeral.'

At that she turned to Nancy, though still ignoring Tilsbury when she gave the maid a beaming smile, 'Why Nancy, I hardly knew you there . . . and looking in the pink these days. The high life in Park Street is suiting you then!'

'I haven't the skivvying to do,' Nancy answered curtly. And yes, she had changed in the past few months. The red of her hair had a glossy hue. And her eyes, which had often been dull with exhaustion when working in Aunt Mercy's house, were now the clearest, sparkling brown.

'You look very well indeed. Put on as much fat I have lost!' Mrs Morrison continued, but more in accusation than any form of compliment. 'Then again, I dare say you've an easier time since you were employed at Claremont Road. Less of that running up and down stairs . . . enough work to wear the hind legs off a donkey.'

'I didn't much mind,' the maid swiftly retorted, which was patently untrue, considering her moodish behaviour most of the time that she was there.

The tension between them was palpable, but then there came a wailing cry from the child who lay two floors above. Mrs Morrison surely heard it, and Nancy's eyes were questioning as she turned to look at Tilsbury. But he spoke not a word, did not bat a lid, and that was when Mrs Morrison bustled back beneath the porch, calling to me from the pavement steps, 'Three o'clock, tomorrow then . . . unless I hear to the contrary. Oh, and you'll need to know my address. Number seventy-six, Besley Street.'

I left Tilsbury and Nancy in the hall, still watching her departure, while I ran back upstairs to the green room, quite breathless when taking my child in my arms and stroking a hand to his tear-streaked cheeks, not noticing when his father appeared to stand in the door behind me.

He said my name and stared into my eyes, his brow creased in lines of suspicion through which, at last, he spoke again. 'Whatever it was that you and that woman were conversing about at the funeral . . . you do understand I cannot risk allowing you to visit her. I will not let you leave this house. I will not let you take this child.'

At that, the baby, grown quiet now, thrust out with a tiny dimpled hand, as if to clutch onto one of my fingers – the finger where the opals gleamed, pearlescent when caught in a shaft of light. The stones that stood for misery.

I lowered my head and kissed his cheek. But was I only playing a part, to prove my maternal devotion, to prove that I really would come back, that I would never leave my son when, defiantly holding his father's gaze, I said with total honesty, 'It really would mean a great deal to me, to see Mrs Morrison again.'

'To contrive with that witch, to deceive me!'

The silence that followed was tortuous. He shook his head and turned away. And, when the door had closed behind, I stood with Charles still in my arms, my back pressed hard against the wood, so hard that my shoulders were aching – aching, then become quite numb. And all the while, I sensed him there. Tilsbury, on the other side. I heard him give a weary sigh, and then his voice. Perhaps a prayer. Those words too indistinct to hear . . .

THE NIGHTMARE – NEVER TOLD

Look here, don't leave me!
If you leave me
I'll insult you by saying,
Oh Madman who wears the fierce elephant's skin!
Oh Madman who ate the poison!
Oh Madman surrounded by the fire of the town's crematorium!
Oh Madman who has me His slave!

I stand with my back against this door, and despair of ever finding a way by which to explain why I can't let her go . . . why I can never give her up. She and I are bound by so much more than the shadows that Mercy always sought. There is the gift of 'all knowing', all joy. The promise of an entire world to be found in the smallest grain of sand. But to know Heaven we must know Hell. To appreciate light we must live in the darkness. To share what is pure we must know degradation. To drink of the nectar of life, we must first taste the bile of our own death.

I have tasted my own mortality on more than one occasion – the last time at the Battle of Sobraon. Three days of solid rain there'd been. When it stopped the air was dense with cloud. It concealed me when I crossed the bridge, when I carried no more than my tulwar – the sword – for my protection, and no idea where harm might lurk with every sound around me then so muffled and distorted.

I could have found the British camp by the stink alone that morning. Coffee, tobacco, urine, shit. In the midst of that squalor I found General Gough, devising his plans for engagement. He was not impressed when I advised for an immediate retreat. At more than one hundred thousand men, the Khalsa far outnumbered ours.

But the outcome was not what I had expected. Such chaos when, within the hour, the river waters flooded up. A great rolling wave tore through the earthworks, taking the bridge, and the thousands of Sikhs who were crossing from the eastern bank. As the mists began to rise, all too clear was the devastation ahead. Men and horses weighed down in their armour stood not a moment's chance of survival. Bodies were jammed beneath boulders and cannon, or dragged into swirling whirlpools. Those who attempted to swim across were stabbed by British bayonets, or scattered with the grapeshot then fired from their muskets. As easy as shooting fish in a barrel. But still, the Sikh war cries filled the air. 'Sat Sri Akal. Sat Sri Akal. Bliss and eternity for the brave'.

I was glad of the roar of cannon fire when it deafened my ears to their agonies, when my eyes were blinded by plumes of smoke and the greasy residue of shot that stank like the foulest rotting eggs. But I saw Harry Hamilton, just nineteen, his golden hair then dark with gore, his forehead gashed open, his hands cut off. He was still warm, but he was dead – as dead I feared myself to be when I turned to see a flashing blade. A searing burn along one cheek. A terrible pressure in my head. I was choking, submerged in the water. And then, the floating. The nothingness. Nothing but stillness, and pain and heat as the midday sun glared down above. The flies that crawled across my eyes. The itching squirm of maggots in flesh then sliced down to the bone. The screams of vultures as they fought to feed on the entrails of the dead.

But, this was no blood-drenched battlefield. The river had washed me far downstream, on to the banks of a funeral ghat, where I had been pulled from the waters to lie beside a cremation fire. The horror of war to be exchanged for what then seemed the flames of hell.

That hell was my salvation – not the day of my death, but of rebirth. The Aghori who gathered round those flames welcomed me into their arms, when I knew not who or what I was, my memory entirely gone. They gave me bhang to ease the pain. I joined them in their ecstasies, lost in the rhythm of their drums and entering those trance-like states in which I need not even breathe, in which my heart could cease to beat – in which I might be thought as dead. I went naked, my flesh smeared in excrement and the ashes gathered from the pyres. I ate the charred flesh of corpses. I drank their blood from human skulls. And all of these things – these depravities – what others may view as the acts of the mad – the mad, or otherwise the damned – they opened my eyes, till then quite blind.

I saw how ephemeral is mankind. I saw that through the flames of cremation every new death is in fact liberation. I saw how, when immersed in such horrors, with nothing viler to endure, a man may become a true aesthete. For did not Shiva create the world, the low as well as the high of it? Did he not create the cosmic dance in which there is no start or end, in which saint and sinner are made as one . . . in which all are saved or destroyed by fire?

The fire of wanting filled my soul. I walked for months through heat and cold, through hunger, thirst and misery. I went into the mountains to seek an ancient Hindoo shrine of which I'd heard such prophecies. And what I found, those secrets – that is what Alice needs to know. Not of the nightmare that came before, but the promise to which that penance led. The glories of a destiny that she and I may one day share – if only she will hear me, if only she will open her eyes, as Shiva once opened his eyes for Parvati – to see the truth of what I am.

237

THE SECRETS OF
A MOUNTAIN SHRINE

Charles was quiet and sleeping again as I rocked him in his cradle. The rhythm of its creak was hypnotic. Back and forth, back and forth went that metronome, and within its beat my thoughts were trapped, going over the same things again and again. The nightmare of Mercy's funeral. That visit of Mrs Morrison. How complicit Nancy continued to be in Tilsbury's deceptions.

When I thought of Nancy the maid appeared, walking into the room and no knock on the door to offer any warning. She stopped before the mirrored armoire where her image was fractured by the cracks, where more than one Nancy appeared to be standing while twisting red curls through her fingers. She gazed at herself for quite some time, and when she spoke her voice was terse. 'I have been asked to pass on a message. Your *husband* would like you to join him for dinner. He's sent me up to care for Charles.'

My eyes fused with hers in those broken reflections. 'I do not wish to eat with *him*! My so-called husband may think—'

That sentence was never completed. Both Nancy and I taken unaware when there came a sudden flapping sound – and a little brown bird flew in through the window, to crash into the glass above her head. From there it made towards the walls, wings beating against them violently as if to escape through the painted trees. Fallen feathers were spiralling round us, through which I leaned over the cradle's edge, thinking to protect my child – looking back to see Nancy waving her arms, trying to chase the bird away. And she very almost succeeded, but rather than flying back out through the window, the part of the sash that had been raised, it smashed into the closed top panes from where a thin trickle of red ran down, to drip on the corpse that lay below.

Nancy and I remained motionless as we stared at that limp and broken thing. When its wing gave a sudden quivering flap, I said, 'Look! I think it's still alive. We should pick it up . . . put it out on the sill. It might come to its senses and fly away.'

Nancy, now alarmingly pale, took a cautious step nearer towards where it lay, and I thought she was going to do as I asked. But instead of lifting the bird in her hands, she raised her foot above its head, stamping down with her heel, and with such force that I was too horrified to speak, only able to watch when she did it again – and again – and again – and again.

During the awful tense silence that followed, while staring down at what remained of that poor creature on the floor, I snatched my sleeping child from his cradle and bundled him into a shawl, and said as calmly as I could, 'Nancy, I shall go downstairs. I shall take Charles with me, and when I come back I hope to find no sign of this . . . of this carnage here.'

I thought of telling Tilsbury, but could not bring myself to speak of the gruesome scene I'd left behind. All through that stilted, uncomfortable dinner I felt sick and struggled to hold my child as he twisted and whined and began to cry. I kept thinking about the murdered bird, and then the look on Nancy's face when I turned to glance back through the green room door, where the maid, unaware that she was seen, was still gazing down at what she'd done – and such a disconcerting smile was playing then upon her lips.

Thankfully, Charles grew calmer, snuggling into my breast to sleep and, when the meal was over and done – not that I'd eaten much more than a morsel – Tilsbury suggested that we go and sit in the drawing room.

I admit, I was apprehensive, thinking of the shadow I'd seen on those walls, thinking about those whisperings. But even that seemed to be preferable to going back up to the green room again, and the horror of Nancy's vicious crime.

After laying the child down on a chair, bolstered between two cushions, I picked up a book from a table nearby, though if asked what it was I could not have said. Tilsbury stood by the garden doors and puffed on the end of a cigar, though I had not noticed him lighting that. Its sweet, woody fragrance filled the air. Its tip glowed as red as the ruby that shone in Parvati's silver crown.

It was then, when I looked at the figurine, that I had the distinct impression that the goddess smiled at me again – though I scolded myself for being so foolish when she was but an effigy.

Tilsbury followed the line of my gaze and walked towards the metal gods. While standing before their table, some ash dropped down from his cigar and fell upon the golden wheel that circled the idol of Shiva. It smouldered there for a moment or two, on one of the jagged golden shapes that so resembled darting flames. I imagined – it could not have been real – that I heard the faintest, crackling hiss and I'm sure that the metal was wavering, as if it had ignited; its gold agleam with real flame. And that was when the baby woke, his little moans now the familiar precursor to the screams of hunger soon to come – and deciding to take him upstairs to feed, I had not even reached the doors when Lucian Tilsbury called my name.

Through his lips there drifted a trail of smoke, smoke that wreathed as if a ghost, when he said that he wished to kiss Charles goodnight. And only then, when he took a step forward, did I notice an idol not seen before. Another new god on the marble top.

Beneath a brass arch made of flowers and leaves, a potbellied creature was sitting cross-legged. He had the most beautiful almond shaped eyes – except they were set in an elephant's head. His ears were made of two long flaps, and instead of a nose he had a trunk that curled all the way down to his lap.

Mini had owned such an idol, but smaller and nowhere near as fine. It used to sit upon a stand that was set to face her bedroom door, from where she said it guarded her from anything or anyone who might seek to enter and do her harm. And about that god, she told this tale:

A long time ago, my thumbling, my sweet, Lord Shiva left his home on Mount Kailash to battle against the demons. And during his absence of many years, Parvati gave birth to a baby son . . . a beautiful boy who was called Ganesh.

Shiva at last returned to his wife. But Ganesh, who did not know the god, saw that fierce warrior at the door and refused to let him come inside, for fear that his mother might be harmed. Shiva then flew into a rage, cutting off the child's head and flinging it into the depths of the jungle. But the god was filled with such remorse when Parvati came to find her son, when she wept to see his lifeless corpse. Hoping to appease her, Shiva went searching for the head, but nowhere could he find it, and seeing a baby elephant, he took that creature's head instead and set it on the child's neck – thus creating the little elephant god who is beloved by us all.

'Ganesh!' I said in the smallest voice.

'Yes, Ganesh.' When Tilsbury said that name he distinctly enounced both syllables, which made it sound somewhat menacing – though I do not think he intended that. No, I am sure he did not mean that.

'Don't you find him appealing?' he asked with a smile. 'Parvati and Shiva's beloved child.'

'I always found him to be a strange hybrid. I always thought it horrible – what a father could do to his own son. I wondered that Parvati could bring herself to love him.'

Did I mean Shiva, or the child?

Clutching my own son closer, I stared at the glinting blade of the axe that was raised in the golden Shiva's hand, and through the corner of my eye I saw Tilsbury throw his cigar to the hearth and then, while lifting up an arm, as if to mirror Shiva's, a finger traced across the mark still vivid on my child's neck.

During that action his father said, 'Parvati will always love her son, just as she loves her husband – even though his betrayals and passions might cause his wife unhappiness.'

'And you mean to act like Shiva?' That was the moment I stepped away, filled with a growing sense of dread, fearing what harm this father might do to his own defenceless son.

'Ganesh brings good luck. He is favoured by all. I believe our son is just as blessed. Don't worry about the old legends, Alice. This is the start of a new one . . . our own. But there is a lesson to be learned. Never use Charles against me. Do not try to make *him* the guard at your door.'

'How could this child guard any door!'

I would not listen to more of this nonsense. Turning away, I made for the hallway, heading back up to the green room. And what a relief it was for me to find a bottle of milk made up, and to see that the bird's remains were gone. No sign that it was ever there.

Nancy was sleeping on the bed, her lips half-parted, her cheeks flushed pink. Her hair gleamed like gold on the pillow – the very vision of innocence, and far lovelier than any one of those women who danced on the posts around her.

Deciding not to wake her, too tired for remonstrations, I fed and changed the baby, then laid him in the cradle, afterwards sitting at his side. I heard Nancy's slow inhalations and the faster breaths of my child close by. I listened for movements down below – waiting for Tilsbury to go to his bed, leaving me free to go to mine.

It must have been well after midnight, by which time the candle had all but burned down, when Nancy lurched up with a dreadful gasp, crying out, 'Oh Alice . . . it's you. Oh, thank goodness. I had such a terrible dream. I couldn't breathe. I thought I was—'

'I didn't mean to frighten you. I didn't want to leave my son.'

'Because of me . . . what I did to that bird?' Nancy appeared to be full of remorse. 'I'm sorry, Alice. Truly, I am. I don't know what came over me. But don't you see? It is a bad omen, for a bird to come into the house like that. They always say it means a death. A bird flew into my mother's room the very day before she died. What if any harm should come to Charles?'

'Oh, Nancy, you must not think such things!' I tried my best to soothe her, though after what I'd heard below – that story of Ganesh still fresh in my mind – I felt anything but calm myself. 'That's only some old wives' tale. The bird lost its way. Nothing more than that.'

And convinced that the maid had been assured, that she loved and would never harm my son, I stood up and walked to the side of the bed where I lifted one of her hands in mine and said, 'I know it must be hard, for you to have lost your family, and in such a way. Perhaps we could be friends. I feel so terribly alone, and I do fear that Charles is in danger here . . . but it's nothing to do with any bird.'

She squeezed my hand in answer. She nodded, and gave me the kindest smile – a look of such complicity. It touched my heart and made me hope that some barrier between us had been breached. And then, almost overcome with exhaustion, I left Nancy in what had been my bed, trusted with the care of my baby son; both of them safely cocooned in bowers of green forest walls.

A candle stub still burned on the nightstand, a shimmer of gold on yellow walls as I stripped off my clothes and pulled on the nightgown that someone – who knew who? – had laid on the pillow. Did my grandmother's nightgown still lie on her pillow, in the Shrine, in the house in Claremont Road?

I let down my hair, but did not brush it out, for I wanted nothing more just then but to climb into bed and draw up the sheets, to lie in the stillness and close my eyes – though all was not as still as I thought. The candle's flame was wavering, caught in something of a breeze, and where its gleam shimmered my eye chanced to follow; seeing again my photograph.

I stretched out an arm and picked it up from its place on the table set nearby – after which I slumped back on the pillows again, from where I stared at my father's face and thought of all that had been lost, until, at last, I fell asleep.

I dreamed of being a child again, laughing and holding

Mini's hand, my other hand grasping my father's, the three of us in a garden where I heard the buzz of insects – then felt a sharp sting in one of my arms. I cried out, and all was darkness, and Papa and Mini, they were gone, and I was quite alone again, nothing before me but endless black tunnels through which I felt compelled to walk as if they would lead me to something I wanted – something I wanted very much.

Spreading my palms over mildewed rock, every blind step that I dared to take was timed with the steady beat of my heart, until I was no longer observing that scene, but was somehow inside it – not myself, but a man – a man whose will was strong and determined, though I tried my best to defy him. I tried my best to open my eyes and, just for a moment, I managed that. For a moment, I was myself again, aware of the yellow of bedroom walls, the flickering dip of the dying flame, and then a voice inside my head . . .

I am lost, in these caves, in this darkness? My bones are aching with the cold. The scar on my cheek is burning. My throat is parched, lips cracked and sore. Is it my fate to die here . . . in this search for a shrine that does not exist beyond the realms of fairy myth?

What is that? That gleaming up ahead? A light at the end of this tunnel. Running towards it, stumbling, breathless, I hear myself laughing. I sound like a madman. But then, what I find leaves me reeling.

A mass of ribbed pillars and arching crests. A sacred bull is carved in stone, its horns stained red and tipped with gold. A god lies prone as if a corpse upon which a goddess is sitting, restoring his life through her gift of sex. Another is a warrior, from whose third and sacred eye a blast of fire is streaming – streaming out towards some steps that rise into the vaults above, where a gap exists – a natural hole – through which I see the night-time sky, and in that sky the full white moon shines down on the head of the Chandrashekhara. The great stone god. Lord Shiva.

This idol stands more than twenty feet high. It is ancient and somewhat crudely made. The features have been shrouded in dusty nets of spiders' webs. But, this is him. I have no doubt. Shiva in his cosmic dance. Shiva, in whose brow once shone the sacred stone, the god's third eye; where now a hole is gaping.

Mists of incense wreathe around the Brahmin sitting at his feet – the priest whose eyes are tightly closed. I inhale the smoke's sweetness and yearn for its bliss, the solace of Soma, white seed of the moon. But how long has this man been dreaming? His flesh looks to be mummified. Matted grey hair grows down to his naval and yet, at his neck, fresh marigolds. The colour of sunshine, here in the darkness.

While staring at that garland, I sense something rustling close behind and, spinning around, I see a snake. The cobra slithers past some bowls that are filled with milk and sandalwood paste. No, not bowls, but human skulls. The chosen vessels of Shiva. I have swallowed from such cups before. I am desperate to drink what these contain – to drink, and quench my burning thirst.

But when I stoop to grab one, I hear the rasping warning, 'Wait! You must wait one moment more. One moment to hold infinity within the palm of your hand . . . to hold Eternity for an hour, the Kingdom of God within your soul. The stars are about to align again, when the Mahadeva will return through the glimmer of sacred white consciousness that may be found in the Koh-i-Noor. Find the stone and you may drink your fill. You may receive the blessing, when celestials will be made as flesh, when Shiva and Parvati will walk again upon this earth, when human souls will be divine.'

'How am to find it?' I set the skull back down, my question more desperate than I had intended, because this could be the answer, the siddhi, the magic for which I search.

Slowly, slowly, he opens his eyes, and says, 'It has long been stolen. We are told it has now left India. Wars have been fought for it. Princes have vaunted it, every one of them hoping to share in its power, every one believing his reward would be found in earthly empires. Their blood fed the Stone. Their souls nurtured its song. Yet, he who returns it to this shrine – that redeemer will be reborn, just as the serpent sheds its scales in the gift of uniting death with life.'

This is what I have dreamed of. If only the legend were true – that a mortal man could be sure of a future where his life lay ahead like an uncoiling serpent, time never-ending, death never coming.

He smiles, as if to confirm my thoughts. He stands, and his movements are languid when reaching out with one of his hands to take the skull then held in mine. With his other he lifts up the garland of flowers. He pushes aside his long grey hair. Grimed are the jagged fingernails that point to a wound upon his breast. Livid and barely healed it is, and when he makes that thrusting punch, when those nails puncture through the skin, I see his eyes widen as if his own action has come as something of a surprise. I hear his groan. I see him fall, sprawling now at Shiva's feet. I hear the arrhythmic pattering sound as his blood drips down, into the skull which the priest is clutching to his breast, like a mother who nuzzles her new-born babe.

He offers the skull to me again, and through his strangled shallow breaths, he says, 'Every thousand years there comes the dawn when the nectar of immortality is churned by the gods and demons alike, when the drops of their brew fall like rain to the earth and the doorway to knowledge is opened up. Drink the host and you will become the next finder. Restore the stone, make the sacrifice, and his spirit will pass from me to you. Let the cycle begin. Let the cycle complete.'

I want this wisdom of which he speaks, whatever the sacrifice must be. I fight against my heaving revulsion, at the acrid odour of the blood, at the fact that I think myself poisoned when my vision is blurring, and then – and then – the most breathtaking, luminous vision it is, when I see the path to eternal life – when, just for a moment, I find myself floating, rising up into the air, rising high above the shrine and riding the stallion of the wind which gallops through the star-lit sky and over the snowy white tips of the mountains where the air is so cold that my fingers grow numb, so numb that I lose my grip on the skull – and find myself back in the cave again, stumbling, falling to the ground, grasping at the rough stone walls which then become glassy, fracturing, to look like the bars of a golden cage.

A small pair of hands is gripping those bars. Small fingers are curled around them. A wrist is wound in coloured beads and seeds of the rudraksha tree. Above, two eyes are staring down at the stone *that lies within that cage. A diamond so large and lustrous that flames seem to stream from its very core, coiling and twisting like snakes under water.*

I look into those eyes again, and reflected there in dilated black pupils I see not one, but two diamonds – two miniature orbs of refracted light.

'Do you see her?' The seer is whispering, his lips held close against my ear. 'She is your Parvati. The chosen one. She will lead you to the sacred stone.'

For five years I have been away from Lahore. Those who I had known before cannot conceal their astonishment – not only to find me living still, but to see my appearance, so gaunt and changed. Last night, I hardly had the strength to meet with those fellow officers who extended an invitation for me to attend the Governor's Dinner. There, I learned that the Koh-i-Noor has indeed been taken to England, claimed at the end of the Punjab wars and gifted to Queen Victoria. This is what I learned from them. In truth, they cared more for questioning me, to draw out those secrets they sense I keep; and then to consider whether or not to have me martialled as a deserter. I did not lie. I told them that I owe my life to the holy men who cared for me when I had not the wit to know my own name, my colour, my creed. But now, with my memory restored, I have returned to my regiment, where it seems one more duty must be performed. The test of a soldier's loyalty.

I have travelled to Chandigarh, to the palace of a rajah who is playing host to Jindan Kaur for the purpose of this meeting. I am here with some other East India man who goes by the name of Willoughby. A talented surgeon by all accounts, and now a revered Political. But Dalhousie is mistaken if he thinks that I, or any man, might exert any influence on this queen. It is true that I found her favour once. She gave me many precious stones. Some were kept, and some were traded. That wealth remains securely kept – should I require the need of it for any future enterprise.

As for the present, I am here to offer the hand of friendship again, to soften the blow when Jindan learns that she must give up every hope of meeting with her son again, that as soon as this evening is over and done she will be escorted back to Nepal – the exile from which she cannot return. Willoughby will claim to hear those grievances that she has voiced regarding the Treaty's personal terms drawn up at the end of the second war – though our mission is really to ascertain the extent of her plots to reclaim the throne. For, even now, from a distance, and despite her incarceration, Jindan still seeks to inveigle those who might infect young Duleep's mind; to remind the Prince of what is lost.

She has not been told that Duleep Singh has converted to the Christian faith and is soon to travel to England. If she did, she would be less serene. But we find her as cool as the milky pearls that wind around her lovely throat. She has taken care to look well tonight. Golden bands circle her arms. Her hair, still black, is sleek with oils which trail a musky fragrance. Even though her face is masked by veils, her eyes are beguilingly painted. Her allure was once irresistible. Her husband, the famous Lion of Punjab, with all of his wrinkles and ugly drooped eye, and his predilection for lovely boys, even he was bound by the spell she cast – though they say he preferred to watch than do, to see his favourite paramour bed the whore become the bride. They say that her child is a bastard, with no real claim to the Golden Throne. But none would have mentioned so much to her and lived to tell the tale again.

Jindan tells many tales tonight. She reclines upon a silken couch and teases at rumours and semi-truths. As the evening draws on to its natural conclusion, when she offers to share her pipe of bhang – Willoughby insults her with his smiling yet haughty refusal. Instead, he asks for lassi, imbibing so much that, when we leave, he is in need of the latrines. Jind waits until he is gone from view, and only then does she touch my cheek and sigh with regret as she strokes the scar. She stares through her lovely lethal eyes and warns that I must be wary, that such an affliction is nothing compared to The Company's treacherous intent; the men who are seeking to trap me with spies. And one such spy is Willoughby.

I bow. I thank her. I kiss her hand. I say that my safety is not her *concern. And with my companion still well out of earshot I tell her of the mountain shrine, and how I must find the Koh-i-Noor, and how, because of that desire, wherever The Company takes him now, her son's fate will be linked to mine.*

Her eyes widen and flash at my stark revelation. She is on the brink of saying more. But our conversation swiftly ends when Willoughby lurches back again, when he offers her his slurred good-night – wishing well for her safe return to Nepal.

Willoughby is completely intoxicated! I have to help him to his rooms, to drag off his jacket and find a chair, upon which he slumps and then points at a table, insisting I look at a photograph. I am tired and impatient for my bed, but still, I decide to humour this bore and lift the folding leather frame – and find myself stunned to see what it contains.

This man and a child at his side. The girl from the vision in the shrine! I turn the frame over in my hands. On the back is a printed label with the name of a French photographer. Underneath the words are inked: 'Dr Charles Willoughby, and Alice. Beloved daughter. London. 1851.'

Willoughby groans and disturbs my thoughts. His head lolls forward onto his breast. He's all right. He is snoring, sleeping now. He'll certainly have a sore head by the morning – which is when I'll come back to collaborate on the writing of our joint report. Yet more worthless scraps to be filed away by the clerks of the East India. And when we are back in Lahore again, I mean to seek his professional advice regarding my hopes of dismissal, perhaps on some trumped up medical grounds. I have served my masters well enough, but I no longer desire or need to remain in the pay of The Company.

When I return, Willoughby is dead! A terrible stench of vomit and blood. A medical officer is leaving the room. He says every object must be burned, to purge all residual infection. The man is a fool. Can he not see? Willoughby has been poisoned. That lassi! I should have guessed last night. And when the officer has gone and, with Willoughby's valet distracted, kneeling there upon the floor and

washing the filth from the corpse's face, I take the opportunity
to steal his master's photograph. And then I also take my leave –
though I pause to glance back from the open door, to ask about the
whereabouts of any surviving relatives, those I may now visit, to
offer my condolences.

The words were fast fading away into silence. A different me,
the Alice me, was struggling to rise to the surface again, gulping
for air in that hot, dark room; weeping for the fate of my father
– for how could I bear to think of him, dying like that, dying
alone? I felt myself poisoned with the shock. I remembered
what Duleep Singh had said when he passed on that message
for Tilsbury. His mother's cynical words of remorse concerning
the death of a mutual friend.

Somewhere, a fly was buzzing, trapped in the bedroom
shutters. The pillow was damp beneath my cheek. I could
almost imagine myself to be back in some steamy tropical place.
My mind was still spinning with all of the colours, the sights, the
smells – the colour red. The colour of blood. The colour of death.
And that voice I'd heard inside my head, it was softer now, and
hushed, and low like the soothing voice of a parent who tries to
pacify a child when it wakes from a nightmare in distress . . .

'I have that picture still, Priyam. My Parvati . . . she still calls to
me.'

My eyes opened to peer through the dull dawn light, to see
the fully clothed man at my side. Against the white of the
pillow, Tilsbury's hair was a shock of black. Dark eyes were
staring into mine, and that moment of truth was strangely raw,
more intimate than anything that we had ever shared before –
because of what he'd shown to me, had given like an offering.

I knew I had not been dreaming when Tilsbury confessed
his past, and some of those secrets – the skull, the blood – I
had seen in other visions too. Though the sense of some vile
depravity had only increased when I saw them again, when he
somehow projected his thoughts into mine, those thoughts
from which I *must* escape – struggling to reclaim my voice, and

eventually managing to say, 'You were there . . . at the death of my father!'

He said nothing, that awful moment only disturbed by the throb in my arm, when I chanced to look down at the small bruised scab and realised what he had done.

'What monster are you?' I struggled to rise, furious and hissing then, 'Do you seek to make me an addict . . . just as you did with my aunt before? Is that the way you murdered her, by sticking your poison in her veins?'

'No! I wanted you to see . . . to enter my mind, to know the truth, just as you did with Prince Duleep.' He was also sitting then, our faces close, and in his eyes a look of anguish when he said, 'As far as Mercy was concerned, your aunt was addicted to her drugs long before we ever met, taking her tinctures to aid her clairvoyance, to open her mind to—'

'To impress *you*! The drug she came to crave the most. The man she was desperate to marry!'

'That marriage was never anything more than a mutually beneficial arrangement. I did not deceive your aunt. I simply complied with her wishes when she first told me of the child. I had to act quickly . . . to think of a way of keeping you . . . of keeping him. I feared, if I acted otherwise, she might think to steal you both away, or confess about the diamond's theft. She threatened as much and more, when she offered her proposal. That was the price of her silence . . . and it seemed the most pragmatic thing. In due course, I would deal with the aftermath and—'

'How? *How* would you deal with it? By letting Mercy discover us? Did you mean for her to see, when we were together, that day of the wedding?'

Again, he looked pained when answering, 'I never intended such a thing. But I do not regret what happened then, or what has happened now, tonight. You need to know my reasons for stealing back the stone . . . what both of us have yet to gain.'

'You really believe that by stealing a diamond, you will somehow be blessed with eternal life!'

'Millions stand in churches each week, kneeling before stained glass pictures and carvings, praying to a man who died on a cross, who . . . so legend tells us, once worked his holy miracles. Didn't he rise from the dead? Don't his worshippers claim he will return, believing that *he* has the power to grant the gift of eternal life, to share his sacred mysteries . . . by eating bread as if his flesh, by drinking wine as if his blood? I cannot hold to such a faith. But I have no objections if others do . . . if it makes them feel safe, if it—'

'Am I supposed to feel safe with *you*, after everything that you have done?'

'The truth is often hard to bear. But would you prefer to be ignorant? You saw something when you were a child . . . at the very same moment I stood in that cave, when your fingers held onto the bars of a cage, when you looked at the Koh-i-Noor . . . when I saw you, from India. And now we shall take the diamond there and—'

'Give the jewel to Prince Duleep? The man whose mother poisoned my father?'

'I have every sympathy with Duleep. What right have the British to raid other lands for nothing more than material gain, to force the natives to bow to their gods, to depose rightful regents from their thrones? If that is not desecration and theft then I would like to know what is! And when that particular wrong has been righted, when Duleep is seen to possess the stone and has drawn an army to his side, then I shall return it to Shiva's shrine, and there I shall receive my boon . . . the destiny that you will share.'

The same blood that had run with the heat of his drug now froze as cold as ice in my veins, for what did he think to share with me, if I went with him to India?

And what could be the sacrifice of which Tilsbury's dreaming priest foretold?

I trembled to think it was my son. My son with the mark upon his throat that looked like the scar from a slashing cut.

A PLAN OF ESCAPE IS HATCHED

Dragging myself from white windings of sheets, I felt sluggish and cold and thick-headed. I sat at the table and looked at the mirror and saw a pallid face peer out. My eyes were dark and glassy. Where tears had leaked across my cheek they might be liquid silver. They made me think of Parvati. The lustrous sheen of her metal form as she danced on the marble table top.

How I wished that my father might enter that mirror, to appear as he'd done in Claremont Road, come then to warn me of Mercy's betrayal; before she was betrayed herself.

How could I begin to trust Tilsbury? How could I even trust myself, when I thought again about last night and how I'd felt when he had gone? He had not tried to touch me, but still I tossed and turned for hours until I slept and then I dreamed, and not about my father's death. I dreamed of a cave with stars above, where my mind danced with visions that filled me with shame, that left me with nothing but remorse; only wanting to be clean again, to close my eyes, to be innocent. But I had seen things that could not be unseen. I had learned of Tilsbury's secrets, the desires that obsessed his mind. Or was that his insanity?

Suddenly, thinking about my son, I ran on upstairs to the green room, and there I found, not Nancy, but the younger maid who worked in the house, who had opened the door on that very first day, and who now looked startled to see me, when I cried, 'Where's Nancy? Why are you here?'

I needed Nancy. Nancy could help me. It distressed me yet further to hear the news, 'She's gone out, ma'am. She asked me to watch the babe, what with you sleeping in so late.'

'What time is it? When will she be back?'

'It's gone two o'clock. She went at noon. I have no idea when she's coming back. I've tried to be quiet. I hope I've not—'

'How can it be that late? Is Mr Tilsbury at home?' It was all I could do to concentrate, overcome as I was with inertia; with a terrible need to sleep again.

'The master said he'd be out till tomorrow.'

'Both of them . . . out? Together then?'

'I don't know, ma'am. I don't think so.' The girl was clearly bewildered, not understanding what might go on in this unconventional marriage of mine, watching while I clasped my hands, while I tried to calm my anxiety, during which act she spoke again. 'You've had a great deal of trouble, ma'am, what with being unwell . . . and the baby, too, and then with what happened to your aunt. If you'd like to go back down and rest, I'm happy enough to stay up here.'

'I'd rather stay here . . . to be with Charles. But please, won't you tell me your name, and then, should I have any need . . .'

'It's Ellen, ma'am.' Her answer was eager, her thin face lit up like the morning sun. 'I do so like being up here with the child. The bonniest babe I ever saw.'

When she'd gone, when the baby slept in the cradle, while I waited for Nancy to return, I looked at my son and I also thought that he was quite the bonniest child. So placid, so still – so perfect he was. He might be a painted idol. And when he finally stirred and woke, when I held him again and kissed his face, I willed my child to smile at me – to know *my* eyes, *my* nose, *my* mouth; to know *I* was his mother; not someone called Nancy, or Ellen.

But Charles was much too young to smile, too innocent for the viper's nest of the world into which he had been born. And what of the dream – the vision that his father had shown to me last night? Could that have been reality?

It was no reality fit for a child. The only Truth I was sure about was the need to protect my son from harm. And if Tilsbury had left the house, then perhaps I could dress and pack some things. And when Nancy returned again, could she be persuaded to lead me out, out through the front, or the kitchen doors?

When Nancy returned, I noticed the smell. The smell of sweat, the smell of sex – and that brazen expression on her face when she walked past the chair in which I was sitting and leaned to look over the edge of the cradle, her voice a pretty lilting song when she said, 'Hello, sweet Charles. I've missed you today, my little man . . .'

'Where have you been?' I was abrupt.

In answer she lifted her eyes to mine. 'Did *you* miss me then . . . while I've been away?'

'Is Tilsbury back? Have you been with him?'

Did she smirk when she heard my voice so slow? Did she sense my stab of jealousy. 'I believe he is in London, making his final arrangements for travelling to India. But me, my ambitions don't stretch so far. Me, I've just been for a walk through town. And really, it's such a lovely day, I went all the way to the river, and I took a ride upon a boat, and I made such a friend of the owner . . .' She broke off. 'You *could* show some interest, not give me that gawping glassy stare, just like your aunt used to do at times.'

Her comment cut me deeply. Is that what I had now become? If not, there was a chance I would, for already my blood was burning with the itching need for Tilsbury's drug, and rubbing at the needle's wound, I asked, 'Why are you telling me these things? What has any of this got to do with me?'

'I've been thinking about what you said last night. It does seem somewhat unfair to me that you're always cooped up inside this house. I thought you might like to join me to-morrow, to take a ride on that same boat while Mr Tilsbury's still away. Would you like to do that, Alice?'

A flicker of hope. Did she mean it? I listened while Nancy continued, 'I thought a boat would be the best. Once he returns and knows you've gone he's bound to alert the authorities, have everyone searching on the roads. After all,' she glanced down at the baby, 'this little prince, he is his son. But if we go to the river, biding our time on the water, it's unlikely he'll think to look so near. And, come the next morning, we'll sail up to London. We'll make ourselves a brand new life.'

'You will be coming with us?'

When I asked that, Nancy swallowed hard. I thought she was about to cry, for her voice was cracked and trembling. 'I know he intends to leave me behind, when he takes you and Charles to India. He told me, before your dinner last night. But I really don't think I could bear that . . . never to see him, or Charles again. He has forced me into this.'

In some agitation I got to my feet. Was Nancy telling me the truth? Is that why she'd acted so queerly last night, when she killed that poor defenceless bird?

I walked toward the window where the creature had died in its quest to escape. No sign of its blood upon the glass through which I looked down at the garden's walls and tried to think more clearly, not to give into the panic I felt when looking back at the maid to ask, 'Then why do we wait? We should leave right now. He drugged me last night. He might do it again. We could go to Mrs Morrison's house – that address she gave us, in Besley Street. I know she'd be willing to help . . .'

'No!' Nancy's answer was adamant. 'Not that old goose. Don't think he wouldn't look there first! He won't be back here till tomorrow night and that gives us all the time we need. You must only do as I tell you, and . . .' she gave me serious look, 'swear that I can trust you.'

'How can you think to doubt me?' I started to twist at Mercy's ring, still stuck quite fast upon my hand; no amount of soap or water having yet helped to ease it off.

'Well, I do know he came to your bed last night. I saw him leaving the room myself. Early this morning it was, when I was heading down to the kitchens to make up a bottle of milk for the baby. So I wonder if you reject his attentions to quite the extent that you pretend . . . or if you *really* want to go.'

My heart was racing. My breaths were constricted. 'I am sure. You need not doubt me. I fear for my future . . . for Charles's too. I know that when Tilsbury is with you, you might almost believe anything he says. But when he's gone, when you start to think . . . Oh, Nancy, I fear that he is mad.'

'What money do you have?' Nancy's mind was on more practical things.

'I have nothing. No money at all. But, there is a ruby necklace. I know where that is kept. And those gemstones, in his study . . . could we take those, do you think? Could we try to sell them?'

Nancy's smiled. 'I'm sure we could. And we won't need to take much baggage. Only the bare essentials. We don't want to be encumbered, and as soon as everything's settled, then we can buy whatever we need.'

And what to do when the gems were gone? What if they were only fakes and had no real value? But then why was I dithering, when Nancy was so brave and bold, when Nancy had it all arranged? And, as far as Mrs Morrison went, I could write and meet up with her afterwards – when everything was 'settled'. For then, I grabbed at Nancy's hands and pressed them hard against my breast, and said, 'Dear Nancy, if you help me in this I shall never forget your kindness. I shall always be grateful and in your debt.'

The maid appeared uncomfortable at such a display of affection. She pulled away with a wary expression and said, very slow and deliberate, 'I only help you to help myself.'

Only later would I understand the full implication of those words.

257

THE BOAT UPON THE RIVER

As surely as night follows day, so our destiny's path is laid out before us, and mine was about to take a turn – though who knew in which direction.

I hardly slept a wink that night. Every creak, every groan that was made in the house, I thought it was Tilsbury come back – or perhaps some spirit left behind to guard me in his absence. But no dream demons loomed in the darkness. The day dawned bright, with azure skies. I dressed in my lightest cotton gown; one that Nancy had brought from Claremont Road at the time of Mercy's funeral. Around one wrist I tied the strings attached to my mother's beaded bag, in which was the necklace of rubies and gold, wrapped in a length of embroidered silk, along with my father's photograph, and what remained of Mini's thread, and the pages torn from the book of gods – though why I thought to keep the last, I really was not sure at all.

How strange for me to realise that I had nothing more to show for all my years in Windsor. But it was enough. I wanted no more. Except, of course, my baby son.

When Charles had been fed and washed and napped, Nancy carried him down the stairs. I followed her to the hallway, and looking in through the drawing room doors I saw the metal deities, and thought I heard the faintest hum – that stuttering, low vibration. I thought about the diamond, for surely it was calling me? Perhaps we should take it with us? But no – I would leave that for Tilsbury. I would take what I needed, and nothing more. And with that decision firmly made, I turned my back. The humming stopped.

Heading back across the hall, I cautiously entered Tilsbury's study, averting my gaze from the evil eye of the crow that watched from its tall glass dome. I dared not glance around the walls for fear of what shadows might observe when I picked up the poker that lay in the hearth and raised it high above my head, before smashing it down through the cabinet door that contained the collection of precious jewels. Dropping the poker to the floor, I reached in through the broken glass, filling my hands with coloured jewels which I then passed back to Nancy – who laid the baby on the chaise before stuffing those treasures into her purse.

With our theft then accomplished I took Charles in my arms, and we left the room where shards of glass sparkled liked ice upon the boards. Nancy looked back from the hallway and gave a wistful sigh. 'See the glisten of that glass . . . as bright as any diamonds. You can never tell what's true, what's false.'

She took a bonnet from the stand. As she tied the ribbons beneath her chin, I realised that very hat had once been worn by Mercy – that the maid must have brought it from Claremont Road, just as she'd brought the tapestry bag which she then lifted from the floor while making the breezy suggestion, 'Well, it's another lovely day. Shall we go on that walk we've been thinking of?'

While Nancy unlocked the house front door I looked back one more time at the drawing room where the gods were still and silent, not making the slightest objection at all when I followed her out beneath the porch.

On the pavement, the maid glanced left, then right, her eyes screwed against the glaring sun before making for the iron gates that led from the street to the Queen's Long Walk. I did wonder why we ventured there, when she'd previously said we would make for the river, but could only presume we would take a route that offered the least chance of being seen.

As we entered The Walk I glanced at the castle, its towers and turrets shimmering pale, though I recalled a winter's night when Tilsbury dressed himself as Herne, when he'd stood upon the snowy walls and howled as if a demon.

Now, that seemed a lifetime ago, and shaking my head to

dispel such thoughts I looked away, across the lawns to where three or four children ran under the trees, laughing and shouting, playing tag. A woman was throwing a ball for her dog which was leaping in circles around her, yapping in vain for its mistress to chase. Two grey horses were drawing a brougham that headed towards us along the drive from the point where The Walk intercepted the highway which lay about half a mile beyond. As the vehicle passed by us, then turned on the gravel, I dreaded that Tilsbury might be inside. For it was his carriage. His driver. The man I'd seen in the stable yards. The man with the leering, grizzled face who now gave Nancy a knowing wink, in response to which she touched my arm, and said, 'When it passes by again, we must make sure to get inside. But don't look back, whatever you do. I've just seen Ellen in the street.'

I did look. I could not help myself, seeing the gate's tall metal spikes that flashed as if they burned with fire – as did the spokes of the carriage wheels when they had slowed sufficiently for Nancy to grab and open the door. Once inside, with the door still hanging wide, her arms stretched out for the child in mine, and somehow I had the presence of mind to thrust Charles towards her, then run alongside, hoisting myself up to join them as the horses began to canter, then gallop towards the open road. We rattled along at such a pace that Nancy was arching her whole body forward, trying to shield the child from harm. When trying to close the banging door, while twisting my head to peer back again, the air rushed like water into my mouth, and my cheeks were whipped and stung by hair that I had not tied back that day. And, it was through those flying strands that I saw Ellen, still at the gates, looking as small as a china doll, two hands clasped tight against her mouth.

We came to a stop in a narrow lane, overgrown with high hedges and brambles. There, I took Charles from Nancy's arms, though I'm not even sure she sensed him gone, such a blank expression on her face.

'Nancy!' I pulled on her arm in concern. She shuddered and

seemed to come to life, and followed when I descended the carriage – with no assistance from the man who had driven us to such a place, who looked down with menace from on high while proffering an open palm, awaiting whatever his payment might be. Nancy dipped a hand into her purse and handed that fellow, not a coin, but one of the stolen gemstones. An amethyst, I think it was. In response, he flashed a black-toothed grin, saying he must be getting back, that she knew well enough where to find the boat. 'So I'd be very much obliged, my love, if you and your friend would fuck off and hide, before there's any trouble here . . . before his nibs returns again.'

Though I was shocked at that crude response, Nancy seemed unaffected, only calling back up with some urgency, 'Ellen was there . . . on The Walk. She's bound to tell Mr Tilsbury. Remember, you promised. You won't say a word?'

'I'm up to scratch with your orders, ma'am. I'll disappear till the nightshift starts. Until then you can give us another kiss. We'll call it a payment on account, in lieu of services to come.'

I could not bear to watch then. The way she so willingly gave her mouth, when he reached down, when she stretched up, and how – when sated with that kiss – he pushed her off, then grinned at me through the blackened stumps of his rotting teeth. 'You later!' he threatened – then whistled, while flicking the reins on the horses' backs: the poor horses, their coats frothed white with sweat, which were now to be pressed into work again.

Still dazed and somewhat disorientated, I followed when Nancy led the way through a gap in a hedge to a field of corn. Our skirts dragged on thistles and rustled through grass as we edged our way around the crop, until we reached a river path where we walked along in the dappled shade cast down through the tunnel of trees around – which meant I no longer had to lift the baby's shawl above his head to protect him from the midday sun.

At last Nancy stopped and pointed out the boat in which we were to hide – which I might have failed to notice, being moored as it was amongst tall reeds, with branches of willow draped around to fall across a tarpaulin roof. I feared it would never be watertight, for in places the woodwork had rotted away and the boat dipped down alarmingly with a great deal of water splashed about, when, with Charles clutched tight against my breast, I clambered clumsily inside. Nancy soon followed after to squat at my side on a low plank bench, with no more than an old stained blanket to offer any comfort. I wondered if she had lain on that when she went to the river the day before. Had she been with the carriage driver? Could that have been the price she paid to secure the use of this vessel now?

She offered to hold the child a while and I willingly placed him in her arms. After that, unsure what to do with my hands, I plucked at loose threads on my reticule while we rocked back and forth in that humid dark cradle, lulled by the watery sounds around – all the suckings and gluggings and soft liquid lappings, the occasional quacking and splashing of ducks. More than once I started, to think I heard the crunch of stones, or the snap of twigs beneath other feet then walking on the river path. But Nancy was calm and unperturbed. With Charles balanced in the crook of one arm she reached down underneath the bench to where she had stashed the tapestry bag. In that there was bread and a flask of beer that she'd taken from a pantry shelf – all the refreshment that we might need during the hours that lay ahead. There were also some bundles of linen rags with which to change and clean the child, and some bottles of milk for him to drink, so that when he woke and was hungry at least we could pacify his cries – though I worried that the milk might sour, and fretted aloud about disease, at which Nancy wiped a teat on her skirts and then looked back to snap at me, 'Would you prefer the child to starve?'

As the afternoon drew on, the air became unbearably hot. When the dusk began to fall and we were less likely to be observed, she pulled off Mercy's bonnet and lifted back the tarpaulin sheet to create a sort of canopy – almost as if we were sitting there within a floating howdah. River mists rose to shroud the banks, and above them, far, far away in the distance, the castle was looming, as high as a mountain. But for us, down there at the water's edge, we must trust to our own guards and battlement walls: the birch and bending willows through which a breeze was whispering, and a cage of leaves streaming around as we looked at the stars in a purple sky. Every one was a sparkling pinhole of hope, but I did not believe they were diamonds. I did not believe they held the gods.

By the time the first rumbles of thunder began, my head was set to explode with the pressure. The baby, back in my arms for the time being, began to whine and squirm about, his tiny fists clenching in distress. In an attempt to soothe him Nancy hummed some pretty tune, and over that came the beat of the rain as fat drops of water pattered on canvas. It was with some reluctance we decided to pull the canvas down – though while Nancy and I were engaged in that task, the child lying safe in the base of the boat, I jumped at a short, sharp tearing sound that might have been fabric caught on thorns. *Dear God, don't let that driver come!*

A night bird gave a screeching cry, at which Nancy looked as alarmed as me. But soon we were sheltered beneath the tent, all three of us hidden from view again. But still, I kept watch through a flap of tarpaulin and saw the path's bushes blaze emerald green when a great bolt of lightning seared through the skies, and that followed by such a thunder roll. I could not help but cry in fright – at which Nancy reached out with her arms and said, 'Here, let me take Charles again. Why don't you try to get some rest.'

I lay back on the bench and closed my eyes, and listened as rainfall became more insistent, such rhythmic torrents splattering down to create a strange and dreamlike mood. I believe Nancy thought I *was* dreaming, though any true sleep was impossible, with the wind so rapidly gaining strength and the boat being buffeted about. Through the barely open slits of my eyes I saw the maid beginning to fidget, as if to find a more comfortable spot. I saw how she lifted that flap of tarpaulin and peered underneath it to see outside, when, whatever she saw upon the path caused her to give a sudden gasp – after which she hauled herself outside, to stand unshielded in the rain, and still with Charles in her arms.

'My baby!' I shrieked. 'Nancy, give him back!' I lunged forward to see her on the prow as more spears of lightning lit up the sky, as her hair was blown around her face to look like a terrible halo of gold.

Whether she heard my plea or not, she did not give an answer. With the baby grasped upon one hip, his head lolling back unnaturally, she was trying to step back to the shore. But somehow the mooring had worked itself loose and the boat had been dragged further onto the river, making it so much harder for Nancy to join the other there: the man who was standing on the path.

Already drenched from the falling rain, his hair lay flattened against his skull. His clothes were plastered close to his body, rendering him like some glistening devil, at whom I yelled through the roar of the storm, 'Tell her to give my child back! I won't let you steal him away from me!'

Tilsbury grabbed the mooring rope and while attempting to steady the boat, called back, 'What theft do you accuse me of? The child is mine. He always was!'

'How did you know where to find us?' I couldn't begin to work it out, to think what on earth was going on.

It was then he turned to Nancy, his eyes meeting hers when he shook his head and said, 'Oh, Nancy. What have you done? Did you not think that Ellen would tell me? My only surprise was how little it took to free your accomplice's wagging tongue. But he asked me to send you a message. He said, in that charming way he has, that you were more than worth the fuck. But, as far as committing murder went . . . well, he is not so keen to play a part in any game so dangerous.'

Another white flash speared through the sky. For a moment the world seemed motionless with only the thrashing of the rain and the terrible wailing of my son to heighten the pain of that awful dilemma. Nancy gave an odd sort of keening sound as she struggled to keep her hold on Charles when, with every attempt she made to jump, the boat's jerking motion held her back. Balanced so precariously, she looked desperate and frightened when glancing towards me, when looking straight into my eyes, she screeched, 'You got what you wanted – you wanted to leave!'

'Nancy,' Tilsbury called out, 'put the child under the covers. Give him to Alice. I'll pull the boat in. I'll—'

'No! Let it drift. Let Alice go. She *wants* to go. I'll bring Charles to you.'

His voice was harsh with anger. 'Did you think to have me change my mind? To take you with me to India? Hadn't I made myself plain enough? You would have been well rewarded, for *every* service rendered. But you have no future in our lives.'

The stark rejection in those words resulted in her answering, 'You would still have needed me – to care for Charles, if nothing else. You made enough use of me before. You could do the same when she was dead . . . when I would have come back to Park Street and said I'd done my very best to try and bring her back to you . . . that in the end she'd left the child . . . gone on alone to London.'

'What?' I was incredulous. A ghastly chill ran through me. Had Nancy planned to kill me?

I fixed on the gleaming of her eyes as they stared through a curtain of dripping hair, when she pleaded again with Tilsbury, 'All I want is to stay with you, with Charles . . . this child that I have come to love . . . this child she *never* wanted. Never . . .'

That was when her voice broke off. Still trapped in that limbo land between the water and the shore she looked up at the raging skies above, her mouth gaping open as if in prayer while the tears were streaming from her eyes. Or were they tears, or were they rain? When she looked back down at me again, she spoke in such a plaintive voice, 'Forgive me, Alice.'

Just that, 'Forgive me, Alice.' And Nancy said not one more word, even though she held my gaze for what seemed to be an eternity, during which she was fumbling with one hand, reaching into the purse tied at her waist, its contents thrown down, underneath the tarpaulin, as if to leave a parting gift. There at my feet, in the base of the boat, there rolled the stolen gemstones, and beside them was the braid of hair that had once been cut from her mother's head.

Having done that, she turned away, to face the shore and Tilsbury. And she seemed to stumble forward, or did she deliberately step out, leaving the solid deck behind, her skirts so heavy with the rain that she sank through the water like a stone?

'No!' I shrieked in horror, dragging myself out, onto the prow, where I lay with my arms stretching down to the water, where there was a moment I saw her, her eyes looking up, back and into mine, her hair floating around her face, and mine falling forwards like dangling ropes through which I cried, 'Nancy . . . give me your hands!'

But she wouldn't do that. She couldn't do that. Not without losing her grip on Charles, my baby held under the surface, to drown along with Nancy. And then there was nothing more to see. Nothing but swirling black water, and a rising stream of bubbles to sparkle, like jewels, on the rain-pitted surface.

In horror, I looked towards the shore where Tilsbury had witnessed everything, his face a frozen mask of shock before he dropped the mooring rope and leapt from the bank to the reeds below: the bank that grew more distant then as the boat began to drift away.

I snatched down to grab at the floating rope and, struggling to stand as best I could, caught hold of an overhanging branch. And while sharp twigs lashed at my cheeks, I summoned every ounce of strength to loop the rope around it, through which action I kept looking back at the shore, panting, shivering, cold with dread, to see Tilsbury splashing his way through the water, frantically groping through the reeds, then plunging down beneath them; only to rise, then dive again.

How many times he did that – more times than I could think to count. But the final time he re-emerged his eyes were blinking through the mud. He was groaning. His mouth was gasping for air. And there in his arms, there was my child.

My heart gave a lurching tip of hope as I watched his father use one hand to clutch at a ladder of tree roots, the means by which he hauled himself back up the bank, onto the path. There, he and the baby lay as the rain washed the slime from their bodies. And I clearly saw my child's face. But his eyes were closed. He did not move – only when Tilsbury turned him, pushing him over, onto his side, while I prayed to whatever god might hear that the water would drain from those tiny lungs. But my son looked all wrong, with his head like that, with his arms and legs so still and limp. And a terrible, pitiful thing it was to hear his father cry his name, to see how he placed his mouth over the child's, hoping to blow some life back in, and how he pummelled at his back to try and force the water out. And then, when every endeavour failed, how Tilsbury tore his jacket off: a pathetic attempt to use that cloth to shield his child from the rain. But all was in vain. My baby had drowned. My baby lay dead upon that bank. And me, still trapped upon the boat, I could only watch that tragedy, and see his father give up hope, and raise his arms to the merciless skies – and howl like Herne the Hunter.

But I, I wept more silently, already mourning what was lost, until his keening ended, and the vulnerable sorrow in Tilsbury's eyes was replaced by something colder, through which he shouted out to me, 'Once . . . only once will I ask you. Come back with me . . . to India.'

My head was spinning. I could not think. When I was able to lift my eyes, spitting bile and vomit from my mouth, I saw him, still standing on the path, still waiting for my answer. And I might have gone with him. I almost relented, for where could I go, who would help me now, and who but a mother should bury her son? But then came the sign to aid me.

While nervously twisting the ring on my finger, the metal grown greasy and wet with the rain, it suddenly slipped, free in my palm. The glittering emeralds and unlucky opals released me from their spell at last.

I hurled that ring into the rain, seeing it skim over black, splashing waters to land in the mud at the feet of the man who so cruelly had used it to own me before. I shouted, 'I am not your wife! You have nothing now that I could want, only to wish it had been *your* fate to drown, and for my son to live. You are cursed. You are the bringer of death. You are truly what you wish to be . . . not the light, but the darkness of Shiva's soul – Shiva the destroyer.'

My answer could not have been any clearer, yet still he offered his reply, 'Shiva destroys to bring new life. Out of the ashes we are reborn.'

He said that while staring down at the ring, and then he stooped forward to pick it up – or so I had imagined. But he had no interest in any such trinket. He threw it into the river. It was my child he lifted, holding that tiny bundle close as he turned his back and walked away, disappearing from view into dark, shrubby thickets, leaving me weeping and alone, with nothing to hear but the hiss of the rain as I crawled back beneath the tarpaulin, my body rocking back and forth, along with the swaying of the boat.

When the first rays of sunlight broke through the clouds and entered the gap in the tent of tarpaulin, they fell upon the scattered stones that lay in the belly of the boat – alongside the braid of auburn hair. I knelt down and gathered up those jewels and placed them in my reticule. The hair, I turned that in my hands, then threw it far out in the water, followed by Mercy's tapestry bag and everything that it contained. A sacrifice for the river gods to act as a prayer for Nancy's soul. And perhaps it would do for my son's as well. To allow them both to rest in peace.

A bird began to sing above, perched on the branch over-hanging the river to which the mooring rope still held. I did not think Nancy would like that song – not with that bird looking so like the one that she had murdered.

Perhaps she'd been right to fear it. Perhaps it *had* come to warn of death.

THE KINDNESS OF THE SISTERS

How I came to be saved, to be in a room surrounded by chintz and flowers and lace, with a bottle of *sal volatile* being waved back and forth beneath my nose, I may now find the courage to relate – though to reach that point in my story I must also return to that wretched place where I witnessed the drowning of my son, the awful memory of which still fills me with such a sense of such distress. A horror that will never leave.

For many hours I sat alone in the filthy wreck of that river boat. I thought to eat some of the bread and drink the beer that Nancy brought, even though to do so made me retch – and again, when I chanced to see the knife, the one concealed amongst the rags which Nancy brought to nap the child. A kitchen knife, and very sharp. The proof of her intention. *I only help you to help myself . . .*

Eventually I forced myself to unwind the rope from its mooring branch and then to fall back on the blanket. As the vessel drifted out on the Thames, it was very peaceful to lie there, not caring how the day would end; whether I would continue to live, or drown like Nancy and my son.

I did not drown, but I did grow ill, hardly able to raise my head from the bench or find the strength to answer when (or so I was later informed) a lock man came across the craft that appeared to be floating with no one aboard it. I do remember a hand on mine, and the loosening of the ribbons that secured the bag still at my wrist, of suspecting that I was being robbed, yet having no will to defend myself. But, fate had smiled on me that day, for that lock man, he was an honest soul, and his only thought to find some means by which to learn my identity.

Inside my bag, he came across the calling card that I had

forgotten. And later that day he delivered me to The Strand on the Green, near Chiswick – which was where the Dalrymple sisters lived.

Their house was built along the Thames, being one of a haphazard row of different heights and widths and shapes, and most with railings and iron gates that led onto a towpath. The Dalrymples' house was bowed at the front and looked a little like a ship, with windows that stretched the whole height of each room, and those on the ground floor opening onto a covered verandah. Above that were the balconies with decorative scrolls of ironwork that spanned the width of the top two floors. But I hardly noted such details then, not until the following year, which was at the end of many months during which those sisters cared for me – for which kindness I feared there would be a price – that, just as with my aunt before, when I first came to live in Claremont Road, they might intend for me to join their spiritualist profession.

Such a concern proved to be false, even had I retained an ability – for in those days my mind was closed. I saw nothing of the dead at all, which seemed the cruellest irony when I was grieving for my son; as desperately as any one of those mourners who'd flocked to Mercy's house, who had entered her parlour and longed to see the children who were lost to them.

The Dalrymple sisters, they still held an interest in matters beyond The Iron Door. They still subscribed to the magazines which Aunt Mercy had also taken, with names like *The Daybreak*, or *The Path of Light*. But, it soon became apparent to me that their own paths of light had darkened; their passion for speaking with the dead then being much diminished.

'It is always a consolation to have evidence for our immortal souls, but it's not been the same since your poor aunt's death,' one or the other would confide when my health had been regained again. 'And that awful case with Mr Home and all his hocus-pocus. Why, we went to consult with the man ourselves, and only by the grace of God were we not subjected to his fraud . . . when he duped that elderly widow of more than sixty thousand pounds, when he claimed to be her husband's ghost, his soul reborn in Home's own flesh! Her son was forced to take legal redress, not only to save his inheritance, but also her reputation.'

'And the Fox sisters . . . those Americans!' Whichever sibling was speaking next was railing at the shame she'd felt when, 'To think that all those rapping sounds . . . what were claimed to be messages from Beyond, and were nothing but ankles, toes and knees, when the sisters' joints went click and clack!'

'They'll suffer for that in years to come. They'll be riddled with rheumatics!' the other sister nodded through a sigh of resignation. 'We fear that we were often duped in such a way ourselves, my dear. This business is plagued with charlatans.'

Thank goodness they were unaware that I had once played a spirit guide, another wicked charlatan who had duped them with false promises – for they were the guardian angels who led me up some narrow stairs to a room where walls were white-washed; as clean and pure as mountain snow. And, in their midst there was a bed, with hanging drapes of palest blue – a bed a child might once have used.

Whoever had slept in there before, that room became my refuge. I often sat for hours on end with nothing other on my mind than the sight of the watery shadows as they played across the ceiling, where I almost believed myself submerged, as if I shared a river grave. It is a morbid memory, but I found some peace in those dark thoughts – in which I felt closer to my son, imagining I heard his cries in the gurgling lap of the rising tides, or whenever it was high enough to ebb against the towpath that ran beneath the window. And once, when lying in the bed, I woke and thought that Charles was there, hearing the flutter of his breaths as they came from the other side of the pillow. My heart nearly broke to see no ghost, only the Dalrymples' dog, a feisty little terrier that liked nothing better than to sneak beneath the sheets and blankets.

For some months my grief pervaded my every single waking hour. And, during that time, the sisters, who I had only scorned before, the two of them took it in turns to sit with me and hold my hand whenever I struggled with fevers, or woke from nightmares drenched in sweat, as wet as the water that filled my dreams, in which a child always drowned.

Fearing the worst, they called in a physician who diagnosed pneumonia – but he assured that I would live, if only I was sensible: if I ate and rested and convalesced. But then he did not know it all. He did not know about the pains that sometimes clawed my belly, or the noxious smelling clots of blood that often stained the cotton rags with which I had to stuff my drawers – which I secretly scrubbed in my washing bowl for fear of upsetting my hosts the more.

I told no one the truth of my malaise. I never spoke about the birth – certainly not in my conscious hours. I only implored the sisters to send no word to Tilsbury. Not to tell him of my whereabouts.

The following summer came around and all of my physical symptoms were gone, though my secret mourning would not heal. I kept that hidden in my heart. But my heart was strong. It lived. It beat. And its rhythm began to call to me, in footsteps on the river path, or through the horns of passing boats, or the raucous screeching of the gulls that settled on the balconies. Whenever the sashes had been raised the air so often smelled of brine I could almost think myself at sea, on a ship, on my way back to India. I began to consider travelling, and with only one intent in mind: to try and find Mini, my ayah, again.

The Dalrymples, they were also keen to have an adventure of their own and to travel as my chaperones. But they did take pains to warn me that we may never find her – with me not having heard a thing since leaving India behind. And I had forgotten my ayah's face. And I no longer knew her voice. My Mini no longer told her tales.

But where there was hope, there was a chance. And that chance began with the letter I wrote, that letter then sealed and posted off to the offices of the East India, in Leadenhall Street, in London. I gave my own particulars and asked if it was possible to obtain any records that they might hold pertaining to my father's staff from those days of his employment at the Residency in Lahore.

I wrote at an old iron table set in the garden at Strand on the Green. Such a glorious sunny afternoon. My ears filled with the sweet liquid song of a blackbird. Bees buzzed around the lavender stems that edged each side of a cobbled path and, at the very end of that, a shanty town of leaning sheds, where the sisters nurtured seeds in trays and spent many hours 'pottering'.

Miss Dalrymple, the raven-haired sister, who I knew by then as Louisa, was sitting close beside me, petting the dog curled in her lap, her face in the shade of the jasmine that formed a bower all around – through which she looked up with a frown of concern. 'I have been considering, Alice. Have you thought any more of your husband . . . about writing to tell Mr Tilsbury that you are here and safe with us . . . now thinking of going to India? Does he not have a right to know your mind? Might there not be some reunion? After all, so many marriages begin with disagreements and—'

'What on earth can you be thinking!' The other sister, the white-haired one, then known to me as Clara, turned back from her place at the garden wall where she had been snipping at the blooms wilting on a rambling rose. 'Do you forget the perilous state in which Alice arrived at our front door? Was that the result of a lover's tiff? Have you forgotten the dreams we had, and how we felt such a sense of dread when sitting at Mercy's funeral? And, that woman, that Mrs Morrison, who used to work at Mercy's house, she had a thing or two to say. Some men are simply not to be trusted, no matter how charming they may seem. Some women – and I include ourselves – are all too easily duped by looks!'

That mention of Mrs Morrison! How guilty it made me feel. I might have had no intention of contacting Lucian Tilsbury, but how often I thought to write to her, and how often I laid down my pen back down, not even knowing how to start – how

273

to explain about my son. Perhaps Nancy's body had been found, her death then common knowledge. But, if not, the secret must remain, for the only other one who knew was my 'husband', Lucian Tilsbury. And surely he would never speak about the horror of that night – to tell of the child of whom few knew for the sake of a girl for whom none cared, with no family to call her own.

Such thoughts were interrupted when Louisa replied to her sister, 'And speaking of other handsome men, have you told Alice the latest news, about Maharajah Duleep Singh, and the months of hoo-ha going on since his mother's death last summer?'

'She is dead?' I could not help my gasp.

'Oh yes, my dear,' said Clara. 'The event took place last August . . . when you were so unwell yourself. We did not want to pester you with any tittle-tattling. But if you hold an interest, I'm sure we can find the newspaper cutting . . .'

And that was how I came to learn the fate of the mother of Duleep Singh, the paper trembling in my hands while reading the words of a letter that had been printed in *The Times*.

Sir, – Her Highness, the Maharanee, Jindkore, of Lahore, mother of his Highness the Maharajah Duleep Singh, died on the 1st current at Abingdon-house, Kensington, in the Hindoo faith, and we understand it is proposed to bury her.

The practice is contrary to the religion of the Sikhs and, as his Highness the Maharajah denies our right to dispose of the body according to our customs, we are constrained, as a matter of conscience, to appeal to the country for protection, and beg you will kindly allow us a place in your spirited journal to enter a public protest against the intended desecration.

Agreeably to our rules, the body ought to be burnt and the ashes given to the Ganges. The thing is simple enough in itself, and, as it infringes no moral or physical law, we certainly cannot believe the wisdom and intelligence of the land would oppose our acting as our religion directs.

Besides, the belief of all religionists is that no funeral is hallowed unless a priest, or, in his absence, a layman of the religion of the deceased officiates at his obsequies.

It is hard, then, her Highness should be deprived of the offices the meanest claim and receive throughout the civilized globe, and that we should be refused the consolation of discharging the last sad duty for our mistress that is the right of all.

We feel we are fulfilling her Highness's wishes, and are satisfied, had she known her dissolution was at hand, she would have left definite instructions for the disposal of her body.

Reiterating our protest in the name of the friends and relations of her Highness the Maharani of the Sikhs in general, both here and abroad, and in the interests of civil and religious liberty,

We have the honour to be, Sir,

Your very obedient servants,

UTCHEEL SINGH, Jageerdar,

KISHEN SINGH, Khutry.

'Who wrote that?' I asked. 'Can it be true that Duleep Singh will not carry out his mother's will?'

Does he no longer wish to reclaim his throne?

'We think it may mean the opposite.' Clara looked pensive, biting down on her lip, as if puzzling over a riddle. 'We hear from Lady Garsington that even though Duleep Singh *appears* to uphold his Christian faith, of late he has taken to Sikhism, the religion of his father. But this is only rumour, and his name must remain unimpeachable here. So others protest on his behalf. Even going so far as to speak of threats regarding the dangers of civil unrest, should his mother's final wishes continue to be neglected. Lady Garsington says that The Company will not risk another Punjab war. And, of course, they must be thinking about the Indian Mutiny. The horrors that resulted then! She thinks the Queen will intervene, and then Duleep *will* be granted permission to make his way back home again . . . to scatter his mother's ashes in one of the sacred rivers.'

The remains of bodies in rivers. Destinies tied to prophecies. I dropped that cutting to the ground and wished I'd never seen it. Not that I was sorry to hear of the Maharani's death. I know that two wrongs do not make a right, but I hoped she had suffered horribly while ravaged by the syphilis. If so, then in some little way, she might have atoned for my father's end.

But what of Duleep, and the diamond? And what about Lucian Tilsbury – and what Tilsbury had done, and what Tilsbury had seen when he'd looked through the bars of a golden cage? Did he still believe the Koh-i-Noor might lead to some great destiny?

THE GHOSTS WHO WALKED
THE RIVER PATH

It was after I'd read the newspaper letter that the strange and upsetting event occurred, after which I knew I could never escape from the glue of the web that Tilsbury spun. Wherever I tried to crawl and hide his fingers would pluck at those silken threads, and I would still feel the thrumming beat as its subtle vibrations sang to me.

That summer it was a habit of ours – the Dalrymple sisters and me – to walk the dog before we dined, and always along the river path where there were fewer houses built, in stretches very overgrown.

On that particular evening, despite the damp and muggy air, we were looking to find the brambles in which we'd seen some blackberries, hoping they might have ripened enough for us to be able to eat them. Such were my simple pleasures then – and, of course, I was only deluding myself to think that I was somehow 'cured': to hear the water's lapping song and yet be able to suppress those memories of another path that ran beside the River Thames.

I had gone on, well ahead of the sisters, and was throwing a stick for the dog to fetch when some drops of rain began to fall. Just a few. I felt sure they would soon pass. I really had no concern at all, until, when lifting a hand to my face to brush away the wetness, somewhere, on the opposite bank of the river, a church's bell began to chime. It rang precisely seven times. I counted every single toll. But the last of those notes lingered on in my ears, and the sound brought a terrible sense of foreboding, and a growing pressure in my head – until I recovered and heard the dog, whining, then growling, then whining again.

Clara was leaning over me. Her one hand was lifting my head from the grass, her breaths coming fast and tremulous. When I looked up, into her face, so distinctly I saw every wrinkle there – the furrowed lines that ploughed her brow, the skin of her eyelids, crêpey and grey. But the eyes within them were filled with light, with such concern, and warmth and love while she did her best to assure me, 'Don't worry, my dear. Louisa has run back home again . . . gone to fetch the smelling salts. You must only lie here and rest a while. You must take just as long as you need.'

Take just as long as you need. I heard another, different voice. I heard more footsteps on the path, expecting Louisa back again. But, those sounds, they came from the other direction, where the river turned and the path was curved, and around that bend there walked a man.

Tall and suited in black he was, with very dark hair reaching down to his shoulders, though some of it was streaked with grey, most thickly at the temples. Following behind, in his wake, a maid was pushing a baby carriage. Although the sun was then low in the sky its canopy had been drawn down. The white lace of the shade appeared luminous and bathed in that light was an infant child, like a little god in a wheeled shrine. Such music I heard in his laughter, while he kicked out with sturdy legs, while dimpled hands were gripping hard onto the vehicle's wicker sides. I noticed his eyes, very large and dark, almost as black as the hair on his head, almost as black as his father's . . .

My heart missed a beat. I could swear it stopped. The next thing I knew it was racing again, making me breathless with all of its thudding when, as if in slow motion, the man turned his head, and his eyes locked with mine, and there was no doubt as to who he was. But then, there never had been.

I think I cried out. The dog barked again. I wrenched my hand free from Clara's grasp and heard her asking in alarm, 'Are you all right, Alice? Are you in pain? Why, whatever's the matter, my dear? You look as if you've seen a ghost!'

Those words were truer than she could know, for the man, the maid, and the child in his carriage just then began to fade away, become lost in green shadows amongst the path's bushes and grown more transparent with every moment, until the vision splintered, no more than shimmering motes of light which dulled and dissolved through drops of rain. Dissolving into nothingness.

I could not shake that vision off. How could I be happy without my son? How could I ever forget him? And his father – wherever he was – that man was still controlling my life. Night after night my every dream was filled with Lucian Tilsbury's face – with his, and the drowned pale features of my beautiful baby boy. The baby I last saw alive when he was held in Nancy's arms. When Nancy stole my child from me. When Nancy tried to steal my life.

The air was so much colder. Burnished leaves of orange and gold had long since drifted from the trees and formed a black and treacherous sludge that lay upon the river path. More than once I slipped and almost fell when walking with the dog alone, and always near the very spot where I had seen my phantom son. I knew that was stupidity, the vision being nothing more than a delusion of my mind. But had not the dog also sensed something upon the path that day?

It was late one afternoon when, returning to the house again, when passing another along The Strand, that I heard someone playing a piano. That tinkling music drifted out through a partly open window. It was the carol, 'Brightest and Best', and to hear that I walked all the faster, my arms hugged tightly to my breast, my fingers grown so cold and numb that I could hardly grip the key to let myself in through the Dalrymples' door. At least that was what I told myself – that the cold was the cause of my shaking hands.

I stood for a while in the hallway, still lost in the memory of those notes, until my attention was suddenly drawn to a package that lay on the table there. It was a large brown envelope, and the name on the front was clear to see. It said, *Miss Alice Willoughby*.

Mini! Snatching it up in excitement I could not wait to look inside, to see what news The Company might have sent to me of India. I confess I thought it somewhat strange not to see any stamp or franking mark. And then I saw the seal on the back. A circle of thick black wax, it was, and in its centre a capital *T*.

I felt such a sense of betrayal to think that one of the sisters – perhaps even both of them – had written to Lucian Tilsbury and told him of my whereabouts. But accusations, they could wait. For then, I rushed on up the stairs and into the room with whitewashed walls. And with the door closed up behind, I tore at the knotting of the string, then ripped the envelope apart, and gasped to see what first emerged – when I reached inside, when my hand drew out the papery sheen of a photograph. No, not one, *two* photographs.

The first was of me when I was a child. The picture that Tilsbury stole from my father. A twin to the other that I kept – except that, here, my father's face remained as nothing but a blur.

The second, that picture was recently made, and, oh, the effect it had me, for it showed the face of the infant boy last seen upon the river path. The same hair. The same eyes stared out at me as those I once knew in a tiny babe.

Could it be true that he still lived? Or was this some imposter – some other boy who looked like Charles, a doppelganger child with whom his father still tormented me?

I would only know if I summoned the courage to read the letter that Tilsbury had written: the last thing to be drawn from that envelope –

Park Street, Windsor

DEAREST ALICE,

I send you a picture of your son. It must come as a shock to see this, but you should know it was not his fate to drown as we feared upon that night. He gave but the semblance of death and revived very shortly afterwards, and despite then ailing for some months, has now recovered thoroughly.

This likeness was taken upon his first birthday. I mean it as a gift for you, to assure you that he is content and well. I hope that you will recognise the very expression of the girl who looks out from another photograph. There is not a day that passes when I do not see my child's face and bemoan the loss of his mother.

I hope that she will join us before we leave for India. That journey, I can no longer delay, for reasons of which you may be aware, regarding our friend, Prince Duleep Singh, and the death of the Maharani.

Will you not change your mind? Do you still refuse the blessings, the chance to enter a heaven on earth; to witness real wonders, real magic, the Truth? You know the truth of who I am, of who and what you are as well, not least what we may yet become. I pray that you will now accept what is your future destiny. You led me to the diamond. Now let the diamond lead you home and reunite you with your son.

Believe me, until such a time,

I do remain, Forever Yours,

L. T.

The picture of Charles I added to everything else in my mother's bag. The rest, I put back in the envelope, screwing that paper in my hands until nothing remained but a crumpled ball. I knelt before the little grate where the fire's coals had burned down low. But the embers were still hot enough to offer up a blast of heat, to devour every single word. Black shadows danced and dipped around, and in the crackling hiss of the flames, were those the sighs of the serpent's regret – the echo of something Tilsbury said when he came to my bed, in Claremont Road?

Let the light pour from me and into you. Through this your own gift is ignited. For now, it will smoulder low in your soul, but one day it will catch and begin to burn, and when that time comes only you will know. Wherever I am, you will find me . . .

I had no hesitation. I started to pack right there and then – what little I had to take away – though the gems from Tilsbury's study, I offered to the Dalrymples. I had hoped to provide some recompense for all their generosity. But they refused to take them, and I had come to be glad of that. I would sell the gems and use their worth to aid me in my enterprise.

When I told the sisters what I planned, Louisa was full of remorse, confessing that she had been the one who wrote to Lucian Tilsbury, but with no malice in her heart, only hoping for my happiness.

I said I was not angry, because now I knew my son's true fate – at which both sisters gaped at me in nothing but astonishment, to hear that I had borne a child; a child who I had left behind.

My turn it was, to then confess. Not everything, but just enough. To tell of the child's illegitimate birth, of how Tilsbury and I had never wed, of how he had trapped me in his deceits, and how those deceits had finally led to a tragedy on the River Thames – since when I was only grateful to them for the kindness they had shown to me; the kindness that had saved my life. But now, I had no other choice but to leave them, to go and find my son.

THE RISE OF THE TEN MAHAVIDYAS

I wrote to Lucian Tilsbury. I told him that I would return. The Dalrymple sisters, they saw me off from the road at the end of The Strand on the Green, their eyes glistening wet with tears when I climbed into the waiting cab, when they made me swear to write with news as soon as I was able.

The journey took most of the day. In parts the road was blocked by snow and the cabman had to dig it clear. One of the horses slipped a shoe. One of the roads was flooded. It was much later than I had expected when we drew up in Claremont Road.

I followed the path to the garden, where I found the key to the kitchen door, still there beneath a flower pot. I left my bag upon the step, then entered the darkness of the house, clinging onto the rise of the banister rails as I made my way to reach the floor where I found what I was looking for.

Outside again, on the pavement, I stood for a while looking back up – up to the window of the room with papered roses on the walls. I almost expected to see myself, still there, still staring wistfully, still waiting for something to happen, to fill the boredom of my days. And higher yet, with no window to see, there was the little attic room, its iron bed covered with old fraying blankets, its cotton sheets worn away into holes, and nothing on the floor beneath but a rug made up of coloured rags. The room where Nancy used to sleep.

Leaving such memories behind, I set out on foot and took a route that led me past the cemetery. The gates were always locked at night, but I lingered there a little while, my hands gripping the railings as I stood beneath branches of dripping leaves and saw through a slowly swirling fog that dismal place where Mercy lay, next to her mother and father – the grandmother I'd thought my friend when I first arrived in Claremont Road.

My grandmother's Shrine had welcomed me. That night it had offered me a gift. But, the place to which I then progressed – about that, I was not so sure.

I trudged on brittle crusts of ice that cracked their warnings underfoot. The air in my lungs grew yet more chill as the fog drew down, now flecked with snow, and so dense I could barely see a thing. But then, I could probably close my eyes and find my way to Park Street. Because Charles, he was my compass point; the magnet that drew me to Tilsbury's side.

I knocked on the door. He opened it. Not a word did either one of us speak as we stared into each other's eyes, as that sudden unexpected spark of something electric fired my nerves. He touched a hand against my cheek to brush away some flakes of ice, and said, 'You're blessed with diamonds.'

I thought about my father's hand, when my father had brushed away the drops of water from a fountain. Now, I felt ice crystals melt through my lashes, running down across my cheeks as Tilsbury led me on into the house.

There my bag was dropped to the floor, along with the rest of the luggage that formed a small mountain in the hall. Everything ready for the trip that he intended we should make.

A sudden claustrophobia – a fear of being imprisoned again when I heard the solid bang of the door, as I stared about through the dreary gloom where only a single candle burned. In its flickering illumination Tilsbury's features were menacing. His hair hung limp about his face, streaked with many strands of grey. Within the shadows that bruised his eyes the whites were red with broken veins. His jaw was unshaven, bristled black. His skin appeared a greyish-blue upon which the scar gleamed silver. It seemed to me that in the course of all the months since we'd last met, this man had aged more than a hundred. It came to my mind: *He looks haunted.*

He held out his arms to embrace me. But, seeing my reluctance he dropped them to his sides again and offered me that old, wry smile. 'Alice . . . I knew that you would come. I knew I only had to wait.'

'Did you?' That echo of my grandmother when I first arrived in Claremont Road, the moment when every nerve in my being was stretched to its very limit, because that was when I sensed the ghost. Not that I saw her, not at first. But the way he suddenly glanced about, and the anxious glitter in his eyes – I knew that Nancy was near at hand, that Nancy was watching, lurking in the shadows. I could feel the extent of her jealousy, the fact that she wanted him to stay, not to leave that house for India.

I said nothing. I feared if I spoke her name then her spirit might be conjured up. Names possess magic. They have their own power. To say hers – well, it might be as fatal as drawing a moth to a candle flame. I did not want to see her. I wanted nothing but my son, and thinking of him, I pleaded, 'Is Charles awake? May I go to him?'

When Tilsbury led me up the stairs, I felt myself almost mesmerised, watching his hand stroke over the rail that was carved to resemble a serpent's tail, seeing the dim green light shine out when we came to the room with forest walls. And that's when he left me, with Ellen, the maid, though I hardly knew her any more. She'd grown much taller than before, this girl who, during the months of my absence, had been tasked with the care of my infant son. Had she also slept in the Jaipur bed, with the whores who writhed around its posts?

I looked for Charles, and there he was, hands gripping the bars of an iron cot. He was bouncing up and down on the mattress, letting out high-pitched squeals of excitement at the sight of this new visitor. But, of course, he did not know me. I was the stranger who reached out her hand to touch the velvety curve of his cheek – and, below, the red that stained his neck. It had not faded, not at all. If anything, it was more distinct, all too clearly visible at the open neck of his nightshirt. But what did that blemish matter? My son looked well. He looked content, just as his father had assured.

Hardly able to breathe for the depth of my feelings, with silent tears upon my cheeks, I lifted him up and into my arms and sank my nose into his hair, inhaling his soapy fragrance, amazed at how solid and heavy he was. I had to sit in a chair by the hearth where he kept straining forward, away from me, more interested in dipping his hands into the water of a bath. In that water were bubbles that glistened like jewels, reflecting the metal of the tin and the light of the fire that burned nearby. The heat from those flames was scorching. Even so, I felt chilled to the bone, finding it hard to concentrate when Ellen started nattering.

'Mr Tilsbury told me you'd be back. I hardly knew what to think at the time . . . when that carriage driver was dismissed . . . when you and Nancy ran away. Will she be coming to India too? There's no other staff here any more. Mr Tilsbury says we'll be setting off as soon as it's light in the morning. And there's only the personal luggage left. The rest of it, he's had shipped off, though there wasn't much he wished to take, only those metal effigies . . . all of them packed up into crates and sent on ahead to the docks.'

I asked, 'You are coming to India too?'

I thought: *This girl has no idea that Nancy died in the Thames that night.*

Ellen looked nervous, nodding back. 'I have no family of my own, and I have grown so fond of Charles.'

I tried to smile, but held my tongue. Hadn't Nancy felt the same? And all the while I gazed at my son, the child who inspired such devotion, whose dark pupils reflected the fire's glow, shining with splinters of orange and gold and – I thought – no, I was sure – I saw something flash through his mirror eyes. The flitting wing of a small brown bird. The liquid sheen of auburn hair – at which Charles struggled from my lap and toddled unsteadily over the rug. And when he began to babble, Ellen laughed indulgently, saying, 'Just hark at all of his "na . . . na . . . na-ing". He does that all the time, you know. What do you suppose he's trying to say?'

I could make no answer; only able to watch when Charles fell to his knees and started to crawl across the boards, making for the very spot where a small brown bird had once been crushed, where now a puddle of water spread. It was too far away from the hearth to be caused by splashes from the bath. It was silty and brackish and green with weed, and there by its side were two watery footprints, and when my son reached them he came to a halt, sitting back on his haunches, stretching up with both hands, and such a sweetly piping sound it was when he began to chant, 'Nancy! Nancy! Nancy!'

I stood up, rushed forward, and hoisted him high, ignoring his angry screams of distress – as if I was stealing his favourite toy. I shouted back at Ellen who was staring in amazement, 'Why would he speak her name like that? Why have you taught him such a thing?'

'Why would I do that?' The girl looked indignant. 'Since that night Mr Tilsbury went looking for you, when he came back here with Charles again, and that little child in such a state – he told us her name should never be spoken. And I swear, ma'am, I've not once disobeyed. This is the first and only time that I have dared to mention her. I hope you'll not think to say otherwise.'

'I'm sorry.' I waited for Charles to grow calmer, his cries become little hiccoughing whimpers, over which I said more calmly, 'Perhaps he was only aping us, with you just having said her name.'

But I knew he wasn't.

Passing the child back to the maid, I returned to that spot by the window, kneeling down upon the floor to circle my palms where the water had puddled; where now there was only the slightest hint of any damp remaining. No stains, or foul water, everything normal, except for a little brown feather, and something else, something small and round.

The glisten of it caught my eye and, at first, I could not believe it – to see those emeralds and opals, the ring I'd thrown at Tilsbury, that had landed at his feet when he'd stood in the mud beside the Thames. But Tilsbury had thrown it into the river. Was Nancy now giving it back to me, as the sign of her presence in the house? Was that why Charles called out her name: the girl who had loved him; been there at his birth? But, my child had been born less than one month when Nancy drowned in the Thames that night. Impossible that he'd remember. Unless she had never gone away.

I drew a handkerchief out of my pocket. The one Aunt Mercy gave to Cook – that Cook then offered back to me. I opened up the clean white folds in which I wrapped the ring and the feather, during which I made my silent plea: *Nancy . . . you can have Tilsbury. But Charles . . . my child . . . he belongs to me.*

As the cloth was placed back in my pocket, Ellen gave me a suspicious look, the maid growing more wary with every passing moment. But she didn't object when I walked to her side to take Charles in my arms again, to hug him hard against my breast as he nestled his head at my shoulder, upon which I rested my cheek a while, until he yawned and I placed him down, back inside the iron cot. There, he rubbed dimpled knuckles against tired eyes, and began to gnaw upon a thumb while I drew up the covers in which he then snuggled, and knelt on the boards to look in through the bars, to see his dark eyes gazing back at mine. His little lids fluttered, then finally closed. I counted his breaths. I stroked his hair. And when he was surely sleeping, I made my way to the floor below.

Every footstep was timed with the thump of my heart, but the gloom did not deter me from the room that spilled blue radiance. There was no fire in its hearth. Any light came from tapers that burned in small jars, on the dresser, and on the floor. Those tapers exuded oily scents, of patchouli and rose and sandalwood.

He was there. He was sitting cross-legged on the bed that looked like a floating ship in the heavens. Above him there glowed the painted stars that glinted from gold, to black, to gold. His eyes were closed. I thought he slept. I thought how different he looked. Somehow then, both old and young. Somehow, just as beautiful and innocent as Charles upstairs.

At his breast, where shirt buttons were open, I clearly saw the inked tattoo – the hooded head of the cobra that lay on Lucian Tilsbury's breast – and there it seemed to guard the pouch that hung from a cord around his neck. While looking at that, from the end of the bed, I felt afraid and hesitant – to think the tattooed snake might live, though its movements were only the rise and fall that echoed the breaths in lungs below. But something, somewhere, was alive – something other than me – something other than him.

It came very quiet, very low, that gentle humming in my ears. It resonated in the boards, vibrations rising through my feet. Looking down, I saw the tiger skin – upon which my blood had once been spilled. I could see the stains of red still there, small drops around the tiger's mouth. Did a growl rise up from between those teeth? Did the tiger speak with Mini's voice: *Remember the goddess Durga. Durga, who rides the tiger. Surrender all actions and duties to her and she shall release thee from thy fears.*

Perhaps Lucian Tilsbury heard that voice. He was shaking his head. He let out a brief groan. One of his hands was closing tight around the pouch upon his breast. And that was the moment he opened his eyes, and that was the moment the humming stopped, as he blinked and looked to be confused – then smiled and reached out a hand, and said, 'Come, Alice. Come, join me.'

I sat at his side, on the mattress edge. I felt the touch of his hand on my shoulder, and I cannot deny the desire I felt. How easy it would have been just then, to be seduced; to be hypnotised in the knowing gaze of Tilsbury's eyes, to forget what I had come to do.

There was a glass of red wine on the stand, a half-empty bottle at its side. He must have noticed me looking at that and asked, 'Will you drink with me tonight?'

I did not want to, but answered, 'Yes . . . and perhaps there is some food as well? I am hungry. The journey took all day.'

'There must be something left in the kitchens. I'll call Ellen . . .'

'No! She's sleeping now. I wouldn't want to disturb her.'

'Then I'll go.' He got up to leave the room, his movements slow but supple, as lithe as any dancer. His feet were bare, soft on the stairs, a muffled and receding beat. And over that I heard my thoughts, an order of such urgency: *Now! You must do it. Now is your chance!*

Hurriedly reaching into my pocket, digging beneath the handkerchief, I drew out the bottle of medicine – the bottle I'd found in Claremont Road when I had gone there earlier – the bottle of Soothing Syrup that I had taken from the Shrine.

My fingers were shaking terribly, but at last I had the stopper out and poured a measure into his glass, hoping the darkness of the room combined with the colour of the wine would conceal any trace of the opiate. And when Tilsbury appeared again, so intense was my anxiety, the fear of him knowing what I'd done, that even though I tried my best to eat the ham and bread he'd brought, I gagged on every mouthful. It was even worse when I sipped the wine that he had poured into my glass, drinking that while watching him, as he drained his own to the very dregs.

I said that I could eat no more and let him take my plate away, setting it on the dresser top – the place where once I'd seen a skull, though no such object now remained.

He joined me on the bed again where, without removing any clothes, we lay as still as effigies, as if we were both made of stone. He looked at me. I looked at him. He stroked the necklace I had worn – the Mughal bridal rubies. The sign of my surrender.

I had to suppress the compulsion then, to touch the scar upon his cheek, to stroke the puckered skin around. And when I looked into his eyes I saw those tiny flecks of gold, those splinters of a glowing light – though I think that illusion was only caused by the painted stars on the ceiling above, the way their reflections glittered in the blackness of his pupils when, almost as if he read my mind, he said, 'You and I shall be remade . . . eternal and infinite as the stars. You and I . . . you and I shall be . . .' *Made one in the light and the darkness. Made one in the good and the bad.*

He kissed me. I gasped when he drew away, when his voice trailed off on a lingering sigh and he lifted a hand to his breast again, to the pouch that was still hanging there. His arm, the one that was tattooed (though I saw none of the inking then, not with the sleeve of his shirt drawn down), that arm was lifted to rest on my belly, and when sufficient time had passed, I tilted my pelvis and arched my back to see if his fingers might respond – as they had done some years before when I lay in my bed in Claremont Road. But the hand remained heavy, as still as the dead, though the proof of the living was in his breaths, those exhalations deep and slow – though slower than they should have been. He did not seem to feel the cold. He did not shiver as I did, even though it must be freezing hard. Each time his breaths were merged with mine they formed a misting lace of gauze. Still, I welcomed the rawness of those hours, the discomfort of fingers and toes grown numb. That cold, it kept me lucid. It kept me alert and on my guard. And when I was sure he would not rouse I lifted his arm and slipped from beneath it and lowered my feet down to the boards – and had not walked more than three steps when I heard the droning hum.

That sensuous creeping through my veins – I knew exactly what it was. The song of the diamond. The sacred stone. The song that had been calling me – calling for so many years. I steeled myself against it, refusing to turn and look back at the bed, staring instead at the ceiling's stars, at what had *not* been there before.

It was something last seen when I was a child, a child with henna-patterned hands, between which, when I held them up, I saw a glowing globe of white. A globe with an aura of spreading gold. A mango moon in a midnight sky. The moon that crowned the head of the god who was sitting on the mountain top.

I heard Tilsbury's breaths, quite even, a regular hushing draw and pull through which the thrumming buzz went on. It grew louder and louder, the vibrations much stronger, circling round me like a cage, within which I found I could not move, stuck as fast as a fly in a spider's web. And the spider was approaching, in the shadowy form of the silhouette that was then rising from the bed, rising up from the body of the man who lay asleep, unconscious still.

Was he dead? Had the medicine killed him? Was this his

soul leaving his flesh, leaving him to come to me? The trident. The drum. The garland of skulls. The palm of an extended hand. The streaming flow of matted hair as the spirit began its cosmic dance, its form growing denser, more distinct, as the shadow loomed across the walls – which no longer looked to be dark blue but appeared to be made of rough grey stone. Upon that stone four waving arms arched high above the vision's head, and every arm was coiled with snakes, though none so large as that which then was writhing at the spectre's throat. Its jaw stretched wide to show its fangs, and bright above, its ruby eyes; mesmeric and entrancing, and—

'*No!*' I protested. 'This is not real. This is nothing but myth and fantasy.'

But in that dream-like moment I felt myself a child again, standing beneath the banyan tree, with the head of a tiger next to mine, and the smell of the tiger's fetid breath, and the eyes of the tiger, alight with life. There was nothing, nothing else in the world but the gleam of those mesmerising orbs, and the swirling stripes of gold and black each side of its enormous jaws. A growling vibration filled my ears, but did not bring a sense of fear. I knew the tiger was my friend, and when it lowered its great head and stretched its forelegs forward, I sensed it was inviting me to climb and ride upon its back. There was a solid tapping sound, like the beating of a drum of war when its razor claws circled the boards. And now it was my shadow that loomed upon the bedroom walls, my silhouette astride the beast's, showered in the spittle that scattered from its yawning jaws, when the tiger gave its violent roar. Through that my arms were flailing. And, oh, so many hands there were. One held a sword. One held a bow, a trident, and—

Was I mad to think those shadows real? Something divine, something born again? Had I truly been infected with Tilsbury's delusions? Whatever demons that goddess slayed, I had to face my own that night – or else for ever be enslaved.

And so I closed my eyes again, and my feet pressed down on the tiger skin, which lay quite lifeless at my feet. I inhaled very deeply and held that breath, clearing my mind of any thought until, in control once more, I looked anew and saw a room where every wall was painted blue, where above my head there was no moon to shine within the golden stars.

Beneath those stars I made my way to stand beside the bed again, touching a hand to Tilsbury's wrist, to feel for the pulse, to be sure he lived. And he did, yet he looked too vulnerable, his breaths coming ragged, much faster now, and an awful groaning in his breast, as he struggled against the tincture's grip; though I think he smiled when I lifted my fingers and traced the scar upon his cheek, when I arched my body forward, about to press my lips to his. But the odour of the opium – that made me think of Mercy. That made me reach for my handkerchief, to open it up, to look inside, at the emeralds of her jealousy, the opals of her sorrow, the little brown feather at their side.

I placed that ring inside the pouch that Tilsbury wore upon his breast. And when my fingers slipped back out and drew the purse strings tightly closed, I wrapped his hand around it, to keep the gift protected. When Tilsbury woke and looked inside then he would know what I had done – that I would never change my mind and go with him to India. Because I was a mother now. A mother must protect her son.

Exhausted and drained of emotion, I finally managed to walk away, though I wonder now, was it my fault, the fire that started in the house – when in my haste to leave that room and return to the one on the floor above, my hems may have caught upon some jars, the oil and burning tapers then being spilled upon the boards?

I know I first smelled burning when I leaned against the green room door, when listening hard and filled with dread at what I might yet find inside, when I heard that drip-drip-dripping sound, like the patter of rain on a canvas roof. But, no time to think of Nancy then, not when the roaring blaze surged up and so quickly the air around me grew thick and grey and dense with smoke.

I rushed inside to save my child – to find Ellen, also sleeping, slumped in a chair beside the hearth. She began to cry when she opened her eyes, coughing on the acrid air as I scooped Charles up into my arms and screamed for her to follow us, as I edged my way past forest walls where branches shimmered, glinting red, as if at any moment they would ignite and start to burn. I'm sure I heard the screech of birds, the fluttering panic of their wings. I'm sure I saw the flashing tail of a deer as it fled through the foliage, heading deeper, deeper into the green.

If only we could leave that way! There was no hope but to make for the landing, stumbling through the choking pall, where the banister rail was smouldering, where embers fell on diamond scales – or drifted down to stairs below. And it might have been the grit in my eyes which were stinging, blurred and wet with tears, but when I looked in through the blue room door, through the furnace that was raging there, I did – I *did* see Nancy – her hair wound in ribbons of river weed, her head a haloed fizz of steam, and the dripping weight of her sodden skirts as she hovered there, above the floor, below the ceiling's golden stars – as Nancy floated in the flames, as if the air was water.

I continued to stare in disbelief when more than one drowned form appeared, a whole line of Nancys in front of the bed, and the shimmering barrier they made. I no longer thought of Durga, only the goddess Parvati – *symbol of fertility and marital devotion . . . through her love Shiva gains immortality. Her yoni calms and nurtures his lingam, which once blighted the earth in passion and fire to burn every living thing in its wake. But, should Shiva dare incur her wrath, then Parvati will call on The Ten Mahavidyas. The furies will rise and wreak revenge.*

Was Nancy – were all these Nancys – my very own Mahavidyas?

This was not the revenge I'd had in mind, but no matter how loud I screamed his name, Tilsbury made no answer. He could not be seen in the midst of those flames. He could not be woken from his dreams, and over my desperate, sobbing groans I heard my son, *his* choking breaths. What choice did I have but to turn away, to pray for the gods to save *his* life, to let us go, to let us live?

I had no idea which way to go, enveloped in that searing smoke, until a hand was cupping my elbow, steering me down, down to the hall where I saw the front door, open wide – and through that rectangle of escape, Ellen, already out there on the pavement. Once at her side I slumped to my knees, gulping on the fresh cool air while she took Charles into her arms. I was vaguely aware of others around us – of women who screamed – of men who called '*fire!*' But those shouts became nothing but echoes to me, as if they belonged to another world, through which I looked back at Tilsbury's house, through the far dimmer glow of the street lamp above, around which there swirled tiny slivers of ice.

And then, I heard the hissing rush – and then, the explosion of breaking glass that crashed from an upper window frame. A sudden shower of molten shards was raining on my face and hands. But my flesh did not burn. There was no pain. I thought they were stars falling down from the heavens. I thought they were glowing diamonds of light, or the droplets of water that sprayed from a fountain that day when I'd held my father's hand, when he'd led me through aisles of red banners and flags. Had he led me that night through red aisles of fire?

That memory was lost again when the screech rang loud above my head. A terrible howling sound it was. Was it just me, or did others see the girl who looked out through the window then, and how she held her two arms wide, as if she was guarding that escape from whatever, *whoever*, might be behind – the fire's illusion of a man, with tongues of fire coiled round his throat, leaping, like serpents, orange, gold. And that forking blaze above his head . . . those flames might very well have been the branching horns of a stag at bay.

I started to shake and could not stop. I plunged a hand into the nest of my pocket, and touched the glassy treasure there. The object I'd stolen from Tilsbury's pouch. The hard, cool gloss of the diamond that only a queen might hold, any man who did so being cursed.

WHO SAYS THE SUN
HAS GONE OUT?

Just as it was with Nancy before, Tilsbury had no funeral. There was no proof that he had died, for no trace of a body was ever found in the burned-out wreck of the Park Street house.

Those figurines of Hindoo gods, all crated and sent on ahead to the docks? I have no idea what became of them. For all I know they are still there, or awaiting collection in India. But I – I did not go there. I did not flee from Windsor, as had been my intention. I returned instead to Claremont Road.

There were investigations. The fire was deemed an accident. Mr Quin, that lawyer of Tilsbury's, he wrote and asked for us to meet, and he gave me the news of investments, all of which would transfer to my own name – should I refrain from mentioning the extent of his personal involvement in any illicit past events. And I did not, and I have not. And I hope you will not think badly of me for no longer wishing to expose the deceit of that fraudulent marriage. I even bought a golden band to wear upon my finger, because I had a child to raise and little choice but to go on with the pretence that first began the day of Mercy's funeral. I donned the black of mourning – to be thought not a bride, but a widow. It saves my reputation now. It gives me a future which is secure.

Another name in exchange for a life.

The first steps I took in that future life led me on a visit to Besley Street where I called on Mrs Morrison. Soon, she was back at Claremont Road (the house which I had come to learn had been gifted to me in my father's will – was never Aunt Mercy's house at all). Mrs Morrison's health was not the best, and she spent much less time in the kitchens. But she did oversee a brand new cook, and the training up of a housemaid, and when not bossing them about, devoted herself to little Charles.

Ellen remained in her role as nurse. It was only fair. She and my son had grown used to each other. He needed the time to settle with me, though I cannot say how relieved I was, the first time he called for his 'Mama', and rarely a mention of Nancy's name, just once or twice, and even then I did not sense her presence near. The only souls in Claremont Road were very much 'the living' – and often joined by the Dalrymples who regaled us with rumour and scandals, which mostly concerned individuals of whom we had never heard at all.

But the news they brought one summer's day, by which time my son was three years old, that *was* of interest to me.

Another cutting from *The Times* was placed into my hands to read – another article about the Maharajah Duleep Singh, who had become a father to a child known as Victor, and Victor had recently been baptised in the chapel at Windsor Castle, during which Christian ceremony Victoria stood as his godmother.

We were sitting in the parlour, the very place where the Queen herself had once taken part in a ceremony of a somewhat darker nature. Since then the room had been transformed, the same with the dreary dining room, where pale green papers lined walls, with drapes and shutters well drawn back to allow in the best of the natural light. There were no spirit circles. No more communing with The Dead – though I could not have been more shocked at that sudden disclosure about Duleep than if the Prince had materialised, right there, before our very eyes.

'He has a son . . . in England?' Since Tilsbury's death I had only imagined Duleep as residing in India, still waiting for the Koh-i-Noor; still hoping to reclaim his throne.

'Oh, good heavens!' Louisa pronounced. 'It was all the talk a few years back. Are you sure we didn't mention it? Lady Garsington was full of little else . . . how the Maharajah met his bride while travelling to India, when he was returning his mother's remains . . .'

297

'And you'll never guess!' Clara broke in, hardly able to contain her glee when she spoke of our exotic friend. 'That bride was not what you might think . . . not some glamorous Indian princess, but a commoner found in Egypt, in Cairo, in a mission school. The illegitimate daughter of a German banker – and her mother an Ethiopian whore!'

'His wife is called Bamba. Bamba means "pink".' Louisa explained with a knowing nod. 'It is due to her fair complexion. By all accounts you'd never tell that she had any blacker blood in her veins.'

'Goodness knows what the Queen must think.' Her sister's words were more subdued. 'Though they always say there is nothing at all that Victoria would not forgive when it comes to her beautiful Duleep. And, of course, he is just as devoted.'

I did not tell my friends the truth. How Duleep had once called the Queen Mrs Fagin. How he had wished to reclaim his throne. Or was that ambition his mother's alone? Had the prince been unduly influenced to rattle the bars of his gilded cage, because of the dreams of another queen, those dreams all to crumble when Jindan died, no more than a handful of ashes left? Or had he waited and hoped in vain, only to think himself betrayed when Tilsbury failed to bring the stone, with no other option remaining then but to make his return to England? Perhaps while still in India, Duleep had considered his future there against the securer privileges that his English Mother Queen bestowed – the life that might be preferable to the gamble of waging another war against The Company in Lahore.

I had no means to know his mind. I had no right to judge the man. In many ways, Duleep was blessed. And so was I, and thinking that, I knew I should follow the prince's lead and be content with what I had. I should not endanger those I loved because of dreams of India, when the threads that tied me to that place – the beaded threads once at my wrist, were gone, and had been gone for years.

Still, I often thought of Mini, and I wished that she could see my son – my very own Maharajah who reigned in Mercy's parlour, along with his doting 'harem': the three old women, the mother and nurse who worshipped the ground on which he walked. He was – he *is* – our beautiful boy, and really quite the happiest child, entirely transformed from those early weeks when, after the fire in Park Street, he lay in a cot at the end of my bed and screamed for his papa for hours on end. There was nothing we did could appease him – until one day, when sorting through the contents of Aunt Mercy's room, Mrs Morrison brought out the gift that had for years been hidden there.

A silver bird in a golden cage, an emerald heart within its breast. And the sounds I'd heard so long ago, the clickings and whirrings that made me so nervous, they only delighted and soothed my son. Charles reached out his hands and smiled, and then began to laugh out loud when we placed the cage on my bedroom hearth, where he could see it from his cot, where he cooed to hear the tinkling notes, and lay on his pillow and slept till dawn – as if he had been hypnotised.

Now, he sleeps in a room all of his own, with quite a different musical box to stand upon the mantel. A gift from the Dalrymples, and one he very much prefers, with little toy soldiers who march around a castle and its fortress walls, with swords and rifles in their hands.

But the silver bird remains with me, and so often I wake and hear its song, and I'm breathless, and I'm gasping for air, and a nightmare is swimming before my eyes; the same dream recurring again and again when:

I walk through the open door of a house, a house that has been destroyed by fire, where a noxious smell is lingering, like the burning ghats in India. I follow that odour, on up the stairs, my hand trailing over the blackened scales that form the banister's serpent rail. I enter the room where light shines in through a gap where a window frame should be, to spread over what remains of the boards where, on a bed of broken glass, there lies the corpse of Tilsbury. I kneel down beside him, carefully, as if afraid that he might wake. I press my cheek against his breast, and though I sense no beating heart, still I listen, still I wait, to hear some precious sign of life. I

*place my lips where his should be. I stroke the brittleness of hands,
now nothing more than cold, charred bones. I think of the first time I
saw those hands, and how those fingers held my own, and how that
touch alarmed me. But now I weep with longing, yearning for their
sweet caress, a poem whispered from my lips:*

> *'Who says the eternal being does not exist?*
> *Who says the sun has gone out?*
> *Someone who climbs up on the roof,*
> *And closes his eyes tight, and says,*
> *I don't see anything.'*

The very last time I had that dream, I knew that I must find a
way of ridding myself of the diamond. For what if my son was
also cursed, just as his father had been before – when he had
tried to see too much, to become like a god though only a man,
when he climbed much too high in the heavens and was burned
by the light of a star?

I lit the candle on the stand. I left the bed and walked to the
hearth where I stared at my mementos. The little brown
feather. Two photographs. The pages once torn from a book
of gods. The ruby necklace. The charred glass beads and the
sacred brown rudraksha seeds – the gifts which Mini gave to me
when she wound a bangle at my wrist and said, *Always wear
this, my dearest . . . it shall be a token of our love. And every time
you touch a bead you shall know that Mini thinks of thee, and that
Mini shall be praying still for her beloved's safe return.*

And finally, there was the cage, the golden bars through
which I reached to touch the silver bird within, silent and quite
motionless when my fingers forced its breast apart to reveal the
secrets of its heart. No longer just an emerald, but next to that a
diamond.

Some flames in the grate below leapt up, bathing my face in
bright flashings of yellow. In the glass of the mirror above the
hearth my face looked haggard, my eyes too dark, both reflecting a crystal of pure white light.

How long did I gaze at the diamond? Long enough for my vision to blur and dissolve, and while lifting my shift to wipe my tears, through the hushing of the fabric, I heard a far-off whisper – *Nothing is permanent. Everything changes. Shiva turns every thorn into blossom. You are the spring flower, a bright sparking of life, always dying and always returning to him. Everything turns and changes, and yet, nothing changes at all.*

THE PRAYER – NEVER ANSWERED

Everything turns and changes. There is no beginning. There is no end. All is Shiva. All is God. Saint and sinner, all are one. All are saved or destroyed by fire.

Every day I light a candle and make an offering, and pray for my dearest's safe return. I pray for the blessed Shiva to enfold my Priyam in his arms, to hold her and love her where I cannot. I wait for her here, in the house in the hills, the place where her father betrayed my trust, when he stole my Beloved from India.

It is here that my Priyam still lives in my heart, where my love shines as brightly as that of a diamond, as pure as the gold in the flame of this candle. And, one day, that light will lure her home – if not in this life, then surely the next, when we are reborn, when my penance is done, when I have atoned for my sins in this: the sins for which I now confess.

My Beloved, she once had a sister – a half-sister who lived but one short month, a death that her father did not disclose when he secretly buried her corpse in Benares, when he placed my own babe in her still warm nest – when he chose to raise the milk-faced child who was born to his Indian bibi bride. The mother become the ayah. The mother never known.

AFTERWORD

While researching the history of the Koh-i-Noor diamond I discovered the story of Maharajah Duleep Singh and his complex relationship with Queen Victoria, the sovereign who claimed his kingdom at the end of the second Anglo Sikh war.

As a child, Duleep was taken away from all that he had known before. Removed from his mother's influence and faith, he converted to Christianity and was then brought to England. The Queen doted on her 'beautiful boy', though there must have been an element of guilt – surely demonstrated by the incident in Buckingham Palace when Duleep posed for a portrait, when Victoria told him to close his eyes and placed the Koh-i-Noor in his hand – the sacred Indian diamond that once signified his sovereignty before it was given as ransom at the time when Duleep was deposed.

The youth's response was recorded as: 'It is to me, Ma'am, the greatest pleasure thus to have the opportunity, as a loyal subject of myself tendering to my sovereign, the Koh-i-Noor.'

But then, what else could he have said? To keep the diamond would have been an open declaration of intending to reclaim his throne.

Duleep appeared to be content. He married in his twenties – to Bamba – a bastard girl who he met in a Cairo Mission school while travelling to India to scatter his mother's remains. The couple returned to England and lived at Elvedon Hall in Suffolk. Victoria acted as godmother to their first son, Prince Victor, who was indeed baptised in her private chapel in Windsor, after which the Queen wrote in her diary: 'I never beheld a lovelier child, a plump little darling with the most splendid dark eyes, but not very dark skin.'

But his father's skin was dark, and beneath it his soul remained Indian. As the years continued to pass, Duleep became dissatisfied with what was then his 'English lot', even writing to Victoria to request the return of the Koh-i-Noor, complaining that the East India Company had failed to make true recompense for the loss of his wealth and sovereignty.

One major cause of such discontent had undoubtedly been his mother who, during her last few years, was permitted to travel to England to live with her son in London, taking that opportunity to remind Duleep of what he'd lost. The Maharani Jindan Kaur was a woman of great character and enormous political influence. Most references to her life in this novel are entirely factual – except for the scene where Tilsbury goes to meet with her in Chandigarh. At that time she was exiled in Nepal and would not have been considered in any further political dealings regarding the ruling of Lahore, or the future of her son.

In later years, after her death, Duleep Singh was influenced by the Russian and Irish dissidents with whom he plotted a 'holy rebellion', intending to lead an army to fight to regain his kingdom, by route of Russia and Afghanistan.

But such efforts were doomed to failure. Duleep was exiled from England and also his native India. Leaving his wife and family, he spent his last years on the continent, in some degree of poverty. However, before his premature death at the age of only fifty-six, he met with Queen Victoria when she visited Grasse in the French Alps – which was where she pardoned the bloated bald prince who she had once loved as her 'beautiful boy'.

In death, Victoria reclaimed him. His corpse was brought back to England and is buried at Elvedon. This is also a place of pilgrimage for those Sikhs who wish to honour the name of the very last king of Lahore.

As far as the Koh-i-Noor is concerned, the diamond was never stolen, despite Duleep's wish to have it back. However, it is true that Prince Albert had the stone cut down, to almost half its original size and that, for a period of time, it was worn by Victoria as a brooch.

It is also true that when Albert died, Victoria consulted with mediums who visited Windsor Castle.

As far as any myths are concerned, the Maharajah was certainly swayed by the well-known prophecy that if the stone were returned to its homeland all foreign invaders would be cast out.

Another Hindu prophecy that dates from the fourteenth century states that 'only a God or Queen may wear it (the diamond) with impunity'; that any man who holds the stone will see his line 'disappear from the light'.

Knowing that, it is somewhat ironic that after Queen Victoria placed the diamond in Duleep's hand, his life then bore all of the signs that he had been blighted by the curse. Despite fathering several children, every one of Duleep's offspring died without any further progeny. His line did indeed disappear from the light.

Another legend concerning the stone says that any queen who owns it will go on to rule the world – which was certainly true for Victoria: the Queen who commanded an empire, who became the Empress of India, and in whose imperial crown that sacred diamond was then set. And there it remains to this very day – despite what is now known as Pakistan frequently making formal requests for its sovereign symbol to be returned.

As to the many stories connecting the stone with Hindu gods, for the purposes of this novel such tales have been much embellished – their threads rewoven to create a fiction that is all my own.

Acknowledgements

In many ways this is a book about faith, but it would never have existed at all without the encouragement and advice of my agent, Isobel Dixon, and my editor, Kate Mills. I would like to thank them both for believing in *The Goddess and The Thief*. It really means so much to me.

I am also indebted to their talented and gracious assistants, Tom Witcomb of the Blake Friedmann Literary Agency, and Jemima Forrester of Orion Books.

And last but not least I give thanks to my husband for his understanding and good cheer whenever it was needed – not to mention his fine barista skills.

The Goddess *and the* Thief

Reading Group Notes

About the Author

Before taking up writing, Essie worked as an illustrator – designing greetings cards, gift wrap and decorative ceramics. Before that, she worked in a Dickensian office in Bloomsbury's Museum Street, employed as an editorial assistant for a book publisher. So, in a way, it almost feels as if she has come full circle, returning to the world of books – her very first love.

Born and raised in Herefordshire, Essie now divides her time between Bow in east London and Windsor.

For Discussion

- How does the author use letters to set the scene?

- What is the significance of the tiger – what does he represent?

- What do you think of Alice?

- How does the author contrast England with India?

- 'Just as the fragrance is in the flower, so the reflection is in the mirror, reflecting who we really are, our pasts, our presents, our future fates.' How important is Mini throughout *The Goddess and the Thief*?

- 'Things are not always what they seem.' How far is this theme explored in the novel?

- 'But that does not mean ghosts don't exist. And as for those who see them – for whom it is more than mere pretence – I wonder to this very day, are we blessed, or are we cursed?' What do you think?

- What significance do rivers have in *The Goddess and the Thief*?

- 'As surely as night follows day, so our destiny's path is laid out before us.' Do you agree?

- Is Alice entirely a product of her time? Does she represent something more? How would a modern Alice have behaved?

In Conversation with Essie Fox

Q *How are you like Alice, and how do you differ from her? What would Alice think of today's world?*

A I believe any writer must infuse some of their own personality into the characters they create. But it is just as important to be an observer, watching the behaviour of others around and then recreating those unique traits in fictional people on the page.

When it comes to Alice – and me – she is somewhat more naive, but then she is very young in the book and her childhood deliberately contained. Even so, she is braver than I could be when placed in such perilous circumstances, when she has no close family or friends to comfort or protect her.

I think we both share a determined streak: a refusal to give in to 'fate' when we know that something is not right. And although some readers have called Alice fickle when it comes to her feelings for Tilsbury, I wanted to show her confusion between what is real and what is not, and how she is torn between sexual desire and a growing repugnance for the fact that this man's overwhelming obsessions (whether physical or spiritual) are a threat to her life and sanity. And, although I remain somewhat dubious of the truth regarding the spiritual elements explored in *The Goddess and the Thief*, unlike me Alice is truly gifted when it comes to seeing 'other worlds'. For her, those worlds are all too real.

In today's world, Alice would never have been so

socially alienated, and therefore at risk from the adults legally entrusted with her care. She would no doubt have gone to school, and there she may well have met with friends in whom she could have confided her fears. Apart from that, it is hard to say how she would behave in the present day – especially when thinking of ghosts or religion, when our views on both matters have changed so much. But one thing would have been very different and that is her unmarried pregnancy, which was such a shameful condition then but is far less stigmatised today. Alice could have had her child and been helped to live independently. In Victorian times she had no choice but to accept the charity of her aunt and consent to all her future plans – otherwise becoming homeless, without any money to live on and at risk of dying on the streets, or falling into prostitution.

Q *'Curiosity was my curse.' Is it yours?*

A Not a curse for me, but a blessing – because any writer needs to be interested in the world around them. New discoveries are exciting, and I also love all the historical research that has to be done before writing my books – those facts from the past which can often be just as relevant to our lives today.

Q *What did you want to explore in* The Goddess and the Thief *that you hadn't visited previously?*

A All three of my Victorian novels deal with obsession, loss and grief. However, *The Goddess and the Thief* explores a wider canvas. In the physical and political world (with the novel having settings in both India and England), there are some hard-hitting historical facts about empire and colonialism. And then there is the spiritual world so vital to this story's plot – all the references to curses, ghosts and gods – all the explicit supernatural references.

Q *'But then, to sit inside that church and to see those emblems of war and destruction displayed side by side with that of the cross, the sign of a peace-loving Christian God – I found that a discomfiting compromise.' Do you share Alice's discomfort?*

A I do. Until writing this novel, although I had been well aware of the Empire's expansion in Victorian times, I was shocked to discover how war was waged beneath the banner of Christian faith. And although many missionaries did travel abroad to do good works in India, it was such a complex arena, where English ambitions were also linked to the accumulation of foreign wealth, either through ransom when wars were won, or else through the prospect of future trade, not to mention the deposition of so many legitimate rulers.

The scene in the novel where Alice sees the emblems of war in Holy Trinity Church is actually based in reality. Windsor's Holy Trinity is unique in serving the local parishioners, but also in being a garrison church. It houses panels on the walls to commemorate the Crimean War, the Egyptian Campaign and the Boer War. It has poles around the gallery bearing regimental colours (flags) from the Royal Horse Guards, the Life Guards and the Coldstream and Irish Guards.

Q Is Alice the physical and mental embodiment of India?

A Alice yearns for the loss of India, which she always feels to be her home, as well as continually being obsessed with her ayah's stories of the gods. She represents some aspects of the spirituality of the Hindu faith, a subject which is reinforced in questions of death and reincarnation, and those scenes when the form of the tiger appears – that creature being a symbol of the physical country of India. Another aspect of the Hindu faith that Alice comes to represent is that of female beauty, fertility, abundance and sex; all elements revered in that faith and the stories of its deities without any sense of the guilt of Eve – although guilt was later introduced through the work of Christian missionaries.

Alice's fate is also a mirror for that of the real-life Duleep Singh, the maharajah so cruelly deposed, parted from his mother when still a child and then exiled to live in England.

Q 'Everything turns and changes, and yet, nothing changes at all.' Do you agree? Is this where your research into the past has led you?

A To a certain extent, this can be true. Mankind is always moving on – with scientific discoveries, or industrial revolutions leading us on to new ways of life. But so often there are truths to be learned from events in our historical pasts. It may take decades or centuries, but every action has a reaction, however long that takes to occur. And then, where religious faith is concerned, there are some truths that never change, turning like the eternal wheel of fire that surrounds Shiva's statue in the book. For those who believe – whatever their faith, whatever its structure or origin – there is the sense that our souls go on, to return to wherever they first came from. Again the illusion of fire is strong: dust to dust, and ash to ashes.

Q *'But to know Heaven we must know Hell. To appreciate light we must live in the darkness. To share what is pure we must know degradation. To drink of the nectar of life, we must first taste the bile of our own death.' Do you agree?*

A Ah, this is very much connected to the Aghori in the book, the extreme sect of Hindus who follow the god Shiva and believe that the only way to move on to a higher spiritual realm is to be prepared to immerse oneself in every aspect of *this* world – the good and also the bad of it.

Personally, I do not believe that we need to experience such things to be aware that they exist – and to try and avoid or put them right. But, as far as Alice is concerned, she does indeed suffer the vilest abuse before she can rise above her fate and find some redemption and hope for the future – to emerge from the darkness and into the light, though her higher plane is here on the earth and not in some other existence.

Q *How did you set about researching* The Goddess and the Thief? *Can you let us into the process a little?*

A I must confess that I have never been to India. To get a sense of place and mood I immersed myself in both factual and fictional writing (much of it from the nineteenth century), and in original correspondence from those soldiers involved in the Indian Campaigns, as well as the wives who followed them. I researched a great many images of the city and landscape around Lahore, as well as Indian works of art. I also read translations of some ancient Hindu texts, and the wonderful sensual stories of the Indian gods and goddesses.

As far as the English settings go, I based this novel in Windsor because I have lived in the town for years and have always been inspired by its architecture and history – as well as some of the local myths, such as that of Herne the Hunter.

Q *'See the glisten of that glass . . . as bright as any diamonds. You can never tell what's true, what's false.' What is the significance of jewels in* The Goddess and the Thief *– both real and false?*

A The main jewel in the novel – the Koh-i-Noor diamond – represents a stolen life and so mirrors the fates of Alice and the maharajah Duleep Singh. It is symbolic of the way in which India's sovereignty was lost, and much of its wealth then 'ransomed' when the diamond was brought to England and gifted to Queen Victoria. The way in which this sacred stone was recut and much reduced in size simply to create more 'sparkle' and a somewhat more fashionable English design, I find to be very poignant.

The use of fake jewels in the novel represents deception and trickery. When Victoria wears the false Koh-i-Noor and believes it to be the real gem, this reflects the fact that she also believes that Duleep is content in his exile in England, when in truth he calls the Queen Mrs Fagan, and longs to reclaim his own stolen throne; to address the wrongs that have been done, both to him and to his mother, Jindan Kaur.

There are also the fake stones worn by Aunt Mercy, who not only lies to her orphaned niece, but also to the clients who visit and pay for false prophecies – and who ultimately deceives herself by believing the lies of Tilsbury.

Q *How do you set about creating the right tone in your writing?*

A This is my third Victorian novel, and during the process of writing all three I have read a great deal of literature pertaining to that period – novels written at the time and some of those more recent works that feature the nineteenth century. This gives me a grounding in tone and style, as to how people spoke or wrote back then, with certain stylistic conventions used to create a believable Victorian world.

I also do a lot of research into the era's history – its fashion and science, politics and faith – basically anything at all that might have affected my characters. I then concentrate on their parts in the plot, how they act and feel and react to events – because, when it comes to the crux of the matter, human nature has not changed so very much. I firmly believe that we share the same needs, the same longings, desires and yearnings as those who lived so long ago.